Prai

"A powerful, moving, touching story that made me cry, made me smile and gave me hope ... A beautiful story of forgiveness, understanding, love and hope for the future ... A definite must-read, you will not want to put this one down."
–*Working Mommy Journal*

"A moving story of courage, strength, hope and second chances! 5 stars plus ... an emotional ride of twists and turns, ups and downs and hope ... I highly recommend this novel, it will surely touch your heart as it did mine." –*Nicole Lavadure*

"I was swept away with so many emotions, I found myself keeping the book firmly in my grasp for hours! Ford made a story so compelling, so wonderful ... I still find myself thinking about it ... do yourself a grand favor and swoop up a copy of this book." –*High Society Book Reviews*

"Brilliant writing ... a heartrending and inspiring story ... Pamela Ford is a smart storyteller who creates memorable characters and a brilliantly crafted setting and atmosphere."
–*Cover Lover Book Reviews*

"I loved this ...touched me deeply, bringing tears to my eyes on several occasions. The characters are realistic, as was the setting and the plot ... The last quarter of the book had me racing through the pages ... Emotional and heartfelt, this novel will please fans of historical fiction and women's fiction."
–*Library of Clean Reads*

"Endearing historical fiction." –*Books, Lattes and Tiaras*

"The historical details made me feel as if I was part of the tale ... I loved the chemistry between Sean and Ailish ... I recommend this book." –*Locks, Hooks and Books*

"A heart wrenching piece of historical fiction ... an emotional rollercoaster of what ifs, hope, anger, faith, fear and more ... if you want to be moved and engrossed in what you read, I recommend A Rush of White Wings." –*Books and Zebras*

"A very moving story of love and loss ...an intense story with truly likable characters ... I will certainly want to read more of this author's books." –*Corinne Rodrigues Reviews*

"This beautiful story that touched on such things as understanding, forgiveness, love, and trust, managed to cause me to shut the book with a smile on my face." –*Pick a Good Book*

"This romantic story with its ups and downs and the heartbreak of it all kept me glued to the pages." –*Pause for Tales*

A RUSH OF WHITE WINGS

OUT OF IRELAND, BOOK TWO

PAMELA FORD

AINE PRESS

BOOKS BY PAMELA FORD

OUT OF IRELAND SERIES

To Ride a White Horse

A Rush of White Wings

CONTINENTAL BREAKFAST CLUB SERIES

Over Easy

Fresh Brewed

Honey Glazed

BACHELOR NEXT DOOR SERIES

Love on the Lane

Dancing on the Drive

Breathless on the Boulevard

Romance on the Road

Kissing on the Corner

A RUSH OF WHITE WINGS

ISBN: 978-1-944792-13-8

Cover design by Robbi Strandemo

Created with Vellum

For my grandmother, Mabel, an Irish lass who knew what it took to keep family together in tough times.

The old man drew his chair near the hearth and settled in to smoke his pipe. As the fire crackled and the flames danced, the door to the stone cottage swung open, and a young boy pattered across the room to climb onto the man's lap and curl into his arms. They stayed that way for minutes, the old man smoking, the child waiting, their lives bound not by blood, but by love.

In a quiet voice still edged with the strength of years long past, the old man told the boy of the Tuatha de Danaan, the Irish Gods. How Oengus Og, the God of Love, gave kisses so sweet they turned into singing birds. How Oengus dreamt, night after night, of a beautiful woman with dark eyes and light hair, and so smitten was he that he searched three years to find her. How he came to learn that her name was Caer and she was the daughter of a faerie king living in a castle beside a lake.

But when Oengus went to declare his love, he found not a maiden but a swan. For every other November on the feast of Samhain, when the veil between worlds was thinnest, Caer transformed into a swan for a full year. So Oengus became a swan to be with her. And they rose into the sky with a rush of white wings, singing a song so beautiful that they became human again and lived a long life together filled with great joy.

CHAPTER ONE

Cohasset, Massachusetts – October 7, 1849

The first nor'easter of the season ushered in the dawn shrieking of death. Outside Cohasset Harbor, the brig St. John floundered in the raging storm. A savage wind and monstrous waves battered the ship as her crew fought to keep from running aground on Grampus Ledge, a rocky shelf just a mile offshore.

Sean Deacey joined the townspeople standing along the water's edge, watching in silent horror. He tightened his collar against the lashing wind and ducked his head as towering breakers burst open upon the rock-lined shore and drenched the gathered crowd with droplets. A chilling cold crept in with the wet, and still the people stayed, lined like sentries along the shore as though their very presence might prevent yet another shipwreck.

A trickle of water traced a path down Sean's back like a single icy claw. He shivered. "That's an Irish flag on the stern," he observed to no one and everyone. His words swirled unheard in the wind and disappeared into the thundering sea.

The old man beside him pulled his brows together in question.

"An Irish flag on the stern," Sean said more loudly.

"Refugees from the famine they're saying," the old man shouted.

"Gone from one hell to another," someone said from behind him.

The words sank into Sean's heart like a chill settles in the lungs. How had it come to be that even within sight of America's shore the Irish were still fighting for their lives?

"My father went to Whitehead to launch the lifeboats." A young girl stepped close to the water and peered southward. "If God be with us, perhaps we won't be needing them."

Sean's gaze skipped over the raging sea to a spider-like metal structure on nearby Minot's Ledge, a lighthouse not yet finished. He'd not give his doubts voice, but if God had been with them, this storm would have waited until the lighthouse was lit.

An anguished cry went up along the shore. Sean jerked his attention back to the brig just as its sails began to shred. He exhaled softly. 'Twould not be long before the captain lost any ability to steer his vessel.

Suddenly, as if an answer to prayers, the ship jolted to a halt and steadied on the chaotic sea.

"They've dropped the anchors," the old man said.

Sean wiped the spray off his face with a gloved hand. "How deep is it there? Will they hold?"

The answer came from someone else, shouted as if intended to reach all the way to the Almighty's ears: "If God be with us."

The wind let out a shriek, like the banshee come to warn of impending death.

"Or luck," another added. "If luck be with us."

So there it was. God or luck. The lives of the Irish were, once again, dependent upon forces beyond their control.

Sean bent his head against the wind. *Not for him. Nay.* It would not be his destiny if he had a word to say of it.

Mountainous waves assaulted the brig, lifted it so high a gasp shot through the crowd. The anchors would never hold in seas like this.

Each new surge of water pushed the brig closer to the ledge. High about the deck, the tattered remains of the sails whipped like frenzied spirits around the spars. Sean's hands curled into fists. "Drop the masts," he muttered. "Now. Drop the masts."

As if his words had swept across the water, the crew cut loose both spars and jettisoned them into the sea. Almost instantly, the anchors caught again. And held.

The ship steadied. A grateful cry went up along the shore, relief that disaster had been averted.

And then someone pointed across the ocean, at a mountain of water curling toward them. Sean's breath hitched. He silently begged the monstrous wave to break along some other shoreline. *Luck, just a wee bit of luck was what they needed now.*

But it was too much to ask, he knew that. For luck had deserted the Irish three years ago when the potato crop first failed and famine had ushered endless death onto Ireland's shores.

The enormous wave picked up the floundering brig, tore her anchors from the seabed and threw her onto the ledge. The ship teetered on the jagged rock before another wave lifted her high and smashed her against the outcropping again. And again. And again. Until finally her back broke and water rushed into her belly to claim the passengers below deck. Within seconds, the boiling sea was peppered with people and baggage and the bodies of those who had already drowned.

Sean looked to the lifeboat inching up the coast, appearing at the top of each crest, then disappearing into each trough, its crew hunched over the oars as they fought to gain ground against the fierce wind and waves. His jaw clenched. They would never make it in time.

Several men tried to launch dories into the surf to attempt a rescue but the breakers were too powerful and drove them back to land. Abandoning the effort, they climbed onto the rocks along the shore in a desperate attempt to pluck survivors from the churning sea. It was a nearly impossible task; each time a wave threw someone against the rocks, the backwash instantly sucked them out to deeper water.

Sean joined the effort anyway. Squinting into the heavy spray, he crept across the drenched rocks to a flat outcropping, then dropped to hands and knees. He swept a dispirited gaze over the waves churning with bodies, the living jumbled among the dead, all of them beyond his reach.

Over the next half hour, rescuers managed to wrest a few people from the ocean, but only one still lived—a woman who had clung to a broken plank to keep her afloat. Though she'd been injured and unconscious when brought ashore, her fingers had to be pried loose from the piece of wood that had saved her life.

Sean spotted a man tumbling toward him on a frothing wave, arms wrapped around a leather satchel, eyes and mouth squeezed shut against the cascade of water. Slanting forward, he stretched out an arm, the tips of his fingers only inches from the other's sleeve. "Give me your hand," he shouted, but his words disintegrated in the howling wind. "Your hand," he bellowed.

The sea swept the man out of reach and hurled him against a nearby rock. His eyes shot open, his terrified gaze meeting Sean's for a heartbeat before the receding surf staked its claim and dragged him like prey, back to deep water. Wave crashed against fierce wave, a battle conjoined, but before Sean could even lament his failure, the ocean was propelling the man toward shore again.

He eyed the wave, gauging where it might deliver its abducted passenger, then slid across the outcropping to position himself, scrubbed a hand over his eyes to clear his vision, and waited, heart pounding, waited, patience straining, waited until—

Sean shot out an arm, seized the man's collar in a tight fist and rolled to one side, leveraging his body to drag the man up and onto the flat stone before the sea could prevail again.

He scrambled to his knees, panting. The man lay on his back, head lolling to one side, arms clamped around the satchel. Blood ran from a deep gash down the side of his face; his battered cheeks were already bruising. The man turned to him, his mouth curving upward, the corners of his eyes crinkling as his smile reached his eyes. Then his lids slid shut and he exhaled his last.

Sean let out a bitter sigh. One more dead to the sea. One more Irishman who shouldn't have died. If he had only abandoned his satchel and reached out a hand, Sean could have pulled him to safety before he received such grievous injuries.

He'd sacrificed his life to save a worn bag full of...what? Sean tugged off his gloves and opened the satchel, stared down at the clothing inside as anger twisted his gut. *He'd died to save these wretched belongings*?

As if determined to prove himself wrong, he thrust a hand into the bag, drew out a threadbare shirt and then a scarf. Spray drenched him and he brushed a sleeve across his face as he pulled back another piece of clothing...

And saw two tiny blue eyes awash in tears come into view.

His mind staggered. A babe? A wee babe? How was this possible? He tugged the fabric lower and uncovered a small mouth, open and squalling, though not a sound could be heard above the thundering wind and sea.

His throat constricted. "Mother of God," he whispered, casting a quick, sorrowed glance upon the man who had given his life not for belongings, but for his child.

With shaking hands, Sean lifted the baby out of the satchel, cradled him against his chest and hunched his back to the wind. "'Twill be all right," he murmured into the child's ear, though he knew the words were a lie. "You're safe. You'll be all right now."

An ache started in his chest, the pain sharp like the puncture of a blade. Old scars, scarcely strong enough to hold his heart together, began to give way, then ripped wide open beneath the weight of a memory; his wife and newborn twin sons had died in Ireland.

A sob wrenched loose from deep in his throat and he dropped his chin to his chest. One way or another, the famine would make orphans of them all.

By nightfall, the ocean had claimed the lives of more than a hundred Irish. Only twenty-one people survived. The captain. Seven crewmembers. And thirteen Irish: eight women, four men, and a baby boy.

Days later, the sea was still pummeling the rocky shore, only sparingly relinquishing its battered dead. Grieving families arrived on the train from Boston to identify deceased family and friends and lay them to rest. Over the next weeks, as the small fishing town tried to move past the tragedy, word gently filtered through Cohasset: no one had claimed the baby.

~

THE SUN ROSE through filigree clouds and bathed the town in a soft light. For an instant, Sean could almost hear his sister Kathleen going on about faerie morns in Ireland, but he shoved away the thought as quickly as it arose. It was easier to keep his mind empty than to remember.

Weary after endless hours of work with little time off, he trudged down the empty street toward the railroad tracks north of Cohasset. He knew he should be grateful that a cow had been hit by the train, and so the tracks were in need of repair and he had work—and income. And he was. But after more than two years in America, laboring almost without end, he was no closer to getting the only thing he wanted—land of his own—than he'd been the day he arrived.

Ahead up the street he spotted the town's only doctor, white head bowed and footsteps slow as though more than age weighed him down this early morn. Sean observed him from a distance and let the thought that had been lingering for days at the back of his mind slide to the fore. Perhaps 'twas a faerie morn after all, for Doctor Foster was one of only a few people who might be able to tell him if the idea he'd been pondering had even a bit of merit.

He hastened his steps to catch up. "A lovely morning," he said as he reached the other's side.

"Is it?" The doctor threw a distracted glance upward. "I'm having trouble finding beauty in a sky that continues to bring so much death to our shoreline."

Sean winced. None who had been present that day had escaped without haunting memories. Even now, weeks later, pieces of the ship and belongings of passengers continued to wash up along the shore. What hope had this town of moving beyond the tragedy when nature kept forcing them back to it?

No doubt the toll on Doctor Foster had been far worse than

on the rest of them. He had tended all the injured, fought to save each one and yet watched most die.

Sean brought his gloved hands together as though gathering his thoughts, then stepped through the opening the man had presented. "Since ye bring up that day, I hope you'll not be minding if I ask...I've been wondering about the babe, the wee lad." His pulse sped up. "Do you know what's to happen with him?"

The doctor's mouth pressed into a straight line. "Perhaps you've heard...we'd hoped he might have relations in Boston who would step forward. But none have. Each day that now passes makes it less likely." He rubbed a hand over his forehead and eyes. "Not even three months old and already he's alone. The family fostering the boy has no interest in keeping him. We've begun seeking a family of his own kind to take him in."

"You mean an Irish family?"

"We prefer that to the orphanage."

Sean's stomach tightened. Only a month had passed and they were already thinking of the orphanage? "Are you having any luck? There are so few Irish in Cohasset..." He didn't need to finish his sentence for both to know what he was saying: *...and most of those families were poor, itinerant railroad workers like Sean.*

"Are you looking for families in Boston, too?" he asked.

"Yes, of course. We've written the appropriate organizations there. The problem is, most Irish can't support the children they already have. And the disease in those slums..." His eyes closed for a beat. "More than half of all Irish children born in Boston die before they're six. One can hardly blame parents for not wanting another mouth to feed—or death to grieve."

Sean struggled to form a response. He'd known conditions in the Irish ghettos were bad, but he hadn't realized how deadly they were. "The child's lost so much already, an orphanage may not be the—"

"Agreed. But all the children there have lost parents one way or another. Having friends with a similar background might be helpful as he grows up." A pained expression crossed the doctor's face, and Sean knew the man didn't believe his own words. "If no relative comes forward, if we can't find a family to take him before another week is out, we'll have no choice."

Sean's brow creased. He'd not have expected the foster family to so quickly want the babe gone. He swallowed hard. "I might be knowing of a family." He tried to sound casual, offhand, but his heart was thrumming an anxious beat.

"What I mean to be saying is, I've a sister in Boston. Kathleen. Married two years now to—" He stopped himself from revealing that Jack was an Englishman. "—to a fine man. He's in shipping, used to be a whaling captain, now he invests in others' voyages." No need to mention that Jack had almost gone bankrupt bringing a ship full of refugees from Ireland nearly three years ago, that he'd been forced to captain one last whaling voyage to pay off investors and save his own financial situation. Those troubles were in the past.

Sean glanced at a passing carriage, waited for it to rumble past and momentarily wondered whether he was stepping too deeply into Kathleen's life without her permission. But what choice had he? Time was running out. He pushed caution to the side. "A nice home they have, a fine life, stability. But no children, though badly they'll be wanting them."

The doctor stopped and faced Sean, the rising sun hitting him full face. He blinked and put a hand to his brow to shield his eyes. "Go on."

"My sister has not been able to carry a child to term," Sean said in a low voice. "Lost her third this past spring. I'll be thinking they would gladly take the babe. A blessing to them he would be."

"You've spoken to them about this? They're in agreement?"

"Not yet. I've not been to Boston in...a while." He opened his palms. "But my sister has long been heartbroken over wanting a child. Not a doubt do I have that she and her husband would take him without hesitation. They would love him like their own, that I can promise ye."

A smile opened the doctor's face, his eyes glistened. He looked up at the sky, now brilliant blue and gold. "Tell me, Sean, have you ever seen a morning so utterly beautiful?" He put a hand on Sean's shoulder. "You have lifted such a burden off my mind. If no one claims the boy by the end of next week, you may take him to your sister."

CHAPTER TWO

Boston, Massachusetts – November 1849

"Happy birthday, Ma." Kathleen smiled over the cacophony of chatter, all the people she loved most in the world together in her dining room. Her husband, Jack. His grandfather. Ma and Da. Her younger brothers and sister—Rory, Tomás, and Nora. Only Sean was absent.

"I'm sorry Sean can't be here," she said. "You know he'd have come but for..." She faltered. "To be sure, the railroad is a demanding master."

She'd posted him a letter about Ma's birthday, had hoped he might attend though she hadn't truly expected him. Two summers ago, he'd left to lay the rails connecting southern Massachusetts with Boston. Since then, he'd visited only once—when that railway opened for passenger travel last April. He claimed he was always working, trying to earn enough money to buy land for a farm of his own. But sometimes she wondered if being with the family reminded him too much of all he'd lost.

Da waved away her apology. "Grateful we are that he has work. At least we'll be knowing he's not starving in Ireland, aye?"

She nodded. Though her family had fled Ireland more than two years previous, the famine still raged there. Despite their good fortune, she couldn't shake the feeling that Sean was slipping away from them. "'Tis just that...with Rory leaving us, going up to Lawrence to work..." She struggled to explain the wistfulness she felt. "I'm afraid this might be the last we're all together for a long while."

Ma patted Kathleen's arm. "Lawrence is but a train ride away. At least we're all alive, just spread out a bit. "*Níl aon suáilce gan a duáilce féin*. There are no unmixed blessings in life, lass."

Rory grinned. "Sean's likely thinking he's been at twenty-six of Ma's birthdays already."

"And the one's the same as the next," Da added.

"Just what is that to mean?" Ma raised her chin in mock offense as Da took her a hand and kissed it.

"You're an Irish rose, no matter what birthday it is, Anna Deacey," he said. "Still as pretty as the day we wed."

"And you're as clever with the words as the day we wed, Micheal Deacey. A regular Thomas Moore ye are. You should have been a writer."

"I'm going to be a writer," Nora announced. "An author—"

"Books?" Tomás twirled his fork as though the idea were preposterous. "What would you write about that anyone would want to read?"

Nora glared at him. "I'd write about what a dunce you are."

"You're the dunce—"

"Have done now, Tomás," Da said. "It's your Ma's birthday. Nora, can you be lending Emma a hand with the dishes now?" He tilted his head toward the cook clearing the table.

Nora began to stack the dirty plates and resumed talking as if she'd had no interruption. "I'll be writing a story about a lass who works in a grand house..."

Tomás gave an eye roll that involved his entire head.

"And she falls in love with a sea captain," Nora continued, ignoring him.

Kathleen threw an amused look at Jack. "Sounds a bit familiar."

Nora picked up the pile of plates. "And she has a brother who thinks he's smart because he's fifteen. But he's not." She stuck out her tongue at Tomás, lifted her nose, and glided regally behind Emma toward the kitchen.

A minute later she burst back into the room, her face flushed pink, mouth working excitedly. "Ma. Da. You'll not be guessing what I just found."

"An idea for a new story?" Tomás let out a snort.

"You have to see—" She gulped out the words. "In the kitchen—"

Every head swiveled toward the doorway just as Sean stepped into the room, a wicker basket hanging over one arm.

"Sean!" His name burst out of them in shocked staccato, like a handful of pebbles bouncing upon a cobblestone walk.

Chairs scraped back in unison, but before anyone could stand, he held up a hand. "Don't get up. Not yet." His expression sparkled and a smile teased the corners of his mouth.

Kathleen froze halfway out of her chair and narrowed her eyes. She'd seen that expression on his face a thousand times when they were young and it always meant mischief. He motioned her to sit, and she lowered herself down. "Seanie, it's beyond grand to have you here, but what are you up to?" She pointed a suspicious finger at him. "I know that look."

He chuckled. "Do you now? Well then, I'll be asking you this. Do you know this look?" He set the basket on the table and reached inside to fold back a yellow blanket, uncovering the face of a sleeping baby.

Kathleen's stomach flopped. A gasp went up around the table. Nora screeched, "You have a baby?"

"Shhhhh, he only just fell asleep." Sean put a finger to his lips and went to stand beside Ma. "Maimeó," he said, calling her *grandmother* for the first time, "I've brought something for your birthday. Your first grandchild. His name is Liam."

Kathleen lifted stunned eyes to her brother. *Sean was a father?* She brought a hand to her chest and slowly stood to gaze down at the child, her throat so knotted she couldn't speak.

As exclamations rang out across the room, Nora bent over the basket. "Liam, I'm your aintín," she cried. "Your favorite aunt."

"Maybe Kathleen is his favorite aunt," Tomás said as he bent toward the basket, but his words carried no bite.

"Shush, the two of you," Jack's grandfather scolded. "Do you want set the child to squalling?"

Liam shifted and yawned, then settled back into slumber. Nora worried her lip with her teeth. "How old is he?" she whispered.

"Three months."

Kathleen blinked back tears, her heart swelling with joy—and breaking from envy. Sean had been a father for three months already. Perhaps she'd been wrong about why he was staying away. Jesus, Mary, and Joseph, 'twould be a blessing twice over if he'd found love again.

She glanced at the hallway expecting to see a woman enter at any moment, his wife.

Ma went to wrap her arms around Sean. "A fine, strong name you've chosen for him. Means *warrior, it does*. This wee babe is destined to have a strong will."

Kathleen ran a soft hand over the fine, dark hair on the boy's head. "He's so beautiful. Be telling me, Seanie, what else have you been keeping from us for...well, perhaps a year or more?" She threw him a grin. "A wife, perhaps?"

"Is she here with you?" Da looked to the kitchen door.

The baby whimpered, and Sean lifted him from the basket. "Kathleen, will you hold him a bit? He's such a tiny thing, I think he gets easily chilled."

She reached for him eagerly, cradled him close as she settled into her chair, her entire being suffused with love for her brother's son. She fussed with the blanket beneath his chin, then shifted sideways to show Jack.

"He's so small," Jack murmured, awed. As he touched a finger to Liam's nose and cheek, all of Kathleen's longing pressed like a weight on her heart.

Liam's lids fluttered open and his dark eyes stared up at her warily, mouth screwed up tight. "Hello, Liam," she crooned, rocking him gently. "I'm your da's sister, no need to be frightened of me." He watched her uncertainly, then his expression relaxed and his face lit up with a broad, toothless smile. Kathleen's heart melted and she let out a laugh.

"Quite the charmer," Jack said. "Congratulations, Sean."

Emotion thickened Kathleen's throat and she swallowed hard. "And your wife? Where is your wife?"

"I've not wed—"

Ma let out a faint sigh. "Och, Sean, every child is a blessing, but don't be telling me you've had this one outside the vows."

"He suits you, Kathleen," Sean said, pointedly avoiding Ma's question.

"Sean," Da admonished, "surely you've a wife coming out to surprise us next, don't you?"

"Nay. I've no wife. This isn't my child."

"You're making no sense," Rory said.

"Then whose is he?" Kathleen tilted her head to look up at her brother.

He beamed at her, his eyes so full of joy Kathleen caught her breath. She'd not seen him so happy in many years.

"He's yours if you want him, Kathleen," he said. "Yours and Jack's."

Her pulse stuttered, missing one beat and then another. Was this another game of his? But nay, the way he was looking at her... faith, could it be true? "You'll not be fooling with me, will you, Sean?" she whispered, afraid of his answer.

He shook his head. "There was a shipwreck outside Cohasset more than a month ago," he said. "The Brig St. John."

"We know of it." Rory set his elbows on the table and rested his chin in his hand as Da added, "Broke apart in sight of the shore,"

"Aye, that's the one. I was there when she went down. Pray to God you never see anything like it." He told them of the storm and the rescue efforts, how he'd pulled the boy's father from the surf and discovered the baby tucked into the satchel and protected by clothing, how another man from the ship identified the baby and his deceased parents and siblings, all of them from the Clark family.

Kathleen couldn't pull her eyes off Sean's face. "Are you saying he has no parents?"

"No family at all. So many Irish came to Cohasset searching for relations who had been on the ship. But none came for him."

"He's an orphan?" Jack's grandfather asked. His eyes rested on Jack, the grandson he'd taken in so many years ago and raised to adulthood.

Sean took the basket off the table and set it on the floor, then drew a chair over to the table and sat down. "Aye. The foster family didna want to keep him, so the authorities were trying to find an Irish family to take him in."

Kathleen felt the universe shudder to a stop.

"I put your names forward," he said. "I hope you'll not be bothered I didn't check with you first."

"Seanie." She blinked back tears. "You'd not have needed to ask." She looked at Jack through blurred eyes and he shook his head.

"Never," he murmured, his gaze on the bundle in Kathleen's arms.

"So, are you saying," she began, "Sean...are you saying that he's ours?" she asked in little more than a whisper.

"He's yours."

Kathleen slid the top edge of the blanket down and touched the soft skin of Liam's throat. *A child? They had a child?* "Just like that, he's ours?"

"Aye. If you want him."

"If we want him?" she asked as though the question were absurd.

Jack put an arm around Kathleen's shoulders and bent over his new son. "Just try to take him from us."

"A baby," Nora exclaimed. "We have a baby!" she shouted into the stunned silence.

Liam began to fuss, and Nora punched her hands onto her hips. "What I'll be meaning, Kathleen, is that *you* have a baby."

Laughter tumbled across the room.

"Liam Montgomery," Jack said. "Has a nice sound to it."

"An English name might serve him better," Jack's grandfather said gruffly. He pushed himself from his chair and hobbled over to size up the boy. "You could call him William."

"He's been through enough already." Irritation wrinkled Jack's brow. "Doesn't need a new name, too."

The old man harrumphed. "The Irish are hated here. Why make his life harder?"

"His surname would be Montgomery. It's English," Kathleen pointed out. "Surely that would be enough."

"Would it? There are Irish with the surname of Montgomery, as well." The old man brushed crumbs off the tablecloth. "I mean only to smooth his path. Would you not want his life easier than yours has been?"

Half a minute passed with no reply. Then Sean lifted a shoulder and said, "An English name might give him other choices than working the railroads and living in a shanty beside the tracks."

Da stiffened. Regret flashed across his face, the guilt he carried from a lifetime of struggling to make his own children's lives easier and almost always failing. Ma reached over to squeeze his hand as she leaned into Kathleen and the baby. "Och, Liam, 'tis so early for you to be learning the hard lessons of this world, but learn them you must someday. *Is minic an fhírinne searbh.* The truth is often bitter."

Kathleen's stomach turned.

"Liam. William," Ma continued in a soft voice. "His name won't be changing what's in his soul."

Kathleen lowered her eyes, the discussion weighing on her, feeling like a betrayal of her country.

"He'll always be your son, no matter what you call him," Da said. "That's what matters, Kathleen."

She looked at Jack and he gave her a nod.

"Sure but you're right," she finally said, the slightest tremor in her voice. "It's only a name. Welcome to our family, sweet William Montgomery." She traced the curve of his chubby cheek with the back of her hand, and he reached up to grasp her finger as if to save himself.

CHAPTER THREE

TWO AND A HALF YEARS LATER

Boston, Massachusetts - March 17, 1852

Kathleen stepped out the front door into a near perfect day, her son in her arms. The sun glittered in a cloudless sky, its rays warming the air, the hint of a cool breeze the only reminder that they had yet to take more than a few steps away from winter.

"Such a lovely morn for a parade, my sweet Will." She spun a circle. "After all that cold, I think we've been blessed with the grandest St. Patrick's Day ever."

The street bustled with people of every age, talking and smiling and laughing—women adorned in green dresses, men wrapped in green scarves, children capped in green bonnets—all moving toward the parade route.

"Jack," she called into the house. "Hurry, it's getting crowded already."

Will gawked at the busy street, then twisted in her arms toward the open doorway and shouted, "Hurry, Papa!"

Kathleen kissed the top of his dark-haired head, grateful every day that Will had come into their lives. "I love you more than a thousand—"

"Frogs," he cried.

"Frogs? Oh, surely I love you more than that." She nuzzled his neck. "Don't forget, Maimeó and Daideó will be meeting us," she said, falling into the Irish endearments for grandmother and grandfather.

Jack came out the door and pretended to be surprised to see his son. "There you are, Will. I've been searching everywhere. Are you ready for the parade?" He raised both hands to the side of his face and played an imaginary fife as he marched in place singing, "Toodle de de do, Toodle de de doo..."

Will bounced in Kathleen's arms. "Papa, my soldiers. Get my soldiers."

"One soldier." Jack rooted around in his pocket and pulled out a red-uniformed tin soldier, musket at the ready. "You can take *one* to the parade. The rest will wait at home."

He hoisted Will onto his shoulders. "What are we going to see today? Horses. And wagons. And drummers. And..."

"Soldiers," Will said breathlessly. "Real soldiers."

"Ah, yes, soldiers. I almost forgot." He grinned at Kathleen. "And—"

"And the gen'ral," Will shouted.

"That's right. The generals will be there. And flowers and bands. And what will the bands be playing?"

"Marts, marts!" Will shouted for *march.* He pounded the top of Jack's head with the soldier as if banging on a drum.

"Will, easy!" Jack stuck a hand up to protect himself, then began to march in place while singing another nonsensical song. Kathleen's heart swelled. She would never tire of watching Jack with his son, this child not of his blood but most surely of his heart.

Will's energy and spirit had been their delight since the day he'd come into their lives. And though his boundless enthusiasm often veered into stubborn bursts of temper, their love for him never wavered.

"Shall we go?" Jack started down the steps, but Kathleen hesitated, her mind caught by something she'd seen—or thought she'd seen—in the crowd far down the street.

She sent her gaze over the path it had just traveled, eyes landing on a man in a dark jacket, head bent against the sun. "Wait a moment," she said, taking Jack's arm. "Faith, but if I didn't know Sean was in Virginia, I'd swear he's coming this way." She pointed down the block. "In the dark jacket. At the end—"

"Everyone's in a dark jacket," Jack replied, but he returned to the porch and followed her finger with his eyes. "He's too thin for Sean."

"It's been two years. He might have changed." She waved an uncertain hand in the air, watching carefully as the man lifted his head, then raised an arm to return the greeting.

"I'll be damned," Jack said.

"Ohl be damned," Will parroted.

Kathleen raised her brows at her husband.

"That's not nice, Will. Don't copy Papa," Jack said, his solemn tone undermined by the smile sneaking up the corner of his mouth.

"Ohl be damned," Will shouted again as Kathleen ran down the steps to meet her brother.

At the sight of his left arm in a sling, she pulled up short. "Seanie! Are you all right? What happened, faith but thank God you're alive. What are you doing here?" She took hold of his other arm and went up on her toes to press a kiss to his cheek. "Oh, no matter, you can tell us everything later. You're here and that's all that matters. Welcome home!"

"Ah, Kathleen, still the same you are," he said, eyes twinkling as he charged up the steps to grasp Jack's hand. "I thought the train was crowded, but Jaysus, will you look at all these people?"

"Jaysus," Will repeated with glee.

"Is this our Will?" Sean rubbed a hand on the boy's back. "What happened to that wee babe I once knew? Such a big lad ye are now."

Will grinned. "Jaysus."

"No, Will, don't be saying that," Kathleen scolded. "Have a care for your words, Sean, he's a quick study. Between you and Jack, the boy will be sounding like a sailor by the time he's three." She gestured at Sean's arm. "Let's go inside."

"And miss the parade?" He mussed Will's hair. "Who would want to miss the parade? I came home for it."

"What happened to your arm?" Jack asked.

"Broke it a month ago."

Kathleen reached out to touch a scar, still pink, puckering the skin on his forehead. "You did more than break your arm. What happened?"

"An accident in the tunnel. Blasting. Laid me up a bit."

"You were inside?"

"Aye. Broke off more rock than we expected." He started down the steps. "You know, Kathleen, if we dally much longer, we'll miss the parade."

"You know, Sean, if you keep changing the subject, it won't stop me from asking questions."

He heaved a sigh and returned to the porch. "Fine. 'Twas

bad, Kathleen. The foreman died and two other men. All friends of mine. Is that enough?"

"Aye." Fear curled in her stomach. "Don't go back, Sean. Let them blast a tunnel through the Blue Ridge Mountains without ye."

"They're making me foreman."

Her eyes widened. "To replace the man who died? Jesus, Mary, and Joseph, a dead Irishman lies beneath every railroad tie. Is that where you want to end up?"

"Some things are better not to think about." He lifted a shoulder. "Besides, I've no choices—"

"Jack can get you on a ship."

"You know I'll be wanting nothing to do with the sea."

She knew. He'd come within a hair's breadth of dying on the voyage over from Ireland and had made clear he'd not venture onto the ocean again.

"It's a raise in pay," Sean said. "If I don't start making more money, I'll be dying of old age before ever I can buy land."

She opened her mouth to protest again, but Jack put a hand on her arm, a quiet reminder that Sean so rarely came home...and not to push him so hard that she pushed him away. She bit her lip and let the topic die.

"Are you hungry? Let me get something to take along." She was inside before he could answer. "Sean's returned," she announced to the cook as she gathered bread and cheese and threw it into a cloth bag. "Broke his arm so I expect he'll be staying a while."

Emma clucked her tongue. "Oh, I can just hear the grandfather now. *Turning into an Irish tenement around here.*"

"He'll say it, but he won't mean it. Not anymore." Jack's grandfather was far different now than the man he'd been when Kathleen first met him. "It's kind of you to stay with him today."

Emma waved the words away. "I've been with him all the years he was healthy. I'll not desert him when he's dying."

Back outside, Kathleen followed Jack and Sean into the throng moving toward the parade route. "Sometimes I'll not understand this country," Sean said after a while. "So many signs proclaiming, *No Irish Need Apply*, but just look how many have come out for an Irish parade."

"I'll be thinking these are mostly Irish," Kathleen replied. "With Ireland in famine now five years, there's a lot of us here."

"America likes a good celebration," Jack said. "Should have been here last fall when they opened the railroad from Boston to Montreal. Closed all the businesses and held a jubilee for three days. Even the President came."

Sean snorted out a laugh. "Imagine the party if ever the railroad runs through to California. By God, that's one I won't be missing. I'd better be celebrating on me own land, by then."

"By God," Will said as though trying out the phrase. "By God," he shouted and threw a fist in the air.

Kathleen rolled her eyes. Sometimes she couldn't even get upset with him.

She spotted Ma right where they'd planned to meet, and knew the exact moment Ma spotted Sean. The older woman's jaw dropped and she rushed forward to gather him close, peppering him with questions and fussing over his injuries until Sean finally interrupted to ask, "Where's Da?"

"Working." Ma lifted Will from Jack's shoulders and gave him a hug.

Kathleen frowned. "I thought he had off."

"Aye." Ma's mouth tightened. "But as you knew, every time he thinks to have even half a day off, they call him in."

Kathleen sighed. She tipped her head back and let her eyes

roam over the buildings on both sides of the street, upper windows filled with the happy faces of women and children, rooftops lined with men watching from on high. Coming to America had saved so many Irish lives, had saved her entire family, but working long day after long day without end would kill them just as surely as the famine would have.

"Here comes the parade," Ma said, bouncing Will in her arms as a row of twelve policemen marching shoulder-to-shoulder came into view, the music of pipes and drums following behind them.

"Up, Papa, up," Will shouted.

Jack swung his son onto his shoulders just as an Irish military company in full regalia came into view, the green Irish flag emblazoned with a harp flying proudly above them. Will raised a hand to his forehead in salute, a move Jack had been practicing with him all week.

A drum and fife company followed, then Irish horse troops, another Irish military company, and more bands. Then came wagons and marchers, each representing a different Irish business or school, fraternal group, or organization. Everything was decorated, some wagons simply, others much more elaborately. Children waved from the wagons and Will waved back and clapped his hands in excitement, as if each new sight had been discovered at this moment for the very first time.

Kathleen reached up to touch her son; her shoulder brushed against Jack, and his eyes met hers. She had never known she could feel so much love.

"A handsome child he is," the young woman beside her said.

She smiled. "Thank you. We're rather fond of him."

The woman returned the smile. "Those eyes. He'll be taking after his father, I'll be guessing."

Kathleen regarded her husband, deep in conversation with Sean. "Perhaps he does, a bit," she said as she turned back. But the woman was gone. She twisted round making a quick search, then gave an unconcerned shrug and returned her attention to the parade. It wasn't uncommon for people to comment about Will, for he was a darling child.

"Mam, Mam. Horses." Will wiggled on Jack's shoulders. "Big horses." He opened his arms wide at the sight of four dappled grays pulling a wagon loaded with iron safes. A sign on the side read: *To keep rogues out*, while another sign attached to an iron grate on the rear said: *To keep rogues in*.

As Kathleen chuckled, Jack reached around her waist and brought her within the protective circle of his arm, his other hand keeping a firm grasp on Will's leg to hold their son safely on his shoulders. "Marts, Papa, marts," Will said as he drummed on his father's head with the tin soldier, and Jack obliged the request without hesitation.

Kathleen looked up to find Sean watching them, his expression wistful. Her heart ached for him, knowing what he'd lost and understanding why it was so hard for him to come home. She wished he would open himself to the idea of meeting someone else.

By the time the parade ended an hour later, Will had fallen asleep in his father's arms. "Will you be coming over, Ma?" Kathleen asked.

"Later perhaps, when your Da is home. He'll want to be seeing Sean, too."

"Later is better," Sean said. "I'll be needing to swing over to Dublin Row, check in at the pubs here."

"Take care for that arm, with all the celebrating," Kathleen said. "You don't want to be hurting it again."

"Ye make a fine mother, Kathleen, but I've got one already."

"Aye, you do," Ma said. "So be minding that arm." She waved a hand. "Go on with ye now. Have fun."

Away from the parade route, the Irish were still celebrating in the streets. But despite the bright sunshine and noise, Will didn't even stir. They mounted the steps to the front door, the comfort of home just seconds away, when a woman's voice called from behind them, "Pardon me, Mr. and Mrs. Montgomery, a moment please."

A young woman stood in the street, her face hidden in the shadow cast by their house. Despite that, Kathleen recognized her immediately. It was the woman from the parade, the one who had commented about Will. *How did she know their name?*

"Yes? Can we help you?" Jack asked.

Kathleen took a step forward, disconcerted by the feeling that something was wrong. "What do you want?"

Jack turned toward her sharply, surprised by her tone. She didn't look at him. "Did you follow us here?" she asked.

"Nay. I followed you *to* the parade."

To the parade. Kathleen's pulse quickened. "Let's go inside," she murmured to Jack.

He didn't move. "What's this about?"

"She talked to me at the parade—"

"My name is Ailish Sullivan," the woman said. "I'll be begging your pardon to be catching you unaware like this. It's just that...I'll not be knowing any way that won't surprise you."

"Surprise us?" Jack frowned. "Have you bad news?"

Foreboding overtook all Kathleen's thoughts. She gripped Jack's arm. "Leave her be. Let's go inside."

"Surprise us about what?" he asked.

Ailish regarded them in silence, her expression locked shut, giving nothing away. After a drawn-out moment, Jack pivoted toward the door. "If you'll excuse us, it's been a long morning. Our little boy needs his nap."

"It's him that I'm here about," Ailish said, stepping forward. She motioned with one hand at Will.

Kathleen's breath stilled.

"He's not your little boy," Ailish continued. "He's my sister's. And I've come to take him home."

CHAPTER FOUR

JACK TURNED SLOWLY BACK. "PARDON ME?"

"That's not possible. Will's mother died," Kathleen said, holding the woman's gaze. "In a shipwreck."

"Aye, that was my sister," Ailish said. "On that ship she was, with her husband and children...God have mercy on their souls. Coming across for a new life." Her eyes drifted to Will, still asleep in Jack's arms, and her expression softened.

A cold draft swept down the street. Kathleen felt it sift through her, cutting across the scars of every baby she'd lost, through the agony of every month she'd ever prayed to find herself with child and hadn't been.

"I'm the boy's nearest living relative," Ailish said. "'Tis my right to have him."

"Nay," Kathleen said on a breath.

"The wreck was two and a half years ago," Jack said, his words taut. "If what you say is true, why didn't you come forward before?"

"I was in Ireland. Stuck there. My sister and her husband were coming across to find work. They were to send money so the rest of us could get passage. When word came that the ship had gone down, that the family..." She trailed off. Clearing her throat, she tried again. "We had no means to come across, not even for one of us."

Fear tripped down Kathleen's spine. The story was a common one among the Irish. Indeed, if not for actions Jack had taken, it would have been her own family's story.

Ailish moved out of the shadow. Her face was thin, her dark eyes weary beyond her years. "The fever took me Mam and Da late in the summer. Then my own husband passed, us only wed for six months. I alone survived."

Kathleen folded her arms against the deepening chill and tried to harden her thoughts. She'd not feel sorry for this woman. How were they to know if her words were even true?

"I sold everything my family had left to buy passage last October." She held out both hands, almost begging. "That wee lad is the only family I have left."

The wind tugged at Kathleen's coat.

"What proof do you have of what you say?" Jack asked.

"His name...his name is Liam Clark."

Kathleen swayed. Her mind returned to the day Sean had brought Will to them, the moment he'd shared the baby's surname...Clark. His name had been Liam Clark.

"That proves nothing," Jack asserted. His words wrenched her back to the present. "You could have gotten that from the newspapers. The names of the survivors were listed along with those of the dead."

"But I didn't. Last week, I took the train to Cohasset to pay my respects to my departed sister. It was then I learned Liam was alive, that he was with you." Ailish's voice trembled. "All the records are at the city hall."

Kathleen's breath came quick and shallow. This couldn't be happening. The authorities had searched for Will's family, had assured them that—

"I'll not be blaming you for taking him in." Ailish took a step forward. "Indeed, I'm grateful you kept him from going into an orphanage. But, now I'm here."

Kathleen took a step back.

Ailish cleared her throat. "I know this is a shock. And sorry I am for bringing it upon you like this, but it would have been a shock no matter how you found out." Her eyes flicked between them, imploring and desperate. "He's the only family I have left. By rights he belongs to me."

Kathleen stared, unable to form a coherent thought.

"Unless you can prove that his mother was your sister, you have no case." Jack tightened his arms around the sleeping child. "Anyone could have gone to Cohasset and retrieved the same information. Anyone could have come here and repeated it. He's our son. You can't have him. We'll not give him up." He shouldered the door open.

"My sister's child he is," Ailish cried.

"Why are ye doing this?" Kathleen fought the urge to raise her voice. "He's happy here. We love him. More than life itself we love him. *He loves us.* We're a family."

"He was my family before he was yours."

"Kathleen, come inside," Jack said under his breath, stepping aside to let her pass.

Ailish's voice followed her over the threshold. "You can't be keeping a child who belongs to someone else. It's the law. I've asked a lawyer."

Fire shot through Kathleen and she spun back, hands fisted, but Jack was blocking the doorway. "Have no doubt, Miss

Sullivan," he said with icy control, "we'll be speaking to a lawyer as well."

Ailish's eyes narrowed and she opened her mouth to say something, then appeared to think better of it. She pulled out a scrap of paper and slowly came up the steps. "The lawyer said I should be giving you this. You can find me here if you'll be wanting to talk...once you've had time to think."

Jack crushed the scrap in his fist and stepped into the house, shutting and locking the door behind him.

Kathleen sought his eyes and assurance. "Jack—"

"Don't worry. We'll speak to an attorney, someone who can help us learn what this is about. It will be fine, Kathleen."

"I love him as much as any child I would have borne."

"I know. I do, too."

"If we lose him..."

"We won't," he said fiercely.

"Papa...marts. Marts, Papa," Will murmured in his sleep. He curled into Jack's chest.

"Hush, little one," Jack handed Kathleen the paper from Ailish, then bent over their son as he headed up the stairs. "Papa's here with you. Your papa's here."

One hand gripping the balustrade, Kathleen waited until they reached the top of the stairs and disappeared down the hallway. Then she dropped onto the bottom step, put her face in her hands and wept.

After settling Will into bed for his nap, Jack joined Kathleen in the parlor. He picked up the book that had been left on the sofa, *A Child's Own Book of Fairytales*, and ran a hand down the binding and across the corners softly rounded from wear.

Against the wall, a rocking horse stood at attention, anticipating its rider. Beside the hearth, a box of tin soldiers waited to be brought to life again. And on the end table, a crumbled scrap of paper holding Ailish Sullivan's address seemed to shout for attention as it threatened everything he loved.

Disbelief settled over him, blurring his senses, jumbling his thoughts. He and Kathleen had forged a life together from his broken roots and her solid ones. They'd taken in a child and loved him as their own. They'd made a family. It was unimaginable to even consider losing Will.

He squeezed the book as though strength alone could change this day, could transform the outcome like coal under pressure becomes a diamond. He lowered himself onto the sofa next to Kathleen, and she leaned into him, seeking refuge. "Jack, what if—"

"We're not going to that place," he said. "We'll get this worked out." He couldn't even fathom what losing Will would do to Kathleen. Not after all the miscarriages. Not after all the hopes that had risen and been brutally crushed time and again. It couldn't happen.

The minutes ticked past as neither of them spoke.

"She may be lying about being Will's aunt," Jack finally said. "It could be a ploy for money. Or she might be...unhinged, mad." He set aside the book and took her hand. "I wouldn't be surprised if an attorney tells us to ignore her."

"What if she's telling the truth? Are you not worried?"

He'd been able to think of nothing else as he lay Will in his bed and tucked him beneath the quilt Kathleen's mother had made for him. "No," he lied. "The address she gave us—it's in one of the worst areas of the North End. She herself said she hasn't any money—"

"So how could she be paying a lawyer?"

"Exactly. I doubt she's gotten a legal opinion at all." He pressed a kiss to Kathleen's knuckles. "Even if she truly is Will's aunt, I suspect we'll discover it's money she's after, not him. Why would she want responsibility for a child when she can't even support herself?"

"Easy enough it is to say that, but you know as well as I, the heart has its own reasons," Kathleen said. "Do you know which attorney we should talk to?"

Jack mulled over her question, unsure how to answer. They needed the best—and couldn't risk making a mistake. "I have an idea, but I want to ask my grandfather for his thoughts." He shook his head. "Though I almost hate to tell him what's happened out of fear worrying will make him take a turn for the worse."

"Who would have ever thought he could love an Irish child so much?"

Jack went to the sideboard, poured a generous amount of whiskey into two glasses and handed one to Kathleen. He took a swallow, welcoming the burn down the back of his throat, relieved to feel a sensation than anger. Or fear.

From the back of the house came the commotion of voices—someone talking to Emma—then footsteps in the hall. Sean stepped into the room.

"I thought ye were going to the pub," Kathleen said.

"So crowded, a body can't even move. I'll be waiting a bit, until some have gone home to sleep off the afternoon drink." He dropped into a chair beside the hearth and cast a puzzled glance between the glass in Kathleen's hand and the decanter on the end table.

"Whiskey, Sean?" Jack poured him two fingers without waiting for a reply.

"Rather early for the two of you, isn't it?"

Kathleen gave him a grim smile and threw back the rest of her drink.

"Tell me you're still celebrating St. Patrick's Day," Sean said. "Before I begin fretting there's something wrong."

"This morning at the parade a woman told me that Will has his father's eyes." Kathleen wrapped her hands around her empty glass. "She wasn't talking about Jack."

Sean frowned. "What are ye saying?"

"Claims her late sister is Will's mother," Jack said. "That Will is the only family she has left."

"I'm not sure I understand. What does she want?"

Jack ran a finger around the rim of his glass, then took a sip to put off answering as long as he could. "Will. She wants our son."

The stillness that followed his words was so encompassing, it almost felt like the air had been sucked from the room and the three of them were hovering in a space between life and death.

"Jaysus!" Sean set his glass on the side table with a thump. "Where has she been these past years?"

"Ireland," Jack said in a flat voice. "Came over in October. Says she didn't know Will was alive until she went to Cohasset."

"Do you believe her?"

Jack shrugged. He didn't know what to believe anymore.

Sean barked out a harsh laugh. "I'll be thinking it's a ruse. For money. Do you think this would be happening if you didna live in this nice house? Like a blazing torch it is, announcing that you have a wee bit of means. Certainly more than the Irish poor have."

"There are far nicer homes all over the city," Kathleen said, though her expression was troubled.

"And I'll be asking you, how many of the owners have taken in an Irish orphan?" He leaned forward. "Think, Kathleen. The

Irish are so despised here, they can't find decent work. If she came across expecting something better and instead found what we found—" He threw his hands in the air. "A struggle to earn a decent wage even after working long hours..."

"Hunger breeds desperation." Jack picked up the scrap of paper from the table and smoothed it flat. His jaw clenched at the sight of the even handwriting. "Ailish Sullivan is her name. She left her address in case we wanted to talk."

"*Negotiate* might be a better word," Sean said. "Whether she's Will's aunt or not, I'll be betting that it's money she's seeking—not a mouth to feed."

Kathleen gave a wry smile. "Jack said very nearly the same thing. We'll be getting a lawyer to help us."

Sean poured himself another whiskey, then took the scrap of paper and gave it a shake. "She invited you to talk." His frown deepened into a scowl. "Why not do that first? Put the question to her straight about what she's after. If it's money she wants, you'll be needing the police—not an attorney."

Jack nodded, grateful for Sean's perspective. "It's a good point. I'll go—"

"Let me," Sean said quietly. "I was in Cohasset when the ship went down. I was there when the bodies were brought out of the ocean, when the dead were identified and buried." His voice dropped. "I brought Will to you. She'll not be able to twist the truth with me." He turned his glass in his fingers.

"I'm his father."

"Aye, but it might be better if the person who talks to her isn't one of Will's parents. I pulled her sister's husband and child from the ocean. If she truly is Will's aunt, perhaps she'll find it easier to trust me." Sean took a swallow of whiskey. I put you in this position. Let me help you get out of it."

CHAPTER FIVE

SEAN STEPPED TO THE SIDE TO GET OUT OF THE WAY OF THREE raggedly-dressed young boys barreling down the walk, playfully shoving one another and screeching with laughter. He absently wondered whether the famine had brought their families here or had they chosen to come because they'd heard the streets were paved with gold?

To the children, the move had probably been an adventure. But he'd be guessing the parents were facing this new existence with despair, having traded green hillsides and ocean horizons for dirty streets and row upon row of tenement housing. A hovel in Ireland in exchange for one in America. Still poor, still hungry, still hated.

'Twas a bitter pill to swallow, that he knew. He'd been here five years already and still the only work he'd been able to get was that which no one else would do: digging canals, building railroads, blasting tunnels through rock. Fourteen-hour days for pauper's wages and still just surviving.

But at least he was alive. And alive, he could have hope.

He stopped in front of a run-down, four-story tenement, one of an unending stretch of nearly identical buildings, all ancient, all decrepit, all home to Irish immigrants searching for a better life. A cacophony of sounds and voices filtered down from open windows above: babies wailing, a man and woman arguing, mothers calling, children playing, someone singing an Irish ballad from so very long ago...

Memories surged through him like a rush of air beneath the wings of a falcon diving at its prey. He felt the sharp prick of homesickness and longing, and roughly shook off the thoughts before the talons sank too deeply into him.

Nerves taut, he dug out the scrap of paper and compared the address on the building to the one Ailish had provided. This was the place.

He stepped into the dark entry and climbed the sagging stairs to the third floor, the acidic odor of urine tingling in his nostrils. The devil take his soul, he may not be close to buying a farm, but at least he was living better than this.

He stopped at the door marked thirty-eight and rapped firmly, anxious to get the discussion started and over with. Behind him, hinges creaked and the raspy voice of an old woman asked, "Are ye wanting something?"

He barely glanced back. "I'm here to see Miss Sullivan."

"Ahh. She might be there. And she might be working. Works all the time, that one." The woman shuffled into the hall and tapped several times on Ailish's door with her cane as if his own knocking hadn't been enough.

"Patience, please," a woman muttered from inside the flat. She tugged at the door, muttering unintelligibly as the lower edge wedged in the frame. Sean stuck out a foot and gave the door a shove to pop it open, then took a quick step back.

A petite woman stood in the doorway, cheeks flushed, dark

hair curled into a knot at her nape, brown eyes glinting with vexation. "Can I be helping you?" Her lingering frustration with the door was evident in her voice.

"I'm here to see Ailish Sullivan," he said.

"I'm Ailish."

"What's this one wanting now?" the old woman demanded.

Ailish narrowed her eyes. "I suppose he wants what all the others want, don't you think?"

The old woman tutted loudly, and Ailish leveled a glare on her until she backed into her apartment and shut the door. Then she raised a mischievous grin and a questioning brow at Sean.

His planned introduction lodged in his throat. He'd pictured someone older, meaner, heavier...uglier. He could almost hear Ma saying, "*Is minic cuma aingeal ar an Diabhal féin. There is often the look of an angel on the Devil himself.*" He glanced away. "I, ah—I'm Sean Deacey—"

"What can I be helping you with, Mr. Deacey?"

He blinked.

"Are you picking up mending?"

Mending? "Nay. "I've come on behalf of Jack and Kathleen—"

"Ahhh. The Montgomerys," she said without surprise.

Her matter-of-fact tone threw him; he'd expected anger at the least. When she said nothing more, he began again. "You told them that...your sister died in the wreck of the brig St. John. In Cohasset."

"Aye. And her family with her. All except Liam."

"Who is it Ailish?" someone called from within the flat.

Sean heard the door behind him creak open again. Nosy old biddy. He didn't want this conversation to become fodder for the gossip mill and somehow affect the outcome. "Could we talk inside?"

Ailish hesitated, then called over her shoulder. "Just

someone for me, Meg. I'll be back in a bit." She grabbed a cloak from a hook inside the door and stepped into the hall. "A fine day for a stroll, would you not agree?" she asked, heading away from him without a backward glance.

He squinted after her. The only thing about this visit that was turning out the way he'd expected was the condition of the building. He followed her down the stairs and out to the street. Though the sun was high, a crisp wind had come up, and it was clear that winter was determined to not yet be counted out. He tugged up his collar and dropped into step beside Ailish.

"I imagine you'll be wondering," she said, eyes forward as they walked shoulder to shoulder, "if the woman who died in the shipwreck is really my sister. Or perhaps you'll be wondering whether I learned a babe survived the wreck and decided to attach myself to him because...who would know whether it was true? And what riches might I collect just by being his relation?" She slowed her steps. "But mostly I think you'll be wondering...how much money will it take to make this woman go away."

Well, there it all was. Sean kept his gaze on the road ahead and debated his response. Any negotiations would surely be easier if they were on friendly terms, so it would be the height of stupidity to accuse her of deceit.

"Aye?" she pressed.

"The truth is what the Montgomerys seek, that's all."

"Ah. The truth," she said, perusing the neighborhood.

Sean followed the sweep of her eyes over the brickwork lacking chunks of mortar and the wood trim covered with flaking paint. Past the ropes strung between buildings, sagging beneath fresh-washed clothing that was permanently soiled from age and wear.

"Here's a truth for your English friends, the Montgomerys,"

she said. "Find an English child to adopt and leave the Irish to the Irish. They've given us slums here in America—why would we give them our children?"

They passed a tavern; rowdy laughter and song wafted through its open door. Someone whistled at Ailish and she ignored both the man and the sound, her only reaction a subtle stiffening of her spine.

Sean clasped his gloved hands together and forged ahead. "I understand why you said...what you just said. But I'll not just be walking away. I've been charged with asking ye, what would it take for you to...what is it you want, Miss Sullivan?"

"To give up Liam? To leave him to be raised as an Englishman, away from any family of his own?"

"Nay, it's not—"

"What I want—faith, they'd likely not even understand," she said, her voice raw. "I want my sister, the one who brushed my hair when I was a child. Who promised we'd raise our children in houses side-by-side. Who came to America to build a new life...and died within sight of the shore." She rubbed a hand across her eyes. "What do I want?" Her words wobbled. "I want the family I've lost. I want the country I left."

Her pain pierced like the barbs of an arrow, sticking beneath his skin and entwining her loss with his. Sean hissed out a breath and jerked his emotions into check. She was likely playing a role, pretending to be the grieving sister as a means of pressuring the family into offering more money. He would be wise to remember that.

"I understand," he said evenly. "But you're here now, we all are, and though your life is not as you hoped it would be..." He almost winced at what he was about to say. "To use your own words...*what would it take for you to go away?*"

She spun to face him, dark eyes flashing. "What do you see when you look at me, Mr. Deacey?"

He frowned, uncertain about how to answer or what she was looking to hear. The wind tugged loose strands of her hair and swirled them around her cheeks, and he almost reached out to tuck them behind her ear.

"Since the cat seems to have taken your tongue, let me answer for you," she said. "What ye don't see is a fool. Nor a mind that is easily swayed from its loyalty." Her eyes narrowed. "You've lost no one, have you?"

Memories crashed forward in his mind. The deaths of his wife and their sons. His inability to save them.

"I thought not," she bit out, as he squeezed the bleeding wound closed.

Her eyes were on everything but him. "Try if ye can, to feel what it's like to pray—to beg—for the lives of the people you love to be spared. And watch those prayers go unanswered." Her voice pitched low. "That was when I prayed for God to take me as well, so I wouldn't have to go on without them. 'Twas not until I went to Cohasset that I understood why that prayer went unanswered, too. I was spared because of my sister's son." She raised her eyes to Sean's, and he knew what her next words would be before she said them.

"I'll accept no money," she said in a quiet voice. "It isn't money I want. It's Liam. He's all I have left. I'll not see him raised in an English household with an English name."

Her words landed like a punch to Sean's gut. He had scant doubt that Ailish was telling the truth. She was Will's aunt.

The news would destroy Kathleen.

It was almost destroying him. The child he'd delivered to his sister and her husband would bring them more anguish than any of Kathleen's miscarriages had.

In desperation, he began to talk, his memories of the shipwreck the only hope he had left of trying to change her mind. "I was in Cohasset when the St. John went down. I pulled Will's—Liam's—father from the ocean. He'd been thrown against the rocks more than once, might have been rescued sooner, but he wouldn't let go of the satchel in his arms. Inside that bag, I found Liam."

Ailish's eyes brimmed with tears.

"He died making sure his son would have a chance for a better life. Liam went to a fine home—and not just an English home. Kathleen Montgomery is me sister. Deacey is her surname. She's Irish," he said, his words coming faster. "Her husband is English, aye, but a good man he is. I hold no love for the English, but Jack is different. Miss Sullivan, the life they've given Liam is better than either of us could ever dream of. He has opportunities, a future secure." He opened his arms wide. "If he stays with them, he'll be able to rise above a life such as this."

Ailish was already shaking her head. "You'll not be understanding," she said. "I promised my sister I would take care of her children if ever anything happened to her."

"With what?" Sean asked gently. "You say you have nothing. How will you care for a child? Will is adored beyond measure. My sister and her husband love him like their own."

Ailish leveled a steely gaze on him. "I love him, too," she said, pressing a fist to her heart. "He is my family. He belongs with me."

"You must be knowing they'll not just hand him over," he said, his voice hardening. "Can you prove your claim? That he truly is your sister's son?"

She caught her lip in her teeth. "I'll find a way. I'm not looking for money. Not a penny do I want—only Liam. Faith, but can you not understand what it is to love a child of your own blood?"

Aye, his brain whispered. *I know.* "My sister and her husband—"

"He's not theirs," Ailish said fiercely. "I'm his family. I have the right to raise him, and by all that is holy, I will." She spun on her heel and began to stride away, her steps long and purposeful, as if determined to put as much space as possible between her and Sean.

"They'll be getting a lawyer," he called after her.

"Ah, well, I'm ahead of them there," she shot back. "And mine has been working for a week already."

Jaw clenched, Sean watched her disappear down the street. He drew in a slow, steady breath and turned for home, his thoughts random and disjointed. He'd come to help Kathleen, but if Ailish was telling the truth—and God help him but he feared she was—what then? If the shoe was on the other foot, would Kathleen not fight with all she had to get the child back? Just as Ailish was doing?

What if both women were right?

CHAPTER SIX

"Your soul to the devil, Sean Deacey!" Ailish muttered as she rammed the door to the flat open with her shoulder. Her mind spooled back over their conversation, coming up with all the things she should have said, all the arguments she should have made to convince Sean that Liam belonged with her, *to persuade the Montgomerys to give him up without a fight.*

"Who was that fine-looking gentleman come to call?" Meg asked from across the room.

Ailish tossed her cloak on a hook. "For God's bright sake, Meg. He may be fine-looking, but he's no gentleman. Not when he's trying to keep me from my own flesh and blood." Sean's visage appeared in her mind, dark hair woven with copper, deep blue eyes like the ocean off the western coast of Ireland. She stomped on the image.

"That's the man who took Liam in?" Meg dropped her mending into her lap.

"Nay. Just a relative sent to find out how much money 'twould take to make me go away."

"Didn't I say they would? Could be the best thing for ye, Ailish."

She tensed. "I'll not be trading Liam for thirty pieces of silver."

"Don't be foolish. Without a husband, how are you to care for a young child?" Meg chided. "Earning barely enough to support yourself. Liam would make eight of us living in this three-room hovel." She stabbed the needle into the cloth, back and through, back and through, as though each thrust underscored the precariousness of their lives. "Keep standing on your principles and there will be two of ye hungry instead of just you."

Ailish went to the window, braced her hands on the sill and rested her forehead on the glass. She'd been lucky to rent a room with Meg and her family, a flat not as crowded as those where so many Irish lived. They'd formed a good friendship these past months. And yet, Meg with four children of her own, couldn't seem to understand why Ailish was so determined to get Liam.

She stared down at the alley, through crisscrossed clotheslines sagging beneath laundry flapping in the air like ghosts of Irish dead. Shoving the sash open, she leaned outside to pull the clothesline toward her, retrieving each garment in turn and piling it on the wooden table.

A group of underdressed children sprinted down the alley, shouting and whooping as they chased each other toward the main street. Would that be Liam's life once she had him? Running wild while she worked?

She rammed the window closed to block the noise and all that it represented. "We'll find a way to get by."

"Like you're getting by now? You came here with nothing. You see how hard it is, how Brian and I struggle to take care of our family." She crossed the room and began to fold the clothing Ailish had brought inside.

"Aye, but there are six of you."

"Ye've not seen the lad since he was a babe just a month out of the womb. He won't even be knowing you."

"So I should just leave him to grow up without knowing his real family?" she challenged. "These people who have him, this Sean Deacey, they lost no one in the famine. Is it fair that they get Liam, too?"

"God knows, I understand what you're saying." Hunched forward, Meg smoothed a shirt open on the table, then straightened and pressed her hands into her lower back. "But look how we live, Ailish. This flat, the work we do. Money could get you on your feet, set you on a path. You'd not have to struggle so."

Aye, but she would lose Liam. How could Meg think such a thing, let alone say it? She opened her mouth to snap out a retort, but Meg waved her silent.

"Could you not bargain with them?" Meg said. "Ask for enough money that it will change your life—but agree to let the boy stay with them only if they allow you to visit him now and again."

"Now and again?" Ailish asked, incredulous. She paced several steps away, wanting suddenly to run out the door and escape this conversation and the truth in Meg's words—a truth she didn't want to hear. "'Tis hardly the same as raising him."

"Do you understand what you're getting yourself into? If they won't give him up, you'll be needing a lawyer. That will cost money. A lot I'll be guessing."

"Don't you think I know?" she snapped. "I spoke to one already. Kind enough he was to offer help for a lesser fee."

"I'm not trying to trouble you, Ailish. But even if the fee is less, how will you pay it?"

"I'll have to be finding a second job."

"And if ye succeed, how will you fit that in?" Meg slapped a hand on the pile of clothing. "You already work long hours at Jordan-Marsh. And if you have a child depending on you..." Meg clucked her tongue in frustration. "A single woman like you would have been better off—"

"As a domestic. Aye, with room and board. We've been through all this before." Perhaps it would have been a better choice, but she hadn't been able to bear the thought of being on call twenty-four hours a day. 'Twas no better than servitude. "At least the store closes every day and I can call a few hours my own."

She stuck her hands on her hips. "Besides, I'd have to be leaving any household job once I had a child. He couldn't be staying in the servants' quarters with the Bridgets," she spat.

"Ailish!" Meg recoiled at Ailish's use of a common derogatory slur for Irish domestics.

"Liam is all I have left," Ailish said, beseeching.

Meg let out a deep sigh of surrender and reached out to brush a hand along Ailish's arm. "You might go up to the next floor and talk to that old woman, Eileen McDonough," she said.

"More mending?" Much as she hated stitching, her spirits rose. Money was money when one was in need.

"She does sewing too, don't you know? Ready-made clothes for the Irish Relief Society. Perhaps she'd have some stitching you could help with." Meg's face brightened. "Ah, and ye might offer to help her with deliveries for some extra coin. Getting long in the tooth she is, and not able to get around like she used to."

~

WILL STOOD beside the bed where his great-grandfather lay propped against the pillows, and marched a tin soldier up the old man's arm. "This the gen'ral," he announced.

"Be gentle," Kathleen cautioned. She pulled a wooden chair near the bed to sit beside Jack in the sun-filled room. Despite the grandfather's illness, he insisted on keeping the curtains open, saying it felt like a coffin when everything was closed up. *I may have one foot in the grave and the other on the edge, but I'm not gone yet*, he'd chided them.

"Where are the soldiers?" the old man asked, his voice weak but steady. "The general must have an army."

"They here," Will shouted. He scooped a handful of soldiers from the box on the floor and flung them onto the grandfather's chest.

Jack grabbed Will's shoulder. "Be careful, Will. You can't be throwing—"

"Let him," the old man wheezed. "No better way to spend the time I have left...than playing with my grandson."

A lump tightened Kathleen's throat. There was a time she would have thought it impossible the old man could love an Irish child. But he loved this one, their Will, beyond measure. It would be heartbreaking to lose him to death with Will so young.

The grandfather pushed back an edge of the blanket to free his hand, then began to stand tin soldiers up on his stomach. "Help me, Will boy. Get these men ready for battle."

Once Will was engrossed in the task, the old man closed his eyes and sank into the pillow. Kathleen watched his chest gently rise and fall, glad that he'd fallen asleep. He'd become so agitated after learning about Ailish, Jack had brought him a whiskey to calm him. Surely the doctor wouldn't approve, but what difference could it make with him growing worse each day?

Sean appeared in the doorway and she breathed out his name, anxious to hear what he'd learned and yet afraid at the same time. "Should talk downstairs?" she whispered.

"No." The grandfather's eyes flicked open. "He's my great-grandson...I want to know." He struggled to sit up, and his movement toppled the soldiers on his chest as though they'd been broadsided by a cannon ball.

Will let out a squawk.

"Sorry, lad." Hand trembling, the old man set up one of the fallen soldiers and reached for another.

Jack motioned Sean into the room. "Did you find her? What did she say?"

Will froze, a soldier clutched in each hand, his expression solemn, as if he knew something of great import was about to be revealed. "What she say?" he echoed.

"She said *set up the army*," the old man rasped with authority. He patted his chest. "Right here. Quick."

Will grinned and began to help his grandfather arrange the soldiers in opposing lines of red and blue. As the boy chattered on about war and battles, oblivious to the skirmish that had been commenced on his behalf, Kathleen nodded at Sean to continue.

He jammed his hands into his pockets and fixed his attention on the opposite wall. "She was there. But what I learned was not quite what we hoped. I'm sorry. I'm glad I went, for at least we know..." He shook his head.

A chill skittered through Kathleen and she wrapped her arms about her waist and waited. An uneasy silence settled over the room, the air suddenly heavy and suffocating. Will's head popped up. Eyes wide in concern, he looked around the room, then smacked a tin soldier against Kathleen's knee. She reached a hand down to protect herself from another blow, but kept her eyes locked on Sean.

"Mam. Mam," Will said, his voice rising. She knew he could sense the tension in the room, knew she should respond to him, but she couldn't tear her eyes off Sean.

Will jabbed the toy into her leg, then forced it into her hand. "Mam! You be the Cor'nel."

"The colonel?" She tried to sound delighted, but her voice quavered. "Line up men. Line them up, Will." She closed the soldier into her fist, pressed the hard edges into her palm until it hurt, as if the physical pain could block the emotional agony of whatever Sean was about to say. "What did you learn?" she whispered.

He began to recount his conversation with Ailish, leaving out Will's name so the boy wouldn't know they were speaking of him. "Her story...we've all heard it before. She's lost her entire family—parents, sister, husband, cousins—"

"Maybe she's a good liar," Jack said.

"I thought of that." Sean pursed his lips. "But if ye'd been there to hear her yourself..." He pulled over a straight-backed chair and sat down. "Hard to think she's lying, for she'll accept no talk of payment."

"None?" Kathleen said on an exhale.

"He's ours," the old man murmured. "What life will he have in a tenement...all those Irish?"

"Grandfather." Jack threw an apologetic look at Kathleen, but she ignored the slight. The old man was dying, and in this moment the only thing that mattered was how much he loved Will.

"You think she's telling the truth," Jack said.

"Aye." Sean scrubbed both hands over his face. "I do."

Kathleen began to tremble. Will stood stock still, looked

between her and Sean, then pitched two soldiers on the floor and kicked one across the room.

"Will Montgomery." Kathleen took hold of his arm. "I think ye'll need to be sitting quietly for a minute or two."

"Nay!" He twisted away from her, shaking his head.

"Can I be the Colonel?" Jack held out a hand. "Isn't it my turn?"

Will scrunched up his mouth as he mulled over the offer, then set a soldier in his father's open palm. Jack marched the man across the quilt. "Attention men, a-tten-tion," he said, making eye contact with Sean.

"While I don't think she's lying," Sean continued with a nod, "I'm not sure she can prove she's the aunt. Seems to me that would work in your favor."

Will let out a frightened screech, as if the stress tangling through the room had winnowed its way inside him. Kathleen reached for her son. This couldn't be real. It couldn't be happening. Sure but she was dreaming, a nightmare. All she had to do was awaken—

Will swung an arm and brushed the soldiers off the bed, eyes wide as they clattered to the wood floor. "Mam, making a mess," he cried. "Big mess."

She pulled him close and planted a kiss on each cheek. "Aye, love, such a mess you've made."

At her unexpected response, he climbed into her lap and burrowed into her embrace. Kathleen slanted a look at her brother. "Sean, it almost sounds like you don't fault what she's doing."

He rubbed hand over the back of his neck and closed his eyes. "Better you know than to ask that, Kathleen. It's not right what she's doing, not with...him...almost three years old. But I'll admit, it's hard for me to blame her overmuch if her story is true.

Think, Kathleen. What if you had been the only member of our family to survive. And then you learned a child of mine was alive? Your only living relative. Would you accept money in exchange for him?"

Kathleen tightened her arms around Will as if her love could keep him safe and part of their family. "Sometimes I hate you, Sean."

"Would you not do exactly as she is doing?" he pressed.

"Aye," she mumbled. "I would fight to get that child with everything I had."

"Even if she's telling the truth, he's been our son far longer than she ever knew him," Jack said, standing. "She's a stranger to him. This won't be a one-sided battle."

"It will be a war," the grandfather rasped.

A disaster, Kathleen thought.

"If we're going to war, we need a plan," Sean said.

Will slid off Kathleen's lap and ran about the room gathering his soldiers, placing them in two facing lines on the rug beside the bed. No one spoke; they just watched him, each trapped in their own thoughts and fears of the road ahead.

"War," Will cried, breaking the silence. He crashed one soldier into another, becoming progressively unrulier as he shouted, "Go away. Go away! I'm the gen'ral." Within seconds, tin soldiers were scattered across the rug. Will sat back on his heels.

"Who won?" the grandfather asked.

Will surveyed the carnage he had wrought, not one soldier, neither red nor blue, left standing. Then he lifted a shoulder in an indifferent shrug and began to set them up again.

CHAPTER SEVEN

"IT DOES APPEAR YOU HAVE A PREDICAMENT." THE PORTLY, SILVER-haired attorney considered them from behind a large mahogany desk so covered with papers and files its glossy surface was hardly visible.

Though Kathleen sat rigidly in her chair, his comment eased the pressure in her mind a bit. *Predicament* wasn't a very threatening word. Certainly nothing remotely like *disaster.* Perhaps this lawyer who had come so highly recommended would have an easy solution.

The man steepled his fingers and tapped his lip. "You asked about my background, whether I had experience that might help you in this case. Let me share some of that first. As you can tell by my appearance—" He gestured at his white hair. "—I've been doing this more than a few years. As you may know, many learn the law by serving an apprenticeship to an attorney. I, however, attended Litchfield Law School. At the time, it was the most prominent law school in the country. It's been closed some twenty years now, but other fine institutions, Harvard and Yale, have taken its place.

He broke off as if caught up in memories, then brought his attention back. "Nonetheless, from Litchfield have come many members of the House of Representatives, senators, governors, cabinet secretaries, Supreme Court justices..."

Kathleen laced her fingers together in her lap and bit the inside of her lip to keep herself from urging him to get on with it. Thaddeus Barker had come highly recommended, albeit with a warning about his proclivity toward long-windedness.

"I studied under Tapping Reeve, not many years before he was named Chief Justice of the Connecticut Supreme Court," Mr. Barker continued. "You may find it interesting...Tapping Reeve's first law student many years ago was none other than Aaron Burr—yes, the man who became Vice President."

Holy Mary, she felt ready to jump out of her skin. Would there be no end to this prattling introduction? She sneaked a glance at Jack, and he narrowed his eyes slightly, urging her, she knew, to be patient.

Mr. Barker chuckled. "Now of course, I was a generation behind Mr. Burr. I actually attended Litchfield with Theron Metcalf who currently sits on the Massachusetts Supreme Court."

Kathleen held back a scream. "It's all very interesting, sir, and I think you qualified beyond measure, but—"

"I understand. You want to know if I can help you. I must apologize. Sometimes I talk to give myself time to think, strange as that may sound." He moved a paperweight off a stack of documents, shuffled through the papers as though searching for something, then frowned and raised his gaze.

"The answer to your question is...perhaps. I wish I could say *yes,* but I won't promise what I'm not sure of. I'll have to do some investigation into the truth about Miss Sullivan's familial relationship to young Will. If she is indeed his aunt—and for your sake, I hope she is not—she very likely has rights." He looked between Jack and Kathleen. "And if it's true she already has an attorney, we've got catching up to do."

Kathleen tried to tamp down her suddenly rising panic. Mr. Barker was considered one of the best attorneys in Boston; surely he would be able to put an end to Miss Sullivan's demands.

"If it turns out that she is the child's aunt, there will have to be a hearing before a judge," he said, his tone even more serious. "I'll make your case. Miss Sullivan's lawyer will make her case. It will be up to the judge to decide what happens with boy."

"We've had Will two and a half years," Jack said. "Miss Sullivan knew him barely a month before his family left Ireland."

"Does it not count for anything that he was alone?" Kathleen slid forward until she was perched on the edge of her chair. "No one wanted him, and we took him in. How can someone just swoop in and lay claim to him now?"

"The law has changed since you got the boy."

Kathleen's heart slammed against her chest. "*What law?*"

Jack expression hardened. "We asked the proper officials what we needed to do to make him part of our family. They said there was no law. That we need only take him into our home and raise him and he would be ours."

"We did exactly as they told us." A hollow opened in Kathleen's chest and she longed to return home, to swoop Will into her arms and dance about the room like they'd done so many times since Sean arrived with him on that chilly November afternoon.

"You did the right thing at the time." The attorney shuffled through his papers again, finally drawing out a single sheet and setting it on top of the pile. "But, last May...May the twenty-fourth, eighteen fifty-one to be precise, the Massachusetts legislature passed the *Adoption of Children Act.* First law of its kind in the nation. Though it was designed to protect the welfare of orphaned children, by doing that it also provides protections for their adoptive parents."

He leaned forward as if to emphasize his next point. "I'll explain. There have been cases of natural parents coming forward years later, demanding their children back. Prior to the passage of this law, the people who took in the child, *the new parents*, had no rights. This law creates what is called...binding adoption. It ensures the child is a legal member of the new family...and that he or she is treated in exactly the same way as any natural-born child, with all the same rights, such as inheritance."

"Will already has that with us," Jack said.

"Not all children have been so lucky. In the past, some people have taken in orphans to get servants. Many were treated badly, underfed, not sent to school."

"But that isn't us," Kathleen said. "Does that count for nothing?" She could hear the desperation in her voice and didn't care.

The lawyer gave them both an appraising look. "It may. Eventually. But the law has requirements. A judge must determine whether the adoptive parents have sufficient ability to bring up the child. And, whether it's proper for the adoption to take place at all."

The child. Will wasn't *the child;* he was their son. He was Will Montgomery, a little boy nearly three who loved soldiers and building blocks and stories and biscuits. A little boy with a spirit so big sometimes it got the better of him.

Bile rose in the back of her throat and she forced it down.

Mr. Barker pushed back his chair and went to stoke the fire in the hearth. The flames flared yellow and orange like a sunset on the horizon sending up fingers of light to meet the falling darkness.

"The law requires that the child's next of kin consents to the adoption," he said in hushed voice, staring into the fire. "If there is no next of kin, the judge of probate will appoint a suitable representative."

Outside the window, the wind blustered across the gray day, smattering the pane with droplets of sleet that sank to the sill in rivulets. *Like an omen*, Kathleen thought.

"They searched for next of kin," Jack said. "They couldn't find any."

"That will be in your favor, I'm sure. But I can't understate this. You don't have a legally binding adoption—"

"'Twasn't even possible then." Kathleen tried to hold her voice level, to sound calm and reasonable.

"I understand." The lawyer's brow creased. "But since next of kin has allegedly stepped forward, we'll have to petition a judge for legal adoption. I would imagine a hearing would be scheduled rather quickly because custody of a child is at stake."

He sat behind his desk again, eyes drooping along with the corners of his mouth. "The new law is clear. The child's welfare must be considered when finalizing an adoption. That means if Miss Sullivan is indeed a member of Will's natural family, our path to success will be narrower. In that case, I believe your best hope will be to convince the judge that it's in Will's best interests to stay with you."

"How do we do that?" Jack asked.

Mr. Barker closed his fingers around the heavy paperweight. "We begin by showing the differences in your living situations.

The quality of your neighborhood, of your home, compared to where Miss Sullivan lives."

"The North End," Kathleen said.

"Exactly. It won't be hard to show that you can give him a more...stable...life."

Kathleen thought of her family's one room cottage in Ireland, the place she'd grown up. Seven of them living in that small home with its single chair and dirt floors and straw on the ground for beds. They'd not had much of anything except each other...and love. "It isn't the grandness of the house that should matter," she said softly.

"If we hope to win, we'll have to argue otherwise," the attorney countered. "We'll also make the case that you're a married couple, while Miss Sullivan would be raising the child alone. A boy needs a father. She has no husband to fill that role." He scratched some notes on a sheet of paper. "Then there is money. How will she support the boy, who will care for him while she works? Obviously, neither of those are issues in your household."

"You plan to show she is unfit to raise him," Jack said.

Mr. Barker sat back in his chair. "Yes. This law is so new, there isn't precedent to rely on for guidance. So first, we'll determine whether she's telling the truth. If she isn't, all this is moot. But if she is, I believe this strategy will give you the best chance of keeping Will. Though I must be clear, I can't guarantee anything."

Kathleen's stomach roiled. She wanted to fight back, wanted to adopt Will legally, to know he would always be their child. "But if we find she truly is his aunt, is there not some—" She faltered, searching for the right word. "Is there not some kinder way to do this? If we purposely tear down Will's own aunt, hurt her just to win...tell me, what does that make us then?"

"It makes you parents who love their son." The attorney clasped his hands together on his desk. "I'd be happy to take this case. Would you like me to move forward?"

Jack's hand tightened around Kathleen's. "Yes."

~

KATHLEEN STOPPED in the doorway to the grandfather's bedroom and let her eyes adjust to the dim light. Ma sat in a chair beside the bed where the old man lay, deep in the slumber of the sick.

"He'll not be happy to find it dark in here when he wakes." Kathleen took the chair beside her mother. "How is he doing?"

"The same. Sleeping mostly. How did your meeting go?"

Kathleen reflected on the discussion they'd had with the attorney. Easy it was to see it would not be a simple path. God save them all if they lost both the oldest and the youngest from the household at the same time. "Not as well as we expected, I would say. Especially if Ailish is telling the truth." She put her elbows on her knees and dropped her head into her hands. "There is a new law..."

By the time she finished recounting what the attorney had told them, Ma's face had flushed red. "Mary, mother of Jesus, she has a case? Are you saying to me that she could get Will? What kind of man would allow that?"

"The judge is bound by the law, Ma. Our only hope is to prove her unfit to raise him."

"Run." The word was hardly more than a murmur.

Kathleen lifted her brows at Ma and turned toward the grandfather. His eyes were closed, his breathing soft with the slow cadence of slumber.

"Run," the old man murmured. "Take the boy." His lids cracked open. "California. Canada." He let out a hacking cough.

Ma moved to wipe his mouth, and he blocked her hand and took the handkerchief from her. "I'm not an invalid. Not yet, anyway. And why the hell is it so dark in here?"

Despite everything, Kathleen smiled. Even as his health failed, the grandfather remained cantankerous, a picture of determination in the face of an overwhelming foe.

"He's your child now. And Jack's," he said, his mouth becoming a hard line. "Leave. None would ever find you."

She considered the idea, warmed to it, embraced it as a solution even as she raced to discard it. "How could we? Jack has his business. I don't think—"

"Think on it too long..." His voice dropped so low, she had to strain to hear him. "...and you'll lose your son." His eyes closed and he was asleep again, each inhale hewed with a jagged edge.

Think too long and you'll lose your son. The words stumbled through Kathleen's thoughts like a drunkard at the end of a party, bouncing from pillar to wall along his path to the door. Her mind grasped hold of the idea, the chance for a shortcut through a landscape lined with steep cliffs on all sides.

Run. It wasn't something she'd even given a thought to. Nor had Jack, she was sure. *Run.* There would be no court hearing. No proving Ailish unfit. No judge's decision. *Run.* They could keep Will, keep their family intact, keep living as they were now.

Could they do such a thing? Should they?

Ma's eyes were on her. "What are ye thinking lass?"

She lifted a casual shoulder to hide her serious consideration. "I'll be thinking that leaving Ireland behind was far harder than this might be. Could it be the answer to our worries?"

Ma brought her palms together as if in prayer. "Or the beginning of new ones," she said. "*Is glas na conic I bhfad uainn.* Distant hills look green."

"Are you saying distant hills are not?" Kathleen snapped, her patience paper thin. "For I'll not be finding the nearby hills too green these days, Ma."

"Wondering is all I'm doing. Would you ever be able to stop looking over your shoulder?"

Kathleen glanced at the double window on the far wall, heavy drapes blocking the afternoon sun from brightening the room. "How would she ever find us?"

"She might not need to." Ma straightened the blankets on the grandfather, lay a gentle hand on his forehead, then motioned Kathleen into the hall.

As soon as the door shut behind them, Kathleen whirled round. "What is it you're saying, Ma?"

"Think, Kathleen. What will you be telling Will when he's older? Will you hide from him that he was born to other parents?"

Kathleen recoiled slightly. "Nay. Why would we do that? 'Tis his right to know."

"Then how will you answer his questions about his other family? Will ye say they're all dead? Ailish included?"

The question stabbed at her, opening a wound she hadn't expected. She held up a hand, not just to hold back the question but to stop her mother from saying anything more. Ma folded Kathleen's hand between both of her own.

"What will happen, lass, when you tell Will that all his natural family died—except his mother's sister? That she came to find him and you ran away with him, kept him from ever knowing her and any family history she might share?"

"Are you wanting us to lose Will?" Kathleen jerked her hand away.

"Och, Kathleen, never. You know that," Ma said. "But the

path you take today cannot help but set you on other paths tomorrow. You must choose wisely."

Kathleen spun away in frustration, spotted her reflection in a mirror on the wall and stopped to stare at the woman looking back at her. Ma came up beside her, their faces side by side, the resemblance obvious.

"Child of mine..." Ma set her palm against Kathleen's cheek, her touch cool, soothing as it had been when Kathleen was young. "Put yourself in Will's place, lass. What if you were to learn this very day that your Da and I hid your natural family from you all these years?"

Kathleen let out a rough exhale. She brushed her fingers over her mother's reflection and then over her own, the nose, the mouth, so much the same. "I would hate you," she whispered, meeting her mother's gaze in the mirror. "Much as I love you, I would hate you."

"Aye. Take Will away from Ailish now, and someday, once you've told him she exists, he may take himself away from you to find her."

CHAPTER EIGHT

THE MORNING OF THE HEARING, KATHLEEN ROSE WITH THE SUN, her nerves fragile, brittle. She felt as if she'd been somehow transformed into crystal, and the mere tap of a pin might shatter her into a thousand pieces.

It had only been a week. Just one week since Ailish appeared at the door and their lives had been upended. A week during which their attorney had gone to Cohasset and located the Irishman who had been on the brig St. John, the man who identified Will...and the bodies of his family. A week during which their lawyer confirmed that the man and Ailish had grown up in the same parish in Ireland and known each other since childhood.

A week that ended with both sides in agreement that Ailish was speaking the truth about her connection to Will.

Though Mr. Barker had said he thought the judge would quickly schedule a hearing, Kathleen never expected it to happen this fast. It was moving so swiftly, sometimes she felt like she was back on the ocean in a storm, ship heeling, sails tearing, water rushing over the rail—and no way to save herself.

She dressed Will and fed him breakfast, not even caring that he threw his last spoonful of porridge on the table. "My sweet boy, you're the best mess maker," she managed to get out before the tears stacking down the back of her throat stopped her from saying more. She brought her eyes to meet Jack's, and they exchanged a hundred words without speaking. There was no need to say aloud what both knew already—this hearing could destroy the rest of their lives.

"Will, let's make a fort for the soldiers." Jack scooped the boy from his high chair and went into the parlor as though this day was no different than any other.

Kathleen watched them from the doorway, both cross-legged on the floor near the hearth, the fire crackling beside them as they stacked wooden blocks into battlements and strategically set up formations of soldiers in preparation for combat. Pressing her lips together tight, she turned away to compose herself, determined not to let the turmoil of this morning touch her son.

She escaped into the kitchen and collapsed against the wall, squeezed the corners of her eyes with her fingers to block her tears. Seconds later, she felt Emma's arms curve around her.

"The place for that boy is here with the two of you," Emma murmured. "I've been praying all week that the judge sees it the same way."

"Kathleen?" Sean's voice preceded his entry into the kitchen. He was already wearing his overcoat. "We'll need to be on our way if we're to talk with the lawyer before it starts."

Emma held out a handkerchief, and Kathleen blotted her eyes and cheeks. She brushed nonexistent lint off the front of her navy wool dress and raised her brows for approval.

"You look perfect. Quite proper." Emma gave her a tremulous smile.

The two women followed Sean toward the main door, only to find Jack still playing with Will in the parlor. Flat on his back, holding his son above him in the air, he swooped the boy from one side to the other as Will flapped his arms and squealed, "I'm flying! I'm flying away."

Spying them waiting, Jack lowered Will to his chest and rolled to his feet with the boy in his arms. "No flying away, my little bird," he said, voice cracking. "Don't fly away."

As he brushed off his trouser legs and shrugged into his overcoat, Emma took Will's hand and motioned them on their way. Necessity forced them out the door into the chilly morning; nervousness sped their steps.

They reached School Street more quickly than expected and found the short, narrow lane already busy with carriages and wagons rumbling upon the cobblestones, the walk crowded with people calling to one another over the din. To Kathleen's relief, they were forced to take the next block at a slower pace, a delay that felt much like a reprieve.

At the cross of Province Street, they stopped shoulder-to-shoulder and gazed up at city hall, an austere three-story stone building where the courthouse was located and the hearing was to take place. Kathleen took hold of Jack's arm to steady herself. *To steady her thoughts.*

It was then she spotted Ma and Da, dressed in their best clothes, waiting near the building entrance. "Jesus, Mary, and Joseph, look at that," she said, incredulous. Her mood lightened. Clutching her skirt, she stepped into the street and dodged between conveyances to get across to her parents. "How do you come to be here? Do you not have to work?" she asked. "Da, they let you take off?"

"Aye, a few hours. *For an urgent matter.*" He set his mouth. "Life and death, I told them. For it is, in a sense."

"Would you think we'd leave you to face this alone?" Ma shook her head as Da straightened his top hat.

"They'll not be thinking a harsh word about the Deacey family if I can help it," he said. "Now let's be getting this over so we can put it behind us."

Kathleen couldn't hold back her grateful smile, nor the hope that rose within her. Their lawyer met them at the door and they huddled for a quick discussion before hanging up their coats and heading into the courtroom.

Inside the door, Kathleen froze.

Rows of mostly-empty pews lined each side of a center aisle leading to the dark wood judge's bench at the head of the room. Two wooden tables, one left and one right, sat in front of the bench. Ailish and her attorney were already seated at one table; the other, Kathleen knew, was for her and Jack.

Mr. Barker tilted his head toward the third row where a man sat alone, head bowed, hat clasped in his hands. "That's the man from the ship. The one who identified the baby," he whispered. "Across the aisle is Dr. Foster, who treated the survivors." He dipped his chin toward three well-dressed young men seated mid-courtroom. "And those are law students, just here to observe."

Kathleen drew a shuddering breath laced with fear and disbelief. Nothing seemed real. Jack gave her hand a gentle tug, and she forced one foot forward and then the next, one deliberate step after another, their footsteps on the wood floor overly loud in the silent room.

They weren't seated at the table more than a minute when a door opened off to one side and the judge swept into the room. A lean man he was, his expression inscrutable, his loose black robe billowing behind him like the sweptback wings of a hooded crow... *a form oft taken by the banshee, the spirit of death.* Kathleen pressed back in her chair.

The judge took his seat at the bench and scanned the room, his eyes briefly lingering on each person before he gaveled the hearing into session. "We are here today to determine the future of a young child," he said in a flat voice. "I have no doubt there are strong feelings on both sides as to what the end result should be. I appreciate that. But the law is clear." He tapped a finger on a thin stack of documents on his desk. "My decision must be based on facts and what is in the best interest of the child."

Kathleen eyed the gavel, inches away from the judge's hand. Its rich dark wood and polished finish couldn't disguise the fact that it was still a hammer, a tool capable of crushing their family.

"Therefore, it is my request," the judge was saying, "that during the initial question and answers phase, both parties and their witnesses restrict themselves to presenting facts...and not embellish answers with emotion. There will be time for personal statements at the end."

With that, the hearing began. By the time all the witnesses had taken the stand and the questions had been asked and answered, by the time all the descriptions of the shipwreck and its aftermath had been dissected, and all the history and details of the Sullivan and Deacey and Montgomery families had been presented, more than three hours had passed.

The judge was thorough, asking for clarification of several points from Sean, Ailish, and the witnesses. He treated each person and their responses with exactly the same brusque focus on detail, so much so, it was impossible to tell which way he might be leaning.

When he had no more questions to ask, he sat back in his

chair and steepled his fingers, saying nothing for so long Kathleen thought her heart might pound through her ribcage. Then he sighed out an anguished breath. "I promised that each of you would have a chance to make a personal statement." His words came slow, his tone weary. "Miss Sullivan, if you'd like to add anything to what has been said on your behalf, you may speak now."

Her lawyer bent toward her, whispering. Then Ailish pressed her palms to the tabletop and rose, her chin high, almost defiant.

"I'll be thanking you for letting me speak, your honor," she said. "As ye've come to learn this morning, I'm not a rich woman. I have no family. There'll be no getting around any of that."

She didn't have to look across the aisle for Kathleen to know Ailish was taking aim at the criticisms their lawyer had leveled against her.

"All my family perished because of a potato blight and a famine over which we had no control. My sister—Liam's mam—would not have been on that brig coming to America if not for the famine in Ireland." A quiver wove through her words. "I canna offer Liam a big family, it's true. Not like he might have known in other times." She paused, as if carefully choosing her next words. "But I can give him his family in memories."

A chill shot through Kathleen.

Ailish nodded as if to reinforce her words. "He'll grow up knowing stories of his mam and da, of his brothers, his grandparents, and their grandparents. He is my family. His mother was my sister." Her face twisted in anguish. "I may be poor in money, that's a truth well told. I may not have a husband, but only because the man I wed died in Ireland from the famine. I may not live in a grand house. But, your honor, I need none of that to love him."

A knot tightened Kathleen's throat.

"I was at me sister's side the day Liam came into this world. I held him when he was just minutes old. I'll be ever grateful that the Montgomerys took him in, cared for him when he had no one else." Her hands curled into soft fists. "But I'm here now. And I'll be asking, pleading, your honor, not to take away the only family I have left. He is my blood. He belongs with me." She lowered herself into her chair and folded her hands on the table.

The judge said nothing for several beats, then fixed his attention on Kathleen and Jack. "Mr. or Mrs. Montgomery? Would one of you like to say something?"

She and Jack had discussed this already. She wanted to speak, needed to. Yet with the moment upon her, she was beset with doubts. What right had she to keep this child? *What right?* Much as she loved him, and she did with every ounce of her being, should she be fighting to keep this child from his own blood relative?

"Kathleen," Jack said, barely audible. "It's your turn."

She stared at him through blurred eyes. Did she have the right to keep someone else's child? *Did she?*

"You may not have birthed him, but you're his mother all the same," Mr. Barker said quietly.

But was that enough? As she hesitated, the attorney grasped her elbow and pushed upward, urging her to her feet.

"For Will," Ma murmured from behind.

Aye, it had to be enough. She owed it to her son to fight for him. She stood and looked directly at Ailish before drawing a deep breath and setting her gaze on the judge

"I was not there when Will was born and christened as Liam. But for two and a half years, I have been with him every day." Her voice grew stronger with each word. "Through the growth of his milk teeth, through illness and fevers, through learning to crawl and walk and talk. With him I've been, as he grew from wee babe to little boy."

She inhaled softly to ground her thoughts, her words. "'Twas a miracle for us, the arrival of Will. We had lived through the loss of three unborn children. I had begun to think my husband and I would never be parents. And then Sean arrived with this child, delivered from the sea."

She fixed her eyes on the judge's gavel again. Its destructive power would not fall on her family if she could help it.

"Families are often made by bonds other than blood. My husband and I are the only mam and da that Will knows. My parents and Jack's grandfather are the only grandparents he knows. He is as much a child of our family as any I might have carried." Her composure wavered and she broke off. When she began to speak again, her voice was brittle. "We love him like our own. We have never thought of him any other way. I'll be asking you, please, with all that I am, let him stay with us. Please let my husband and I raise him to become a man worthy of the two families that call him son." She sank into her chair unable to say more.

A long, heavy silence followed. As the judge bent low over the document on his desk, Kathleen cast a series of fragmented prayers and desperate promises silently into the universe.

The judge lifted his head and looked directly at her. "This is a difficult case in many ways," he said, his voice more compassionate than it had been all day. She felt a glimmer of hope and chided herself for thinking of the banshee when first he'd arrived.

"There is nothing more unwavering, more compelling than the unconditional love of a mother for her child. I have not a doubt that you love this boy, Mrs. Montgomery." He shifted his gaze to Ailish. "Nor do I doubt that you loved this child as a newborn, Miss Sullivan. But..." His shoulders drooped. "You knew him for just a month before his parents left Ireland. I do not intend criticism when I say that, after all this time, he'll not remember you. If we are to look at this rationally, neither will you know him."

Kathleen's pulse quickened and she cast a sideways glance at Jack.

"But your honor—" Ailish protested.

The judge smacked the desk with the gavel to silence her. "Patience please, Miss Sullivan. There is another truth I cannot ignore. That is the fact that you are the boy's only blood relative. You and he share ancestry—and that is no insignificant matter. Indeed, throughout history, ancestry has generally been one of the most important considerations in legal decisions. Often it has been the only consideration."

Kathleen rubbed a nervous finger over her wedding ring.

"But times are different," he continued. "The law now says that, in cases of adoption, the welfare of the child must be taken into consideration." He studied the ceiling as though answers might be written there. "But what does that mean when two women make a claim upon the same child—two women, both speaking honestly of their love."

He spread his hands wide, palm up. "I do not believe that poverty makes one a lesser parent, nor does it make one less capable of loving a child. Mr. and Mrs. Montgomery, I suspect you would agree with me, though your lawyer makes the case otherwise."

After a hesitation, they both nodded. Jack took Kathleen's hand under the table. Only the heat of his palm betrayed his worry.

"Still, one cannot discount the value of being raised in a

prosperous home. Nor can one ignore the importance of a male child being raised with a father present. And yet, if I am to be fair, Miss Sullivan should not be penalized for the fact that her husband passed on. In time, she may well marry again."

The judge's brows drew together and he rubbed the back of his neck as though tormented by a deep pain. "So...let us address the questions on the table. In order for Mr. and Mrs. Montgomery to legally adopt the child, the next of kin—in this case, Miss Sullivan—must give consent for the child to be adopted." He paused. "Will you give your consent, Miss Sullivan?"

"Nay." The word came out razor-sharp.

Prickling crawled across Kathleen's chest and up her back. Her palms dampened. Faith, but were the walls moving in or was she just imagining it?

"Without consent, I cannot force an adoption unless I find that it is best for the welfare of the child. Miss Sullivan may be poor, but she is not unfit. She is the child's aunt. She has a steady work as a clerk—"

"Aye," she said nodding.

"And she has made arrangements for someone to care for the boy while she works," the judge said. "Most importantly, she loves him."

All Kathleen could hear was a buzzing sound, like thousands of bees had been let loose in the room. He couldn't be taking away her son. He couldn't. She sank against Jack.

"Mrs. Montgomery, would you like a few minutes recess?" the judge asked.

She shook her head. Tears slipped down her cheeks and her feelings poured out of her in the form of words. "Your honor, I beg you. No one could love this child more than we do. There are songs that he loves to hear at bedtime. And stories. And we have special games, just him and me. I tell him sometimes that a kiss is stuck in my throat."

"Kathleen," Jack murmured.

"And then I cough and pretend the kiss has escaped and I put it on his cheek." She gasped out a sob.

"Mrs. Montgomery," the judge said.

His tone frightened her, full of pity it was, like he didn't understand and didn't care to try. She pushed forward. "And then I pretend that another kiss is escaping and another, and I kiss him and he giggles and I laugh and cover his cheeks with kisses because, oh sir, you cannot know how much I love him."

A hush settled over the room like night fog.

"I believe I have a reasonable grasp of how much you do." His lips turned thoughtfully down. "I'm sure he loves you as well. Which is why I am not going to remove him from your custody today."

Kathleen gasped. Jack's head swiveled toward their attorney.

"One of the imperatives of the new law is that the welfare of the child must be protected," the judge said slowly, as if carefully choosing each word. "The boy has already suffered the trauma of losing two parents. I see nothing positive in putting him through that a second time."

"But, your honor—" Ailish's attorney jumped to his feet. "If you accept that the child is Miss Sullivan's nephew and that she is fit to raise him...and if she does not agree to the adoption, which she does not, then you must give the boy over to her."

The judge thumped down the gavel. "I think we can all agree that taking a young child from a happy and loving home and giving him into the custody of a person he doesn't know is quite possibly the definition of cruel." He glared at the attorney until the man took his seat again.

"Indeed, we have no notion if the boy will take to Miss

Sullivan—or she to him. We do not know if she will enjoy raising a child as an unmarried woman—or if the job will be more than she can handle. Without answers to these questions, I must fall back on my duty to the law, which is to protect the child."

The muscles in his jaw clenched. "I am a pragmatic man. And this is a nearly impossible situation. Which informs me that, as anxious as everyone is for a decision, patience must rule the day. I'll not disrupt the boy's life on a whim. Therefore, my ruling is this. The boy will stay in the custody of the Montgomery family for the next month."

A gasp went up across the courtroom. Jack gave Kathleen's hand a squeeze as though to say, *we haven't lost him yet.*

"Over the course of that month, Miss Sullivan will take him on outings twice each week so they can become better acquainted. In order to eliminate any distress the child might experience over being taken from his home by a stranger, a member of the Montgomery family will accompany Miss Sullivan and the boy on each excursion. A chaperone, if you will."

Not a muscle moved in the courtroom.

"My goal is to encourage interaction between the boy and his aunt, to see whether a bond will develop. Therefore, it would be best if the accompanying family member is an adult other than Mr. or Mrs. Montgomery. In fact, I require it."

His expression was steadfast, his tone countenancing no dissent. "I would prefer that the same family member attend each outing to help minimize distractions that might interfere with the child and Miss Sullivan getting to know one another."

He pursed his lips and sized up the two attorneys. "I suggest the lawyers get together to create a schedule that works for both parties. In thirty days, I want written reports from both sides detailing how the visitations have gone and how the relationship between the boy and his aunt has progressed. Once I have thoroughly read those reports, I will rule on custody."

He slammed the gavel on the desk and exited the room.

Kathleen put a hand to her throat. Let the lawyers talk. She was going home to her son.

CHAPTER NINE

LATE THAT EVENING, SEAN EXITED MURPHY'S PUB AND STOPPED outside to drew several deep breaths of crisp air into his lungs in an effort to steady his mind and balance his steps. Not because of the ale he'd drunk, but because today's hearing had turned everything on its head. He'd hoped the drink would dull his feelings over the ruling, but somehow it had only made the pain worse.

He pulled his wool scarf closer and looked in the direction of home, contemplating the route that would take him there. A path down streets lined with businesses and pubs gradually giving way to quiet houses filled with families.

Home.

Kathleen and Jack's home. Not his.

Ma always said, *Home is where you hang your hat.* For him, that was now a shack near the railroad tracks, a place so spare it made him forget he'd ever had a home. Made him forget that his wife and their sons were buried in Ireland in graves unmarked by headstones. There'd been no money for such things with the famine.

Several drunk patrons burst through the door behind him and spilled into the street. "Sean, lad, you're still here?" one shouted. "Come along, we'll be going to Paddy's."

The last thing he needed was more drink. He waved them off, but didn't move.

Though the family was likely abed at home, he didn't want to be there, didn't want to be reminded by everything he saw, everything he touched, that Kathleen could lose her son like he'd lost his. He wished he'd never told the doctor in Cohasset where Kathleen and Jack lived. Wished they had moved away years ago so they couldn't to be found. Wished he had never asked to bring the boy here at all.

He let out a sigh. Nay, he didn't wish that last one.

Gray clouds scudded across the night sky like wafts of smoke rising from smokers' pipes and borne away by the wind. He buttoned his coat, tossed another look in the direction of Jack and Kathleen's home, and set off the opposite way, wanting only to travel an empty path with no destination.

He walked aimlessly, gradually becoming aware of a growing sense of squalor, a roughening of the neighborhood. Even the wind seemed uglier as it tugged at his coat and chilled his face. Street after cramped street was the same—three and four-story buildings, fouled and dirty, squatting in the darkness like the surly Fomhóraigh giants of Irish legend. Aye, he could almost see them hunched in the night, those monstrous, malevolent beings of chaos, disease, and death.

Nervously, he shook off the superstition and kept moving, steps slowing as one street of tenements blended into another and another, and a thought shoved its way forward—that every room of every building was overfilled with Irish immigrants barely surviving. Easy it was to see the streets of Boston had not been paved with gold for the Irish.

He glanced around to get his bearings, realizing then that he was not two buildings away from where Ailish lived. Perhaps his anger brought him here. To be sure, he hadn't planned it. His eyes went to the third floor where faint light shone from behind tattered curtains. Though he knew the dimly-lit windows didn't open into Ailish's flat—hers was at the back of the building—still he couldn't contain the frustration that spilled through him. How could she think what lay ahead would be good for Will?

He stared upward as if the intensity of his feelings could penetrate the building and reach into Ailish's soul. Did she not see how difficult her own life was in this country? Could she not see she would doom Will to the same if he came to live with her? That any dreams he had would die beneath a lifetime working on the railroads or the factory floor or in the iron works? All for a pittance. Never a hope of getting ahead.

Perhaps Ma would be able to soften Ailish's determination to take Will away. She'd volunteered to be the chaperone on the visitations. "Have done with your worries," she'd told them after the hearing. "I've a friend in the head housekeeper. Been kind to me, she has. If God be with us, she'll be letting me adjust my work hours so I can be free at the right times."

If God be with us. How many times had he heard that before? He'd wait to see if it came to pass.

A piece of newspaper swirled into the air beside him and he jerked back with a start, his thoughts clearing. Jaysus, what an idiot he'd been to come here. How would he explain himself should Ailish spot him outside her building? If she were to think he'd come to threaten her and report such a thing to the judge, it might push everything in the wrong direction.

He spun on his heel and headed for home. The tails of his

scarf whipped in the wind and he tucked them beneath his collar, thrust his hands in the pockets of his coat, and bent his head against the wind.

~

AILISH WANDERED up one street and down the next, reluctant to return home though exhaustion weighed heavy upon her. She'd put in twelve hours of work after the hearing. Day had long ago faded into night, and the bright glow of early spring had slipped back into the somber chill of winter. She hugged her cloak close and kept moving. Tired, hungry, and unsettled, she couldn't escape the fear that while everything seemed to be going the way she wanted, somehow it would go wrong in the end. She drew her hood up and stopped a block away from the house where Liam lived with the Montgomerys. Though she hadn't let herself admit it, she'd known all along this was her destination.

Lanterns glowed behind the lace curtains of the solemn brick house, two floors of rooms for just one family. It wasn't the kind of home an immigrant Irishwoman could ever hope to have. Not unless, like Kathleen Montgomery, that woman was lucky enough to marry an Englishman. *Or unlikely enough.* 'Twas all in one's perspective.

And now, after committing the absolute sin of wedding an Englishman, Kathleen Montgomery was fighting to keep Liam, to raise him in that household with an English bastard as his father. Liam's real mam was probably rolling in her grave at the very idea.

She moved nearer the house, eyes locked on the warmth of those windows.

Their lawyer had been right when he'd said Ailish couldn't provide Liam with all the material things the Montgomerys could. But she could give him something more valuable—his heritage, the very reason he was on this earth at all.

He had a right to know about the day the landlord's brigade tore his parents' home to the ground and forced the family onto the road with two young sons—and a babe on the way. How they'd had to move in with his grandparents and Ailish and her husband. How once Liam was born, the family had pooled what little coin it had to buy passage to America for his family. *How his mam and da had risked everything—and lost everything—to bring him to America.*

She wanted Liam to know that his mother loved him so well, she'd made Ailish promise to care for him if anything ever went wrong. It was a promise she was determined to fulfill. "I'm trying," she muttered into the wind. "Faith, but I'm trying."

Out of the darkness a man appeared down the block, shoulders hunched, hands deep in his pockets. She dipped her head and hurried away in the opposite direction. Though it was unlikely she'd be spotted out here in the shadows, best not to risk being seen, even by a neighbor. She hadn't lost in court, but she hadn't won either. No need to be caught outside the Montgomery home and somehow prejudice the judge against her.

One more month. She just needed to make it through the next month and prove to the judge that she and Liam had developed a bond. Then she and her nephew could move forward together.

And she would have a family again.

CHAPTER TEN

THOUGH THE TREES WERE STILL BARE, THE GRASS WAS BEGINNING to green and the sun-brightened air smelled clean and light. Kathleen waited on a bench in the Boston Common for Ma to arrive so they could go together to meet with the lawyer. She turned her face into the breeze and thought to herself that even the dirt smelled fresh.

"Where's Jack?" Ma asked when she arrived. She dropped onto the bench, her face flushed.

"A problem at the wharf. One of the dock boys arrived with a message just as we were to leave. I told him to go, that we didn't need three of us to deliver the visitation schedule."

Ma pulled the thin scarf off her head and wadded it between her palms. "Och, 'tis trouble we have, Kathleen. I'll not even be knowing how to tell you." Her voice shook with anger. "The head housekeeper changed her mind. Stopped me right before I left and said I couldn't be switching me hours."

"Ma, what?" Kathleen felt as though the air had been squeezed from her lungs. "You told her about Will, didn't you?"

"Aye, she knows. When first I asked off, I explained everything. She said there would be no trouble. But now she says it was a mistake. That others had heard of it and were asking for changes themselves. And if she were to let me do it, then she'd have no reason to deny anyone else." She let out a harsh laugh. "Convinced herself, she did, that the household would fall into chaos if she allowed changes to the work schedule." Ma drew in a long, slow breath. "And then she told me I was a hard worker and that she'd hate to lose me, but there were plenty of other Irish willing to take me job if I didna want it."

"I thought she was your friend."

"As did I."

Kathleen stared at her mother, despair beginning to roil her gut. "The lawyer thinks we're coming today with the details—the name of a chaperone, a plan. What will we tell him?"

"Ah, Kathleen, I'm sorry to tell you, I can't even be coming to the meeting. I have to go right back." Ma's mouth tightened into a straight line. "I've half a notion to quit—"

"You know Jack and I would help—"

"Nay. We'll support our family ourselves. When we are old and frail and have no other choice, perhaps then 'twill be different."

The discussion had been broached before and always ended the same. Kathleen sighed. "Well, then, ye can't be leaving your job, Ma. It's a good situation even if the housekeeper isn't the friend you thought her to be. What about Da?" she asked, knowing the question was foolish.

Ma got to her feet. "The same trouble as me, only less time off to begin with."

Kathleen bit her lip hard. Such a lovely day in the park, everyone going somewhere, each with their own troubles no doubt, but surely none fighting a battle to keep their child. Such a lovely day...and suddenly the only scent of spring that she could discern was that of mud. Wet, sloppy mud.

She stood and headed out of the park with her mother. "If only Rory were here."

"If wishes were horses, beggars would ride," Ma muttered. "Perhaps one of the younger two—"

"The judge said it should be an adult. Nora is but thirteen and Tomás only two years older. I'll not be thinking the judge will be pleased with either choice. Besides, they shouldn't be missing school."

"'Twill have to be Sean then."

He'd never agree to it—and she'd not ask him. "Ma, you know as well as I, he's going back to Virginia within days. To that foreman job they're holding for him."

"What's a few more weeks?"

Their paths about to diverge, they stopped across from the park at a corner bordering the Granary Burying Grounds where so many heroes of the Revolution had been laid to rest. Kathleen fixed her gaze on the tall white obelisk near the center, a twenty-foot memorial to the parents of Benjamin Franklin, the man who drafted the Declaration of Independence and signed the Constitution. So much he'd accomplished, yet even *his* life had not been untroubled.

His only living son—*William*—had been a loyalist who moved to England when it became clear that Britain wouldn't win the war. That son, born in America, finished out his life in England. And his father, born in England, finished out his life in America. The two men never reconciled.

"Kathleen?"

She hauled herself back to the conversation. "How can I ask Sean to stay? The job is a promotion. A raise. He's got his own goals. If he's not there when the railroad needs him, someone else will get it."

"'Tis his family that's needing him now."

Pain pricked her heart. She glanced again at the obelisk, so tall it stood apart and alone in the cemetery. How had Benjamin Franklin withstood the years of separation from his son, never to see him again? Had he spent the rest of his life filled with longing?

"Nay, I can't ask that of him. All he talks of is buying land. He's lost so much already, I can't bear to be the reason Sean loses his dreams again."

MR. BARKER SET his elbows on his desk and clasped his hands together. "Go on."

"Even though my mother can't do all the visitations, I've thought of a solution." Kathleen controlled the rush of her words and spoke with feigned confidence to prevent her misgivings from showing. "Would it not be grand if a different person accompanied Miss Sullivan and Will on each visit? 'Twould be a fine way for her to get to know Will's whole family. My ma could go once and then my Da...and my younger brother and sister..."

Doubt flicked across Mr. Barker's face, and Kathleen pushed forward before he could voice disapproval. "Emma our cook has been part of Will's life from the first. Sure but she'd happily chaperone once or twice." She forced a hopeful grin.

As if whisking away a layer of dust, the lawyer swept his palm over the only section of desktop that wasn't covered by papers, then brushed both hands together. "It's a thought, certainly," he finally said. "And if it's our only option, then we have no choice. But surely you remember, the judge was quite clear as to his expectations. He wanted the framework to be the same for each visit: the chaperone must be an adult, and it should be the same person each time."

The reality of what they were discussing tore at the veneer of calm she was fighting to maintain. *They were speaking of her son's life, making preparations for the possibility of giving him to someone else.* The blood rushed in her ears.

"I do remember." She pressed her hands into the armrests of her chair. "But we've been thrown crosswise by me mother's employer. In light of that, could we not ask the judge for a bit of leeway?"

He let out a sigh. "I can try. Do you have a list of names and a schedule?"

"Not yet. I'll need to checks the dates with each person."

"As soon as you can, please. I want to avoid looking like we're trying to delay. The last thing we need is the judge to decide this has gotten too complicated and simply hand Will over to Miss Sullivan."

The room tilted. "Could he do that?"

"This law is so new...he has wide latitude to do whatever he deems fit." He gave her a thin smile. "There is no precedent to guide him. Every judge who finds himself facing an unusual adoption proceeding will have to, in essence, interpret the law himself until more cases are on the books."

"But his order for visitations...ye thought 'twas in our favor, did you not?"

He nodded. "Yes, but I will admit I was shocked. I had feared he would strictly interpret the law and immediately give custody to Miss Sullivan."

Kathleen's throat went dry. He'd not said anything like this after the hearing.

"But when he ordered a transition period," Mr. Barker continued, "I knew he was searching for a way to gain more information to guide his decision. It's a novel concept, a lifeline I didn't expect us to get."

"A lifeline?" She blinked, shocked. "From your words that day, I've been thinking we were in a better place than that."

Mr. Barker hesitated. "I'm not entirely sure what place we're in. I don't believe the judge sees Miss Sullivan's home as the best choice for Will. And I remain convinced that as long as you and your husband have custody, there's a reasonable chance you will keep him." He braced his hands on the desk and leaned forward as if to emphasize his next words. "But we need to ensure the judge stays on our side."

"If you don't mind, sir, what exactly are you saying?"

"Don't create complications. Don't ask the judge to bend his order to help your family. Don't give him a reason to set aside his original ruling and apply a strict reading of the law. If that happens, I can almost promise it won't go well for you."

He held his thumb and index finger a pinch apart. "I don't want us to lose even this much goodwill. I know this judge. He's brusque, but fair. This tiny margin might be all we need to prevail."

Her thoughts charged forward as she considered and discarded options, her mind leaping against the confines of the judge's ruling like a caged animal seeking escape. In truth she knew she had but one choice, and it wasn't one she embraced lightly. Indeed, she would give anything to have a bit of time to talk to Jack and her family, to get their support and make sure she was doing the right thing. But she didn't. And she'd not risk angering the judge when he'd ordered visitations to begin this week.

"That being the case, sir," she began slowly, "you can be

telling the judge that—" She hesitated, sent a quick prayer of contrition skyward and began again. "Tell him that me own brother, Sean Deacey, who is at this time staying with us, will accompany Miss Sullivan on all the visitations with Will."

"YOUR MA CAN'T HELP?" Jack shot a look of alarm at Sean.

"Nay." Kathleen went to the sideboard and picked up the decanter of whiskey, her grip firm to stop the trembling of her hands. She was going to need a wee bit of something to bolster her courage before she confessed what she'd said to the lawyer.

Jack sat forward on the sofa, utterly handsome in the late afternoon light. A man of honor he was. A believer in right and wrong and good and bad. He'd not ever lived the life of a people scorned, but his eyes were open enough to see the hatred, and his heart big enough to despise it. She hoped she would not disappoint him with what she'd done.

"What did Barker say when you told him?" he pressed. "Are we to come up with another plan?"

She poured a drink for herself, then refilled both men's glasses. Jack slid over to make room for her beside him, but she went to stand with her back to the hearth as though chilled from being out and about.

In truth, her blood felt to be on fire.

"So? Tell us." Sean lifted the glass to his lips.

"Indeed I will," she said, stalling. "At first, I offered to make a schedule, changing up Ma and Da, Tomás and Nora...even Emma, though she isn't family but feels like it." She sipped her whiskey as though she had all the time in the world.

"And? Did he think the judge would approve?" Jack eyed her curiously, and she avoided directly meeting his gaze.

She linked her fingers around her glass. The moment of truth was fast coming upon her. "He worried that asking to change the order might work against us. The judge might think us overly difficult and decide it simpler to give Will over to Miss Sullivan right away. *Apply a strict reading of the law* is the way Mr. Barker put it."

"With no trial period?" Jack asked, stunned. "No chance to see whether she likes him? Or he likes her?"

Sean's expression hadn't changed, but his eyes were fixed on Will's box of tin soldiers. A muscle worked in his clenched jaw.

"Aye. I didn't want to do anything that might cause the judge to make a sudden decision. So..." She threw an uncertain glance at her brother. "I said we had no trouble meeting the terms of the ruling."

Jack cocked his head. "Good. But then who—"

"I wanted to make sure we weren't starting out with our feet in a hole," she said defensively.

Sean drained his whiskey. She could feel his eyes on her as she removed the stopper from the decanter, splashed more into her own glass and went over to refill his.

"Kathleen...?" Jack's voice was full of question.

She cleared her throat. "I said to tell the judge we'd have no problem complying with his order."

"But we do have a problem."

"Nay, we do not." Her mouth turned down in a contrite frown. "At least I'll be hoping not. What I said was...I said that me brother, Sean Deacey, would be accompanying Miss Sullivan on all the visitations."

"Sean?" Jack coughed.

Sean's jaw went slack for a heartbeat. "Sweet Jaysus, Kathleen, why would you say that? I'll not even be here."

She fixed pleading eyes on her brother. "Hoping I was, Seanie, that you would agree. It's just a month."

"Kathleen. You know I'd be helping if I could," he said irritably, but she thought she heard a thaw in his opposition, a softening immediately masked by an unyielding countenance. "John Kelley's holding the foreman job, waiting on my return."

"Could you not write him to say your arm needs more healing? Ask if he could hold the job a little longer."

"God knows I understand why you did it," Jack cut in. "But, Kathleen, you can't force this on Sean. Opportunities like he's been offered don't come often to an Irishman in this country."

She pretended to examine a painting on the wall as she scrambled to find an argument that might win Sean over. "If we meet all the terms of the ruling, it will likely improve our chances of keeping Will."

"Barker said that?" Jack asked.

"In...in a way. What he said was, if we didn't meet the terms, it could hurt us. Knowing that, why would we risk such a thing?"

"Far be it for me to dash your hopes." Sean set his glass aside and pushed himself to his feet. "But despite what Mr. Barker says, I'll be thinking the judge's final decision will be based on whether Will gets along with Miss Sullivan—not whether the same person accompanies her on all the visits." He went to the doorway and leaned against the frame, arms folded across his chest.

"Don't you think I'll be knowing it's a long hope?" She felt sick with fear that she would lose this struggle. "But if, in the end, we are forced to give Will up, let me never have to wonder if this one thing is what caused us to lose him. Please Seanie..."

His face was taut, his jaw set. She went to stand directly in front of him. "Remember that morning in Ireland when you said I had to go to America to save the family—and I refused?" she said. "In the end, I did what was right. I left Ireland though I didn't want to, *for the family.* All I'll be asking is that you..."

Guilt stabbed at her. How could she ask him to postpone his dreams so she might have a chance at keeping hers? "I know you must return to the railroad. I know this job will get you closer to buying land. But please, Sean, one month, that's all I'm asking. Then nothing else, ever. I'll promise ye that, I will."

He didn't look at her and she didn't move, all her hope caught in the breath she was holding. His silence made her desperate, and she pushed past a boundary she normally respected. "If you were to know that something as simple as this would give you a sliver of a chance of saving your boys, would you not ask the same of me?"

He loosed an exhale. And though his expression remained steely, his eyes no longer glinted with ire. He dropped into a chair by the hearth and let his head fall against the back, one hand on the armrest, the other reaching for his whiskey. "Fine. One month I'll stay. But God be helping you Kathleen, if John Kelly gives the foreman job to someone else."

CHAPTER ELEVEN

"Now you'll watch him close, Sean, aye?" Kathleen fretted. "Make sure he doesn't dash into the street. Be holding his hand —" A line appeared between her brows. "He's got so much energy, he's apt to start running when you least expect it."

Sean took hold of Kathleen's shoulders and gave them a reassuring squeeze. He wished he could tell her what she longed to hear—that this first visitation wouldn't be the next step on the path to losing her son. But he couldn't. So instead, he promised her what he could: "I'll keep him safe. Have no worries of that."

They were all seeking assurances of one thing or another. His own, he hoped, would arrive soon in a letter from John Kelly saying he would hold the foreman job open for Sean.

Jack wrapped an arm around Kathleen's waist. "Sean, what you've done for us since the beginning, what you're doing now...thank you." His voice was rough, his expression bleak.

"I'll do my best," he replied, though what he meant by that was anyone's guess. Ahead lay a month of torture with an uncertain ending, all because Ailish Sullivan had put her own desires above all else, with no care to the wounds she was inflicting on this family.

Outrage tightened his chest and he tamped it down. Anger wouldn't be his ally in this war, kindness would. His goal, as they all had decided, was to make Ailish his friend. He needed to get her to trust him—and by extension, the family—so she might come to realize the best place for Will was with Kathleen and Jack.

"Have fun today, my sweet lad." Kathleen knelt in front of her son. "Remember, I love you more than a thousand—"

"Spiders!" he said, eyes bright and sparkling.

"Spiders?" Her smile wavered. "All right. More than a thousand spiders. Now you listen to Uncle Sean and be doing what he tells ye, aye?"

Will bobbed his head up and down and wiggled his arms. "Mam you come. And Papa. Going on *a-venture*!"

Kathleen blanched. She'd always found his mispronunciation of *adventure* sweet. Now it surely made her heart ache.

Jack bent to tug the corners of Will's collar together and press a kiss to his son's forehead. "Mam and I will come on a-venture another time. Do you have your bag of corn?"

Sean held up a small cloth sack, the drawstring top cinched tight. "Right here."

Will stomped his feet in excitement.

"I'll be thinking you're ready to go, lad." Sean swung the boy into his arms and stepped outside as Will leaned over his shoulder, waving and shouting, "Bye Mam, bye Mam, bye Papa, bye, bye, bye," with such enthusiasm, it almost made farewell seem like a joyous occasion.

"Goodbye," they called back in unison.

Sean didn't need to turn around to know that his sister was

weeping. He didn't need to turn around to know that Jack's face had had paled.

Clamping his teeth together as if to bite back his feelings, he set off down the walk, one resolute footstep after another.

AILISH PACED near the pond in the Public Garden, stomach tumbling in anticipation. Though the day was cool and the sun mostly hidden by slow moving banks of dirty clouds, a trickle of sweat slipped between her breasts. She smoothed her hair back from her forehead, wiped a hand across her mouth, then licked her lips.

It hardly seemed right that she should have to prove a bond to her own nephew in order to raise him. She was his next of kin after all. She loved him. What more was needed? It had seemed clear to her at the hearing that he should be given over to her without delay. And though her lawyer held the same belief, he'd urged her not to protest the ruling. "*This is not a judge to ruffle,*" he'd said, advising that the fastest path to custody was unquestioning compliance with the order.

So, *compliance without complaint* was her goal. She would do whatever it took to get to know Liam, to make him like her, to prove to the judge that hers was the family where he belonged. *Family*. Her stomach leapt. Beginning today, she had a family again.

Her gaze roamed the park, past the leafless trees, over the grass just beginning to green and the bare flower beds, past the smattering of people strolling the paths and pushing carriages and hurrying on their way somewhere. She hadn't cared when the lawyer told her Sean Deacey would be bringing Liam. It made no matter to her who came on the visitations so long as Liam was there.

But whoever it was, they were late—and that was a bit worrying.

Meg had asked what she would do if they didn't come, and Ailish had waved the concern away. "Of course, they'll come," she'd said. "Respectable people they are. And respectable people follow the law."

Not that other people didn't follow the law, but it wasn't so simple a question sometimes. The famine had made choices stark for the Irish: Heed the law and let your family starve. Break the law and help them live another day.

If God were to weigh in, she wondered, which would he say was the more righteous path?

She scanned the park again. *What if they didn't come? What then?*

A screech fractured her thoughts, startling her, and she pivoted round to see Liam racing down the path, Sean striding several steps behind. Her mouth broke into a smile so wide her cheeks hurt. She hadn't seen the boy since the day of the parade, but to know that he was so happy to see her...could it be that he actually remembered her from his earliest days of babyhood?

She opened her arms and bent forward intending to scoop him into her embrace, but he dodged past her and charged to the edge of the pond, shouting, "Good noon ducks!"

Mortified, she straightened, cheeks flaming. Was that the shadow of a smirk on Sean Deacey's face? Resentment tingled across the back of her neck. The devil take him straight to hell. "Good afternoon, Mr. Deacey," she said in a stiff voice.

"Miss Sullivan," he replied. "A fine day it is."

Liam hopped from foot to foot, jabbering at the ducks that had gathered in the water along the shore. Ailish tipped her head in his direction. "Quite a lot of energy, he has," she said just to say something.

"The ducks are his favorite."

"Good to know." Though her tone was friendly, she bristled inside. This was her nephew, her sister's son, her own family. It was disconcerting that this stranger knew Liam better than she did.

Awkwardness killed their conversation and both focused their attention on the boy as he cavorted along the bank beside the quacking ducks. "Uncle Sean!" He raced back to them. "They hungry. Get the corn."

"In a bit, lad, a wee bit. First, I'll be wanting you to meet someone." He swung the boy high in the air, then brought him down against his chest. "Will, this is...uh...this is your Aunt Ailish. Can you say Ailish?"

"Aish." Will's gaze stayed firmly locked on the pond.

She bent her head near his and carefully enunciated each syllable. "Aaay-lish."

"Aish."

Sean chuckled, and Ailish narrowed her eyes. "Aye, that's right, Ailish. And I'll already be knowing who you are." She reached out both hands in welcome. "You're Liam."

He stared at her. So did his uncle.

She patted the boy's arm. "Your name...is Liam," she said.

"No." He swung his head left to right in protest. "No Leem," he said, training his eyes on the ducks.

"Careful," Sean warned. "Has a bit of a temper, he does."

His words pinched. "He was the sweetest of babes, Mr. Deacey. He can't have changed so much now, could he?" She smiled at the boy. "Could you Liam?"

He eyed her suspiciously, as if contemplating his reply. "No."

"You see?" she said, feeling vindicated. "Even he says he hasn't changed."

"He says *no* a lot."

She tousled the boy's hair. "You see, Liam, your name is Will. And your name is also Liam. They're the same. Liam. William."

"And you think he'll be understanding this?"

"Why wouldn't he?"

"Because he's a child, and he came here to see the ducks." Sean chuckled again. "Not change his name."

"Will," the boy said.

The corners of Sean's mouth quirked, sending Ailish's resentment surging.

"Aye, your name is Will," she pressed, determined to prove Sean wrong. "But in Ireland, it's Liam. Your own Mam and Da called you that. Liam." She took him from Sean, and the weight of him in her arms, the mere feel of him, sent a swell of happiness through her. "Liam, I hear you like the ducks."

He grunted and tried to twist free, but she held tight. "Liam, do you like ducks?"

"Not Leem." He smacked a fist against her shoulder.

"Liam!"

"Will, no hitting." Sean grabbed the boy's hand. "Miss Sullivan, perhaps you should be leaving aside the name until he knows you better. There's no rush."

No rush? Almost three years had passed since Liam's birth. She scowled. "Have ye raised any children yourself?" she asked, her scorn barely hidden.

His hesitation was all the answer she needed. "I thought not."

"He's so young, I'm just thinking he'll not understand. Or even care," Sean said. "Not yet three—"

"I know his age," she snapped as she gripped the wiggling boy tighter. "I was at his birth."

"I'm just saying—"

"And I'm saying it's not too early for him to know that his real family named him Liam."

The boy's arms shot straight into the air and he let out an ear-splitting scream. "Not Leem!" he shouted. "Not Leem!" He arched his back and batted her face and chest with his fists.

Shocked, she let him slide to the ground.

"Not Leem!" he howled, swinging at her legs. Sudden tears streamed from his eyes and he threw himself onto his stomach, wailing.

As others in the park began to glance around seeking the source of the unholy noise, Ailish took an embarrassed step back and raised her brows at Sean. He gave a shrug as if to say, *I warned you*. "The lad knows his own mind," he said over the commotion.

"Or perhaps he's spoiled."

Sean's expression hardened, and he knelt to take the boy into his arms. "And just how many children have *you* raised, Miss Sullivan?"

Her eyes widened. She opened her mouth to snap back at him, but Will's screeching had reached such a crescendo it seemed pointless.

"Will, scaring the ducks, you are," Sean said in his regular voice. "You know what happens when there's too much noise."

As the boy's chest heaved with great sobs, Ailish allowed herself a smirk. Spoiled, certainly. Or over-coddled.

"Have done with your crying or there'll be no ducks left." Sean drew a handkerchief from his pocket and began to wipe off the boy's face. "And then we'll have to be going home."

Will sucked in a ragged breath and lay an accusing glare on Ailish.

"There ye go. That's a good lad." Sean set him on his feet and gave his face a final swipe with the handkerchief. "You're fine now, aye?"

Lower lip still trembling, Liam gave his uncle a tremulous smile and pointed at the ducks on the pond. Jealousy stole into Ailish's heart. Spoiled or not, the boy certainly responded to his uncle.

"Lucky you are, they're still here," Sean said. "Let's be showing your Aunt Ailish how we feed them." He poured some corn from the drawstring bag into Will's outstretched hand. The boy greedily closed his fist around the kernels.

"You'll need to be sharing those." Sean gestured toward Ailish. "With your aintín."

Will scrunched up his mouth as if considering whether to comply, then finally opened his palm to Ailish. She took several pieces. "Thank you...Will," she said.

Without a word, he went to the water's edge and hurled the rest of his corn at waiting ducks, then looked over his shoulder at Ailish.

"Like this?" She came to his side and scattered her corn into the water.

Will beamed. "More corn, Uncle Sean."

As soon as Sean obliged him, Will swept his arm in a wide arc, releasing his fistful of kernels all at once. As the corn pattered upon the water and the ducks chased down the snack, he paced the edge of the pond, giggling, his fury at Ailish already a distant memory.

She found herself as charmed as she was shaken. Clearly he'd grown out of some of his sweet temperament—just as his older brothers had. Faith, but she'd forgotten what a handful they'd been, those older two, *God's blessing on their souls*. Her sister's husband had been the only one able to make them behave.

"He's stubborn. Not one to like change," Sean offered, jarring her back to the present.

As strong-willed as his brothers, she almost said, but didn't.

"We've wondered if the shipwreck was the reason...losing his parents when he was just a babe..." Sean squinted, as if gauging her response. "He was with strangers for a month before Kathleen and Jack took him in. Perhaps it's why he fights back so."

"All the more reason he should be with his real family." The words came out more harshly than she intended, and regret reared its head. She squashed the emotion beneath righteousness; her words were nothing more than the truth.

Will raced back for more corn.

"Don't be throwing them all at once or we'll run out too soon," Sean warned. "One at a time...like this." He tossed a single kernel into the pond and waited as three ducks went after it.

"One?" the boy asked, clearly unconvinced of the merits of the method. He threw a kernel at the ducks.

"See?" Sean said to Ailish. "It's not so hard to get him to behave. All in the approach."

Will closed his fingers around the corn in his palm and reared back. "Oh—no—" Ailish lunged at him just as he heaved all his corn into the pond. As a gaggle of quacking ducks jostled for the snack, Will let out a shout of joy and clapped his hands. "Need corn," he shouted. "More corn!"

"As you can see, Miss Sullivan," Sean said dryly, "it's all in the approach."

A laugh tried to burble out of her and she slapped a hand

over her mouth to hold it in. "Thank you, Mr. Deacey. I do see how effective the right approach can be."

Sean handed her the sack of corn. "You should probably be doing this with him. I'll step back."

She nodded, touched by the kindness of the gesture. She filled Will's open palm and knelt beside him so she could intervene if he tried to throw them all at once. "Remember, one at a time, Will. No need to hurry," she said as they tossed the kernels, piece by piece.

"Well done, Miss Sullivan," Sean called from behind her.

She threw an appreciative glance over her shoulder, met his grin with one of her own. "You can call me Ailish if you'd like." She turned back just in time to see a fistful of kernels sail above the pond like the seeds of a dandelion puff released on the wind. "Will!" She slapped her hands atop her head in mock dismay.

A chuckle from Sean danced forward with the spirit of an Irish jig. "My friends," he said as he came up next to her, "call me Sean."

CHAPTER TWELVE

KATHLEEN STOOD AT THE SIDE OF WILL'S BED IN THE DARKENED room and let herself relax into the stillness of her son's slumber, so gentle she could hardly see his chest move. Such a difference from an hour ago when he'd protested vehemently against going to bed. Now, he lay on his back, blanket tossed to the side, arms and legs splayed as though sleep had overtaken him right in the middle of play.

Love slammed into her with such force, she gasped and set a hand on the bedpost for support. What she wouldn't give to go back to the time before Ailish had broken into their lives.

Last night she'd dreamed that a thief had gotten into their house and though she knew he was there, she'd been unable to cry out, powerless to stop him from stealing everything they valued.

Tears sprang to her eyes and she dashed them away with the back of her hand. Weeping would solve nothing; what they needed was an end to this nightmare. She gently brought her son's arms to his sides and tucked the blanket close. As she brushed a wisp of hair from his forehead, she pressed this image of him into her mind, imprinting the tiniest of details, things that wouldn't matter to anyone else—his soft intake of air, the tiny curve of his nose, his dark lashes against his cheeks. She'd been doing this often lately, deliberately memorizing moments so that no matter what happened, Will would be with her forever.

Almost a week had passed since the judge ordered the visitations with Ailish. The second outing had been earlier this very day—another afternoon in the park with the ducks. Sean reported it had gone better this time than the last. For Will's sake, she was glad—or at least trying to be. Feeding the ducks had been something they'd done together since before he could crawl. She would hate for his favorite *a-venture* to become tainted for him.

As it suddenly had become for her.

Jealousy skittered though her, bitter and ugly, and she gripped the bedpost as if to squeeze the life out of the emotion before it could take root and grow.

Footsteps sounded in the hall, then the door creaked open. Jack stepped to her side, to gaze upon their son and wrap Kathleen in his arms. They stayed like that for a long minute, watching Will sleep, holding one another close as though the strength of their love could prevent their family from fracturing.

"I asked Sean...pushed him to tell me..." Jack said in a ragged voice. "I know it's been only two visits, but I asked if he'd seen any sign Ailish might be softening about us keeping Will."

Her heart nearly shattered. Jack had weathered so much loss already. He'd been but a child of eight when his father took his own life and his mother abandoned him to his grandfather. Now, that beloved grandfather lay dying in the next room, and Ailish was fighting to take away his only child.

Will rolled over groggily, and Kathleen straightened his blanket and smoothed the corners. "What did he say?" she whispered. "Anything different?"

"Just more about Will's temper. She doesn't know how to handle him. It can't hurt for her to see he's not always...easy to pacify. That she would have a lifetime of—"

"Battles?" Kathleen frowned at the thought of Will's stubborn nature. "Remember what Ma said the day Sean brought him? His name means *warrior*."

"Well, I would say he's fulfilled the prophecy." Jack took her hand and started for the door. "Perhaps his temperament will be what saves us."

Downstairs, they found Sean in a chair in the parlor, staring into space, an open book in his lap, the dying fire the only light in the room. Kathleen studied him in concern. The book had been given to him by his foreman just days before the man died in the explosion that injured Sean. Now he seemed to be reading it every chance he got. "Are you all right, Sean?"

"Just thinking. And running from me thoughts."

"I know the feeling." Jack went to add wood to the fire.

Kathleen knew it, too. How one thought ran over the last and smashed into the next. How the more she tried to rein in her fears, the more they ran wild. It was a bit like trying to corral rabbits scattering across a spring hillside.

"You'll ruin your eyes reading in the dark." She raised the wick on the oil lamp on the end table.

"In truth, I'll be reading far less than reflecting."

She dropped into the chair opposite. "On what?" she asked softly, almost afraid of the answer. He'd been so distant these past few years, even though he was with them now, she still feared someday he would drift away forever.

"Time. The passage of time...death...grief..."

She put a hand to her heart. Moira and his sons were never far from his consciousness, that she knew, but this book he'd been given, written by a man she'd never heard of —Henry David Thoreau—seemed to bring out such melancholy in him. "Are ye sure that book is the best thing for you?"

He gave her a look. "Aye."

"What's the title again?" Jack asked as he tended the fire. "Perhaps I'll read it when you finish." The small flames roared suddenly upward, crackling with ferocity, and he took a quick step back.

"*A Week on the Concord and Merrimack Rivers.*" Sean shut the book and held it with both hands. "He wrote it after his brother died. About a boat trip they took together. But in truth, it's about far more than that."

Kathleen nodded and no one spoke, each of them caught in their thoughts, the book's relevancy to their own situation not hard to see. A grim silence stole over the room like a shadow in the late afternoon deepens as the sun drops low.

Sean cleared his throat, breaking the quiet. "How about some dominoes?" he asked. "I believe I'm still the champion."

Kathleen caught her breath. *Dominoes?* "Jesus, Mary, and Joseph, are ye mad? Do you think we should just go on like nothing has changed? When over every moment hangs the possibility we could lose—?" She couldn't bring herself to finish the sentence.

"I know it feels wrong." Sean inclined his chin in acknowledgement, ran a palm along the spine of his book. "Grief...is a shadow, this Thoreau says. And light, the only cure. There's a pall over this house—"

"As well there should be," she snapped, not wanting to hear any more.

"Nay. It will kill the two of you. In spirit, if not in body. What good are you to Will if every day is clouded by grief?"

"A fine one you are to talk. So, you're thinking we should just pretend—"

"Not pretend—"

Kathleen huffed out a breath.

"He's right, Kathleen," Jack said. "We can't keep on like this. We understand why life has changed in our home, but Will doesn't. Nor should he. For our son's sake, we must do our best to return to normal. I should go back to work. You should continue volunteering."

"And I should keep talking of buying land." Sean retrieved the box of dominoes off the shelf near the hearth and weighed it in his hands.

"'Tis not so easy to shut off feelings such as these," Kathleen muttered.

"You forget how well I know that. Doesn't matter if my boys lived one day or two years. Doesn't matter if they died five years past or last week. Love is love." Sean lifted the top off the box.

Kathleen's eyes drifted to the stairs leading to the bedroom where Will lay soundly sleeping, blissfully unaware of the storm that had swept into their lives, disrupting everything, perhaps forever.

"Loss is loss," Jack murmured, reminding her of what she already knew but had somehow forgotten.

Regret clamped down upon her heart. "Ah, Seanie, sorry I am. Sometimes I'll be feeling like I'm losing myself, like I've been swept unknowing into the otherworld, deep underground where everything is different, where even I'm different...and the faeries won't let me go home."

"Perhaps I've been sent to save you. *Again.*" Sean gave her a cocky grin. "The first time I had to rescue her, Jack, I was only five."

"*Rescue* is overstating it just a bit." She got up to retrieve a stray tin soldier lying in a dark corner and return him to his blue-coated battalion along the baseboard.

Sean laughed. "I fished ye out of a peat bog. If that isn't a rescue—"

"'Twas hardly more than a puddle, but if it makes you feel better, call it a rescue then." She turned to face him, serious now, hands on her hips. "Something's been weighing on me, Sean...sitting in my thoughts like a blackbird ready to poke out me eyes. I'm wondering if you know..." She almost couldn't bring herself to voice the question that had haunted her since Ailish came into their lives. "Do you think Ailish has other reasons for doing this, or does she truly care about Will?"

"It's only been two visits." Sean rearranged the dominoes in the box without looking up.

"Humor me, then, with a guess. Your intuition."

He scrubbed a hand over his jaw. "She may not know him well, but care for him she does. I'm sorry, Kathleen. She knew him when first he came into this world. He's all she has left. It's a fierce love she feels, I'm afraid."

His words were both a blade in her side and a balm on her heart. A lump squeezed her throat. "Don't be sorry. It may be bittersweet to know, but in truth, it eases my fears. For if it comes to pass that we lose our son, we can ask nothing better for him than to be loved."

The fire cast shadows against the wall as it illuminated the tin soldiers standing at attention along the baseboard. Tomorrow, another war would take place, the general in full command. At some point, a ball would fall upon the enemy soldiers and knock them over in one fell swoop. Juice would be drunk, perhaps spilled. Lunch would be devoured. A nap would be had.

As long as Will was with them, life should go on the same as it always had. He must not know the pressures they were feeling.

She brought pensive eyes to Sean's, her agony allayed, as least for a while. "I'll be thinking we should set those dominoes out on the table," she said. "It's time to be finding out who the true champion is."

CHAPTER THIRTEEN

"My soul to the devil, not again." Ailish sprinted toward Jordan-Marsh, the large department store where she worked, one hand plastered against her head in a desperate attempt to keep the twist at her nape from coming completely apart, the other clutching the front of her cloak as it billowed behind her like an empty sail.

"Jesus, Mary, Joseph, and all the saints," she puffed as she ran, "if ye'll be caring for me at all, don't be letting me get caught." She gritted her teeth. If not for the Montgomerys' objection to giving up Will, she wouldn't be having to pay a lawyer. Which meant she wouldn't be having to make deliveries for Eileen, the old woman upstairs, just to earn some extra coin.

And she wouldn't be late to work yet again.

She slipped into the back entry and hung her cloak on a hook, relieved that everyone was already on the sales floor. Another minute or two and she would be in her place, no one the wiser. She hurried across the storeroom, re-pinning her disheveled hair with both hands as she went. If her luck held—

The door to the sales floor opened, and the store manager stepped through. Ailish sent up a prayer that he would assume she'd been on time and was simply taking care of things in the storeroom. "A good morning to you, sir," she said, flashing a bright smile.

He frowned and crossed his arms over his chest, the movement tightening the vest under his suit jacket and emphasizing his portly belly. "You're late, Miss Sullivan," he said in a troubled voice. "Again."

Though he'd always been friendly to her, suddenly his crisp pressed slacks and jacket, even his too-tight vest, had a slightly menacing feel, like a fresh suit of armor donned before a conflict.

"I'm sorry sir, truly I am. The woman on the floor above asked if I might deliver a bag of sewing for her. She's old and has trouble getting about, you see—"

"Regardless, you're required to be here on time. I've warned you twice before already." His gaze was everywhere but on her. "We are a business. If the shelves aren't stocked, if the staff isn't present when we open the doors, how successful can we be?"

"I understand." She tried to still the nervous tapping of her heart. Once this month was past, once the judge made his final ruling and she'd paid the attorney's bill, she had to find a way to survive without taking on so much side work.

"I'm sorry, sir. Truly." She clasped her hands behind her back. "When I agreed to make the delivery, I didn't know the distance I'd be needing to walk. Took far longer than I thought. I'll not be helping with morning drop-offs again." She waited for him to unfold his arms and give a curt nod, an unspoken signal that Ailish should get to work.

Seconds passed and she dropped her chin, studied the unfinished wood floor of the storeroom, the grain weaving across the boards like serpents twining underfoot. Unease slithered up her spine. "It won't happen again," she said with conviction. "I'll be promising you that."

She considered bringing up Liam, then decided against it. She'd seen others lose their jobs when family problems interfered too much with their work. This manager had already been kind enough to let her take a couple of hours off for each visitation.

"I'm glad to hear it," he said, and she raised hopeful eyes.

He let out a frustrated sigh. "But even if I were to let this pass, an issue has been brought to my attention from another of the girls. As you know, the store's policy is to hire only married women. I've been told you're a widow. Which means, technically..."

You're not a married woman, she finished in her mind.

The manager cleared his throat. "What I mean to say is, do you have a husband, Miss Sullivan?" he asked, an understanding expression on his face, a desperate note in his voice. "Else I have no choice, much as it pains me. You know the company policy—married women only. Single women pose too much temptation for male customers."

Her thoughts churned. Without a job, she couldn't pay an attorney. Without an attorney, she'd lose her chance to get Liam. She couldn't get fired. How had he learned the truth? Should she lie outright about a husband? Would he believe her?

No matter which way she turned, it seemed she was damned.

Her eyes slid over the shelves lining the storeroom walls, stacked with products, everything pristine and dust free. *Kept clean by women.* She felt a rush of heat, like a wave of fever. Women could clean houses and cook food and work in factories, but let an unmarried woman work in a store and suddenly men couldn't control themselves? It was beyond absurd.

Stay calm and reasonable, she reminded herself. She must be calm and reasonable if she was to have any hope of bringing the manager to her side. "I'll be asking you, sir, to reconsider," she said, purposely avoiding the question of a husband. "I'll soon be supporting not just myself, but me young nephew as I've mentioned, who will be coming to live with me. I need this job. Please, if you'll—"

"Ailish, I'm sorry. I don't set the rules. I merely carry them out. Your tardiness I might be able to overlook if I had your absolute assurance it wouldn't happen again. Reliable employees are a necessity in any business, but especially in such a large store—"

"I can assure you I'll not be late again." This couldn't be happening. Somehow she had to convince him to keep her on. "You can rely on me."

His face softened. "I know you've not been long in this country, and I've been pleased with your work...considering that so many Irish have such an aversion to labor."

Despite her vow to stay composed, Ailish bristled. Even those who should know better harbored false beliefs about the Irish. "I'm but trying to make a better life for myself," she said stiffly. "Working nights as well as days."

"I wish there were something I could do, but your lack of a husband can't be overcome," he said, hurrying his words. "I don't own the company. I have no choice but to let you go."

She reached out both hands in supplication, knowing full well the odds were stacked against her. She'd heard about how strictly the store enforced its policies. Now she knew for fact—nothing short of a living husband would save her. Still, she had no choice but to try. For if she got to the final hearing without a job and the judge thought she couldn't provide a secure home for Liam, she had no doubt how he would rule.

"It's true, my husband passed on," she began slowly, grasping for any idea that would keep her in this job until the final hearing. "The truth is..." *What? What could she say that would change his mind?* "The truth is...I'm...engaged. Soon to be wed."

For God's bright sake, she didn't actually say that, did she? Suddenly everything was becoming ever more complicated. "And so," she continued, having nowhere else to go, "since I was married already—that husband gone, *God rest his soul*—and with another wedding coming up soon, I'll not be long without a husband."

Heaven and earth forgive her this falsehood, but it was for Liam's sake she did it. Such foolishness anyway these men believed, that single women were temptresses, as though men were ruled by their lusting and had no control over themselves.

"The problem is Lent," she said. "In the Catholic church, none may wed during the Lenten season. Once Easter has passed, we—my betrothed and I—will be married."

The manager looked down as he adjusted the lapels on his coat. "I'm sorry. You're a good worker and I hate to lose you. But the owner will not bend the rules for an Irish. Once you're married, I would be happy to have you back."

She couldn't breathe. In the span of a few minutes she had lost all her income except the pittance she got delivering mending for Eileen.

Panic roiled her stomach. She was to have another visitation with Liam and Sean this very afternoon. If Sean were to learn she lost her job, what would stop him from telling his family? And who could blame him for doing it? 'Twould be the perfect weapon to use against her.

And what of her own lawyer? Nay, he couldn't be finding out either. She couldn't risk that he might step away from the case fearing she'd not be able to pay even the small amount they'd agreed upon.

"I'm sorry, Miss Sullivan. Ailish." The manager put a hand on her back and urged her in the direction of the exterior door.

She forced herself to cross the storeroom and step outside into the early morning light. The Montgomerys be damned. If they'd given up Liam when she'd come to claim him, she'd not have any of this trouble.

The heavy wood door clunked shut behind her; the latch dropped into place with finality. She sank against the building, the cold stone a welcome support for her suddenly weak legs.

She had lost her job.

She'd not felt so alone since the day she left Ireland. Foundering. Afraid. *Broken*. She'd sought a new life in this country, a chance to start over. But no one had warned her of the prejudice that slashed through the fabric of Boston, the hatred so many harbored against anyone not of the same religion or nationality.

Why had no one warned her that the English were still ruling America long after the Revolution? That the Protestants had proclaimed sovereignty as though God himself had declared the Irish inferior simply because...they were Irish and Catholic?

She pushed herself away from the wall, squared her shoulders and started for home. They'd not win; she couldn't let them. She had Liam to fight for, a promise made to her sister. She would find another job and begin again. And once she prevailed, once the judge ruled that Liam belonged with her, she would waste no more time in America before returning with him to Ireland.

CHAPTER FOURTEEN

SEAN STROLLED WITH AILISH DOWN CENTRAL WHARF, WILL between them holding each of their hands. The wharf, vital to Boston's seaport and teeming with activity, jutted nearly a quarter mile into the harbor, its center crammed with some fifty warehouses, four-stories each, its outer stone walls lined with docked vessels. The shouts of workers mingled with the creaking of wheels and the clatter of hooves as cargo was transferred from ships to wagons to warehouses. Owners stood talking with captains, and captains directed their crews ,and no matter what direction one looked, there was movement and action.

"I'll be guessing we can keep his attention occupied here," Sean said, although, thus far, Will had been most entertained by simply jumping into the air and letting himself swing from their hands. Each jump was accompanied by a joyous laugh. And each laugh drove a jagged reminder into Sean of what was at stake—Will's future, Kathleen and Jack's family.

"Perhaps with so many new things to see, he'll be able to hold his temper in check," Ailish commented.

Her words rankled. Even when he knew that forging a friendship with her was a means to an end, it wasn't always so easy to do.

Will jumped again and Ailish let out a sharp laugh. "Such a silly boy," she said, sounding peevish rather than amused.

He cast a sidelong glance her way. She didn't seem pleased to be here today, hadn't been very happy when first she saw Will. Could it be she was beginning to realize how her life would change if she had responsibility for a child not yet three?

Might she be starting to reconsider the path she had chosen?

If there was even a small chance she was having second thoughts, he had to try harder. He groped for something pleasant to say, something unthreatening and friendly, finally coming out with, "Seems to be getting colder again." *The weather was the best he could do?* "Almost feels like snow." He mentally winced. Such a paragon of dazzling conversation. Somehow, he knew Kathleen would not be impressed by his effort.

"Snow?" Will asked. "More snow?"

"Wouldn't that just be a grand cap to me day," Ailish mumbled. "I thought the snow was done now that we've passed into April."

"Not always." He gave her an appraising look. Hard to believe the weather could cause such dismay. Perhaps another topic would be better received. He pointed at an octagonal cupola rising from a tall building near the middle of the wharf. "That's where the telescope is," he said. "In that little room on the roof. Not a prettier view of the countryside, they say."

"*They?* And you think *they'll* just be letting us use it?" Ailish snipped. "Irish rabble off the street?"

He blinked, taken aback. She was out of sorts today, that was sure. "It's for public use."

"We'll find out, won't we?" She dropped her head back. "Have ye ever stopped to look at the American sky?"

He peered up at the blue-gray clouds stretching endlessly outward, grainy and uneven like the rock he'd been blasting in the mountains of Virginia. "Aye," he said cautiously.

"Such a promise it is, that sky. Hanging over all of Boston...the whole country I'd venture. But ye need only look beneath it—and not very deep—to see the lie."

"Lie lie," Will sang as he swung between them.

"I'll not be following you."

Ailish let out a snort. "The truth is, Sean, the promise of America doesna shine on everyone. Sure but you know that already. How long have you been here?"

"Near on five years."

"That's four years, seven months more than me. Tell me, has it gotten better in those five years? The work? The pay? *The contempt...?*"

What was this about? Sean searched her eyes, noticing for the first time how dark they were, rich earthy brown with hints of bronze. Inherited, perhaps, from a Spanish ancestor centuries ago, when Spain sent men to help Ireland in its endless battle against English repression.

Ailish's brows snapped upward in question.

"Nay," he admitted. "In some ways, things may be getting worse." An anti-immigrant political movement had taken root in America and was growing quickly. Though its members hated all immigrants, they particularly despised the Irish. "So many Irish have come across the last few years, some fear we're going to steal America and give it to the pope."

"And how are we to do that?" she scoffed. "We can't even take our own wee country back from the English."

"Stop." Will pulled his hands free and planted them on his hips. "No fighting."

"We're not fighting," Ailish said. "We're—"

"Going to see the telescope." Sean grabbed Will's hand. "Come on."

A few minutes later, after being reassured by a woman at the door that the telescope was indeed free for public use, they climbed several flights of stairs to the cupola. Sean aimed the telescope toward the harbor and showed Will how to look through the eyepiece.

"Boats," the boy cried, as if he'd never seen a ship before. "Lookit Aish, boats!"

She bent to take a quick peek. "It was in a boat like that I sailed over the ocean."

Will straightened, eyes round with wonder, as if he couldn't believe she had done something so exciting.

"I came across the ocean on a big boat, too," Sean offered.

The boy lifted one shoulder in an unimpressed shrug. Sean widened his eyes and let his mouth drop open in mock offense. *"A very big boat,"* he added.

Will shrugged again, drawing a genuine laugh out of Ailish. The sound brought a smile to Sean's face. "Well, then, let's have a look at the city." As he swiveled the telescope and made sure Will could see properly, Ailish stepped to the open-air window.

"'Twas a day not unlike this when I arrived here," she said in a voice so low she could have been speaking to herself.

Alone, Sean thought. *Possibly sick. Certainly hungry. Most likely afraid and broke.* It was a rare Irishman who didn't finish the journey in exactly the same state. "Are ye homesick much?"

When she didn't immediately reply, he knew the answer.

"That I am," she finally said. "But for the way Ireland was before the famine struck."

Sean bent over Will and pointed into the distance. "Look for our house, lad. That way." He stepped closer to Ailish. "I used to feel the same. Helps if you remind yourself we were always under the English heel there."

"As we just discussed, we're under it here as well." She paced the perimeter of the small octagonal room. "What real opportunity is here for the Irish? Only the jobs no one else wants. Building the railroads for someone else to ride. Working the docks to bring goods ashore so that someone else—people with money—can buy them. Cleaning grand houses for someone else's leisure. At least in Ireland I felt like I belonged. It was *my* country."

The despair in her voice rattled him, her words reminding him of things similar complaints he'd made himself, bitter thoughts he tried to bury when they arose. For if he yielded to such thinking, he would have no reason to keep holding onto the dream of owning land. "You haven't even been gone a year. You're still hurting. *Grief passes in its own time*, me ma would say."

Ailish's expression hardened. "What do you or your ma know of grief? Your family made it here. They all survived."

Though she'd thrown this accusation at him before, he flinched as if it were a fresh blow, his mind sliding back to the winter day Moira died, a steady snow falling outside, dropping like a dusty shroud over his family, his life, his country. He carried Moira and his boys deep in his heart, thought of them nearly every day. But he owed their story to no one.

"'Tis easy to start anew," Ailish continued, her tone sour, "as long as the people you love are near. No such luck was there for me. In that rocky soil of Ireland, I buried everyone I loved."

A group of people entered the cupola, and their

exclamations about the view filled the small space with welcome distraction. Sean lifted Will from the telescope so others could use it and went to stand near Ailish looking out over the dark water of the bay.

"Next week will be my sister's birthday," she said.

The commotion around them, so many people chattering at once, created a sense of privacy, a wall behind which they could speak without being overheard.

"I was four when she was born. Just a young girl, but I was her protector from that day forward. 'Twas my idea that she leave Ireland. I thought America would save her family, save all of us." She rested her hands on the sill and leaned forward to catch the sun on her face. "Instead she's buried in Cohasset. Her husband lost to the ocean. And her only living son too young to remember her."

Ailish's pain sharpened the ache in his chest. "I'm sorry." He wanted to turn away.

Giorraíonn beirt bóthar. Two shorten the road, Ma whispered in his mind. Nay, he didna need another's grief to bear beside his own.

"Go down. Let's go down." Will patted Sean's cheeks with his hand. "Uncle Sean," he said, patting harder.

"In a minute."

Ailish appeared not to have heard, her gaze trained in the direction of Cohasset—and her thoughts, he knew, fixed on the memory of her sister. Sean watched her, his mind arguing with itself. He owed this woman nothing, least of all, understanding.

Nothing.

And then a breath hissed out from between his teeth, a quiet surrender. "We didn't all get to America," he said in a low voice. "My wife, Moira—"

"You're married?"

He struggled to voice the words that didn't want to come. "I was. She didna make it here." He boosted Will higher in his arms. "She died in childbirth, weak from the famine. And my sons, two wee lads, were already gone when they were born."

Ailish let out a sharp exhale and reached out to touch his arm. "God rest their souls. I'm sorry. I was thinking you were one of the lucky—"

"I'll be thinking there are few Irish who've had any luck these past years."

Will leaned out to rap a fist against Ailish's arm. "Go down now?"

"Will doesn't even know his real Mam and Da are gone," Ailish said. "Perhaps it is the babes who are the lucky ones, not even knowing what they've lost."

She started for the stairwell, and Sean watched her go. Jaysus, could it be that she was no different than the rest of the Irish, *than him*, just seeking some way out from under the pain? He followed her down the stairs.

"I've been reading a book," he said when they were outside again.

"You can read?" she asked, impressed. Will ran out ahead to watch a row of men hauling wooden barrels up the gangplank of a ship.

"Aye. And you?"

She hesitated. The din of the wharf filled the space where she would have replied. "Not as well as I'd wish," she finally said.

He gave an empathetic nod. The poor had few opportunities in Ireland and many got little schooling. If not for Ma's insistence, he might not have learned to read very well himself.

"What of this book?" she asked.

"Ah..." Suddenly he felt embarrassed to have brought it up.

"The author, it's just that he sees things differently...life and death—"

"What good is that?" she scoffed. "You may look at death however ye want, and still the dead remain dead. Change what you call it even, and it changes not the truth of it."

"Aye. But a different view might make it easier to bear," he said, pushing back. How did he explain that the man's writings filled a hollow Sean had felt since leaving Ireland? After losing Moira and their sons and his country...after years of working on the railroad, blasting tunnels through mountains, inhaling gunpowder and rock dust, laying thousands of rails in the heat and the cold, and living in a shack beside the tracks...how did he explain the hope he got from Thoreau's words?

Ailish quickened her steps to catch up with Will. "Claims to be a miracle worker, does he?" she bit out as they reached the boy.

"Nay. Just a man trying to get past his own brother's death."

"Mother of God, yet another of the unlucky." She let out a weary sigh. "I'm glad you've found words that bring you solace. I hold no hope that I'll ever be so fortunate." She bent toward Will, exclaiming over the length of the ship and the height of its two masts.

Sean understood her bitterness. For years he'd held tight to his anger, stoked it even.

When the foreman first offered him Thoreau's book, he'd wanted no advice, had pushed it away, refusing to open it. Only guilt finally made him take it up, a self-imposed penance for surviving the explosion when his friend had not. He rubbed his injured arm.

"The author lives in Concord I'm told. Not twenty miles north," he said, as Ailish turned to look at him. "He's giving a lecture tomorrow night in Boston. At Cochituate Hall. Ye might..." His thoughts stumbled at the invisible wall he was scaling. And for what reason? Friendship? To force assistance upon Ailish that she wasn't even seeking? "Ye might find it interesting..."

"A lecture?" An edge had returned to her voice. "And you'll be going to hear him?" She straightened and brushed off her hands, one against the other.

"Aye."

Her eyes flashed, the brown rich and vibrant in the sun. She let out a derisive snort. "I'll be having no time for lectures."

CHAPTER FIFTEEN

AILISH TRUDGED THROUGH THE SNOW BLANKETING THE SIDEWALK and bent her head against the white flakes furiously falling, swirling in gusts of wind like faeries dancing in the dark. She let her gaze sneak into the windows of homes she passed, the soft firelight within a cruel reminder that she'd lost her job and the scant comforts she enjoyed would not be hers for long on her meager earnings from mending.

Beneath the glow of the street lamps, the falling white soon lost its magic, seeming more and more like a curtain dropping between acts of a stage play—between the acts of her life—marking in so many ways the end of the lovely first days of early spring and a vengeful return to winter.

"In this weather you're going out?" Meg had asked, incredulous, before she left. "Who is it you're going to hear?"

Ailish hadn't replied. She had no good reason to give...only a vague hope that perhaps the comfort Sean got from the Mr. Thoreau's words might also be there for her. If she could but find a way to calm the rage that seemed to hover just beneath the surface of her skin waiting to explode at any moment, perhaps she could find her way back to who she used to be.

By the time she reached Cochituate Hall, she was covered in a layer of white—and more than several minutes late. She rushed into the building and down the hall to the room where a sign indicated the lecture was to take place.

"Twenty-five cents," the doorman said, holding out a hand.

She skidded to a halt. "There's a fee?"

"Of course. The speaker needs to be paid."

"I didn't know—" She peeked into the lecture room and stifled the urge to roll her eyes. Row upon row of empty seats greeted her, only four other attendees in the room. If this man had such valuable thoughts to offer, where was his audience?

SEAN GLANCED AROUND THE ROOM, surprised at the low attendance. The weather had made the going slow; maybe some would arrive late. Or perhaps everyone else was smarter than he. If the event was cancelled, all he would have gained this night was cold feet from a slog in the snow, already several inches deep.

A middle-aged man came to the front of the room at took up the spot behind the podium. "I'm Bronson Alcott," he said. "I'm happy to introduce Mr. Henry David Thoreau, writer and natural philosopher. Mr. Thoreau will lecture this evening on the book he's soon to publish...insights he learned while living alone in the woods, in a one-room house on Walden Pond. No subject suits Mr. Thoreau better, and perhaps no man in the world is better qualified than he to treat that subject profitably."

Mr. Thoreau stepped to the podium to a smattering of applause from the sparse audience. With his clean-shaven face and light brown hair carelessly shoved across his forehead, he hardly seemed older than Sean himself. How could a man of so few years have acquired such deep insight?

Sean leaned forward eagerly, determined not to miss a word. But as Thoreau began to speak, thanking them for attending, the sound of a voices, a quiet stir, pushed into his consciousness and he half-turned to see a woman engaged in discussion with the doorman. Though snow covered her cloak and her head was bent, he recognized her instantly: Ailish.

An amazed grin snapped across his face and he quickly swallowed it down. He waited for her to look into the room and spot him, alone like an island in a sea of empty seats. Ailish raised her head just as Thoreau began the lecture: *"The mass of men lead lives of quiet desperation...I went to the pond because I wished to live deliberately...to see if I could learn what it had to teach, and not, when I came to die, discover I had not lived."*

Ailish threw a glare across the room; her eyes fell on Sean for a furious heartbeat before she back-stepped into the corridor and disappeared from view. He hesitated for a second before throwing a regretful glance at the podium and hurrying into the hall after her. Thoreau's words followed him out: *"I first took up my abode in the woods, which by accident, was on Independence Day, or the Fourth of July, 1845..."*

"Ailish," Sean called softly.

She whirled back, ruffled. "Ye didn't say there's a fee," she challenged, cheeks flushed red. "No entry without twenty-five cents. I can't...I don't have that with me."

Like a caged bird escaping to freedom, Mr. Thoreau's words soared over the doorman: *"...living is so dear, I wanted to live deep and suck out all the marrow of life...."*

Sean wavered, torn between a desire not to miss any of the

lecture, and his reluctance—nearly as compelling—not to abandon Ailish in the hallway.

"Men say that a stitch in time saves nine, and so they take a thousand stitches today to save nine tomorrow."

"Stupid of me to forget." He stuck a hand in his pocket and withdrew several coins. "You can repay me later."

"Let us spend one day as deliberately as nature and not be thrown off the track by every mosquito's wing that falls on the rails."

"Ye'll be misunderstanding me." Ailish took several steps back. "I've…not the funds to pay at all," she said, eyes downcast as she made the obviously reluctant confession.

Thoreau's words beckoned him to return: *"To be awake is to be alive. We must learn how to reawaken and keep ourselves awake, not by using mechanical aides, but by having an infinite expectation of what the dawn will bring…"*

He gritted his teeth and made a quick decision. "I'll pay, then. You'll be my guest."

"…there is nothing more encouraging than the unquestionable ability of a man to improve his life through his own efforts…"

"I'll not be putting myself in your debt," Ailish said, raising her chin.

"Heaven is under our feet as well as over our heads. If the day and the night are such that you greet them with joy…that is your success."

Frustration roared through him like a train at top speed. Jaysus, but this woman was a test. "Consider it a gift."

"However mean your life may be, meet it and live it to its best. Do not shun it and call it names. The fault-finder will find faults even in paradise."

Ailish turned from Sean to send her gaze through the open doorway, as if hearing Thoreau's words for the first time.

"Love your life, poor as it is. You may have some pleasant, glorious

hours, even in a poor house. The setting sun is reflected from the windows of the almshouse as brightly as from the rich man's abode..."

A disbelieving huff shot out of her. "This is his truth? The words that console you? Sounds, he does, like those who wish to rinse away their guilt over paying low wages."

"His meaning is deeper. You're missing the point." Aggravation shadowed his words. "And Ailish, need I point out, we're missing the lecture."

"Cultivate poverty like a garden herb, like sage. Do not trouble yourself much to get new things, whether clothes or friends. Things do not change, we change."

"You're thinking this man can help me?"

At this point, he was having his doubts. "Ailish, it's a Godforsaken night to be out, yet here you are. Either go in or not, but let's spend no more time in his hall." He took firm hold of her elbow and steered her toward the open doorway.

"Could a greater miracle take place than for us to look though each other's eyes for an instant?"

She snatched her arm away. "Nay. Be keeping your money." Striding to the entrance, she pushed through into the snowy night. The door thudded shut behind her.

Sean scowled. He understood not wanting to accept charity, but she was already here. Why not stay a bit, give the man a chance before rushing away? Exhaling softly, he went into the room and slid into a seat just inside the door.

"My nearest neighbor is more than a mile away, and my horizon is bounded by woods. I have a distant view of the railroad where it touches the pond..."

Thoreau paused to take a sip of water. *"We do not ride on the railroad; it rides upon us... Those cross-ties that underlie the railroad? Each one is a man and the rails are laid on them so the cars run smoothly...so that if a few have the pleasure of riding on a rail, the rest have the misfortune of being ridden upon."*

Sean sat back in his chair. Was he not making the same point as Ailish had yesterday? That none of the Irish owned their own lives?

He listened rapt for the next hour as Thoreau railed against the old way, asserting that no person—whether born wealthy or a common man—should be forced into a life preordained by birth. Instead, each should be allowed to choose their own path.

Elbows on knees, hands clasped together, Sean's spirit soared as Thoreau's final words wrapped around him like a promise: *"This I have learned, by my experiment in the woods...if one advances confidently in the direction of his dreams, and endeavors to live the life which he has imagined, he will meet with a success unexpected."*

By the time he was tramping home through the still falling snow, Sean's mind churned with all that he'd heard. Thoreau's ideas were uplifting, but his words were often complex and it could be challenging to decipher his meaning.

If only Ailish had stayed, they might work through it together. A pang of regret traced a line along a scar in his heart; he should have ignored her protests and paid the fee, not given her the opening to refuse.

He brushed a gloved hand across the snowflakes sticking to his face and chided himself for being a wishful fool. As Ma was inclined to say, *Bheir aon fhear each gu uisge, ach cha toir a dhà-dheug air òl. One man can lead a horse to the water, but twelve cannot make it drink.*

Aye, true enough. Especially, he was finding, when it came to Ailish.

CHAPTER SIXTEEN

THE WOOD PLANK FLOOR CREAKED UNDERFOOT AS KATHLEEN crossed the back room of the Irish Relief Society. She passed the sorting tables stacked with newly-delivered garments and ran a hand over a small shirt, sea blue in color, the workmanship excellent. It would be perfect for Will in the coming summer.

Her heart stilled, and she crushed the thought. She'd not be planning ahead, not yet. "The seamstresses have been busy," she said aloud to divert her mind.

Sean had been right about getting back to normal life; it felt good to be here again, busy with something else for a few hours. She'd begun volunteering after her first miscarriage to keep herself from dwelling on her loss. It had given her such purpose, she continued even after Will came into their lives.

She stepped onto the sales floor with its racks and shelves of ready-made clothing, everything from trousers, shirts, and coats, to dresses and skirts, to gloves and hosiery, boots and shoes, and more. A gray-haired woman folding clothes at a table near the front window raised a hand in greeting. "Did you see all the new garments?" she called.

"Aye. And not a moment too soon," Kathleen replied. "With spring nearly upon us, there will be ever more ships bringing Irish across."

Before an hour passed, the two women had moved most of the new garments onto the sales floor, folded and arranged and added them to the appropriate areas, and opened for business. A steady stream of customers came and went, some just browsing but most buying. Kathleen hurried toward a harried woman with three young boys who were digging through stacks of clothing on the shelves along the back wall, discarding garments as quickly as they unfolded them.

"A lovely morning to you. Can I be helping?" she asked pleasantly, hoping to put a quick end to the family's chaotic search.

"We're looking for warmer things. Men's and boy's trousers and shirts," the woman said. "Off to Canada we're going. I'm hearing it's frigid, even in high summer."

Kathleen searched through the stacked garments, determined to find what the family needed before her children destroyed the back of the store. She held up a wool shirt. "How is this for size?" She pulled out another. "Or this?"

"The first will do." The woman let out a discouraged sigh. "My sorrow indeed, but sometimes it's all just too much. We've been here just a year and already leaving. Feels a bit like we're *An Lucht Siúil*, the Travellers, moving from place to place, staying nowhere long enough to call anywhere home."

The Travellers. It had been years since Kathleen had thought of them, the Irish gypsies who spent their lives wandering across the country in caravans. Faith, but what had become of them during the famine?

"Have you family in Canada?" she asked, holding out a shirt that might fit one of the boys.

The woman shook her head. "My husband wants to get out before we're pushed out."

Kathleen wondered whether the family wasn't overreacting. While it was true the Irish weren't being welcomed with open arms in Boston, they weren't being pushed out. Her skepticism must have shown on her face, for the woman raised knowing brows. "You've not heard of the *Know Nothings*?"

She shook her head. "We've had...family issues to deal with of late."

The woman put a hand on Kathleen's arm and dropped her voice. "A political group it is. Hate the Irish, they do."

"There's nothing new in that. Much of Boston has little use for us already." She shook open a pair of wool trousers and held them up for approval.

"Ah, but it is new. They're aiming to take rights away from immigrants. From Catholics." A balled-up shirt hit her square in the chest and she broke off. "Be done with that now!" she snapped at her sons. "All of you, go sit along that far wall until I come get you." She let out an exasperated sigh, then handed over a stack of wool shirts and trousers. "We'll take these."

Kathleen wrapped the clothes in brown paper and tied the package with a piece of rough string. A thread of unease wove through her. "What did you say that group is called?" she asked.

"*Know Nothings.* Best you be keeping an ear cocked. Don't be letting their name fool you. They know plenty." She took the package and ushered her brood outside, the boys trailing behind her like skittish fawns.

Disconcerted, Kathleen almost called her back to ask more questions, then stopped herself. There were always rumors of one type or another going around, most of them not anywhere near the truth. Sometimes it seemed as if people didn't have anything better to do than make things up.

She returned to the disordered mess the customer had left behind and began to fold and stack garments. "What was she going on about?" the older woman asked, lending a hand with the folding.

"Rumors. A political group called the *Know Nothings*. Have you heard of them?" A child's sea blue shirt tumbled to the wood floor, and she swooped a quick hand down to save it.

"Nay. But I've scant interest in politics."

"Nor I," Kathleen said softly. But just the same, she'd be sure to ask Jack and Sean if they'd heard anything of this group.

The bell on the front door jangled and the other woman went forward to offer assistance. Kathleen finished organizing one shelf and moved on to the next.

"I've three ready-made shirts to deliver from Eileen McDonough," a young woman said, her voice vaguely familiar.

"Excellent. I'll get the payment."

"She asked that you add it to her tally and she'll collect at the end of the week."

Kathleen tilted her head, but didn't turn round. The last thing she wanted was to run into an acquaintance who might ask about Will. She had no desire to share her troubles, nor did she want to have to hide them either.

"I've heard you offer help to the Irish here," the young woman said.

"Can you stitch? We pay a fair wage to Irish women to make the garments we sell. All the money we earn goes to aid programs for the Irish."

"'Tis food I'll be needing right now," the other said in a strained voice. "A wee bit of potatoes or oatmeal would be enough to hold me."

Kathleen caught her breath. *Ailish?* Jesus, Mary, and Joseph, it couldn't be. She peeked over her shoulder, but the woman was facing the other way. Nay, it wasn't possible. Ailish wouldn't be looking for food, she had a fine job at Jordan-Marsh as a clerk on the sales floor. The lawyer had confirmed it.

"You're not the first to ask about food, but I'm sorry to tell ye, all we have is clothing. Can you stitch at all?" the older woman asked.

"I'll be helping Mrs. McDonough with mending. But stitching is not my strongest skill."

Kathleen tried to sharpen her hearing. Either her imagination was running wild or Ailish was in the store. She took several light steps to escape into the backroom, turning slightly to glance back as she crossed the threshold. The sun-filled windows illuminated the front of the store, and though she could see only the woman's profile, recognition hit like a slap to the face.

Ailish.

She nudged the door nearly closed, leaving a thin gap through which she could listen but not be seen.

"Try the Charitable Irish Society," her fellow volunteer was saying. "They might provide some coin to see you through."

"I didn't expect Boston to be like this. Some days I'm nearly as hungry as I was at home. I know 'tisn't right of me to compare..." Her voice dropped so low Kathleen couldn't make out the rest of her words.

"If you can mend decently, I'll be betting you can stitch a garment. Think on it."

After another exchange too quiet for Kathleen to hear, the bells on the door jangled. Frozen with shock, she stared at the sliver of open space between the edge of the door and the frame. If Ailish wasn't earning enough to feed herself, how could she feed Will? If the judge gave her custody, would there be days Will would go hungry?

She peeked out to make sure Ailish was gone, then stepped onto the sales floor.

"Breaks my heart," the other woman said as Kathleen neared. "So many coming across for a better life. It's not so easy to find in Boston."

Kathleen barely heard her. What did this information mean for Will? For her and Jack? *For their lawyer?*

"I hear New York isn't so set against the Irish, "the other continued. "Not like Boston. Perhaps I should have told her to go there."

"Aye," Kathleen muttered uncharitably. "Send her there. Anywhere but Boston."

"YOU MEAN she's going hungry? Here?" Sean surged to his feet and paced across the parlor, coming to a halt in a wide swath of afternoon sun striping the carpet in front of the window. He rubbed a hand over the nape of his neck.

After living through the famine in Ireland and nearly dying on the voyage over, it enraged him that so many Irish had to struggle to survive in this country. It was no wonder she didn't want to spend twenty-five cents on a lecture when she didn't have enough to eat.

"That's what it sounded like," Kathleen said. "She didn't seem to have work other than mending. Jack, might this be information our lawyer should know?"

"*She's going hungry, Kathleen,*" Sean said, his voice taut.

"And she's trying to take my child, Sean," she shot back. "Whose side are you on?"

"Easy, both of you." Jack held up a palm. "We have enough trouble without fighting each other, too." He let out a quiet curse and sat back in his chair. "I don't know whether this means anything for us. My guess is, she's still employed at the store. Just using a great deal of her earnings to pay her lawyer."

"Which means she's going hungry in order to pay him."

Kathleen settled a harsh look on him. "This was her choice, Sean, all of it."

"Aye." He braced both hands against the mantle and bowed his head, choosing his words carefully. "But as I've spent time with her, I've come to see...she's not evil, not like you're thinking." He faced his sister. "Alone she is. Angry. Lost everyone she loved. If not for the famine, none of this would have happened. She wouldn't be fighting for Will because his parents wouldn't have died off the coast of Cohasset...because they'd never have left Ireland in the first place."

Kathleen's expression froze. He knew he was taking this too far, that he should quit talking. Instead, he reached out with both hands. "For that matter, without the famine we would never have left either—"

"Nay! I hear your words, Sean, but you're asking too much." She made an exasperated sound. "I can't feel sympathy for her. *I won't.* I haven't that within me. *Will is my son.*" She glanced toward the stairwell as if to underscore her claim to the child napping upstairs.

A despondent silence settled over the room, and Sean dropped into a chair beside the hearth. 'Twas a troubled place he found himself lately, able to see the point of view of both women, able to understand how much Will meant to each of them—and yet, unable to fathom the right answer. All he knew for certain was that no matter how the judge ruled, someone would be left devastated for the rest of their lives.

Kathleen went to stand at the window overlooking the street, the glass frosted from the unseasonable cold. She pressed the fingers of one hand into the pane; perfect circles melted beneath each fingertip. "Will thinks it's magic when he does this," she said, though they all knew it already. She scraped a fingernail through the frost, the sound a sharp squeak.

"A woman came into the store today." She turned and rested her back against the sill. "Warned me about a new political group. The *Know Nothings*. Have ye heard of them?"

Sean exchanged a weighted look with Jack. Though he didn't want to lie to Kathleen, he could think of few good reasons to lay another burden on her shoulders.

Jack's brow furrowed and he heaved a sigh. "They're not new," he said. "Remember that rally against the Irish the first spring you were here?"

"Five years ago? I thought they went away."

"A lot of us hoped that was the case. But they were spreading quietly. In the background in New York, Boston, Philadelphia...they've joined together under the banner of the American Party."

"*Know Nothings* is what people call them," Sean interjected, "because whenever they're asked what they stand for, they say: *I know nothing*."

"What do they stand for?" she asked. "Hating the Irish?"

Jack nodded. "And the Italians and the Germans... They play on people's fears. Claim immigrants steal jobs and bring crime."

"Why haven't you told me?"

"Because no one knew if the group would come to anything. And lately, you've had other things to worry about."

"I can fret about two things as easily as one." She pushed herself away from the sill and stepped across the room. "The woman told me their goal is to take away the rights of Catholics. Is that true?"

"They claim the Pope is moving the Vatican here so he can overthrow America and turn it into a Catholic country," Sean said, avoiding answering her question directly.

"That's absurd."

"Aye." He rubbed an uneasy hand on the armrest. "So much of what they say is lies, but people believe them. Their numbers keep rising, more and faster each day."

"And what of Catholic rights?" Kathleen pushed.

"That woman was correct," Jack answered. "They intend to keep full rights for Protestants—and take all rights away from Catholics."

"'Twill take more than talk to do that." She looked at Jack. "They'd have to get elected."

"I'm told that's the plan." Jack's gaze moved around the room, not settling on anything for long. "From what I've heard, they'll be running candidates at all levels of government next year."

Kathleen picked up the newspaper from the table, gave it a shake and tossed it back where it had been. "And neither of you saw fit to tell me?"

Will let out a cry from the second floor, as though his mother's dismay had drifted on the still air all the way up to him. Mouth tight, Kathleen started for the staircase. Jack was instantly on his feet and after her, his hand on her arm, his head bending low until his forehead touched hers. "I would have told you, but for this thing with Will."

She softened into him and Sean looked away, their subtle intimacy almost too painful to watch. He waited until Kathleen was upstairs and Jack back in his chair before voicing the question that had been troubling him for weeks. "What are you hearing?" he asked, his tone muted to prevent his words from carrying. "Can they win election?"

Jack poured whiskey from a decanter into two glasses and handed one to Sean. "As you know, their numbers are growing quickly. In every state. Massachusetts is one of the worst." He lifted the glass to his mouth and took a swallow. "If they maintain this momentum, the answer is yes. Men who are more intelligent than I on these matters fear the Know Nothings have a real chance."

"Jaysus. If they win, could they prevent the Irish from buying land? From owning it if they've already bought it?"

"If they gain control of the government, my guess is they'll be able to do whatever they want."

Sean curled his hand into a tight fist sending an ache stabbing into his injured forearm. It was like a return to the past, an echo of what England did to Ireland. Made it illegal for the Irish to own property. Stole all the land owned by Irish Catholics and gave it to English Protestants.

"And what is it, specifically, they'll be wanting?" Kathleen asked from the doorway.

"Where's Will?" Sean asked, stalling.

"Asleep. Making noise in his dreams." She shot them both an irritated look. "Don't even think of hiding what you're speaking of."

Jack threw a wry grin at Sean. "Your sister..."

"Aye. Well, you went and married her."

"And?" Kathleen challenged. "What do they mean when they say they want to take away rights?"

"I've no proof, just rumor." Jack exhaled. "They want to make it harder for Catholics to become citizens, twenty-one years in the country for citizenship instead of five." He shoved a hand through his hair. "Anyone born on foreign soil can never vote or hold office. No Catholic, even native born, can ever hold office—"

"Sean and I have lived this already, in Ireland." There was a sliver of panic in her expression. "I can figure well enough what all this would mean for him and me. But what about Will? What would this mean for his future?"

Her fear seeped into Sean as if it were his own.

Jack locked eyes with her. "If the Know Nothings prevail," he said finally, "Liam Clark, an Irish Catholic immigrant, will be an unwelcome, second-class citizen in this country. While Will Montgomery would have all the privileges accorded a Protestant of English ancestry."

CHAPTER SEVENTEEN

THE WIND BLUSTERED SNOW OFF THE GROUND AND INTO CIRCLES IN the air, the temperature dropped by the minute. It appeared that spring would not come to Boston until it had fought off winter time and again. Ailish glanced at Will in the sled Sean was pulling, his small body cocooned in heavy clothing, a wool scarf around his neck, arms straight out to either side like sticks on a snowman, and cheeks so red his face was nearly a ripe tomato. As she smiled at the sight, her lower lip cracked—and the wind whipped around her as if celebrating her discomfort.

She muttered a curse in her mind. Such a fierce day, perhaps they should have postponed this visitation, especially with Will so young. She'd not have expected the snowstorm two nights ago to lead to such bitter weather, not in April. She exhaled, her breath like vapor, and hunched her shoulders against the cold. A shiver rippled through her.

Sean had not once spoken of the lecture, nor her refusal to borrow twenty-five cents—or her churlish departure. Despite the icy bite of the wind, her face heated. Under other circumstances, she would apologize for her abrupt exit and explain her behavior. But she dared not broach the subject for she couldn't risk his family learning how dire her situation had become.

An ache gnawed at her stomach, reminding her how little she'd eaten these past days—and how unsuccessful her efforts at finding a new job had been. She was grateful to have mending and sewing to do, though patience and neat stitches had never come easily to her. Though she was becoming more skilled stitch by stitch, still she was slow and her earnings meager—and her sleep was paying the price for her hunger. She'd awakened during the night to dreams of steaming potatoes and bread straight from the oven and butter freshly churned. The memory sent her stomach rumbling and she wrapped her arms around her waist to press against the pangs.

"Are you cold?" Sean's breath curled out of him, silver gray like the smoke from an old man's pipe.

Cold? Aye. Hungry and defeated, as well.

Without awaiting her answer, he put an arm around her shoulder and pulled her against his side. Startled, she twisted away. "Will appears quite frozen," she said. "And I'm chilled to the bone. Perhaps it would be best to end this visit early."

The wind grabbed her words and flung them into the air, broken into delicate lace like so many snowflakes. Sean squinted at her and shook his head.

"Be looking at Will's face," she said loudly. She bent to tug the boy's scarf higher to cover more of his cheeks. "It will be no good if he gets sick. We're near your home, aren't we?"

"You want to shorten the visit?" he asked, taken aback.

"Aye. Are you not feeling the cold? My lips are frozen. My legs, I hardly feel them. And my toes...I'll be thinking I no longer have them any longer, just five blocks of ice on the end of each foot."

"Why didn't you say something?"

"I'm saying something now. If I'm this done in, what must our Will be feeling? He needs to get out of this weather." A chatter rattled her teeth.

Sean gave Will a dubious look. "I can hardly believe he's anything but overheated, bundled up as he is." He brought his gaze back to Ailish. "But you on the other hand..." He bent to look her full in the face, his blue eyes glistening in the cold, his cheeks painted crimson by the wind. Faith, but 'twas a face to drown in. She blinked, shocked at the thought.

He cupped her cheeks with his gloved hands as if to protect her from the turbulent gusts, and she caught her breath at the tenderness of his touch, the kindness, the way this simple gesture made her feel sheltered, accepted in a way she hadn't felt in so long...

Batting away the feelings that had leapt to life inside her, she took a step back and let the cold rise between them like a barrier. "For God's bright sake, now me eyes are running from this icy air." She brushed a rough hand across her lids and gestured at Will. "You must be getting him home. Fools we've been today, bringing a young child out in this weather."

A shiver ripped through her and she clenched her teeth together to keep them from chattering. She took another step back, eager to put more space between her and Sean. "I'll be on me way now, for I've a distance to go before I'm home."

Sean didn't move as she walked away. Didn't speak. Just stared after her, stunned. She'd ended the visitation early, had given up her time with Will—for Will's sake.

As she moved further down the block, a dark figure alone on such a brittle day, words slipped unbidden into his mind, something Ma had said often when he was a child: *Ní heaspa do díth carad. There is no need like the lack of a friend.*

He planted his feet on the snowy walk to hold his ground against the wind pushing at him, its frigid claws scraping his cheeks. It was dangerous outside today, not just for Will. And Ailish was far from where she lived, from the tenement she called home...*where she likely had nothing to eat.*

Still he didn't move, just squinted after her until she had shrunk small in the distance, until Will screeched, "Pull!", until he saw clearly the answer to the question that had been hovering beneath his consciousness since the famine began and England had stood by as Ireland starved: *What do any of us owe each other?*

He took a step.

What do we owe each other when the need is so clear?

He knew the answer, had always known it. Even that night at the lecture when Ailish had refused his help, when he'd told himself it was enough that he'd tried to help her.

What we owed one another was a chance. Or two. Or even three. Enough chances to get it right. And a hand, if it was needed, along the way.

He took another step and then another and another, each faster than the last until he was running along the walk, the sled careening behind him, Will screaming in excitement. They nearly plowed down a man bundled in a long overcoat, and Sean shouted an apology over his shoulder.

Up ahead, Ailish whirled round, no doubt alarmed at the

screeching coming upon her, the sound more like a rusty door creaking open than a child's joy. Her eyes widened, her jaw dropped in disbelief as Sean skidded toward her, the slick walk preventing him from stopping. She shrieked and leapt out of the way just in time.

As Will shouted his delight, Ailish bent over the sled and shook a teasing finger at him. "So much noise. I thought it could only be the pooka, chasing me home."

The boy pulled his scarf below his chin and let out a roar worthy of an evil goblin. "I a pooka," he cried. "Run, Uncle Sean!"

Sean raised a brow at Ailish. "I'll be thinking that one day you'll be sorry you told him he was the most feared faerie in all of Ireland."

She laughed. "I thought you were going home."

"Aye. But I wanted to ask you—"

Will roared loud and long, and Sean leaned down to reposition the boy's scarf, pulling it up over his cheeks and nose to quiet him. "What I wanted to ask was..." he began. "What I mean is, our house is so close, come get warm before you go the rest of the way. Have a bite to eat."

A startled laugh burst out of her. "Are ye trying to make your family hate you? They'll not be welcoming me there."

"No one is home. The cook is off. Kathleen is volunteering all afternoon. She makes sure to be out of the house, busy, when we're gone on these visits. Jack is at the wharf. They'll never know you were there."

"It's kind of you to be offering, but no." She gave her head a firm shake. "I'll not be coming over."

"Emma baked bread this morning. And we've fresh cider."

A light flared in her eyes. Hunger. He'd seen it so many times before. Had felt it himself. He took her hand and gently pulled her along. "Come. You'll be thawed and fed and on your way before anyone ever knows."

~

KATHLEEN DUCKED her head against the wind and hurried up the steps to the Cathedral of the Holy Cross. She'd told Jack and Sean she was volunteering at the Irish Relief Society this afternoon, and though she had put in a few hours there, it wasn't the full reason she'd insisted on going out in this weather today.

Nay, the truth was deeper. And Jesus, Mary, and Joseph, but all these actions might not even be necessary if she had some way of knowing that single hour...*the special hour* in each day when one's dearest wish, whatever it was, would be granted. But the only way of learning that hour was to catch a faerie, and she had no hope of doing that in America. Indeed, she'd likely no hope of doing that in Ireland either.

So she'd taken matters into her own hands.

She tugged at the church's heavy door, pushed it open with her shoulder just enough to let her steal inside before it banged shut. An instant hush enveloped her. After the fierceness of the weather outside, the stillness of the church and the dull light filtering through the windows imbued the nave with the quietude of sunset, that moment when the wind dies leaving all of nature as still as a painting.

She waited for her eyes to adjust to the dimness, then went forward to make a modest donation and light a candle, to drop to her knees and pray to God, to Mary and Jesus, to all the saints, and to every one of her dead relations for divine intervention in this matter with Will.

She didn't wish to be seeming selfish, but was it too much to expect of the God who'd brought Will to them, to also expect him to make sure the lad stayed with them?

"I'm sorry for thinking that last," she muttered and crossed herself. "But can ye not see why this might be troubling me?" She crossed herself again. "Och, forgive me, sorry I am, truly. But I can't stop from wondering how you can be allowing this—"

She broke off and headed for the door. Best if she left the church before she dug herself a hole straight into hell.

Fifteen minutes later, she stood outside the three-story red brick building that housed Mr. Barker's law office, doubts tugging at her decision like the wind was pulling at her cloak. She drew a fortifying breath, squared her shoulders, and stepped inside.

"Mrs. Montgomery, what a pleasant surprise." The lawyer shook his pen into the inkpot and set it aside. "What can I do for you on this wintry spring afternoon?"

Her misgivings leapt to the fore again. Perhaps she should have told Jack she was coming here. She loosened her scarf and removed her gloves before taking a seat in one of the leather wing chairs facing the desk. *Too late now for second guesses.*

"I'll be confessing, Mr. Barker, that I'm worried about Miss Sullivan's ability to support Will," she said evenly.

His brow creased. "Have you new information or just a concern about her situation in general?"

"New information, perhaps." The tension she'd been holding in her neck eased, so relieved was she to give this over to him, to let him decide if it was worthy of investigation. After all, she had no proof Ailish was out of work, just suspicions. "I volunteer at the Irish Relief Society..." Doubt sent a queasy wave through her gut and she trailed off, waiting a beat before beginning again. "Not two days ago, Miss Sullivan came in asking for food. Said she was doing mending to earn money."

Guilt took a seat alongside doubt. What if Jack and Sean were right? That Ailish was only doing what so many other Irish were forced to do to survive—earn extra money any way they could? She rubbed a finger over her wedding ring, twisted it back and forth. "If she can't feed herself," she asked in a thin voice, "how will she feed Will? Might this be something to share with the judge?"

"Hunger is quite prevalent among the Irish, as you know," the lawyer said softly. "I understand your concerns. But consider this from the judge's vantage. He may take a favorable view of Miss Sullivan working a second job, thinking it shows how hard she's working to make a life for herself."

Kathleen clasped her hands in her lap, squeezing her fingers until they hurt. "I'm not trying to create stories where none exist. I know you confirmed her employment before the hearing, but I'm wondering if perhaps we shouldn't check again."

The lawyer waited.

"If she's lost her job at the store, it would explain..." Her guilt swiveled into self-loathing. The Irish were often fired for no reason other than the whims of their employers. If that had happened to Ailish, how fair was Kathleen being?

It was for Will she was doing this. Her son.

"It would explain," she said in a stronger voice, "why she was asking for food."

"I'll make some inquiries," Mr. Barker said. "If she's lost steady work, it may be information for us to hold in our back pocket until closer to the hearing."

Their meeting over, Kathleen let herself out into the cold and headed home, her mind a battlefield of doubts and uncertainties. Was she a loving mother fighting to protect her child and family? Or was she a selfish monster using every means possible to keep her son from knowing his only living blood relative?

By the time she stepped into the foyer, she felt as though her soul had frozen. She closed the door wearily and hung up her cloak, wondering who she would be when this was over.

The sound of Will's giggling drifted down the hall, drawing a smile to her face. Such a relief it was to know the boys were home early from the visitation.

Home. This was Will's home and he was here and all was well. Her doubts lifted along with her mood. Surely she had done the right thing bringing the information to the lawyer.

She went into the kitchen, her steps so light she was almost dancing—and froze at the threshold. Sean and Ailish sat across from one another at the table, rows of tin soldiers lined along the dark oak grain. Will bounced on Ailish's lap, snuffling with excitement as he shouted, "The gen'ral shoot them."

Jealousy soured her stomach. Her son was sharing his beloved soldiers with Ailish. The soldiers she and Jack had given him. The soldiers that barely ever left his side.

And Sean had made it possible.

Her gaze locked on her brother. "Hello," she said stiffly, a hundred questions in that single word.

He lunged to his feet, mouth twisted as if in pain. "'Twas so bitter cold outside—"

"Mam!" Will scrambled to the floor and flung himself against Kathleen's legs. She picked him up and pressed a kiss to his cheek.

Head down, eyes averted, Ailish started for the cloak rack near the back door.

"Mam! I show Aish my soldiers." He wiggled from her grasp and chased after Ailish. "We have war."

"Aye, lad, a big war," Kathleen said with forced enthusiasm, her voice so stilted, she knew she was fooling no one but Will.

"It's my doing, Kathleen," Sean said. "We ended the visit early because of the cold. I insisted Ailish come in—"

"Aish!" Will tugged at her cloak as she tried to put it on. "The gen'ral waiting."

"You finish the war," she said. "I'll need to be going home now."

"But..." His lower lip quivered. "Mam, stop Aish," he cried.

Kathleen's heart wrenched. To Will, Ailish was just a new friend. He had no idea what any of this meant, no idea why Ailish suddenly wanted to leave.

"Mam," Will insisted.

"He loves make believe," she offered, acquiescing, her eyes on the opposing armies lined across the table. "Especially with his soldiers. Makes up tales of battles..." She managed the ghost of a smile. "But no matter what, the blue general always wins." An ache squeezed her chest. Why had she not stopped talking after the first sentence?

"Reminds me he does, of his grandfather. Me own Da," Ailish murmured. "A storyteller he was—" Pain flickered through her eyes and she dipped her head apologetically. "I'm sorry."

Kathleen felt the edges of her anger soften, like a snowflake as it melts on a warm cobblestone. "Perhaps that's where Will gets it."

"Mam, I show Aish my room," Will said, both hands still clutching Ailish's cloak.

"Not today." Ailish reached down to break his grip.

Sean swept the soldiers off the table into the box. "Will, let's set up a war in the parlor."

"No! Mam, please I show Aish?" Will begged. "Please."

Her cheeks flushed. He'd never asked to show his room to anyone except family.

But what was Ailish, if not his family?

The tightening began in her chest and spread across her back, squeezing her lungs. She smoothed her hair with trembling hands. "Let him show you," she said. "He loves his room."

Upstairs, Will patted the blue and green patchwork quilt spread neatly over his bed, the coverlet Kathleen and Ma had made shortly after Sean brought the orphaned babe from Cohasset. "This mine," he said proudly.

"It's lovely." Ailish turned slowly and took in the entire room. "So lucky you are, young Will. To have a room such as this. Thank you for showing me."

In that instant, Kathleen saw the space through Ailish's eyes, a gaze that would have been her own just five years ago. Guilt trickled through her again. In the tenement Ailish rented, whole families likely lived in a space the size of Will's bedroom.

"Time to get on my way," Ailish said. "'Tis getting late and dusk will make it even colder." She hurried down the stairs and was quickly gone, the door shut behind her like she'd never been there at all.

Except she had, Kathleen's mind whispered. She followed Will into the parlor, watched him plop onto the rug and dump out his soldiers. How could it be that, now, even the inside of the home they shared with Will had been breached by the woman who was determined to tear their family apart?

She motioned Sean into the foyer. "What were you thinking, bringing her here like that?"

"I told you—"

"Would she have frozen to death on the street?"

Sean exhaled.

She rubbed her hands over her face as if to wipe away the emotions raging within her. "Forgive me. I know you meant nothing by it. I just...I hardly know anymore what's right. It was such a shock..."

"I didn't expect you'd be home. 'Twas the cold. And I was hoping, like we've all said, if she sees me as a friend, perhaps she might decide to give up this fight." He spread his hands wide, his expression conflicted. "Do you know how much I wish I could change this?" he asked under his breath. "Sometimes I wonder if it might have been better if I'd never brought him in the first place."

"Oh Seanie, don't every think that. Even if I'd known in advance that we would lose him, never would I give up the years we've had." Her eyes burned with unshed tears. "Life offers us no promises, though you know as well as I, we all go along hoping we'll get them anyway."

She let out a small sound, a hiccup caught before it became a sob. "If Jack and I had been able to have a child of our own...who is to say he would have survived the cholera epidemic two years ago? Who is to say we'd have had him in our lives any longer than we've had Will?"

From the parlor came the sound of her son playing, his child's voice barking commands like a brigadier general, "Aaah-tention. 'Tention, men. Line up. Soldiers, marts, marts, march."

It took her a moment to realize he'd pronounced *march* correctly for the first time. She bit her lip and ordered herself not to cry.

CHAPTER EIGHTEEN

FINALLY, SPRING HAD PUSHED WINTER OUT FOR GOOD. *AND NOT A day too soon*, Sean thought as he followed Will through the park, picnic basket in hand. How quickly the weather had changed. He tipped his head back to let the sun strike him full in the face, to inhale the scent of warm earth and clean air. For a heartbeat, he was back in Ireland, on hands and knees pressing seed potatoes into shallow trenches in the garden, Moira smiling at him from the doorway of their whitewashed stone cottage.

"Ducks!" Will shouted as they neared the pond.

And then Ireland was gone and he was back in Boston's Public Garden, green buds bright with sun-kissed highlights, purple and blue and white crocuses dotting the lawn like scattered gems, daffodils dancing like faeries in yellow dresses.

Words from Thoreau's book inched forward in his mind —*nature seemed to have adorned herself*—and though he tried to call up the rest of the sentence, it eluded him. He'd brought the book along to show Ailish in case the opportunity presented itself; he could always seek out the rest of the passage before she arrived. Or not. It was enough to think of nature as being adorned on a soft day such as this, like so many in Ireland had been, as close to perfect as one might get...*without Moira.*

The devil take him, why did she hover in his mind today?

He set down the basket and spread a blanket on the ground in the sun not far from the pond. As he smoothed out the wrinkles, Will threw himself across the cloth and sprawled onto his back, stretching arms and legs outward like a star.

Sean swept a hand through the air. "Move yourself over, lad, this isn't your bed. Once Ailish arrives, there's three of us that need to fit here."

"I'm hungry."

"We'll be eating soon enough." Though it was early in the season to be picnicking, he'd packed a basket anyway, for he had no illusions that Ailish's situation had improved in the week since Kathleen spotted her at the Relief Society.

He sat cross-legged beside the boy and pulled Thoreau's book from the basket, absently flipping through the pages, half searching for the turn of phrase that had teased his memory. Will twisted onto his stomach, chin propped in his hand as he surveyed the surrounding area and jabbered on about people and things as though cataloguing all there was to see and do in the park. Breaking off suddenly, he shouted, "Aish!" and jumped to his feet.

He raced across the lawn, and she knelt to greet him, her mouth curving up in a broad smile, tendrils of dark hair swirling about her face in the buoyant breeze. Sean watched, captivated, as she cupped Will's cheeks and kissed his brow, then gathered him into her arms and spun a circle. Both their heads were thrown back, and though he couldn't hear their words, the joy was unmistakable.

Something inside him let go, shifted, softened the way light sneaks into a room around the edges of a shade and mellows the darkness.

Will pointed in his direction, and Ailish waved a carefree hand above her head.

She seemed different somehow. He put away the book and waved back.

Will took Ailish's hand and began to drag her toward Sean, hopping and skipping along the path, gesturing and chattering, no doubt sharing every thought that popped into his head. Ailish focused on him as if his words were the most important thing—the only thing—in the world.

"Having a picnic," Will sang as they neared.

Ailish smiled at Sean and called out, "Hello."

Something shifted inside him again. He grinned. "Hello."

"I hear we'll be having a picnic."

"It's still cool, I know, but I thought the ducks shouldn't be the only ones lucky enough to eat in the park. Are you hungry?"

"Aye. This is a lovely surprise. Thank you."

Will threw himself onto the blanket and Ailish sat beside him. "So young Will, what is it we'll be having today?" she asked.

"Corn."

"Corn?"

"The ducks are having corn," Sean said. "We're having *cornbread*."

"Corn-bread. Corn-bread," Will repeated as if imprinting the word in his brain.

Sean opened the basket. "And chicken and apples and carrots and cider," he said as he lifted each item out. "And for dessert—" He held up the last item.

"Biscuits!" Will clapped his hands. "You like biscuits?"

Sean took out his pocket knife and began to slice up an apple.

"Very much," she said. "Did you know that some people call them cookies?"

"I make biscuits with Emma," the boy said in a voice puffed with importance. "You help, Aish?"

"That sounds fun." She filled a plate and set it in front of him.

"You come my house again?"

"I'm so hungry I might eat everything in this basket," she said, tactfully ignoring his question.

"Come to my house?" he beseeched, not to be put off.

"Aye, someday she can," Sean said, offering Ailish a cup of cider. "It's easier sometimes with this lad not to climb every mountain he puts in front of ye. If you'll be understanding my meaning."

He tapped a finger on the edge of Will's plate. "Now be done with your talking and get on with your eating or the ants might soon be carrying away your food."

Will was finished before Sean and Ailish had hardly begun. "The ducks hungry," he said, bending over the basket and lifting out the sack of corn.

A hint of a smile danced at Ailish's lips.

"Be still, lad. Wait until everyone is done." He gave Ailish a wink. "None would ever say that patience is his gift."

"'Tisn't easy for most children." She patted the blanket. "Come sit by me, Will. I'll be done in a lick and we'll go feed the ducks together."

He plopped down beside her, let himself fall flat onto his back, then pressed the bottom of his shoes against the side of the basket. After a few seconds, he began to push the basket off the blanket, ever so slowly as if no one would notice the gradual movement.

"Will, stop that," Sean warned around a mouthful of food. "If you'll be wanting to feed the ducks, you—"

"What do you see up there?" Ailish took a last bite of chicken, then set her plate aside and dropped her head back to inspect the sky. "You know what I see? That big white cloud there..."

She pointed at a swollen puff loitering high above them, a flock of smaller clouds surrounding it. "That looks like...I'll be guessing it's a..." She twirled a hand and threw a pleading look at Sean for assistance.

"A...horse," he managed to get out just as she said, "A turtle."

He choked back a laugh. One was as good as the other to a young child, but in truth, the cloud was far more like a turtle than a horse.

"Your uncle is right. That's a horse. One of the white horses of the Irish gods," Ailish said in a hushed voice. "Fleet as the wind she is, made of fire and flame and magic. Riding out to Tir Na Nog, a magical island far away on the western ocean where the faeries live forever."

The lilt on her words filled him with yearning. She was definitely different today. Calmer, more accepting, enjoying Will instead of trying to make him be something he wasn't.

Or perhaps it was that he was seeing her in a different way.

"White horses." Will pointed at an overstuffed cloud passing overhead. "Fat white horses."

"Aye," Ailish answered. "So many white horses. Sometimes if ye look carefully, ye'll see them on the water, running in the waves." She made swooping motions with her hands as though her arms were swells rising and falling on the sea, and Sean found himself as mesmerized by her words as Will was. "And sometimes if you're very lucky, like today, ye'll see them high in the clouds."

Her eyes met Sean's, and he felt the connection of shared history and common dreams. A fragment of a sentence came to him, another passage from Thoreau. *"And the clouds,"* he said as the wind played with the white shapes, blowing and tugging the fluffs across the light blue sky, *"seem a fit drapery to hang over fairyland."*

"That's lovely," she said. "What is—"

"Pigs!" Will shot an arm upward. "See there—pigs."

"I think you're right." She exchanged a grin with Sean as though they held a secret no one else knew. "White pigs...everywhere."

It struck him then, though he'd not say it to Kathleen—not yet and maybe never—it was easy to see that if Ailish got Will, she would be a fine mother to him.

Just as Kathleen already was, his mind retorted.

And yet, had it not been Kathleen herself who said, *we can ask nothing better for him than to be loved?*

He watched Ailish as she leaned toward Will and the two discussed cloud pigs in all seriousness. It was obvious that Will liked her. Sean could hardly fault him, for he'd come to like her, too.

God help them all to survive this nightmare. Hard it was to be knowing what was right when the lines were blurred almost beyond recognition.

"What was that ye were just saying? About fairyland?" Ailish asked.

He considered her question, wondered whether it was wise to draw Thoreau into their discussion. With things going so well, he didn't want to make the moment uncomfortable by reminding her of that night at the lecture. Still, he could hardly lie about where he'd gotten the phrase. "It's from the book I was telling you of—"

"The river trip?" Her lips took a thoughtful turn. "I thought that book was about death."

"Aye. And life and—" He frowned. "What were you thinking, it was a bleak funeral story?"

"Something like that."

He chuckled and threw caution aside. "More a philosopher he is, than anything else. With a poet's heart perhaps." He searched for the right words, treading carefully. "What he does is...he takes things you think you've got somewhat figured out...life, death, religion, nature...and makes you see that somehow, you got it all wrong."

"And you like that?"

He knew better than to try to explain, for he never did the man justice no matter how hard he tried. Still, maybe this time would be different. He opened his mouth and closed it, then started again. "I like that he sees life..." He blew out a frustrated breath. "...in a way that gives me hope."

HOPE. She'd not had much of that these past few years. "Perhaps I should have stayed to hear his lecture after all," she said, surprised to feel a twinge of regret, a touch of envy. Avoiding Sean's eyes, she took the biscuits from the basket and handed one to Will.

"He makes you see, not from here," Sean said, pressing two fingers to his forehead, "but here." He put a hand to his heart.

She wondered if that was even possible for her anymore. Stretching out her legs, she rested back on her hands and watched Will march around on the grass, alternately taking bites of biscuit for himself and throwing chunks to the ducks that were following him like he was leading a parade. Faith, but he reminded her so very much of his brothers. "I'll not be thinking biscuits are the best for ducks," she called.

He gifted her with an incredulous frown before throwing another piece to his feathered friends. "Ducks like biscuits," he announced.

To be sure, he was exactly like his brothers had been.

"Ducks like corn!" Sean chased the boy, swung him upside down and threw him over his shoulder like a sack. "I found a big bag of corn, Ailish. Shall we feed it to the ducks?"

Will let out a screech. "I not corn!"

She caught her breath at the beauty of this young boy and his uncle, at the love and trust between them. Sean's laughing eyes met hers, inviting her to join in this game they had obviously played before.

"A fine idea it is." She stood and brushed off her skirt. "Let's dump that corn in the pond right away."

"Not corn. Not corn," Will shouted, giggling as Sean marched to the edge of the water.

"Ailish, do you hear something?" he asked, turning left and right as Will collapsed on his shoulder in full-throated laughter. "It's not the corn talking, is it?"

"How can corn talk?" She patted Will's back.

"No feed me ducks. Not corn!"

"Not corn?" Sean swung Will to the ground.

"I Will." The boy stomped his feet.

"I'm so sorry," Sean said. "Are you sure you're not corn?"

Will charged back to the blanket and retrieved the bag of corn. "This corn," he shouted, triumphantly holding it aloft.

"Do you play this often?" Ailish asked.

"I'm not in Boston much. But his da does—"

"You mean Jack," she said, holding his gaze.

His face fell, and she felt a prick of embarrassment over pointing out his error.

"Sorry," he said. "Jack. Jack plays it with him."

Sean took the sack from Will, shifted it from one hand to the other as though weighing its value, like gold. He dumped some kernels into the boy's palm, then handed the bag to Ailish. "I'll pack up the picnic."

She knew the gesture was one of kindness, a deliberate choice to give her time alone with Will. Regret jabbed her again over her comment about Jack. Though these people weren't Will's real family, at least he hadn't spent the past two years in an orphanage. At least he'd been cared for and loved.

Not just loved, but cherished.

Unsettled, she turned toward the pond just as Will swung his fistful of kernels over the water with all the force he could muster. Momentum carried him forward and he teetered in the sunshine on the edge of the shore, arms twirling as he tried to keep himself from falling in. She lifted the front of her skirt and sprinted toward him, knowing it would be a miracle if she got there in time.

He landed in the pond with a plop and a splash, and she hit the water in much the same way, gasping as the icy liquid soaked through her clothes. Scrambling to get her feet beneath her in the three-foot depth, she grabbed his jacket in her fist and lifted the screeching boy into her arms. "You're all right. You're all right," she shouted over his cries.

Sean was already at the water's edge, arms outstretched. As she handed Will up to him, his eyes danced and he said, "I think we were wrong, Ailish. This is a big bag of corn after all."

He set a shivering Will on the ground, then reached out a hand to help Ailish up the muddy bank. Her foot caught the hem of her skirt throwing her off balance, and Sean grabbed hold of both her arms and pulled her the rest of the way up. "Don't worry," he said, "I've got you."

For a heartbeat, she wished he meant something more than he did. She'd been on her own since the loss of her family. It would be nice, now and again, to have someone to catch her when she stumbled in this new life of hers. The breeze swept over her and a shiver rippled down her spine.

"What smells?" Will wrinkled his nose.

"*You do.*" Sean picked several wet, brown leaves off the boy's sleeve before wrapping the picnic blanket around his shoulders. "Time for a bath, lad. Wait 'till your mam hears—" He winced and corrected himself. "Kathleen hears you were in the pond."

Ailish felt the full force of her regret. "Nay, it's fine. A natural mistake. She's the only mam he knows." She dried her hands on the blanket. "I'll see you in a few days, Will, when we're not both soaking wet."

"And smelly," Sean added.

She opened her eyes wide in mock offense. "Smelly, you say. Well, Mr. Deacey, I must be telling you that despite my unplanned swim, today has been grand. Thank you for the picnic...and for telling me about Mr. Thoreau. Perhaps I'll even stay to hear him speak next time."

"I have his book with me...if you'd like to borrow it." Sean dug it out of the basket. "I've read it through already."

She took the book in her hands, turned it over twice. Books were valuable things. Costly. And he would lend this one to her? "Are you sure?"

"Of course. I trust you."

It wasn't lost on her that he was trusting the woman who was trying to break up his family. She ran her palm over the book's cover, the edges lightly worn. "I'll give it back as soon as I'm done. But be warned, I may know how to read, but I'm not quick about it."

"The more time to ponder his words then. I'll be interested in knowing if they catch you like they did me."

She jerked her eyes up to his. Catch her? To keep her from falling? Had this man somehow heard her thoughts just minutes ago? Or was he just as lost as she was?

CHAPTER NINETEEN

THE LIGHT IN THE GRANDFATHER'S ROOM FELT FADED, DULL, LIKE dusk on an overcast day, the curtains closed to hold back the brightness of the afternoon so the old man could sleep. Kathleen sat in a chair beside the bed, the dim glow of an oil lamp illuminating the book she had been quietly reading aloud: *The Whale; or Moby Dick.*

She read though she wasn't sure the old man could hear her, just knew that his breathing stayed more settled when there were voices in the room.

This was a new book, released just the previous fall. Jack had thought the story would interest his grandfather, since both he and Jack had spent many years aboard whaling vessels. But for her, the story rekindled memories of the worst of that business—the brutal method of killing whales with a spear to the blowhole, the repulsive sweet-rotten stench of boiling blubber, the ship's deck slippery with whale oil and blood.

She let her eyes run again over the passage she had just read aloud: *For there is no folly of the beast of the earth which is not infinitely outdone by the madness of men.*

Whale killing was just one folly of many. She had no doubt that a list of the follies of men—and women as well—might take a full day to recite. For one could use no other word but madness to describe this battle over Will, this quest to determine *his best welfare*, as the judge put it. It could be nothing other than madness that left adults fighting over a child who knew not that it was even happening.

She rested a hand on the bed where the old man lay, waiting for whatever came next, so little time left for him on this earth. He'd survived much in his long life, had overcome the pain of losing his only son to suicide, had taken in his fatherless grandson and raised him to be a fine, principled man. And yet, despite all that he'd done and achieved, death would call for him soon.

"Does it not all seem pointless?" she said faintly, for her own ears alone. "We fight to build a life, a future, make a difference...but no matter what, death comes, even to dreams."

"Kathleen!" The whispered reprimand snapped across the room like a whip.

She jerked her head up to see Ma in the doorway.

"You're to be guiding him to the next world," she said, frowning as she neared the bed. "Not filling him full of regrets about this one. No life is wasted. Who is to know what impact his existence may have upon generations to come?" Ma straightened the old man's blanket, then lowered herself into a chair beside Kathleen. "How is he today?"

She let the book fall closed and gave Ma a cheerless smile, reluctant to voice her opinion about his condition in case he might be able to hear.

Ma's head dropped forward, a silent acknowledgement of the

message in Kathleen's silence—that the grandfather would not long be with them.

"Sean told me what happened," Ma said after a pause. "Ailish being here in the house."

"Sean is a fool."

"Feels terrible he does. He meant no harm, Kathleen. You told him you'd be gone all afternoon."

"Aye." She slumped back in the chair. "It's not just that she was here that troubles me. It's the idea that Sean should become her friend. I know we all thought it best...but easy it is to speak such words and far more difficult to live them." Her stomach tightened as she neared the crux of her fear. "I'm afraid my son will come to see Ailish as just another member of our family. So if she wins, 'twill be easier for him to leave us. Already he goes happily with Sean on those visits."

Ma reached across the space between their chairs and put her hand over Kathleen's. "I know. I feel the same. But much as it pains you, try to remind yourself that the happier Will is with her, the less he will be hurt if she, God forbid, wins custody in the end."

"You want to make it easy for her to take my son," Kathleen said, though she knew the accusation false before it left her mouth.

"Nay. I want to make it easier on Will if he is forced to go. The final hearing is less than two weeks away. This isn't about you or Ailish anymore. 'Tis about Will. I know you would do anything to protect him." Ma's voice, always so strong and steady, quavered. "You need to be protecting him now the best way you can—by making sure he's not afraid to go with her if it should come to that."

"I can't."

Ma gave Kathleen's hand a squeeze. "Would you rather have

him weeping for you, night after night, and you not there to comfort him? Do you want him scarred a second time over losing his mother? All because you refused to encourage friendship?" Tears slipped down Ma's weathered cheeks. "Kathleen, lass, we are all dying here now. We mustn't let Will die too."

She closed her eyes as if it would block Ma from saying more. "My life I would give for him, to keep him from ever experiencing pain. But this woman, this Ailish...she may have rights under the new law, but I'll be wondering, has she a heart? Sean claims she does, says she's hurting. But I ask you Ma, if she has a heart, how can she be doing this to a child? Why should I do anything to help her?"

"It's revenge you want, is it?" Ma let her head fall against the back of the chair. "That will only hurt Will in the end. Would you soothe your own needs before your son's?"

Kathleen stared at the ceiling, shadowed and dark like her mood. "Nay," she whispered.

"Then choose your moves wisely, lass."

"I can't bear the thought of losing him, Ma." Her voice was barely more than a whisper. "But if we should, I want to know he's happy. That he's laughing, playing with his soldiers, telling his stories...even when he's not with us."

"So then, it isn't just Sean who should become her friend," Ma said softly, her words tinged with compassion.

"I don't know if I can."

"You can because you must. Not for Ailish. Not for the judge. But for Will. *For your son.*"

"The best..." Faint words cut through their discussion, and both women swiveled toward the bed. The grandfather's eyes were closed, his intake of air barely discernible. Kathleen threw a questioning look at her mother.

"...best laid schemes." Though the old man's voice trembled with weakness, it still held an edge. "Kath...leen. Do you remember...?"

He'd spoken those words to her years ago, when he'd thought Jack was to wed Emily Cuthbert and Kathleen was to wed Danny O'Sheehan—and neither marriage had come to pass. It had been a turning point for the old man, the beginning of his acceptance of the Irish as human beings.

"Aye," she answered. "The best laid schemes of mice and men often go awry."

"Good," the old man rasped. "Don't worry...not...this time." Each word was less clear than the last, each syllable more labored.

She waited for more, bent forward, eyes on his chest searching for movement. Her pulse began to race. Was he breathing or not? It couldn't be that he passed on at this very moment. "Sir?" she whispered.

A ragged, rattling sound wrenched out of him, and she sat back, startled.

"Don't...worry..." he murmured, his breath labored. "Don't worry..." His words slid out of him on a long exhale. Then the muscles in his face slackened. And his shoulders eased and his body softened as his life escaped its earthbound tether.

Tears filled Kathleen's eyes and she pressed her lips together to hold back a sob. To the end, he was fighting for their family.

Ma made the sign of the cross and bowed her head. "*Ar dheas Dé go raibh a anam. May his soul be on the right hand of God.*"

Kathleen blinked to clear her vision, then went to the window and pushed open the sash so his spirit could begin its journey to the afterlife.

~

"MEG!" Ailish lifted the front of her skirt and took the hallway stairs two at a time. She couldn't believe that luck had laid its hand so heavily on her shoulder. "Meg!" Hands wrapped around the doorknob, she struggled to force open the stuck door, finally kicking the bottom corner with her toe to pop it free.

The door banged against the far wall, and Meg lurched out of her chair, mending flying from her lap. "Upon my soul, what's wrong? Has someone died?"

Ailish danced into the room. "Nay. It's fine news I'll be having. The best ever. I've found work," she declared.

"A job? Better news I couldn't be asking for you," Meg exclaimed. "Where?"

Out of the corner of her eye, Ailish saw the old woman from across the hall shuffle to their open doorway. Nosy old biddy. It would be fine for her to know things, but she'd too many opinions to share and they were always contrary. Ailish didn't acknowledge her, just narrowed her eyes at Meg and scrunched up her face as if to say, *Play along with me.*

"A place over on North Street," she said, lying. "They tell me the name was changed just a few months ago. Used to be called Ann Street."

"Ann Street?" a shocked voice said from the doorway.

Ailish's mouth quirked as she pretended she hadn't heard. "The pay, oh Meg, you'll be loving the wage I'll be earning. I met a woman who told me they needed girls at some of the businesses there. So, in I went and was hired straight away."

"Sounds grand. Perhaps I can get work, too. Anything would be better than this." Giving a dramatic sigh, Meg swooped her mending off the floor and tossed it carelessly on the chair as though she were done with such menial work.

"Gambling dens, dance halls, and brothels," the old woman

exclaimed, shaking her finger. "Och, that's the best you'll be finding on Ann Street."

"They said I'd be dancing with the gentlemen who come round." Ailish purposely misunderstood the other's meaning. She grabbed Meg and began to waltz with her about the room. "Perhaps I'll be meeting a man to wed."

"Pah," the old woman sniped. "You'll be meeting sailors fresh off the ocean with their pockets full of money. Seeking out wifely diversions, they are—not wives—and paying for them up and down Ann Street."

Ailish let go of Meg and pivoted to face the other. "That's not what they told me," she said with wide-eyed innocence. "And I've always liked a man who loves the sea. Think of the places they'll have been, the stories they'll have to tell—"

"It's about *you* they'll be telling the stories."

"Indeed?" Ailish curtsied to Meg, and Meg bowed to her. "Then I'll have to be on my very best behavior. All I can say is, it's just such a relief to finally be earning a fair wage."

"Ailish, promise you'll help me get hired on as well," Meg said.

"Foolish girls. Heads full of mischief." The old woman clucked her tongue and went back across the hall.

Ailish pushed the door shut, and both women burst into laughter. "Serves her right," Meg said as she dropped into a chair.

Ailish sank into the one beside her. "Did you see her face? Oh, it was worth every second."

"Wouldn't have mattered what job you got," Meg said, "she'd have found something wrong with it."

"Aye. Still, best I go tell her the truth soon, before the entire North End thinks the two of us have joined the ladies of Ann Street."

Meg chuckled. "But you did get a job, aye?"

"At Chandler and Company." Ailish grinned. The establishment was one of the largest dry goods stores in Boston, a high-end retail and wholesale house. So big it was, some fifty salespeople worked the floor every day. "I'm to start in a week. On the sales floor."

"On the floor?" Meg's brow furrowed. "Do they not have the same rule? That female clerks must be married?"

Ailish hesitated, almost afraid to admit what she'd done. She wasn't proud of herself, but desperation created its own rules. "I said I was engaged. And he believed me."

"Ailish..."

"The hearing for Liam is next week." Surely Meg understood what was at stake. "If I haven't a job, I'll have no hope of getting him. I have to be working."

Her plan was simple, though she'd not speak it aloud. She'd keep her head down and hang onto this job as long as she could. If they learned the truth and she was fired, she'd find another job. Whatever it took. Because once she paid the lawyer, she would immediately begin saving her money again. This time for passage to Ireland for her and Liam.

CHAPTER TWENTY

"Lucky your grandfather was, even in death," Da said as he took the stool between Jack and Sean at the bar in Murphy's Pub. "All this rain on his funeral means he'll be going straight to heaven."

Between the low cloud cover outside and the dim light inside the small tavern, it could have been late evening instead of mid-afternoon. The smell of pipe smoke sifting through the air only served to make the time seem later. Sean held up four fingers for the barkeep; seconds later, the lean, silver-haired man planted a foamy pint of ale in front of each of them.

"Who gets the fourth?" he asked, holding up the glass, a frothy head capping the dark ale.

"Put it right here." Sean patted the bar to his left, where an empty barstool awaited an occupant. He tilted his head toward Jack. "For his grandfather."

Once the barkeep had gone to serve another customer, Sean raised his glass to toast the empty seat. Jack and Da followed suit. "To a fine man, who'll not be forgotten," he said. "The blessing of grace be with him. May his life be rewarded by a short road to heaven."

"And may we be a long time following him," Da added. The three tapped their glasses together and each took a hearty swallow of ale.

Jack lifted his glass again. "He never gave up on me even when times were bleak. Took me in—" His voice cracked. "Was more of a father to me than my own was. Rest in peace, grandfather."

"Maireann an chraobh ar an bhfál ach ní mhaireann an lámh du chuir," Da murmured.

"*The branch lives on the hedge, but the hand that planted it is dead,*" Sean translated. "Your grandfather will live on in you, Jack."

The funeral had taken place earlier that afternoon. They'd expected it to be a small affair because of the grandfather's age, but apparently the old man was more well-known than they'd realized. Afterward, they'd all gone to the house for a luncheon and drinks. And later, when most everyone had left and the women had taken over the parlor, the three of them headed to Murphy's Pub to hold a private Irish wake.

"A nice service, it was," Da said for about the fourth time that day. "I'll be thinking your grandfather would be pleased by the homily."

"A very proper send-off," Sean added, for perhaps the fourth time as well.

Another customer interrupted to ask about the empty chair, and Da shooed him away. "It's taken can't ye see?"

"What was it the priest said near the end?" Jack took a swallow of ale. "Something about a life making mistakes is more honorable and useful than a life spent doing nothing at all. Such a charitable thought."

"Aye. May God grant us all enough time to make the mistakes that make us better people." Sean lifted his glass and the others joined him.

"Rousing as Father Andrew's homily was, I'll have to admit, he was a wee bit long-winded," Da said. He took a drink as though needing succor to revisit the memory.

"A wee bit?" Jack snorted. "I half expected my grandfather to stand up in the coffin and shout at the man to get on with it."

Sean slapped a hand on the bar. "I half expected him to stand up and protest against his service being performed in a Catholic church."

"There's that, too." Jack eyed the empty chair beside him. "I owe him my life, loved him like a father. But many's the time he didn't make it easy for Kathleen...although, to be fair, he got far better with time." He set his elbows on the bar and grinned. "Still, it seemed only right that a Catholic priest be the man to send his soul to its eternal rest."

"Saint Peter will be happy to see him, regardless of who did the sending," Da pointed out. "Perhaps delayed a touch by a brief spell in purgatory, penance for his unkind thoughts about the Irish."

"Purgatory?" Sean raised a brow at Da to warn him off the topic. They were speaking of Jack's grandfather after all; no reason to raise doubts about the next leg of the man's journey, even if he did end up with a detour along the way. "Da, don't be forgetting now, the rain today means he'll go straight to heaven."

"And where is purgatory, I'll be asking you? Right outside heaven's gate. I didn't say he'd be staying there long, just long enough to atone—"

"Jaysus, Da."

"Gentlemen, not to worry." Jack waved a hand. "We Protestants don't believe in purgatory."

Da gestured with his glass. "True. But how are we to know whose rules are being followed, when it was a Catholic priest—"

Sean elbowed his father in the side. "I think what we'll be needing now is some whiskey." He got the barkeep's attention and placed the order, determined to let the discussion about purgatory rest in peace.

"Whiskey. *Uisce beatha, the water of life,*" the bartender said as he poured a short glass for each man. He set his eyes on the untouched pint of ale in front of the empty stool. "And the fourth? For his grandfather as well?"

"Aye," Sean said. "Set it up." He finished off his ale and reached for a whiskey. The others did the same, raising their glasses in unison at the empty chair before taking a sip.

"Ahhh," Jack said. "The Irish do know how to make whiskey."

"Right you are," Da said. "We're good at making poitín, too, with fermented potatoes. But if I never have another glass of poitín as long as I live, 'twill be too soon." He took another sip, his expression growing pensive. "But I'll be missing those days...so many old friends now gone from this earth." He looked at the empty chair and set a hand on Jack's shoulder. "He was a good man."

Jack nodded and cleared his throat. "I'm glad he passed on before the judge made his final ruling. He loved Will more than I would have thought possible. Told Kathleen we should go to California or Canada. Start over where no one would find us."

"Could you do that?" Da asked.

"Spend my life wondering whether what we'd done was right? I don't know. I'd never want Will to learn we'd kept him from his natural family." He gripped his glass in both hands and stared into the amber liquid as if seeking an answer. "It's one thing if the judge decides we get to keep him. It's another if we steal him away. Besides, what would we do in California?"

"Pan for gold," Sean deadpanned.

"Me and a hundred thousand others."

An unrestrained laugh went up between them, as though the tensions they'd been carrying had finally broken free.

"If there's any gold left." Sean downed the rest of his whiskey, welcoming the heat into his stomach, his veins, his head.

The barkeep refilled their glasses, tipping his chin toward the one for Jack's grandfather. "What about him?"

"Leave it," Sean said. "You could get land out there, Jack. To farm."

"I don't know the first thing about farming. You're the one who needs to get the land."

"Land where?" the barkeep asked as he wiped down a nearby section of counter. "Are you talking about the land they're giving away out west?"

"Cohasset," Da answered as Jack said, "California."

Sean froze with his glass halfway to his mouth. "They're giving away land out west?" He set his glass down so quickly, whiskey splashed over the lip and onto the bar. "Who's giving away land?" he asked.

"The government," the barkeep answered. "In the Oregon Territory. Free land, north of California."

Sean gave a disbelieving grunt. "Free? Aye, as long as ye have a bag of gold from Sutter's Mill."

"It's just what I've heard. Men drink, they talk, I listen. Especially when they say the government is giving away land—"

"Why would they do that?" Jack asked.

"To get people to settle there. It's grand country, is what I'm hearing. Golden valleys. Bluffs like Ireland. Green hillsides..."

Longing swept through Sean, images of home, of Moira, of

the country he hadn't seen in five years—and would likely never see again.

The bartender's gaze drifted past them as if he were actually seeing the place. "They say the oceans stretch to the horizon, deep blue like the Irish sky just before sunset, white horses riding the crest of every wave."

"The Tuatha dé Danann," Da said wistfully.

And then all Sean could see was the light on Ailish's face as she told Will about the Irish gods and their white horses. "And the land itself?" he asked as his mind ran from the memory of that afternoon. "Do you know anything of that?"

"They say the black soil of Oregon is bottomless. And the rain plentiful." The barkeep topped off their whiskeys.

Black soil was the best growing dirt there was. "And they're giving land away? To anyone?" he asked skeptically. He braced both hands on the bar and bent forward. "Even the Irish?"

"Now be casting your eyes on me customers here," the man said, amused. "It was here that I heard it. Do you see any but Irish in this pub? Why would they be talking of it if they couldn't be getting it?" With that, he went to refill some pints for patrons at the far end of the bar.

Sean swirled a finger in the whiskey he'd spilled on the bar. Back in Ireland, the English government had taken almost all the land owned by Catholics and gave it to the Protestants. Why would the American government do the opposite? Especially when the Irish were so unwelcome in this country?

It sounded too good to be true. And yet...

He turned to Jack. "This Oregon Territory. Do you know anything of it?"

"A little. Wild country, untamed. There's a lot of it out there."

Sean took a drink, savored the burn down his throat as he pondered the possibility of a future that didn't involve working years on the railroad to save enough money for a few acres. *What if he could get land now? For free.*

Ridiculous.

The bartender wandered back their way. "I almost forgot an important piece. Have you a wife?" he asked.

Sean shook his head.

"Well, I suggest you find one. If these men were to be believed, you get double the land if you're married."

Sean let out a snort. "Now I'll be knowing for certain it's not true."

"I have a wife," Da offered. "How much land are we talking? One acre? Ten?"

The barkeep shrugged. "That's all I know. Too old I am myself to be chasing a rumor to the other side of a country this big. Dreams are for young men."

Someone at the other end of the bar waved for a refill, and he ambled away.

"Can't be real." Sean squinted after the man, wanting desperately to believe his words true, and resisting the temptation with every ounce of his being.

"If it was, you'd think I'd have heard something of it," Jack said.

"What you're both forgetting is that this is America." Da lifted his glass as if toasting the whole country. "When they said the streets were paved with gold, perhaps this is what they meant."

"Da, nobody gives away land. Especially not the government."

"Maybe here they do. If you could be getting land to farm right now, what would ye do, Seanie?"

Sean eyed his father for a long second, then threw back the

rest of his whiskey. "I'd be off to the Oregon Territory before you could shake your fist."

"Well then, find out, lad. You owe it to yourself to see if it's true."

"And if it is? What then, Da? If they're giving away land on the ocean as lovely as that in Ireland, are you with me?"

The sparkle in Da's eyes took fifteen years off his face. "Ach, I don't know, Sean. You want to know if I'd exchange fourteen-hour days in a factory for a piece of land of me own?" He chuckled. "Are you forgetting what the priest said this morning? Is gairid ár gcairt ar an seo."

Sean blinked. "*Our lease on life is short.*" Thoughts of Moira filled his mind again. Thoughts of Ailish. Of her sister. And of Ireland and all its buried dead. So many lives cut far too short. "So, Da, what say you?"

"You need not even ask, Sean. If it's true, I'm with you."

CHAPTER TWENTY-ONE

THE BRAKES SQUEALED AS THE TRAIN PULLED INTO COHASSET station, steam filling the air with gray smoke. Ailish braced her feet against the floor and tightened her arms around Will to keep from sliding off the wooden bench during the stop. Though the boy had already slept the entire two-hour trip, he barely stirred as their journey came to an end.

She couldn't believe Sean had brought them here, that he'd gone so far as to purchase tickets in advance so she couldn't refuse. She glanced at him gazing out the window, let her eyes follow his past the peaked roof that extended over the track so passengers could disembark protected from the weather, past the people milling about the platform (some awaiting travelers who were arriving, others no doubt, planning to take the train on its return journey to Boston), past the road that led to the cemetery where her sister rested.

The train let loose a final blast of smoke as though it were a giant beast exhaling before settling down to rest. For some reason, today Cohasset felt like the beginning of this railway line instead of its end.

"I still don't understand what Cohasset has to do with Mr. Montgomery's grandfather, *God's blessings on his soul,*" she said to Sean. "But I'll be thanking you again nonetheless, for bringing us here."

As passengers gathered their belongings and began to disembark, Sean lifted Will from her lap and stepped back to let her exit ahead of him. "Is it not your sister's birthday this week?" he asked, following her toward the door.

And what had her sister to do with the dead grandfather? "'Tis next week, not this."

"Ahhh. Forgive my mistake, then."

"Pray be telling me," she said over her shoulder, "what has her birthday to do with the old man's passing?"

Will began to rub his eyes, slowly coming awake. "Toot toot," he mumbled, repeating the sound he'd been making as they set off on their journey.

"Ye can be thanking the priest from the funeral," Sean said. "Talking he was about how we're each given a short time on this earth. Set me to thinking of all the Irish who got even less than we did."

Reaching the door, Ailish took the offered hand of the brakeman and stepped off the train to the smells of smoke and burning coal. She brushed at the specks of soot landing on her cloak as if she could sweep away the memories Sean's words had just shaken loose.

Sean came up beside her, let Will slide to the ground and took him firmly by the hand. "Since you're her older sister, I thought ye might want to be here to remember the day of her birth." He shot her a self-deprecating grin. "Even though it's next week and not this."

She found herself momentarily unable to respond, touched yet again by his unexpected kindness. "I'm sure she'll not be bothered by the error. Nor am I."

They left the shade of the platform and stepped into the brightness of unbroken sun, the day still cool enough to remind them that not a week ago, winter had reigned in its full glory. Warmed by the walk, Ailish opened the top of her cloak. "This trip will be naught but an adventure to Will, but his being here might mean something to his mam, God rest her soul." She brushed a hand through the boy's hair, the color identical to his mother's. "And it means very much to me. Thank you."

The cemetery afforded a peaceful view of the harbor, the grass-covered ground sloping gently toward the water's edge. Large trees dotted the property, dark branches covered with pale green buds just beginning to open. Despite the calling of the birds to one another and a steady breeze off the ocean, the property had a stillness, a sanctity.

"Do you hear the robins, Will?" She pointed toward a nearby tree. "They're God's bird. 'Twas the robin that plucked the sharpest thorn from Christ's brow. And when he did, the wee bird's breast was dyed red with the Savior's blood. It has stayed red always, so we would know the robin is blessed and must be protected."

Will gave a slow nod as if he understood the solemn meaning of her words. Then he threw a hand in the air and yelled, "Hello robin bird, hello!"

"Not so loud, Will," Sean said gently. "This is a quiet place."

"Let him be." Ailish filled her lungs with the salt-tinged air, held it deep and low, then let it out slowly. "If my sister's spirit is here, she'll find joy in the life of him."

The boy charged across the lawn, zigzagging between gravestones, arms outstretched so the tips of his fingers could graze every marker he passed. "Toot, toot," he shouted with each touch, his voice getting progressively louder.

Ailish pointed toward the water. "The dead are buried in a mass grave, unmarked, the groundskeeper told me. Near the shore. Seems only right that those whose bodies were retrieved should rest close to those who were never found."

They stopped at the edge of a shallow beach, light brown sand reaching out to an ocean that sparkled as though the stars had dropped into the sea and were winking from beneath the surface. In the distance, a rocky outcropping peeked in and out of the waves, beckoning and warning at the same time.

"So many came from Boston in the days after the wreck," Sean said. "Searching for relations and friends who had been on the ship. For each who got good news, there were so many others who—" He shook his head as though recoiling from the memory.

Ailish clasped her hands together and bowed her head. Beside her, Will knelt in the grass and poked an anthill with a stick. She was grateful he didn't understand why they were here, and that even a cemetery was a place of wonder to a child. "Blessings on the souls of the dead," she murmured. "And dear sister, may he grant you a generous share of eternity."

After a moment, she turned to Sean. "Will ye tell me of the day it happened?"

He loosed a breath. "Nay. You'll not want to see those pictures in your mind as you fall asleep. Or when you wake in the dark hours of the night. I'd not wish it upon my most hated enemy." He picked a stone from the grass and side armed it over the water. "Knowing more won't soothe your pain, Ailish. It will only give you thoughts you'll soon wish you could banish. Be glad those memories don't haunt you." He stared into the distance, eyes trained on something, or perhaps nothing, the sorrow in his expression a harsh contrast to the tranquility around them.

"I only meant to honor the dead by hearing their story. Making sure they aren't forgotten by keeping them alive within me."

"Moira used to say something like that," he said without looking at her. "How we all live within each other. That we are all the same though we are all different."

"Tell me about your Moira. Not how she died. But how she lived."

He searched her face as if wondering whether she could be trusted with the memories of the woman he'd wed.

"Have you told anyone since then?" she asked. The surf rolled onto the shore and returned to sea, came in and went out again, and she knew his answer before he voiced it.

"Not more than a bit."

"Tell me if you'd like. Here in this place commemorating death, it would be a fine way honor the best of her life."

Will sauntered onto the beach collecting bits of driftwood and piling it together, paying no notice to the tide creeping up the sand—until a wave climbed high as if determined to catch him. He let out a shriek and scampered away.

Sean shoved his hands into his jacket pockets and lowered his eyes. "Moira was...you could be saying she was my anchor. Not that she kept me tethered, but that she kept me grounded. No matter how far I went, I always knew where home was."

Ailish softened inside at his love, so obvious, for his wife.

"Many a summer I sailed to Newfoundland to work the cod fisheries..." He scuffed his toe against a rock poking through the ground, kicked it loose. "Hard enough it was to leave, but the voyage home seemed an eternity, knowing she'd be waiting. Even with the potato blight, all the death, I never thought...never expected...always thought we'd live to see our plans through and be raising a family here in America." He drew a ragged breath.

"I'll be guessing she had a lovely smile," she said, giving him space to refocus.

His eyes stayed fixed on the water. "Aye. Quick with it she was. And blue eyes, like a clear sky when the sun first rises. The color rose on his cheeks and he gave his head a shake. "Now I'll be sounding the hopeless romantic."

"Nay. You sound like a man who loved his wife. Honoring the best of her."

He cocked his head. "She used to say to me, *Seanie, you're the best part of me.* Except, I always knew she had it backward—Moira was far more the best part of *me*."

Tears stung Ailish's eyes and she ducked her head to hide them, waved a hand at Will and called, "Stay back from the water." She swallowed down her emotions, succeeding with all but one: envy. Jesus, Mary, and Joseph, but what she would have given to be loved by her husband the way Sean loved Moira.

THE MORNING after the trip to Cohasset, Sean left the house early, determined to learn the truth about the supposed land giveaway in the Oregon Territory. He feared it was one of those stories that began as a rumor and grew larger with each retelling—false from beginning to end. Still, he'd not be fool enough to toss it aside until he knew for sure. This was America after all, not Ireland, and things were supposed to be different here.

"Luck will surely have been on my side if it turns out true," he muttered as he pulled open the door to City Hall. He'd come to realize when he was in Cohasset with Ailish, that he would never be able to settle there no matter who got custody of Will. If

Jack and Kathleen lost, every day in Cohasset would be a reminder of their loss. And even if they prevailed, the town would forever be stained with the memory of these troubles.

He stepped into the building, onto the marble floor inside, cool silence enveloping him as he waited for his eyes to adjust to the dim light. The door shut behind him with a dull clunk, propelling him forward to the main desk to ask for help.

"Federal Land Office," the man there said without raising an eyebrow. "Down the hall on the left. They know all about it."

Jaysus, could it actually be true? For the first time since hearing of the land giveaway, Sean felt the thrill of real possibility. Minutes later he got the confirmation he'd never expected to hear.

"It's called the Donation Land Claim Act," a balding man assured him from behind the counter in the Land Office. "Signed into law more than a year ago. What would you like to know?"

Questions flooded his mind. How could this be possible? When had a country ever given away land except as the spoils of war? Could he get enough for a real farm? Not just an acre to grow potatoes, but enough for other crops as well? He forced his thoughts to focus.

"How much land can a man get...is ten acres possible?" His heart picked up its beat. He knew he was expecting much.

"Ten?" A younger man at a nearby desk leaned back in his chair and joined the conversation.

Sean's hopes plummeted.

"You could ask for ten," the older man replied, "but why would you do that when they're giving away three hundred and twenty?"

"*Three hundred and twenty?*" The words burst from Sean before he could stop them.

"Married couples get double, six hundred and forty."

His mouth went dry. "But...why?" He could barely fathom the idea of owning so much land. In Ireland, they'd been allowed to rent only a tiny plot—less than an acre—to grow crops for the entire family.

"The government wants people to settle there," the younger answered eagerly. "My brother went west for the gold rush. Didn't find gold, but he got land in Oregon. A lot of it—"

"But there are residency requirements," the other interjected. "Are you asking for yourself or someone already out there? To get that much land, you have to have lived in the Territory before December first, 1850—"

Oh, there it was. Rules, always rules. It was already more than a year past that date. "And if you haven't?"

"You can still get land, just not as much." The younger man came to the counter. "You get half the acreage if you arrive after 1850. That's what my brother did."

A hundred and sixty acres? Sean tried to force his careening thoughts into order. "You're saying, if I go to the Oregon Territory today, I can get one hundred sixty acres of land. *For free*?"

Both men grinned, clearly enjoying Sean's reaction. "Yes," the older said. "Double for married couples—three hundred and twenty acres. Have you a wife?"

"Nay."

"Perhaps you should be finding one."

Sean nodded, stunned. Wait until Da heard all of this.

"Now, as for going there today..." The older man unrolled a map and ran a finger over a marked route. "Takes four months to get to the Territory by wagon train. It's a long trip through rough country."

Sean ignored the travel advice. He had another question,

perhaps the most important of all. "This land...is it available to anyone?" *Even the Irish?* he wanted to add, but held back, reluctant to draw attention to his nationality.

"There are a couple of restrictions."

Of course.

The older man took a document from a stack on the desk and read aloud, "Land is available for any white settlers or half-breed Indians. Hawaiians and Negroes are excluded."

"What about the Irish?" Sean asked, almost afraid of the answer. With so much discrimination against the Irish in this country, he couldn't believe they would be allowed to get land.

"You're white aren't you?"

"Aye," he hesitantly replied.

"Then you can get land."

Sean gaped at them. The Irish were denied jobs in America because they were...Irish. But they could get hundreds of acres of land for free because their skin was...white? This was a strange country indeed.

"There are a few other requirements." The man spun the page around so Sean could see it, then pointed to a paragraph.

"Recipients must be at least eighteen years of age," Sean read aloud. "Must be an American citizen or must have declared according to law the intention to become a citizen." Easy enough. He lifted his head, still struggling to believe the land giveaway was real. "Once you're in the Territory, how do you get the land?"

"Pretty simple. You stake a claim. Once you've worked the land for four years, you get the title."

"Why four years?"

"Keeps speculators from grabbing land and selling it," the younger man explained.

Sean nodded. "But I choose the land I want?" His mind

sprinted ahead, already planning. "What of the Indians? I've heard stories...is the Territory safe?" More worried he was for Ma and Da and his younger siblings than he was for himself.

"There hasn't been much of a problem." The older man gave his head a firm shake. "The government is negotiating treaties to make sure everything is done fairly. Trading other land to the Indians in exchange for farmland."

Sean considered the answer. There wasn't an Irishman alive who didn't know of the English invasion of Ireland two hundred years before, when all of their land was stolen and given to Protestant landlords. "They're not stealing it, are they?" In his quest for land, he'd not let himself embrace the very actions he'd despised his entire life.

"No. It's definitely an exchange. Everything has been negotiated." The man penciled some notes on a scrap of paper. "If you're serious about this, you'll need to get to Missouri soon and catch on with a wagon train. Most leave in May. Wait until June and it will be too late to get across the Rocky Mountains before winter sets in."

"Best to hurry," the younger added. "My brother writes that it's gotten as bad as the gold rush. The last to arrive will get the worst land—or none at all."

CHAPTER TWENTY-TWO

KATHLEEN HANDED SEAN A DECK OF CARDS AND TOOK A SEAT AT the round parlor table with Jack and her parents.

"I'll deal and barkeep for the first game, aye?" Sean said. "What's your pleasure?"

"Whist." She threw him a breezy smile in an effort to make the moment feel as ordinary as possible. They were three weeks into the month of visitations ordered by the judge, marching ever closer to his final decision. And though they were all doing their best to pretend life was normal, with each passing week the tension increased, as though a steel trap pressing its teeth into one's foot.

"Whist it is." He removed the jokers from the deck, then shuffled the cards, his gaze gliding around the table like a professional gambler eyeing the competition. "Teams are Ma and Da against Jack and Kathleen."

"Fine, fine." Da drummed his fingers on the table.

"Anxious to be getting on with the game are you, Da?"

Kathleen teased. It wasn't like him to be showing such impatience.

"Aye. Deal them, Sean," he said. "And don't be keeping us waiting. What did you find out?"

"About what?" Kathleen eyed her brother curiously. What were these two up to?

Ignoring them both, Sean passed out the entire deck, then flipped the last card face up on the table. "Five of clubs," he announced, the corners of his mouth tugging upward as he pressed a finger to the card. "If I'll be remembering it right, Da, the five of clubs prophecies success—business success. Five Irish clovers is the sign that all our dreams are coming true."

Ma made a face and rubbed her forehead as if Sean had lost his wits. "Best you leave the readings to The Travellers, Sean," she said, picking up her cards. "'Tis the six of clubs that predicts business success. The five means a new friend and a successful marriage. I believe your Da has both those already. Aye?" She perused her cards.

"A new friend and successful marriage?" Kathleen fanned her cards and fluttered them flirtatiously. "Indeed, tell us more, Seanie."

He let out a disgusted snort. "This is nonsense—"

"Aye," Da almost roared. "Sean—"

"What are the two of you getting up to?" Kathleen asked warily. "Something's in the works, I can tell—"

"Da, are ye ready for this? Truly ready? Because everything he told us...it's all true," Sean said.

"All of it?" Jack asked.

"You know what he's talking about?" Kathleen narrowed her eyes at her husband.

Sean pointed a finger at Da. "It's better than any of us could make up. A man can get over a hundred acres. *Free.*"

Da's jaw dropped.

Kathleen eyed them suspiciously. "Of what are you speaking?"

"One hundred sixty acres to be precise," Sean continued, paying her no notice. "In the Oregon Territory. And, please be excusing me ladies, I spoke wrong." He gave a deferential nod of the chin to Ma. "Even the women can get free land. Wives get a hundred and sixty acres, too."

No one moved. Sean gestured expansively with one hand. "Are we to be playing whist tonight or not?"

All four gaped at him in stunned silence.

"You know this for fact?" Da asked. "Absolute true fact?"

"Aye."

"And are you going?"

"Going?" Kathleen exploded, her throat aching with sudden emotion. "You're already that far along and we only just learned of it a minute ago?"

Sean lifted his tumbler to his lips and caught her gaze over the edge of the glass. Her stomach tumbled with foreboding. "Well, Kathleen," he said, "I've been pondering me choices. I can stay in the east, building the railroad, saving my pennies, hoping someday I'll have enough to buy a few acres of land." He lifted his left arm, healed but still weak. "And praying I don't get caught in a cave-in worse than the one that did this."

Ma rearranged the cards in her hand as though concentrating on them would somehow prevent this conversation from unfolding.

"And if I stay, what then?" Sean looked around the table into each of their faces, one at a time. "What happens if the *Know Nothings* win office in Massachusetts? Will they pass laws forbidding the Irish—forbidding all immigrants—from buying land? Will they take land away from immigrants who already own it?"

"Do you actually think that could happen? In America?" Kathleen asked, unwilling to believe it.

"It aligns with what they stand for," Jack said, his voice tired. He played a card to start the game. "I wouldn't doubt they would try. Support for the party is growing quickly. If they win enough seats, they can do whatever they want."

Da's eyes were locked on Sean, his expression hopeful. "But if you go to Oregon, the land would be yours *now*. More land than you could buy even if you saved for the next twenty years."

"And no threat of losing it," Sean said. "The Know Nothings are rising on the east coast, not the west."

A look passed between them, an asking of permission and a granting of it, though they all knew Sean would never have had to ask. He was a man grown, with his own choices to make; he'd had to leave the family more than once already.

Kathleen stared at her cards, at this feeble attempt to maintain their regular life, when now it seemed that change would be foisted upon them no matter how they tried to hold it at bay. "You've already decided, haven't you?" she asked.

Sean ignored the question. "Ma, it's your play."

"Doesn't seem there's much of a decision to be made," Jack said thoughtfully.

"How soon would you be leaving? If you go." Ma played a card, and Kathleen followed, then Da tossed one on the table as if he just wanted to get past his turn.

"I'll be wondering now...do you know if anyone can get land?" Da asked. "Even men my age?"

Ma's head snapped up. "Micheal?"

"Da, you didn't want to leave Ireland and now ye would pack

up and leave Boston?" Kathleen exclaimed, incredulous. 'Twas happening too fast, all of it. Ailish, the Know Nothings, Oregon... "Jesus, Mary, and Joseph, how can you—"

"Stop fretting, lass, I'm but asking a few questions. Only a fool wouldn't do the same."

"But Da, we're all here in Boston. And we're facing this thing with Will that we don't know what will happen..." She cast desperate eyes upon her mother. "Ma, did you know of this?"

"Nay. This is new to me this very instant. But even so, your da..." She put a hand on her husband's arm and a somber smile curved her lips. "Your da is a man of the land, you know that."

Kathleen carefully set her cards face down on the table. "I just thought...because we were here...together. We survived the famine—"

The stillness in the room lay heavy on her chest, like a weight squeezing out her air.

"You know Boston isn't an easy place for the Irish, Kathleen," Jack said gently. "It's why we changed Liam's name to Will. It cannot help but get worse with the rise of the Know Nothings." He played a card as if the move would lower the emotions in the room and return the tenor to normalcy.

"Have you a plan, Sean?" Ma's voice sounded loud in the silence. "How will you be getting to Oregon?"

"A wagon train out of Missouri. The last ones leave at the end of May." He slid his chair out from the table and paced across the room. "I'll need to be there a week early—two weeks even better—to buy a wagon and oxen to pull it, get provisions for the trip."

Kathleen stared at him, speechless.

"And getting to Missouri itself won't be easy—"

"It's already the middle of April," she cried. "What about Will?"

He shoved a hand through his hair. "I'll not be leaving until the visitations are over. But then I'll have no time to waste for the trains don't go through to Missouri. The route is a mishmash of unconnected railways, each with a different owner and prone to delays. Accidents, broken rails, animals on the tracks—"

"What of the stagecoach?" Da sat back in his chair and set his cards on the table.

"The trains are fastest. But parts of the trip will have to be by stage and I'm told the roads are rutted and muddy..."

"That will make a tight schedule tighter," Da said as if to himself.

Kathleen gave him a sharp frown. She knew the toll working in the factory took on her father, how much he hated the Irish ghettos, squalid and teeming with too many people, so unlike the open fields and hillsides of home. And yet he couldn't actually be thinking of going, could he?

"He's asking a few questions, that's all," Ma said gently as if reading her mind.

"There's much to consider," Da added. "And not a lot of time."

Sean pulled the stopper from the decanter of whiskey and went around the table refilling their glasses before taking his chair again. Ma watched him with thoughtful eyes. "Sometimes when least you expect it," she said, "a path appears. And if your spirit is open, you'll know it for the gift it is."

Kathleen perused her cards. "So many gifts I've been receiving lately, I can't begin to decide where first to be thankful." She could hear the petulance in her voice and didn't care.

"Kathleen," Ma said softly, "this world has never been kind to the Irish. Perhaps the voyage to America was only the first leg of the journey God planned for us." She reached across the table to lay her hand atop her daughter's. "Don't be forgetting now, *Is fada an bóthar nach mbíonn casadh ann.* It's a long road that has no turning."

CHAPTER TWENTY-THREE

IT WAS HARD TO BELIEVE SHE WAS ALREADY ON HER SEVENTH visitation, and before another week would pass the judge would make his final ruling. Ailish stood a short distance away from Will, her hands wrapped around a small leather ball.

"Throw it, Aish," the boy shouted as if she were halfway across the park. "Throw it!"

She grinned. The connection between them had improved so much since their first visit. They were friends now and had fun together, she liked him and he liked her. It could only get better from here. Surely the judge would see how far they'd come and decide Will belonged with her.

Bending slightly at the waist, she swung her arm back and forth like a pendulum, finally letting the ball fly in an underhanded toss that went up...up...and over Will's head.

"A bit too much follow through I'll be guessing," Sean said as the ball hit the ground and rolled away. He made an exaggerated lunge after it. "Quick, Will, it's escaping."

As soon as the boy took up the chase, Sean pulled back and threw a wink at Ailish. "Works every time."

Though she knew the wink wasn't personal, still her pulse fluttered and her cheeks began to heat. She turned away to watch Will and hide her face. "I've been wondering," she said finally, just to break the silence, "are Mr. Thoreau's words as lovely in person as they are in print?"

"You like the book then?"

She nodded. "Sometimes it's a bit of a struggle to understand what he's saying, but other times his words can fair lift the curtain from the window, make you see things in a way you never did. Like the dew on the leaves or each drop of water in a stream...a wee tiny ant or even the heavens themselves..." Mortification crawled up her spine. For God's bright sake, why was she jabbering on like this?

She gestured toward Will, skipping and spinning his way back to them, shouting unintelligibly as he held the ball aloft. "Apparently he's just clinched a victory of some sort."

"All of life is a tournament for that lad." Sean motioned him in. "As to Mr. Thoreau...aye, he speaks as well as he writes. But you're right, sometimes it takes extra thought to discern his meaning. That night at the lecture, he read from a new book he's writing about living in the woods. On a place called Walden Pond."

"Walden Pond," she mused. "Perhaps 'tis good I didn't stay. Just hearing of it makes me long for home. Lately I'll even be missing all the rain." She could almost see the hills of Ireland, green and fresh, a steadily falling drizzle coating everything with shimmering silver. "His words so often remind me of what I've left behind."

"Aye. Or perhaps he's showing us that there are other places in the world as fine as those we left behind."

She cocked her head. Was he trying to convince her of that —or himself? "Being in a place that looks like home isn't the same as being home."

Will skidded to a halt in front of them, his face scrunched up in fierce determination as he windmilled his arm round and round, ball clutched tight. Sean held up a hand. "Wait, Will, don't—"

The ball smacked into his shin with a dull thud. A laugh burbled out of Ailish and she pressed a fist to her mouth to squelch it. "Careful, Will," she said. "Someone could get hurt."

"Someone just did," Sean muttered as he rubbed his leg. "Good God, lad, where'd you get that strength? And that aim?"

"His da was quite skilled at hurling so perhaps he comes by it naturally."

"I didn't even know Jack played." Sean scooped up the ball and tossed it to her. His face fell the moment he realized his error. "Ah, sorry again," he said. "You meant his other da."

She sighed. "Sure I'll be wishing I'd never raised the point in the first place. It's not what's most important." She faced Will, eager to put the discussion to rest. "Ready, lad? Put your hands together." She lofted the ball toward him, and t though he threw his hands in the air and jumped several times, the ball escaped over his head again. Without any urging, he set off after it, short legs churning.

Ailish flashed a warning scowl at Sean. "Not a word do I want to hear about my throwing skill."

"Nay, I was thinking of what you said before." His gaze flicked across the park, eyes following Will on his mad dash. "A new place won't be exactly the same as the one left behind, not the land nor the people...but if it reminds you of home, might it not ease the pain of never going back?"

She shrugged. "Perhaps. If you've accepted that you'll never go back." That wasn't the case for her; she was going back. She put her hands on her hips and squinted at him. "But what are we talking of? Is it Ireland? Or somewhere else?"

He wearily rubbed his temples. "A bit of both, I'll be guessing. There's a program giving away land..." He explained what he'd learned about the Oregon Territory.

"Well now," she said, "I think I'll be knowing why you're having so much trouble with the decision." She took a couple of steps toward him and wagged a teasing finger. "It's the number of acres that's holding ye back—one hundred sixty. That could never feel like home. If you want it to feel like home, you must insist on only half an acre. Certainly no more than one."

He laughed. "Aye. And it must be covered with rocks that need picking before I can plant. Then I'll be knowing the true feeling of home."

She felt a touch of yearning, the tickle of a dream stirring awake inside her. "What they're giving away in Oregon, Sean, it's enough for a real farm. A landholder's farm, not a cottier's. What's to hold you back?" She nudged his arm. "It can't be that you dread giving up railroad work."

"Nay, of course not. There's a greater issue. It's the reason you're here today." Will ran up to them, panting, and Sean swung him into the air. "What I mean is, leaving family behind, choosing to leave them and knowing they'll live on but not as part of your life...it's almost as painful as losing them to death."

Will snuggled in and rested his head on his uncle's shoulder as he caught his breath.

"All the time I've been away working, my family was just a train ride away," Sean said. "But I didn't make time to take that ride. And now..."

He was speaking of regrets. Surely he knew he wasn't alone with life's regrets. When she thought of what she would give to have some moments back, to do them over, to choose differently, it almost made her heart hurt. "If you go, you fear you'll never see your family again," she said softly.

He nodded.

"At least you'll know they're alive." The words sounded harsher than she intended them.

"Aye. But to know they're alive and it's beyond your means to see them is a kind of death in another form." He said nothing for several long moments. "Ailish, it's what Jack and Kathleen will feel if they lose..." He looked down at the child in his arms. "Could you not reconsider...what you're doing to their family?"

Her breath caught in her throat, all her fear and pain twisted into a knot squeezing her lungs. She swallowed hard. "I...know this is hurting them. I wish it wasn't. I will be forever grateful for all that they've done for Liam. *Will.* But, please, Sean, I can't. I'm sorry."

After a long beat, he let Will slide to the ground. "Shall we do something else, lad?"

"Ducks!" Will took off in the direction of the pond, spinning circles as he went.

"A shocking decision," Sean said with a lopsided smile as they followed the boy.

Ailish exhaled, relieved they had left the subject of Will's future behind. "Surely you've heard talk of building a railroad from east coast to west," she offered. "Perhaps it won't be long before it's done and people can travel more easily across the country."

"We've all heard of it. But Ailish, there are mountains all across the west. If you knew what it took to blast a tunnel through such rock...I'll not expect them to be connecting the two coasts anytime soon."

Will sprinted ahead, each time straying just far enough to

feel a burst of panic before he spun round and galloped back to them, gleefully tagging Sean's legs as if to confirm he was still there before racing away again. Here in the park, Sean was his anchor, his foundation, his safety, his security, *his home.*

Ailish's chest tightened defensively. Given time, she could be that for Will, too.

"Much as I pretend there's a choice to be made, I know I have to go to Oregon. *I want to go,*" Sean said.

"Tell yourself it's just a river trip you're setting off on. Like Mr. Thoreau and his brother."

"Aye. Albeit a much longer one," he said with a grin. "Perhaps before I leave, I should make a pilgrimage to Concord."

"For what?"

"To stand at the place where he launched his boat and know that, like him...*I'll be sailing up a river with a pleasant wind; new lands, new people, new thoughts to find,*" he said, quoting loosely from the beginning of the book. He cocked his head. "The more I think on the idea, the better I like it. Concord is but twenty miles away. I may never get another chance."

His smile lit his eyes so fully, she felt a tug of yearning. "If that's the case, I'll have to be getting your book back to you. For surely you'll want it along when you stand where he set off..." She grinned and pulled out a bit of what she remembered from the same passage. "*...the flags and bulrushes curtseying God-speed.*"

A slow smile opened Sean's face as he recognized the words. "Oh, lass, don't be telling me it's taken root in your soul."

"Perhaps a bit," she admitted.

He threw back his head and laughed. "Why don't you come with me?"

"With Will?" She shook her head even as the idea grabbed hold of her imagination.

"Me ma always says adventures are better shared. *Giorraíonn beirt bóther. Two shorten the road."* He nudged his shoulder playfully against hers as if they were children.

Up ahead, Will stood at the edge of the pond, waving his arms and talking to the ducks gathering around him begging for a handout. Will spun back, "Hurrrrrry," he shouted. "They hungry!"

"I think it might be easier to go without Will," Sean said slowly. "Can you get a few hours off another day? We can take the train."

She blinked. She'd have no problem taking the time off, for she'd not yet started her new job. But she had little money and none to spare for train tickets. "I'm sure they'd let me have the time," she lied, "but I haven't the coin. Stretched thin I am, making ends meet." There was no need to mention she had a lawyer who needed payment as well.

"Ah." Sean pulled out the bag of corn and filled Will's outstretched palm. "I've a bit of money saved...I could buy your ticket."

"Now you're talking foolishness." She placed her attention on Will. "Remember, one piece at a time," she called as he ran back to the pond.

"One man's foolishness is another's grand idea. I'll be buying two tickets. Because that's what I want to do."

"And you always do just what you want?" She raised a brow.

He shrugged. "For my friends, aye."

He thought of her as a friend? The woman who was determined to take Will from his family? Warmth did a slow waltz through her veins. Flustered, she didn't reply.

"I'd like to have someone along," Sean said. "Come with me. Keep me company."

At the bank of the pond, Will danced from one foot to the other. "One at a time," he sang as he tossed a kernel to a mallard.

"One at a time." He threw another piece. "One at a time, one at a time," he sang as he hurled all the corn into the air at once. It pattered onto the pond like hail, and the ducks made a ruckus chasing after it.

"Will!" Ailish stuck her hands on her hips and glared at Sean. "And does he, too, just do what he wants...always?"

"He's quite determined."

"Takes after his Uncle, I'll be guessing."

"Does that mean you'll be coming to Concord with me?"

Her stomach slipped sideways. What was to hold her back? They were friends, hadn't he just said so? Her new job didn't yet require her presence. And the book had captured her imagination, given her hope when she'd thought she'd never feel such a thing again.

But was going with Sean wise, with the hearing just a week off? Might spending a day with him somehow hurt her petition for Will?

What could be the harm? her soul whispered. *Two friends spending the day together.*

Her mouth curved upward as she met his eyes. "Does it mean I'll be coming with you?" she asked. "I'll be guessing it does."

CHAPTER TWENTY-FOUR

SEAN LEANED OVER AILISH TO LOOK OUT THE TRAIN WINDOW. Shouldn't be long and they would be in Concord; twenty miles had become a short distance with the railroads.

"Do you see that body of water there?" He pointed at a small lake visible through the trees, the silvery fog of early morning obscuring its surface. "Sure it must be Walden Pond. Where Thoreau lived. He said the tracks run along the shore."

"How awful it must have been when the train came through. Him being in the woods, nature all around, and then suddenly all that noise and smoke tearing up the peace."

The train whistle sounded, announcing their arrival.

"Aye. And a whistle shrieking loud enough to wake animals in their dens," Sean said.

As the train drew to a halt at the station, he picked up the basket of food he'd brought and stepped down to the platform, holding out a hand to help Ailish with the steps. "Welcome to Concord," he said formally, as though he were mayor of the city.

"Thank you for the welcome, kind sir." She grinned. "Now

could you be steering me in the direction of the riverbank where Mr. Henry David Thoreau and his brother launched their boat on the start of their fabled voyage?"

Sean looked ahead to the main street, cluttered with carriages and people, both sides lined with shops and businesses. They would have to ask around, but how hard could it be to find out? Thoreau still lived in Concord, after all.

Before fifteen minutes had passed, they discovered just how difficult it would be. They'd stopped in six businesses and found no one who could help them. In fact, few knew Mr. Thoreau had taken a river trip—or written a book about it.

"'Twas thirteen years ago," Sean said as they exited the bank after being dismissed by a cheerless banker. "Perhaps too many years have gone by."

Ailish skipped forward and gave a knowing nod. "Do you know what I'm thinking?"

"That we've made this trip in vain?"

"Nay. I'm thinking that banker was a leprechaun," she declared.

He snorted out a laugh. "Leprechauns don't like to be around people. Or so I've heard."

"In Ireland, aye. But who knows here? Be listening to me now, Sean." Ailish tucked her hand into the crook of his arm as though they were old friends out for a stroll.

He slanted a curious glance her way, memories of Moira cascading through him—memories and longing. "I'm listening," he said and forced the thoughts away.

"Think of him now. Short and round he was, right plump like a leprechaun."

"Even so, he's much taller than any leprechaun I've heard of," Sean pointed out.

"Everything's bigger in America, don't you know?" she said,

mischief in her eyes. "Did you notice how cross he was? Bad-tempered, like every leprechaun. They're known for it. And the fact he's a banker? That seals it." She dusted off her hands as if to countenance no dissent. "Banking is what they do. Leprechauns are the bankers of the faerie world."

"Ahhh...so, then what's he doing in America?" Sean smiled confidently, certain he'd just laid a boulder in her path.

She grinned back. "Perhaps he heard about the gold in California and came across hoping to get a potful."

A laugh burst out of him and he conceded defeat. "All I can say is he'd better join a wagon train soon or he'll not be getting to California this year."

They went into the stately Middlesex hotel and crossed the elegant lobby to approach a woman at the main desk with their questions. As Sean spoke, her expression grew so puzzled, he was certain she would quickly send them on their way. Instead, she tapped her lower lip thoughtfully. "I've heard of that book," she said slowly. "But I don't think many copies were sold. As for where they set off, I can't help you. I've never heard mention of it."

She gave the room a quick once-over, then bent forward as if to share a secret. Her voice dropped to a whisper. "I shouldn't be talking out of school, but Mr. Thoreau lives right over on Main Street. I don't recommend you knock on his door, but if you linger about the area, you might be fortunate enough to cross paths and you can ask him yourself."

Sean saw a crease form between Ailish's eyes. He was glad to know she had the same opinion as he about lingering on Main Street lying in wait for Mr. Thoreau.

"Why not just go out to Walden Pond?" the woman continued. "I daresay you'll find more to see there than at the riverbank. It's but a half hour walk."

"But he wrote about his river trip," Ailish protested.

"From what I hear, he's writing about the pond, too." The woman pursed her lips thoughtfully. "May I ask, is it just Mr. Thoreau's haunts you're after? Or are you interested in others?"

Others? "Others would be grand," he said without any idea what she was talking about.

The woman bent forward again, whispering conspiratorially. "I'll deny it if you say you heard this from me, but Ralph Waldo Emerson and his family live over on Lexington. And Nathanial Hawthorne—you've heard of him, yes?—is renting the Emerson ancestral home, the old manse on Monument Street. Next to the Old North Bridge." She stopped talking when a man came down the stairs and crossed the lobby. As soon as he exited the front door, she dove in again, speaking faster.

"Bronson Alcott and his family live at Hillside House, which is also on Lexington, but a ways further out than the Emersons. But rumor has it that..." Her voice dropped so low Sean had to strain to hear. "...Mr. Hawthorne is purchasing the property from the Alcotts and plans to rename it, *The Wayside.*"

She straightened and smoothed back her hair. "Concord has been quite the destination for writers these past twenty years. Creative people, coming and going all the time. Would you like to know others?"

"Nay, that's enough. Thank you." Sean made a quick decision. "I think we'll take your advice and go to Walden Pond." He looked at Ailish and she gave a quick nod, the corners of her mouth twitching. "If you'll just point us that direction."

The woman came from behind the desk and went to a window overlooking the street. "Head back down Main Street, then go left onto Walden. It's just a mile and a half out. Once you see the clearing along the shore of the pond, you'll know you're in the right place. His cabin has been taken down already, but it sat in the woods along that beach."

Voicing grateful thank-yous, they escaped out the door and hurried in the direction of Walden Street. "We must look quite learned. Intellectuals, I would think," Ailish said lightly. "Have ye heard of any of those people?"

"Nay. Important writers they are, I'll be guessing. But who has time for reading when there's a railroad to be built? If not for my foreman, I wouldn't even know of Mr. Thoreau."

"If not for you, neither would I." The smile on Ailish's lips filled her eyes. "And I'll be thinking me life is richer because of it."

"Your life is richer because of meeting me?" He lifted an eyebrow, and a long dormant place deep in his chest felt a flicker of life. "Such a fine thing to hear from a pretty lass." He reached for her arm and she danced away, laughing and waving a dismissive hand.

"Your soul to the devil, Sean Deacey," she said. "That isn't what I meant and you well know it."

He laughed with her and looked ahead at the road stretching out in front of them, a small curve blocking the view of what lay next. Aye, he knew it wasn't what she meant, but even so, the tension that seemed to live in his shoulders eased for the first time in a long while.

On either side of the road, the meadow waved at them with the colors of early spring, purple and white wildflowers bouncing in the breeze like children at play. "Reminds me of Ireland it does," Ailish said. "Walking along an empty road, the fields all greening with the coming of warm weather. Are you disappointed we'll not be finding our way to the river?"

Disappointed? At that moment, with her beside him, the sky overhead glimmering silky blue in the sun, the meadow on either of the road greeting them with the newborn colors of spring he felt not even a twinge of regret. He opened his palms. "How could I be disappointed in this?"

Ailish stepped off the hard-packed road and picked a handful of white wildflowers, petals open like starbursts. She tucked the flowers beneath the belt of her dress. "Memories of when times were better help me forget what Ireland has become."

Without thinking, Sean reached out and took her hand. He knew the weight she carried—the guilt that came from having survived when so many others had not. "It gets easier the longer you're gone," he said. "At least in some ways."

She studied their joined hands, her eyes downcast for so long he began to wonder if he'd overstepped propriety. Then she raised her chin. "Have you ever felt like...none of what's happened is real. And you've only gone away for a visit and everyone you love is still at home waiting for you to return?"

He pushed away the buried memories that tried to spring to life with her words. "Aye. Even after five years, it happens sometimes. The thought sneaks in, catches me unaware. And for a heartbeat I think I'm in America to work, and Moira is in Ireland waiting for the money I'll be sending so she can soon come across and join me."

Ailish pressed her hand against his, palm to palm, as if to leave no space for the loneliness that thoughts of Moira provoked. They walked in comfortable silence, the songs of the sparrows and robins filling the air like a choir welcoming them to the woods.

Ahead through the trees lay the clearing they'd been told about, and they stepped off the road onto a worn path bounded by stately pines and budding hardwood trees and a forest floor dappled with wildflowers of blue and purple and white.

As they broke out of woods at the edge of the beach, Walden Pond lay before them, the silver mist rising from its surface turning to lace as it dissipated beneath the heat of the sun. Childhood memories leapt forward in his mind, stories told around the hearth of Irish gods and fairies and magic.

"Surely 'tis enchanted," Ailish said softly. "Making light I was, when I said the banker was a leprechaun. But this...Sean, do you think there could be faeries in America after all?"

"If there are, they would surely be at a place like this. On a morning such as this." The view was so otherworldly, it was hard to think it anything but enchanted. "When you're inside a tunnel all the day long, blasting rock and breathing black dust like air, it's easy to forget what a faerie morn looks like." He felt again the aching loss of his wife, and curled the fingers of one hand into a fist, nails pressing sharply into his palm.

"Perhaps that's why we're seeing one today. So we don't forget." Ailish scooped up a handful of sand and let it sift through her fingers until it had returned to the beach, each grain indistinguishable from the rest. "So many Irish perished in Ireland, so many left the country. So few remain to remember the legends...perhaps the faeries want to make sure we don't forget them."

In the distance a church bell chimed the hour as though marking the passage of the dead and their rise into heaven, the sound both mournful and joyous at once. Suddenly the silence of the pond was broken by the singing of larks and warblers in the trees and the quacking of ducks as they glided onto the water.

Ailish pointed along the shore. Sean followed her finger to a nearby inlet where two large white swans, black bills extending to their ebony eyes like masks, cavorted like dancers at a masquerade. She stretched out her arms and turned a slow circle. "It's no wonder Mr. Thoreau came here to stay. All around us life is renewing itself." She stripped off her shoes and stockings and let them fall into the sand.

A flower dropped from her waistband, and Sean picked it up. "What are you doing?"

"Going in."

"It'll be freezing."

"Come with me." She stepped across the sand toward the water, one hand trailing behind her, motioning him to follow.

She was so different than Moira had been, more impulsive... He waved her away with the flower, its petals shaking like a burst of life in the air. "You go ahead."

She put her hands on her hips and faced him. "Sean Deacey, there's magic here today, can you not feel it? A chance to be renewed. Are you not wanting such a thing—or would you rather every day be the same as the last has been up to now?" She lifted the front of her skirt, stepped into the water to her ankles and let out a shriek.

"Is that the sound of you being *renewed?*" Sean grinned. "I'll remind you there was snow on the ground two weeks ago."

"Think what you like. I'll be finding it...refreshing. Like dipping your feet in the river on a hot summer afternoon."

He lay back his head and laughed out loud. And she laughed in reply, the sounds mingling, connecting the two of them, making him want to be next to her, feel the water that was touching her skin also touching his.

But he didn't move.

Squirrels chased up a nearby tree, chattering as they scampered noisily through the branches above him.

"You're missing out, Sean," Ailish coaxed. She swept one foot, then the other across the surface of the water. "The longer I'm in here, the more and more renewed I'm feeling. Like my life is soon to change and move in directions I've never dreamed of."

She strolled through the shallow water, moving away down the beach without looking back. Suddenly he didn't want her going any further without him.

He pulled off his shoes, rolled up his trouser legs, and chased across the sand to splash into the pond beside her. The icy water shot an ache through his feet and he let out a curse. "I'd say it's a bit more bracing than refreshing."

Ailish kicked a foot, sprinkling his bare calves with droplets.

"Be warned," he said. "I've bigger feet. I can move a lot more water than you."

"Warning noted." Her eyes sparkled. She pushed up her sleeve, then reached into the clear water and retrieved a small stone, light gray with speckles of black. "Looks like a sparrow's egg." She handed it to him and swept a foot over the water again. "We used to live near a pond like this. From the time I was a wee lass, I've always loved the water."

He could see that. He closed his hand around the stone and let it fall into his pocket. "Are you sure you're not a *maighdeann-ròin,* a seal maiden?" he teased. Irish legend told of seals that became humans when they stepped from the water, only returning to seal form when they went back to the sea.

"If I were, I'd not admit it." She hitched her skirt over one arm and waded deeper, her legs still visible through the pristine water. She closed her eyes and tipped her face to the sun.

His gaze slid up the gentle curve of her neck and he had the sudden urge to press a kiss to the soft skin of her throat. He pulled his eyes away. Moira had been gone too long. For why else would he have such thoughts about the woman who might soon destroy his sister's life.

Ailish dipped a hand into the water and brushed it across

her face, let it drip over her dark hair, the droplets sparkling in the sun like diamonds.

Heat thrummed through his blood. He followed her into deeper water, came up close behind her. Could it be that she truly was one of the maighdeann-ròin and had bewitched him? "Are ye tempting me," he murmured, "to join ye beneath the sea?"

She lifted her face to him, water glistening on her pink cheekbones, a light in her eyes, a warmth that filled him with sudden longing. "Are you tempting me to stay on the land?" she asked, her voice low.

The world stopped. There was no movement, no sound, no cold, no heat, no air, nothing except him and Ailish and the pond and the fading fog...and the Good People. For surely the faeries were here among them, casting their magic over this moment, over the two of them, over their hearts and souls and free will.

And would it be so bad if they were?

He brought a hand up to cup her cheek, to run his fingers along her jaw, to brush his thumb over her lips.

The sun crested the tops of the trees and its golden heat dissolved the remaining mist, burning off the mischief that had seeped into his mind. He drew his hand away and took a step back. This couldn't be. Not this moment. Not them. Not ever.

CHAPTER TWENTY-FIVE

SEAN TOOK A STEP BACK. "BEST WE GET OUT OF THE WATER BEFORE our feet turn purple. Let's see if the path goes all the way around the pond."

Ailish followed him to the beach, felt the stiffness in his silence as they dried their feet and donned their socks and shoes. Regret stumbled through her over what had just happened between them on the lake. She should have known better than to let herself act so free. Faith, but there was just something about Sean that made her soften even when she was determined to hold a hard edge.

If she were in Ireland, she'd be putting such feelings up to faerie mischief. And perhaps that's what it was, even here in America.

And yet.

She fell into step behind him on the trail, eyes trained downward to spot roots and rocks in the path. Bounded by tangled underbrush and sprawling grapevines, the trail was easy to see. Sean shoved aside some low branches and held them out of the way so they didn't whip back against her, and she murmured her thanks.

Despite everything, despite the battle front she'd opened with his family, he had never been anything but kind to her. Which, if she was truthful, was more than she could say for herself.

She sighed out an exhale. 'Twas foolhardy to think like this, to allow feelings for Sean to kindle. For the fight over Will would create an unscalable wall between them. No matter who won in the end, there would be grief. Sean would never be able to forgive her for taking Will from his family. Nor, should the judge rule for the Montgomerys, would she ever forgive them for keeping her from her sister's son.

The trail forked and Sean stopped, looking one way and then the other. Ailish frowned; the branches and thickets seemed much the same in either direction. "Left seems to follow the shore, which is surely more scenic," she offered when he made no move. "I'll be guessing both end up in the same place."

Taking her suggestion, he set off along the shore, stopping many long minutes later, blocked by a wide patch of prickly evergreens clogging the forest floor. After a beat, he stepped to the side and swept out one arm with a partial bow and a big grin. "Ladies first."

"It appears I might have been wrong," she said with an impertinent smile.

"Hard as that is to believe."

She laughed, relieved that the uneasiness hanging over them had passed. Retracing their steps, they followed the path in the other direction. By the time they reached a narrow inlet at the far end of the pond, the sun was high and the view back to Thoreau's beach, stunning. The water shone azure in the sun, its smooth surface ruffled in spots by a light wind. Framed by dark tree trunks and thick pines, it was like a gem in an elegant setting.

"Let's rest here a bit," she said. "So peaceful it is, the memory will soothe my soul for months."

Sean spread a blanket on the small beach and they settled comfortably beside each other, facing the lake. "Are you hungry?" he asked as he took bread and cheese from the basket. "Or thirsty?" He held up a bottle of claret and two small glasses. "I thought we'd toast Mr. Thoreau at the river. But this spot is just as grand."

"Perhaps even better."

"A lass after me own heart." He filled both glasses, handed one to Ailish and raised the other high. "To Henry David Thoreau. Writer, adventurer, philosopher."

"And poet." Ailish tapped her glass against Sean's, took a sip, and savored the claret as it warmed all the way to her stomach. "This moment feels like something he wrote about in the book." She inhaled the scent of pine, remembering the rhythm of Thoreau's words, the way he put them together so that they flowed with spirit and meaning. "So lyrical it was...something like...*we seem to be floating on the currents of our dreams.*" She shook her head, frustrated. "I'm not doing the man's talent a service at all."

Without a word, Sean took the book from the basket and handed it over.

"I should have known you'd have it along." She thumbed through the pages. "Early on, it was," she muttered, scanning the beginning of the book until she found what she was seeking. "Here is is...*We seemed to be embarked on the placid current of our dreams, floating from past to future,*" she read aloud.

She gave the book back to Sean, set her palms on the ground

behind her and let her weight rest back. "I'm thinking it was life he was hinting at, not just his river trip. Like you setting off for the Oregon Territory."

"*Embarked on the current of my dreams.*" Though his tone was light she could see the strain of the decision still lay heavy upon him.

Yearning whispered through her, a longing to begin anew again, this time in a place too fresh to be marred by block after block of four-story tenement buildings lined up like barricades against a better life. "Can you tell me what ye know of the trip west?"

He fashioned loose sandwiches from bread and cheese and handed her one. "The wagon trains leave from Missouri. So first I'll have to be getting there."

"By train?" she questioned around a bite of food.

"Train and stagecoach. Once I reach St. Louis, I'll travel five days by river steamer up to Independence. Then I'll be a week or two in Independence to buy everything I'll need for the trip."

She tilted her head. "I thought I was leaping into the unknown leaving Ireland. And all I did was board one ship." The memory of that day rose up and she pushed back against it. She'd not be needing reminders of standing at the ship's rail alone, no one to see her off because all her family had died.

They spent the next hour sipping claret, snacking on bread and cheese, and talking only a bit—and even that of nothing important, just the easygoing give and take one expends on a lazy day without any responsibilities. Between the trill of the birds, the soft breeze, the afternoon warmth, and the wine, Ailish found her eyelids drooping. She lay back and closed her eyes. "Doesn't matter where in the world you find yourself," she murmured, "the sun always feels the same."

Her thoughts drifted, one sliding over the next as sleep

beckoned. She forced her lids open and peeked at Sean, sitting beside her with elbows on knees, eyes trained across the pond. His dark hair glistened in the sunlight; dark stubble covered his jaw. A handsome man he was, but not overly so. Still there was something about him that was so appealing...

She sliced off the thought before her mind could take it further. In another time, under other circumstances, she might be allowed to find him attractive. In another time, under other circumstances, he might feel the same way about her. But he had his own concerns to worry after—and she had hers. She closed her eyes to bury her growing attraction.

It seemed only a few minutes later when a loud rumbling hurtled her to consciousness. She blinked her eyes open and stared up at a purple-navy sky, shot through with icicles of gold and orange. Confusion muddled her mind.

The rumbling grew louder and she lurched to sitting just as a southbound train roared across a nearby rise like some ancient beast, its dark shape silhouetted against the bright horizon.

She drew her brows together, squinting as she tried to make sense of the moment. It looked like sunset. But it couldn't be. Not yet. She'd only just fallen asleep. She stared after the train, at the whiff of misty gray smoke that trailed behind it shading a piece of the sky, brilliant with the light of the sinking sun.

Jesus, Mary, and Joseph, the last train to Boston departed in the early evening. They couldn't have missed their train. They couldn't. *What time was it?*

She reached for Sean's arm.

SEAN CAME AWAKE WITH A START, instantly on high alert. He shot to sitting. "What? What's wrong?"

Ailish pointed to the west, at the sun low on the horizon. "A train just passed, going south. Could we have missed our ride home?"

As her words sunk in, he let loose a curse. "Are you serious?" He scrambled to his feet and went to the water's edge to get an uninterrupted view of the western sky. Orange and purple and pink greeted him, the sun a brilliant ball sinking lower by the second. His stomach turned.

How could he have fallen asleep for so long? "It's sunset," he said, his voice tense. "I'll not be needing to know the time to know we've missed the last train."

Ailish came to stand beside him, her unspoken question hovering between them: *What are we going to do now?* He scowled. She'd not like what he had to say. Their choices were few—and none of them good. "We'll have to wait for the morning train," he said.

"I thought as much. But what of tonight? I've no coin to let a room. Have you?"

Did he seem like the type of man who could afford to carry enough money to cover unplanned overnight stays? He resisted the urge to say as much aloud. It wasn't Ailish's fault they'd missed the train. "Spent everything I brought on the tickets."

The path around the lake was already deep in shadows, and he knew the trek out would not be easy once the woods was pitched into darkness. "Best we get on our way. Perhaps someone in town will take us in for the night," he said, not confident of that outcome. Not with such widespread distrust of the Irish.

"You think to convince me of the kindness of strangers?" Ailish asked as if he were lacking basic sense. "Are you dreaming still? What do you think will happen when two Irish arrive in

Concord in the dark, on foot, asking for someone to take them in *free of charge?*"

She inhaled sharply. "I promise we'll not be getting welcoming greetings and open doors from the fine people of Concord. Nay, what we'll be hearing is one bolt after another slamming into place as they secure their homes against us."

He stepped across the sand with no destination. She was right. Didn't matter where the Irish went, but lies about them always preceded their arrival. Was it too much to hope that the Oregon Territory was too far west and too desperate for settlers to care about his nationality?

Ailish followed him. Her stomach rumbled and she clasped her hands over her belly.

"We've food at least," he said more brightly than he felt. "I packed extra in case we were hungry on the train ride home." He returned to the edge of the pond, the last rays of the sun reflecting gold in the still water. They didn't have many choices.

In truth, they had none.

"I'll be thinking, perhaps we should stay here the night. Like Mr. Thoreau," he said.

"He had a cabin." Her expression was unreadable in the deepening shadows, but he knew for certain she wasn't smiling.

"Hear me out, lass."

"He had a hearth, too."

"I'll make us a fire." He took out his pocket knife and flipped open the blade. "I've spent many a night outside building the railroad. 'Tis not so bad. The forest sounds soothe you to sleep like a lullaby, and the light of the rising sun brings you awake slowly, like a mother's touch."

"A lover's touch?" she asked, shocked.

"*Mother's* touch. I said *mother's touch.*"

She didn't reply.

"You can have the blanket," he said. "I'll be fine in my coat."

She sighed. "Don't be foolish. If we have a fire..." She gave him a pointed look as if she didn't fully believe he'd be able to deliver fire, "...my cloak will be enough for me, as well. We can share the blanket."

She scrutinized the nearby woods and he followed her gaze into the thick patches of charcoal, purple, and black closing in around them. "Did you never worry about animals?" she asked.

"Nay. They're as afraid of us as we are of them."

"And...what of the sheerie?"

He blinked. The sheerie were all over Ireland, radiant faeries no larger than an infant whose greatest joy was to bring misfortune, even death, to humans. How was he to reassure Ailish about the sheerie when he didn't know himself? "There are no sheerie in America," he said firmly.

"How do ye know?

"Be reasonable. Don't ye think we'd hear their cries? So shrill they are, they'd be ringing in our ears."

"Have you a crucifix?" She reached out a hand.

"Nay, but Ailish—"

"If a water sheerie is about and determined to lead us astray, we'll be needing a means of protecting ourselves."

He let out a sigh. "My own grandmother told me if you haven't a crucifix, you need only put your coat on inside out and loudly recite the Lord's Prayer to scare them away."

"She told ye that, did she?"

"Aye. And I'll be trusting my Maimeó, blessings on her resting soul."

Ailish dipped her chin. "As will I then."

"Don't be worrying, lass. We'll be safe here tonight. We've food, some wine, and a blanket." He gave her a cheeky grin. "And you've me. I promise I'll keep you safe this night."

"I'll be holding you to it," she said softly.

Somewhere deep in his mind a thought tried to rise, a wish that his promise to keep her safe was for more than just this night. He stomped it down and went into the woods to gather kindling and weathered wood and find a rock to strike his knife blade against to create a spark.

CHAPTER TWENTY-SIX

THE FIRE HAD DIED TO EMBERS, ITS HEAT ALMOST GONE. SEAN shivered awake and listened to the sounds of the night; the quiet rustling on the forest floor, the chirp of crickets, the croak of frogs. An owl hooted, another answered, a whip-poor-will called again and again. He turned toward Ailish, only to find her no longer on the blanket beside him.

Pushing up on his elbows, he squinted into the murky night, lit only by a silver crescent moon and a star-encrusted sky. He saw her then at the water's edge, a gray shadow almost indiscernible in the shadows. He rolled to his feet and went to her.

"It's a new moon," she murmured as if she'd felt his presence before he got close.

"It's the middle of the night."

"The cold woke me." She gestured toward the moon, its crescent shape perfectly mirrored in the quiet surface of the pond. "See how it's just a slice of light? That's the moon beginning anew."

"A growing moon, I've heard it called," he said after a while.

"Means the same. After the full moon wanes, there's a day or two with no moon at all. Then it's born once more, arriving like a newborn babe, just a sliver of what it will become." She gestured upward with one hand. "Grows a bit each day until it's round and full—and then gone again. And on it goes."

He stepped closer, mesmerized by her words and the lilt caressing every syllable.

"All living things have a cycle, birth to death. But the moon..." Ailish shivered and crossed her arms against the cold. "Lucky she is to be reborn, a fresh start every month."

Sean retrieved the blanket and wrapped it around her shoulders, then went to nurture the fire, blowing gently on the embers, adding twigs and pinecones and larger pieces of weathered wood until the charred pieces flared and flames rose to devour the kindling.

"My grandmother always said the new moon is a time for new beginnings," Ailish said so quietly she might have been talking to herself. "Second chances. To plant seeds for a new future. I'd like to believe that. But I keep wondering...how many times can one person keep starting over?" Her voice ached with wistfulness.

He wished he had an answer.

The air smelled of smoke and dry leaves and pine needles and damp earth; the promise of life and death and change. Always change. He stepped away from the fire and lay his head back, let his gaze pass across the sky. The darkness stretched out, infinite it seemed. And yet it was not. For thousands of tiny shards of light punctured the blackness as if to show there were many paths forward through the night.

Anticipation fluttered through him, the prospect of change, a future unknown but waiting. Perhaps 'twas due to his thoughts of going to Oregon. Perhaps ’twas Ailish here beside him. Perhaps ‘twas the forest and the night and the talk of faeries and the sheerie and the new moon.

“Could it be you’re just looking at it wrong?” he asked. “Nothing ever stays the same, much as we wish it.” Shadows from the fire capered across nearby trees. “I think we’re often starting over, even when we don’t realize it.”

Not until she brushed a hand across her eyes did he realize she was weeping. He crossed the space between them and drew her into his arms. She leaned into him, rested her head on his chest, and he smoothed her hair and wished again that he knew what words to say.

“When I learned Liam was alive,” she said against his chest. “I was desperate, frightened I’d not be able to find him, afraid I’d lose him when I did. I swear, I didn’t set out to hurt your family. Sometimes I feel like the more I try to hold onto the memories and honor those who are gone, the more lost I become. Like I’m suffocating and can’t find my way to the air.” She fell silent, and the sounds of the night slid forward to fill the space. “God and Mary forgive me for asking such a thing, but how much of this life do I owe the dead?”

Her words shook free a memory he’d long contained...the day after Moira’s death, when his every inhale had seemed to press the air out of him instead of in, each breath so shallow he’d been driven to his knees gasping.

His heart began to pound. And as if she could hear its frantic beat, Ailish lifted her head from his chest and whispered, “Might it be that this new moon is for starting over?”

Neither of them moved. He could feel the heat of her filling him, stoking a want he had long denied. He brought a hand up to wipe the tears from her cheek, brushed his thumb across her lips and over her chin and down her throat. She shivered, and desire surged within him. It had been five years since Moira passed, five years since he'd been this close to a woman.

He traced the curve of her eyes and the arch of her brows, smoothed a palm gently over her hair, then cupped her face in his hands and lowered his head.

This was Moira and this was Ailish and this was all the dreams he'd suppressed for so many years.

He brushed his lips across hers, and she softened in his arms and kissed him back, leaned into him, her heartbeat melding with his. He pulled her closer and deepened the kiss. She tasted of wine and winter fading...and wayward impulses.

Her hands slid up his chest and around his neck, her fingers twined in his hair, each touch singeing him as though he were made of embers sparking to life. The blanket fell from her shoulders to the sand.

Moira, his mind murmured.

"Ailish," he whispered, putting the old memories away.

AT THE SOUND of her name on his lips, she pulled back, disquieted, eyes locked on his in the darkness. Cool night air filtered between them like a wall, a line not to be crossed. A warning it was, she knew. *Stay away,* the chill air whispered. *He is not meant for you.*

"I'll not be taking liberties, will I?" he asked.

Even with his face masked by shadows, she knew the choice was hers to make or not.

In that instant, the space between them felt less like a boundary and more like a void, forlorn and empty. And though the warning flared again like a torch, she set her misgivings aside, wanting only to recapture the feeling of belonging with him, the sense that at least one thing in the world was as simple as it always had been.

"I was a married woman. I'm no maid with my honor to protect." She picked up the blanket and went to spread it on the sand near the blazing fire, unclasped her cloak and let it fall to the ground.

Sean closed the space between them, his jacket open and then off. He drew her close, took her mouth with his and kissed her hard, lips slanting across hers until she had to come up for air—and even then she couldn't fill her lungs. For his tongue was teasing the lobe of her ear and searing a trail down the sensitive skin of her throat, and slowly, so slowly his hands were opening the front of her dress, his fingers skimming inside with each button undone to touch her over her chemise.

He eased her dress off her shoulders and down her arms, let it slide to the ground to pool at her feet. Then his hands followed its path along the arch of her spine, over the curve of her buttocks, each touch burning with heat, the chemise hardly more than a wisp of air between them. His fingers were on her belly, her waist, teasing her breasts until a whimper grew deep in her throat and escaped between barely parted lips.

He tugged his shirt loose from his waistband, then opened the buttons at the front of his trousers and slide his pants low on his hips and off. Her skin tingled, her breathing stumbled. He pulled his shirt over his head and he was suddenly naked, his desire obvious, the glow of the fire painting him with shades of gold and black as though he were not fully of this earth.

She reached for him, let her hands skim over the dark hair on his chest and the flat plan of his stomach as he drew her close, his calloused fingers kissing her soft skin, sliding beneath her shift to cup her buttocks, one hand stroking the inside of her thigh, fingers touching her so intimately she gasped out his name. He kissed her eyes, her jaw, her throat, as he inched her shift above her breasts, bent to circle their tips with his tongue, teasing every inch of her body to exquisite tightness. Then he stripped off her chemise and dropped it to the sand.

Mouths still joined, he eased her down to the blanket and she arched up to meet him, letting his body fill her with his heat, his need. Beneath the sliver of a new moon and its promise of new beginnings, beside the blazing fire wrapping them in a cocoon of warmth, he loved her then. One lost soul seeking solace with another.

And later, when their passion was spent and he'd drawn her back against his chest and wrapped them both in the blanket, she held onto his arm and let her tears fall quietly, dripping her regrets into the sand.

CHAPTER TWENTY-SEVEN

"Emma was here with the sunrise and she hasn't seen Sean yet either." Kathleen paced across Jack's study, unable to contain her concern. She spun back to face her husband at his desk, papers spread around him as he worked. "He couldn't have come home last night and left again so early. What if something happened to him? Set upon by a gang of thieves? I should have known that plan of his was foolish. To go to Concord and find the river from that book? What if he drowned? I should have spoken out against it instead of encouraging him to go."

"You couldn't have stopped him—and you probably shouldn't have. He's a grown man, Kathleen. Perhaps he stopped at the pub." Jack shrugged and lifted a brow. "And met someone."

She let out a snort. "I might grant you that if he were someone else. But ye'll be knowing as well as I, he's been trapped by his grief these past years. Might as well be living in a cave." She rested her hands on the desk and dropped her head.

Today was the last visitation for Will and Ailish before the final hearing.

And Sean was nowhere to be found.

"I'll just be wanting us to have done everything exactly as the judge ordered," she said. "Making no difficulties. I want him to know we abide by our word, we're honest people that he'd want to leave a child—" She broke off, her voice shaking.

Jack drew her onto his lap and curled her in his arms. She rested her head against his chest and tried to be comforted by the steady beat of his heart.

"Don't let your worry get ahead of you," he said, rubbing her back. "We've done everything the judge asked. Remember what your Ma's been saying all along..."

"*In the end, all will be as it was meant to be.*" She scraped a hand over her face and tried to ease the tightening beneath her breastbone. "That's all well and good as long as Sean is back in time for the last visit. But what if he isn't?"

"We've been told the judge is a fair man. I can't believe he would remove Will over one missed visit. Indeed, a fair man wouldn't want to take him away at all, not from loving parents and a stable home." He put his hands on her shoulders and looked into her face. "Do you honestly think Sean wouldn't move heaven and hell to be here for Will?"

She met his eyes, so dark they were almost black, eyes she'd once thought belonged to the devil—how wrong she had been—and felt the strength of his conviction. "You're right of course."

The entrance door slammed in the foyer. "And a grand good morning to you, too," Emma called.

"I'm starving," Sean answered jauntily.

"Apparently he wasn't set upon by brigands." Kathleen flung herself off Jack's lap.

"Go easy, Kathleen."

"Aye. First I'll hug him. Then I'll hang him."

"Fresh made bread in the oven," Emma was saying. "Here, let me have that basket."

Kathleen raced into the foyer and positioned herself in front of her brother so he couldn't move forward. She swallowed down her anger and calmly asked, "Are you all right?"

He eyed her warily. "Aye."

She popped her hands onto her hips. "Then where have you been? I've half lost me wits worrying over ye. Afraid you were hurt...and knowing today is your last meeting with Ailish—"

Sean held up a palm. "Slow down, Kathleen. You've let your imagination run wild. You knew I was going to Concord."

"Aye, yesterday that was. In case you haven't noticed, 'tis now the next morning."

"I missed the return train and had to stay the night."

"You missed the train?" She couldn't keep the surprise from her voice.

"Fell asleep by the pond where Mr. Thoreau lived. When I woke it was already—"

"I thought you went to see a river."

"Aye. But then I went to see a pond." He moved to one side and went around her, heading down the hallway as though the conversation was over.

She stared after him, eyes narrowed. He'd been rhapsodizing about Mr. Thoreau since arriving in Boston. Talked on and on about the man's lecture for days after attending it. And now, after returning from a visit to the man's home city, *and his special river*, he had nothing to say?

She followed him into the kitchen, stepping through the doorway just as he was thanking Emma for packing so much food for him yesterday. He took a biscuit from a plate on the counter. "You saved me from going hungry when I missed the train."

Emma removed two steaming loaves of bread from the oven.

"And how *was* Concord?" Kathleen leaned against the door frame, arms crossed over her chest. "And the river where Thoreau set off in his dory?"

"We actually didn't see the river because—"

"We?" The word shot out of her wrapped in surprise. Jesus, Mary, and Joseph, perhaps Jack was right—there was a woman. To be sure, it was more believable than him missing the train and sleeping on the shore of a pond. If it was true...oh, she hoped for his sake it was.

Sean blanched. "I—I didn't see the river."

"You said *we*."

He lifted one shoulder and rolled his eyes as if to warn her against reading something into nothing. "I'm more than a wee bit tired, for the night was long and plenty cold. As you might be guessing, I didn't sleep well."

So now he was trying to put her off from learning the truth? She'd known him for twenty-five years; without a doubt he was hiding something. Her gaze settled on the basket, tucked into a corner on the floor near Emma. Striding forward quickly so he couldn't stop her, she whipped open the lid. An empty bottle lay nestled in a blanket. Aha! She triumphantly lifted the bottle. "You drank this claret all by yourself?"

"What else was I to do once I missed the train?"

Emma's low chuckle wafted across the room on the scent of fresh baked bread.

"You drank it alone?" Kathleen pressed.

Sean cut a slice off one of the cooling loaves and slathered it with butter, purposely ignoring her.

Fine. She'd get at the truth one way or another. She closed

one eye and peered into the empty bottle, turned it round in her hands before setting it on the worktable. "Seanie," she said softly, taking a less combative approach, "have you met someone?"

He frowned.

"I wouldn't be upset. 'Twould be lovely news," she said. "Much as I loved Moira, nothing would make me happier than to know—"

"Enough, Kathleen. Be done with it. I went to Concord to see the places of Mr. Thoreau—"

"With a woman?"

He let out a sharp exhale. "If I answer that, will you stop pestering me?"

She nodded, beaming. In the midst of all the troubles with Will, a relationship for Sean was like seeing a dancing beacon of light. Ma would be beside herself with happiness. She twirled a hand at him to continue.

"All right, then, here's the truth. I was alone. Now, Kathleen, if you don't mind, I'll be catching a few winks of sleep before today's visitation." He went into the hall, letting the door bang shut behind him.

"The devil take my soul he was alone. He's not fooling me." Kathleen lifted the blanket from the basket, then let out a triumphant sound at the sight of two glasses nestled underneath. Grinning, she held them up to show Emma. "Met a woman, hasn't he?"

"If he has, he's not told me."

"No matter. He's met someone. I'm sure of it. I feared so long that he would buy himself a piece of land and hide away, buried beneath grief the rest of his life." She clinked the two glasses together as if a toast had been raised. "But today, Emma? Today is a fine, fine day."

CHAPTER TWENTY-EIGHT

LEADEN CLOUDS SCUTTLED PAST OVERHEAD, SOMBER GRAY PILLOWS plump with moisture, threatening to unleash a downpour but delivering only a smattering of drops on the back of a gusting wind. Ailish glanced upward. If they were lucky, they'd only get a little wet. And if they were unlucky...

She took Will's hand. "Sure and we're tempting fate being out here today."

"It isn't just today that we've tempted fate, lass," Sean said with a wink.

Her breath hitched. They'd not spoken about what transpired between them last night. Not a word on the chilly early morning walk from Walden Pond to the Concord railway station, nor on the train ride back to Boston. She'd tried to find a way to broach the subject but soon gave up. For how was she to tell him she'd begun the day thinking of him in one way, and by the time the sun rose this morning her feelings had changed, had grown? And what would it mean, what would she do, if he were to say he didn't feel the same?

She gave him a sidelong glance, but his eyes were fixed on the street ahead. When several minutes passed and he said nothing more, she suspected that he realized a discussion would be useless—they could talk for days about last evening and still the basic problem remained unchanged.

It didn't matter whether the faeries had meddled in their lives or if they'd made decisions of their own free will. It didn't matter if they'd been influenced by the power of the moon or they'd simply been caught up in the loneliness of their lives. None of it made a difference when they both knew, in the end, Ailish's goal was to take Will from Sean's sister.

No matter what happened with the judge, no matter how much last night had seemed like a chance for a new beginning, the truth was, taking Will would devastate Sean's family.

A gust of wind swirled around them sprinkling everything with droplets again. The scent of the sea lingered on the easterly breeze, and for an instant she was on a ship on the ocean, her face to America and hope, her back to Ireland and the death scourging its hillsides. She'd thought she was leaving pain behind, but she'd been wrong. It had followed her here.

She brushed back her hair, parts of it now damp from the dusting of rogue raindrops, and pulled up the hood of her cloak. She gestured at Sean's closed umbrella. "Are you planning to use that at all or is it just for appearances?"

He stopped suddenly and planted his feet, brandishing the umbrella like a broadsword. "Fear not," he said, "for I am bound by oath to protect you and the boy."

As if mocking him, the clouds unleashed a heavier round of drops, splattering the walk, the cobbled street, their heads and arms and shoulders and faces. Will squealed in delight and bounced up and down, arms raised skyward as if he were a magician calling down a deluge.

"Now might be a fine time for that protection," Ailish said, smiling.

Sean moved to open the umbrella and it stuck, closed. He struggled to force the mechanism to work, and failing, gave it an irritated shake. "Jaysus," he muttered as the rainfall intensified.

Will's eyes widened. "Jaysus!" he shouted at the top of his lungs. Jumping in circles, head back, hands high, he tried to catch fat drops of rain in his open mouth between shouts of, "Jaysus!"

"Will! Don't be taking the Lord's name." Ailish tried to maintain a stern expression, but a chuckle forced its way out. Any moment the sky was going to burst wide open, and they would be caught outside with a broken umbrella and a cursing two-and-a-half-year-old.

"Are you finding this funny?" Sean asked.

She pressed a fist to her quirking lips. "Perhaps we should find shelter before—"

The clouds opened with a vengeance, severing her words. Not rain, but hail. A barrage of pea-sized balls of ice hammered down like pebbles, hitting the street with a steady staccato and pinging on the metal rooftops. Will scooped a handful off the ground and hurled it into the air like kernels for the ducks.

"This way." Sean handed Ailish the umbrella, threw Will over his shoulder and took off running.

"I corn, Aish," the boy yelled. "Sack of corn."

Head down, one hand on top of her hood as if fingers spread wide would be enough to protect her, Ailish chased after them. Sean rounded a corner, charged into a building and set Will on his feet in the enclosed entry.

At the sight of the tall storefront windows, Ailish skidded to a stop. Her gaze shot to the store name gracing the top of the building, shouting like a town crier that this was the place for all those with money to find an assortment of goods from around the world: Chandler & Company.

Here? He wanted to wait out the weather here? The place where she was to begin working in only a few days? *The place where she'd lied about being engaged?*

If the manager spotted her and came over to talk, Sean could destroy her ruse in seconds. Faith, but she couldn't go inside, couldn't risk losing this job. She had to be employed or she'd not have a chance at the hearing tomorrow.

Though she knew she must seem mad standing out in the falling hail, she pretended to be distracted by a passing carriage. An instant later, she felt a firm hand on her arm. "Come inside," Sean said. "We can browse about until the weather lets up."

He tried to pull her forward and she set her feet, slipping on a smattering of tiny ice balls. "High-end clientele is who they're wanting here," she protested. "Not the likes of you and me."

The hail ended as quickly as it began, and then the rain started again, a steady downfall that turned the hail into a slushy mess. Will waved at her through the window in the door.

She grasped for a reason, any reason, to stay outside. "They'll not approve of us wandering the store with no intention of spending money."

"How will they know that?" Sean asked. "Maybe I'll buy something."

"I think there's an awning we can stand under..." She threw a glance back the way they'd just come.

"Ailish, we're here now."

She opened her mouth to protest again, her thoughts tumbling like branches in a flooded stream, one catching upon the next until they dammed up, stopping all progress.

"Explain to me out of the rain." He herded her into the entryway, one hand snaking out to prevent Will from sneaking past them through the open door. The boy let out a shriek of frustration as his uncle moved him to the far side of the entryway. "Be still with ye now," Sean commanded, voice countenancing no pushback. "For just one minute, stay put."

He turned his attention to Ailish. "The boy's not yet three, so I'll be understanding why he wants to be out in the rain. What's your excuse?"

She pushed off her hood, brushed the dampness off her shoulders, and tried to come up with a reply that didn't make her sound daft. The last thing she needed at the hearing tomorrow was questions about her mental stability.

Sean gave her a reassuring smile.

She flushed. Could she trust him with the truth? Should she? If only they'd talked about last night even a bit so she knew what he was feeling. She rubbed her hands together to warm them, the chill in her fingertips reminding her how easy it was to get hurt when one wasn't careful.

Nay, she couldn't risk telling him everything. But perhaps a piece of the truth would be enough to make him agree to take shelter elsewhere. "It's simple actually," she began. "I'm to start a job here...in a few days."

Surprise flitted over his face. "Here? You're going to work here?" His words were oddly tinged with both confusion and delight. "That's grand news."

"Left my other job," she said, hoping to fend off questions before he asked them. "So ye can be seeing why I'd rather not—"

Behind them, the glass-paned door leading to the sales floor opened and she broke off, waiting as two women came into the entryway, chatting loudly, each retrieving an umbrella from the stand before heading into the drenching rain. As the door whooshed quietly shut behind them, she finished her thought.

"I haven't even had my first day, so I'm afraid it might be awkward to go in now."

"I'd think they'd be glad to see you patronizing the store."

"Perhaps once I've started. Please, Sean, if you don't mind, I'd rather not."

He nodded. "Another time then," he said, though she knew his words were without meaning. The hearing was tomorrow and he would be heading west not long after. There would never be another time for the two of them.

"Will, lad, you get your wish," he said, pivoting. "We're going outside—" He turned a full circle. "Did he sneak out with those ladies?"

"Nay, I watched them leave. He must have slipped into the store when they came out."

"If Kathleen learns I've lost him she'll have my hide." Sean pulled open the door to the sales floor and charged inside, and disappearing down the nearest aisle, a forest of fabrics and ribbons and lace.

Ailish hesitated, conflicted. For God's bright sake, why did these things always happen to her? She thrust aside her fear of getting caught in her lies and followed him in.

CHAPTER TWENTY-NINE

HEAD DOWN TO HIDE HER FACE, AILISH HURRIED ACROSS THE store to the opposite wall and began her search in a row filled with elegant linens and damask napkins and doilies. Moving quickly, she peeked beneath displays, under shelves, and behind counters—anywhere a young boy might think an adventure lay. "Will," she called softly. "Will."

She didn't even want to think about the possibility that he had let himself out another door. Or that a stranger might have carried him away.

How could this have happened? How could she have let it happen? Even if they found Will after just a few minutes, even if Sean said they were equally at fault, she knew this episode would not sit well with the judge were he to learn of it.

Rushing past parasols and gloves and hosiery and into the ready-made apparel section, she tried to swallow her rising panic. He couldn't be gone. Children didn't just disappear.

She met up with Sean at the middle of the store. "I've been down every aisle from here to the wall," she said, gesturing.

"He must have gone outside." Sean shook his head in disbelief. "Where else could—"

A delighted screech and a round of giggles fluttered toward them from somewhere across the sales floor. "That's him," Ailish exclaimed, lifting the front of her skirt and running toward the sound, Sean right behind her. "It has to be." She'd never been so glad Will had such an exuberant spirit. Rounding the end of the aisle, she spotted him near the back of the store clutching the hand of the store manager.

Her steps slowed. *The devil take her soul, did it have to be the manager?* She sent up a prayer that he wouldn't recognize her. "Will," she called.

"Aish!" He pulled his hand free and ran toward her shouting, "I got present. For you." He opened his fist to reveal a length of turquoise ribbon crushed into a ball.

She crouched beside him to accept the gift and bring it against her heart, reveling in the joy of finding him and the love that threatened to overwhelm her. "It's beautiful, Will. Thank you."

Sean scooped the boy into his arms. "What were you thinking, lad, running off like that?" he admonished. "We thought you were lost forever."

"Not forever," Will chirped.

"He told one of the girls he was buying presents." The manager smiled. "She gave him that ribbon and brought him to my office. We were just setting out to find you."

"We only turned our backs a moment—"

"Miss Sullivan, isn't it?" he asked.

Her stomach dropped like a rock in a pond. "Aye. Hello." She could think of absolutely nothing to say.

"Is this the nephew you were telling me about?"

Heat crawled up her chest and prickled under her arms. God

help her if the man revealed any more of her interview in front of Sean. She nodded. "This is Will."

"Thank you for taking care of him," Sean said.

"Just part of the fine service we offer here." The manager grinned and stuck a hand out to Sean. "I assume you must be—"

"Sean Deacey," he said at the exact moment the manager said, "Miss Sullivan's betrothed. My congratulations to both of you. We're looking forward to having her on our staff."

Sean tipped his head slightly and looked at her, his expression unreadable. Clearly, it was time to escape this store before her whole world exploded. She patted Will on the back, her eyes steadfast on the manager. "If you'll excuse us," she said, "we must be getting on our way. Thank you again for helping with Will."

Outside, the rain had tapered to a sporadic drizzle, and the clouds were beginning to break. Will stomped into a puddle as though there were no more important task than splashing water in every direction.

"I wish the world was as simple as he sees it," she murmured.

The air hung heavy between them with things unsaid.

"Ailish, are you to wed?" Sean asked suddenly.

She could almost hear the other questions that lay beneath this one. Why had she never spoken of her upcoming nuptials? What had last night been about...her talk of new beginnings and starting over, their physical joining?

She kicked a foot into a puddle, watched the ripples travel outward over its surface. If only she could be honest, explain that she'd lost her other job, that she'd told a wee lie to get hired again. She wanted to tell him. He deserved to know the truth. But could she risk it?

Faith, but this was about more than just the two of them; it was about Will.

If she admitted she lied about being betrothed, she'd be handing the Montgomerys the very weapon that could destroy her chance of getting Will. They'd merely have to tell the store manager that she wasn't engaged and she would be fired before she'd even worked a day. She would go to the hearing with no means of supporting a child, and no income but the pittance she earned from mending.

She cleared her throat and cast her eyes downward. "I'm sorry, Sean, for not being honest from the start. 'Tis the real reason I didn't want to go into the store. I didn't want to risk you finding out about my betrothal and—"

"Jaysus, Ailish...what was last night?" A mirthless laugh slipped out of him, and her stomach wrenched.

"Does it matter?" She was beginning to despise herself. But she had no other choice. She'd be an idiot to share her secret and expect him to keep it. "You're moving so far away, across the country." She lifted her chin high, determined to seem fiercely independent. "And I'll be going the other direction. Back to Ireland, with Will or without, once the judge makes his decision."

She took hold of the boy's arm and tugged him out of the puddle. "Enough of that, Will, you're getting all wet."

"Ireland?" A bewildered look shot across Sean's face and he shoved a hand through his hair. "You just came across. Why would you be going back?"

"Things are not as bad as when you left."

Sean frowned. "Is that where he is? Your betrothed? Ailish, last night, I thought you and I..."

The anguish in his voice made her doubt herself. Perhaps she should tell him the truth. Perhaps she could trust him.

And if she was wrong? If he betrayed her confidence and exposed her lie to the manager, if she lost this job and thus, lost her chance at gaining custody of Liam, she would regret this decision the rest of her life. She couldn't lose sight of the fact that, no matter how much she might wish it otherwise, Sean's loyalty was to his sister and his family.

Last night had been an unforgivable mistake, and she needed to destroy any thoughts either of them had that it might have meant something more. Too many bridges had already been burned between his family and hers.

And she had been the one lighting the fires.

"I should not have—we should not have..." She tried to form a coherent argument. "With the hearing ahead, neither of us were thinking straight. I should have been knowing when I woke in the night, 'twas the faeries doing. Sowing confusion is what the Good People are known for." She felt ill. "Best it would be if we put it behind us. Accept that it happened because we were bewitched."

Will pounded on Sean's leg. "My feets wet," he said, reaching both hands upward.

Sean pointed at a nearby puddle and gave the boy a nudge. "There's a big one you missed." He turned back to Ailish. "Bewitched? Perhaps I was. But not by the faeries." He watched Will stomping in the puddle. "Do you love this other man?"

Her heart crumbled. How could it be that she had found everything she ever wanted—and not be able to have it? Surely, Sean wouldn't betray her. Surely. But if she was wrong...

She drew a slow breath and resisted the urge to confess the truth. "I did love him. I still do," she said with a steady voice. "Besides, all of this—" She waved a hand between them. "'Tis pointless to even consider. Tomorrow everything will change for your family. Or mine. And sure as the sun will rise in the morn, no matter which way the decision goes, there will not be a place for either of us on the other side."

~

He'd put Moira aside last night. Though he'd buried her five years ago, last evening he'd finally let her rest.

In the slowly darkening dusk, day melting into night, Sean sat on the outside steps and dropped his head into his hands. A long-buried ache rose in his newly unbound heart. He'd peeled off the wrappings, bandages laid down over years, made room to move forward with someone else. And she was promised to another.

He was a fool. How had he thought there could be something between them when the truth was, they weren't friends, not really. They were soldiers in a war, engaged in an uneasy truce, and Will was the spoils that would go to the victor.

He heard the door open, looked up as Kathleen sat beside him on the steps.

"What will ye be doing out here?" she asked. "Worrying about tomorrow like the rest of us?"

He lifted one shoulder in a shrug. He didn't want to tell Kathleen all that he'd learned from Ailish this day, had been putting it off, trying to convince himself there was no benefit to her and Jack knowing.

But it wasn't his place to make such choices for them. They had a right to know if for no other reason than to be prepared should the judge rule against them.

"Ailish has found work," he said simply. "At Chandler and Company. And she's to wed—so there will soon be a man in her household. I tell you only because it means neither point will make an effective argument with the judge any longer."

"You know this for certain?"

"Aye. The store manager confirmed both points when we went inside to get out of the rain."

Kathleen blinked several times, then began to stand. "I should tell Jack—"

"There's more, Kathleen. She's going back to Ireland." He clasped his hands together and rested his elbows on his knees. Amidst the climbing shadows, memories of Walden Pond rose in his mind like a flock of birds taking flight.

Kathleen sank to the stoop again. "But she only just came across. And Ireland is still struggling."

"Her betrothed is there. When I think back to other things she's said, I should have realized it before. Many's the time she lamented being here."

"There's no future in Ireland," Kathleen said bitterly, and Sean knew that even after five years his sister longed for her home country as much as he did.

"Even still, some go back."

"And if she gets Will? She'll take him to live in a country destroyed, bound by laws that keep him forever under the English heel?"

He wished he didn't have to be the bearer of such news. "So she says."

"I've tried, Seanie, to be understanding of how it must feel to be her. To have lost everyone. To know that you have but one blood relation left." She balled her hands into fists in her lap. "But the path of understanding should stretch both ways. Has she ever expressed a word of caring, a wee bit of compassion for how it feels to be the parents who might lose their son?"

Her words pierced like a well-placed knife between the ribs. So intent he'd been on befriending Ailish...and then friendship had evolved into attraction and he'd been so caught up in his own feelings... "There were moments, glimpses of caring..."

Kathleen let out an almost inaudible keen. "If she prevails tomorrow, what will leaving this country do for Will? Why would she think it good for such a young boy to be ripped away from the only family he's known with nary a glance backward." She gripped Sean's arm. "Could she really do that?"

Despite all the time he'd spent with Ailish, he had no answer. All he knew was that last night she'd joined with him, had spoken of new beginnings and the future—and all the while she'd been betrothed to another.

He suspected that someone who could do all that would have little care for a young boy's heart—or his family left behind. But though his suspicion weighed heavy on him, he kept the thought to himself, for there was nothing to be gained by voicing it to Kathleen.

"She can't win," he said. "The judge doesn't want her to win. Why else would he have ordered these visitations?" He put an arm around his sister's shoulders and hoped with his entire being that he was right.

CHAPTER THIRTY

KATHLEEN BRUSHED DAMP PALMS OVER THE FRONT OF HER PLAIN gray dress, smoothing wrinkles that didn't exist. Today was the final hearing, the day the judge would decide whether she and Jack got to keep Will. She swallowed hard and faced her husband. "How do I look?" she asked, a slight tremor in her voice betraying the terror she was trying to control.

There was such tenderness in his eyes. "Like a woman who loves her son very much."

A half sob escaped her. "I'm so afraid, Jack." She tried to tamp down her spiking panic, the fear coiling around her. "If the judge takes Will from us, I'm not strong enough. I can't—"

"Yes, you are. You're the strongest person I know." He crossed the room and wrapped her in his arms, crushed her close as if to draw her pain onto himself. "We'll make it through this. The three of us—you, me, and Will—together we'll survive this." He pushed her gently back. "It's time to go."

She drew her fingers across her burning eyes.

"Mam! Mam!" Will charged into the room with all the energy

of a toddler and wrapped himself around her legs, clinging as though he hadn't seen her in days rather than minutes. "Play with me!"

He had to be reacting to the tension in the house this morning, though he knew not what it was about. She picked him up and kissed one cheek and then the other, over and again as he giggled. "How's my favorite boy this fine day?" she asked, wishing the only thing she had to do at that moment was sit on the floor and play with him.

Jack wrapped his arms around both of them at once, and Kathleen softened into him. If only his embrace was all they needed to remain a family. If only the hearing was already past. If only the judge had already ruled in their favor and they knew they would be keeping Will. If only...

Will twisted sideways and reached for his father, wiggling until Kathleen handed him over. "Papa, let's play fighting," he said as Jack curved around him. "Not hugs, Papa. Fight."

"Always war," Kathleen admonished, but her words were gentle and her chest tight with love.

"I'll take him down to Emma." Jack set him on his feet and they headed for the door, Will's small hand clasped within his large one, the little boy galloping and jumping and chattering about his soldiers.

She bit her lip to keep from breaking down, to prevent panicked words from spilling out of her mouth and frightening her son. But when Jack and Will stepped into the hall, when their exit suddenly seemed like an omen portending a permanent exodus, her pulse began to drum a rhythm in her ears so loud she could hear nothing except her own voice calling out, "Jack...?"

He turned, his expression so grim she wanted to weep for

what this was doing to him. They had yearned for a child so long, and Will had been such a gift, an answer to their prayers.

I'm so afraid, her mind whispered, but she kept the words locked in her throat.

As though knowing her thoughts, Jack came back into the room, cupped her face in his hands and kissed her hard. He smiled against her mouth, then pulled back to grin at her with complete and utter confidence. *Grinned.* Her heart swelled, her lips curving upward in response.

"Have faith in the judge's wisdom," he said. "Have faith that he will recognize the best thing for Will is to remain with our family."

THE WALLS of the courtroom seemed closer than they had at the first hearing, more confining. Kathleen followed Jack to the front row and took a seat beside their attorney. Turning slightly, she nodded at Sean and her parents, seated in the row directly behind her. Da reached forward to place a supportive hand on her shoulder, and though she appreciated his intentions, it did nothing to allay her fear.

Across the aisle, Ailish sat beside her attorney, simply dressed in a dark skirt and white blouse, her hair tied back with a pale turquoise ribbon.

Kathleen wanted to hate her.

But she couldn't, not if she was honest with herself. It wasn't hard to understand why Ailish had come forward, not hard to know the pain of all she'd lost. Faith, but if their places were reversed, Kathleen knew without a doubt that she would overturn heaven and hell for Will.

At the front of the room, the judge sat quietly behind the raised desk, his eyes locked on some distant spot above their heads. Only when he dropped his chin and put his hands together, did Kathleen realize he was praying. Her heart pulsed in her throat. Was it guidance that he was seeking? Did he not know what to do?

He raised his head, his expression almost mournful. "We are here today to determine who should raise the boy born as Liam Clark, now known as Will Montgomery."

Kathleen gripped Jack's hand.

"I'll begin with a question for the lawyers," the judge said, addressing the two men sitting across the aisle from one another, almost mirror images in their white shirts and dark suits. "Has the boy been taken on the visitations with his aunt that I ordered?"

Both lawyers answered in the affirmative.

The judge leafed through some papers, stopped to read for a minute, then raised his head. "Miss Sullivan, after spending the last month getting to know the boy, I first need to ask...do you still desire custody of him?"

"Yes, your honor," Ailish said.

"Since you are the child's next of kin, I must also ask, will you give consent for the boy to be legally adopted by Mr. and Mrs. Montgomery?"

"No, your honor."

Though Kathleen had not expected a different reply, Ailish's answer landed like a blow to the stomach.

"And are you aware of all that it takes to raise a child?" the judge asked.

Ailish hesitated. "I was married in Ireland. My husband died before we had any children. But I am well acquainted with caring for children because I helped my sister in the years before they left for America. I promised I would care for her boys if ever she could not." Her voice had a rough edge, as if she'd not slept long the night before. "I know what it is to love a child. I understand what it takes to raise one."

Kathleen looked at her fingers, entwined with Jack's. The two of them up against one of her, fighting over one wee boy. *There could be no solution today that would make them all happy.* One family would leave here in pain. And neither family would ever forget.

The judge set his mouth. Time seemed to tick past in long minutes, though she knew it was likely only a series of seconds.

"I believe you have the best of intentions, Miss Sullivan," he said. "But it's been brought to my attention that you may no longer have a job with which to support the boy. Is this true?"

Ailish started. She turned to her attorney, then back to the front of the courtroom. "It's true, sir, that I...left my previous job. But tomorrow I begin a better position at Chandler and Company, the dry goods store. I also intend to keep taking in mending for extra funds."

"I have affirmation from Chandler's that Miss Sullivan is to start tomorrow." Her attorney went forward to deliver a letter to the bench.

As the judge scanned the sheet, Ailish slid to the front of her chair. "He is my sister's son," she said as if the point needed repeating. "I will do whatever I must to ensure he has what he needs, that he has a good life."

The judge turned to Kathleen and Jack's lawyer. "Is the chaperone in attendance?"

Kathleen's chin jerked up. What could he want with Sean?

"Aye." Her brother raised a hand and stood.

"I understand you accompanied Miss Sullivan and the boy on the visitations. Is that correct?"

"Aye. All of them."

"Can you tell me briefly, how the visits went?"

Kathleen shifted so she could see Sean better.

"Most of the time we went to the park—"

The judge shook his head. "No. What I'm asking is, how did things go between Miss Sullivan and the boy?"

"Sorry." Sean dipped his head, embarrassed. "It was harder in the beginning. She wanted to call him *Liam,* and he was having none of it. It took a couple of visits, but in time, they got to know one another." His gaze darted toward Ailish. "They became...friends. He calls her Aish."

"And you?" the judge asked. "Did you also get to know her?"

"Me?" Sean's cheeks flared red.

"Yes." The judge sounded irritated. "You've accompanied Miss Sullivan and the boy on eight visitations. Surely you got to know her in some way."

"Of course." Sean clasped his hands behind his back.

"You must have drawn some conclusions about her yourself. I realize you're a member of the Montgomery family, but I'd like to know your honest thoughts about Miss Sullivan's ability to raise this child. About her character."

Their lawyer had given no indication Sean would be called upon to answer questions about the visitations, let alone to vouch for Ailish's character. It hardly made sense, with him being on the opposite side of this battle. Kathleen caught his eye, and he gave a nearly imperceptible shake of the head as though to say he was just as puzzled as she.

Sean loosed a breath. "I found Miss Sullivan to be a...fine person," he said in a low voice. "Very pleasant."

"What about her ability to raise the boy?"

Sean took hold of the pew in front of him. "He's her nephew," he said so quietly Kathleen almost couldn't make out his words.

"Speak up, please," the judge said.

"Will is her nephew. Why wouldn't she have the ability to raise him?" His voice cracked. "But my sister, Kathleen Montgomery, is the mam he knows and loves. She's already raising him—"

"I'm asking about Miss Sullivan," the judge snapped.

"She hasn't known him but four weeks, your honor," Jack interjected, leaning forward. Their lawyer took hold of his arm as if to caution him. "We've known him more than two years." Though his voice was strong and steady, Kathleen could hear an underpinning of pain.

The judge smacked his gavel on the table, a crack so sharp it rang in the room like a single peal of a church bell after a funeral. He ordered Sean to sit.

"The Massachusetts adoption law passed in May of last year is quite clear in its requirements," he began, his tone strained. "As the judge presiding over the proposed adoption of William Montgomery, also known as Liam Clark, I am required to make several determinations, all of which involve ascertaining what is best for the welfare of the child." He leafed through his papers, stacking them neatly before continuing.

"I find that, despite Miss Sullivan's lower social standing compared to that of Mr. and Mrs. Montgomery, both parties have sufficient ability to raise the boy." He paused. "Next, the law requires that the natural parents—or next of kin if the parents are deceased—must agree to give the child up for adoption." His eyes flicked to Ailish. "In this case, the next of kin, Miss Sullivan, has declined to give that consent."

Kathleen's eyes drifted to a window along the wall, to a view of the building next door, its bricks laid in straight lines, one upon the next upon the next. What was the message of such precision, such perfection? Do everything right, and you may build something that will never fail. *Until it does.* She forced her attention to the front of the room, to the man who held her son's future in his hands.

"Finally, the law requires me to determine if it is fit and proper for the adoption to take place," the judge said. He placed his palm on the stack of papers as though the answer lay within those sheets.

Jack's fingers tightened around Kathleen's.

"I wish every child could be as blessed as this one has been," the judge continued, "with so many who love him and want to give him a home. What a world that would be." He stopped and drew a breath. "That said, the law must guide my decision. The state passed the adoption statute, the first of its kind in this great nation, to protect children. Based on the tenets of that law, based on Miss Sullivan's decision not to consent to the adoption, I have no choice but to award custody of William Montgomery, Liam Clark, to Ailish Sullivan."

A gasp went up across the courtroom, punctuated with exclamations of disbelief. Kathleen collapsed against Jack. She could hardly hear over the roar in her ears.

"Your honor." Their lawyer stood. "Surely you can't believe it best for this child to be removed from the home he's known for more than two years."

The judge leveled a stern expression on the man. "Nor do I think it best to deny him from knowing—and being raised by—his only living relative. We have a law—"

"That says you must do what is best for the welfare of the child," their lawyer protested.

The judge held up his index finger. "The law first says the child belongs with its next of kin. Only if that living situation is detrimental, can I legally remove the child." His mouth tightened. "The transfer of the child should occur as soon as possible, preferably today. I leave it to the lawyers to work out the details." He banged the gavel on his desk and brought his eyes to rest on Kathleen and Jack.

"Mr. and Mrs. Montgomery, I offer my deepest apologies. I wish there were a better solution. Young Will was lucky to have you for the time that he did." He pinched the bridge of his nose and closed his eyes. "This is perhaps a poor time to raise the subject, but...when you are ready, there are many worthy children in The Home for Little Wanderers. Some have been abandoned, others are orphans. Last year, a train carried thirty Boston orphans to New Hampshire and Vermont to find homes. *There are other children in need.*"

Kathleen's eyes flooded with tears; her chest ached as if her heart had physically broken. Did he think that one child was interchangeable with the next? That as long as you had one, you'd not miss any others you might have lost?

"You're right," Jack said in a rough voice. Arm around Kathleen's waist, he helped her to her feet. "It's not the time to speak of this."

CHAPTER THIRTY-ONE

KATHLEEN STOOD ON THE LANDING HALFWAY DOWN THE STAIRS, gazing out the window at the empty street below, a satchel of Will's clothing clutched in her arms as if the tightness of her grasp could prevent the rest of this nightmare from unfolding.

An hour ago, she and Jack had told their son he would be going to live with Ailish. They had smiled and tried to make the change sound like something wonderful, even called it an a-venture, but it had taken every ounce of Kathleen's self-control not to weep in front of him. Especially when he wrongly assumed that she and Jack would also be going to Ailish's—and asked if Ailish could come to sleep at their house sometimes, too.

He hadn't understood what they were telling him.

They hadn't actually expected him to.

She could hear Will showing his tin soldiers to everyone in the parlor—Ma and Da, Sean and Nora and Rory, the lawyer and his assistant—and explaining that some soldiers were privates or maybe colonels, but the most important one was the general because, "*He has a horse*."

A knot lodged in her throat.

After the hearing, everyone had agreed that the physical exchange would best be handled by the lawyers, instead of forcing Kathleen and Jack to hand Will to Ailish. Their attorney had arrived a few minutes ago to collect Will and his belongings so he could deliver both to Ailish's attorney, who would then take Will to Ailish.

Like he was a purchase from a store, she thought. A frantic sob escaped her. How could this be happening? Why hadn't they listened to Jack's grandfather when he said to take Will and run as far away as they could get?

She lay her palm against the glass of the window and remembered the day, years past, when she had stood at this spot praying for a sign about whether her life was meant to be with Danny or with Jack.

"I'll not be needing a sign this time," she murmured, blinking away the tears cresting in her eyes. "Dear God, I'll be needing a miracle. Just a small one, the size of a wee boy." She squeezed the satchel to her chest as if it were her son and clenched her teeth to keep herself from weeping.

Jack came down the stairs with a second bag of Will's things and stopped beside her. She saw the dampness on his cheekbones and reached up to wipe it away. "How can we be doing this?" she asked as he shook his head.

"What will happen when he wakes in the night from a bad dream? Or when he gets so determined about what he wants and angry because nothing else will do? What will happen when he throws his food on the floor or says words he shouldn't be saying?" she whispered fiercely. Her face contorted as she fought to contain her agony "What will happen when it comes time to go to school, when he makes new friends, and meets a lass and falls in love and weds, when his wife bears his child and we aren't there for any—"

Jack pressed a hand to her mouth. "Shhh, Kathleen. Don't. Don't think of it."

"Will he forget us?"

He closed his eyes a moment. "I'm sure he won't."

"But what—"

"Kathleen, stop. It's not your heart alone that's breaking. I wanted to be the father to Will my father never was to me. And now he's to have a stranger for a father—or perhaps none at all."

At a creak on the stair, both turned. Ma came up to the landing, each step slow, one hand gripping the rail as if her legs might give out without the support. "The lawyer is asking after you." She eyed the two satchels. "Is this everything now?"

"As long as we don't go down, he's still our son," Kathleen whispered.

Ma's mouth twisted as she fought back her grief. "Och, lass, he'll always be your son, no matter what. In this life and the next."

Tears burned at the back of Kathleen's eyes and she blinked them away, determined that Will would not see her weep and realize this wasn't an a-venture after all.

"I'm so sorry, Kathleen. There is no cure for the pain but to go through it," Ma said, her voice shuddering. "You must be going down now. For there's no hope of getting to the other side if you don't begin the journey."

Jack took both satchels and started down the stairs. The women followed, leaning into one another all the way to the foyer, each step searing the memory into Kathleen's soul. Within minutes, Will's soldiers and blocks had been stuffed into one of the satchels, and he'd been bundled into his coat. Their lawyer motioned his assistant out the front door. "Take your time," he said to the family. "We'll wait outside."

"Going on a-venture," Will announced as the door closed behind them.

"That you are," Ma said in a voice falsely bright. She picked him up and kissed both his cheeks. "My sweet lad, I'll be loving you always." Her voice quavered. "The days on this earth seem slow, but in the passing of time, they're but a wink. We'll see you again in a wink, my sweetest boy."

Tomás took him from Ma, then Nora took him from Tomás, and he was passed around the room like that, each making him giggle over some silly thing, and kissing and hugging him as they moved him along. Da reached for him and roughly cleared his throat. "You be a good lad. Be well and safe," he said.

"Too much hugs," Will protested. He squirmed until Da set him on his feet, and they all laughed too loud and too hard, their mirth quickly silenced by tears of despair trailing down their cheeks like they were standing beneath a drizzling Irish sky.

"She'll have her hands full, she will," Ma said.

Sean knelt beside Will. "I'll be betting Ailish will take you to see the ducks. So I got you some corn." He tucked a small bag into the satchel, then pulled Will into his arms and raised his eyes to Kathleen's. "I'm sorry."

She knelt on the floor beside them. "My precious boy," she said, unable to still the shaking of her voice, "don't ever be forgetting how much I love you. More than a thousand ants, I do." She swept him close and tried to memorize the feel of him in her arms.

Will stretched away, giggling. "Mam. Too much hugs."

Jack swooped him up. "One more hug," he said in a rough voice. "A big hug for Papa. I love you, Will."

"Can you tell Papa?" Kathleen could hardly get the words

out, her eyes on her husband, on the muscles working in his jaw and the blinking of his eyes. "Tell Papa, too."

Will threw his arms around Jack's neck. "Love you Papa. A thousand ants."

~

WILL WAS GONE. Had been gone for nearly three hours already. Sean sat in the parlor across from Jack, each with a glass of whiskey in hand, a half-empty decanter in front of them. Neither spoke. Even if he'd wanted to, Sean could think of nothing to say. Ma and Da had gone home with the older children not long ago, leaving the house entombed in a silence broken only by the sound of Kathleen's footsteps as she wandered from room to room.

Some irrational side of Sean kept hoping that Will would jump out from a hiding place and surprise them, and Ailish would step forward to admit the whole thing had been mistake.

And then he'd remind himself he was thinking of Ailish as the woman he wanted her to be, not the woman she was. How had he failed to notice the difference?

It felt like poison had seeped into his veins, his blood black with bitterness. The grief in the family was so heavy, it was almost as if Will had died. Worse perhaps than death it was, for at least death brought a natural end. Losing Will to Ailish denied them that.

Kathleen stopped in the doorway, and Jack set a hand on the sofa next to him. "Come sit."

She didn't move, disconsolate.

He held up his glass and said, "What butter and whiskey won't cure there's no cure for."

"I can't believe you remember that," she said softly.

"I was already in love with you, though I wouldn't have admitted it then, even to myself."

The look that passed between them was so tender, Sean dropped his gaze to his glass, turned it in his hands, then took a drink and emptied his mind of Ailish. Jack poured a whiskey for Kathleen and though she took a swallow, grimacing at the burn of it, still she didn't sit.

"If I don't keep moving, my thoughts race all the worse," she said. "I can't seem to stop my mind from chasing round and round, like a dog after its own tail, the same words repeating themselves over and over: *She'll be taking him to Ireland and we'll never see him again.*"

She paced into the foyer and back. "I know things are a little better in Ireland, but the famine isn't over." She gulped the whiskey too fast and let out a cough. "Sean, might she just be talking? Could it be she's doing what we all do, say that we're going home someday though in our hearts we know it won't ever happen."

"It seemed like she more homesick, missing Ireland worse," he said, shaking his head. "Said it often. When we went to Concord, she—"

"Concord?" Kathleen shot out. "I thought you went alone."

Sean felt the color drain from his face. How could he be so stupid? Between the pain and the despair and the disbelief—*and the whiskey*—he wasn't thinking straight. He refilled his glass and held a silent debate in his mind. Should he admit the truth? Lie? Would it make a difference? With Ailish planning to return to Ireland, would it matter? *Did anything anymore?*

"Sean?" she pressed.

"Aye," he said finally. "Ailish went to Concord with me."

"Sean..." Jack set his glass on the table, incredulous.

Kathleen strode toward Sean, glass held high as if she were

going to throw the contents in his face. She stopped and lowered her arm. "I can hardly believe this. You spent time with her on a day you didn't have to?"

And then her eyes widened as if all the pieces suddenly snapped into place. "Ailish is the woman I was so happy you were seeing? Ailish?" Her voice rose with each word. "Jesus, Mary, and Joseph, Sean, you spent the night with Ailish?"

"In the woods. We missed the train and had no—"

"She wanted to take our child," Kathleen spat. "In the end, she did exactly that. Why would you be spending extra time with her?"

He stared dumbly, no answer to give. Why had he done it? Why had he pursued a woman he could never have? "We became friends," he said. "We both liked Thoreau's writings—" His mind whispered a passage from the book: *My friend shall forever be my friend, and reflect a ray of God to me.*

"Don't be playing with me now, Sean. How could she know about Mr. Thoreau? She just came out of Ireland. People in America don't even know of the man."

"I told her of him."

Kathleen's mouth set in a hard line. "Of course ye did."

"I'm sorry." Sean rubbed his temple. "It was just one day. I was trying to befriend her like we all talked about. If she and I were friends, maybe it might make her...stop." He let his head fall back against the chair. "That's all it was. One day. It meant nothing."

"God help ye if it did."

His chest constricted, his breath suddenly shallow with the lie.

One day. And one night. And a memory he'd never be able to extinguish even if he wanted to. After believing he'd never care for anyone again, he'd lost his heart to a woman he'd known all along he could never have. Unbidden, the rest of the passage from Thoreau's book slipped into his mind: *as I love nature, as I love singing birds, and flowing rivers, and morning, and evening, and summer, I love thee, my friend.*

He downed his whiskey and refilled his glass.

THE FLAT SEEMED SMALLER than it ever had before. Shabbier. Dingier. Ailish took the satchels from her lawyer and nudged Will over the threshold. "My thanks to you, sir, for all you did to help me," she said. "I'm sure my late sister, *God's blessings on her soul*, is grateful as well."

"Is this him?" Meg hurried to the door and knelt so she was at eye level with Will. "Welcome, young Will. It's good to have you here with us."

Ailish shut the door and set a hand on Will's shoulder. "Will, this is Meg. She has four children, so just be thinking of all the fun you'll have here."

He eyed Meg silently and his lower lip quivered.

"'Twill be like having brothers and sisters," Meg said in a singsong voice, though her downturned lips betrayed her concern.

"Where's Mam?" Will demanded.

"I'll not be certain he quite understands what's happening." Ailish set the satchels aside and lifted Will into her arms, giving him a couple of cheerful bounces. "Let's go see your new bedroom."

She carried him down the hall to a narrow room with a straw-filled mattress on the floor in a corner, a worn quilt stretched smooth on the top. Though it was nothing like he was used to, children seldom noticed such things. "That's your new bed," she chirped. "It's my bed, too. Not everyone is so lucky as we are to have such a nice place to sleep." She set him on his feet and patted the mattress. "If ever you have a bad dream and wake in the night, I'll be right there with you."

Will ran solemn eyes around the nearly empty room, over the bed, the floor, the walls, the door, the ceiling. It struck Ailish again how barren the space was compared to the Montgomery home. He'd had a bed and room of his own, a thick comforter, a carpet on the floor.

How was she to compete with all of that?

But she didn't have to. Not anymore. Will belonged to her. Money and possessions weren't what made a family, and shame on her for giving such a thought entry into her mind. "Come, Will, let's get out your soldiers and show them to Meg."

CHAPTER THIRTY-TWO

EXHAUSTION, AIDED BY A DOSE OF LAUDANUM, HAD SENT Kathleen into a deep, dreamless slumber the first night without Will. The second night, even laudanum wasn't enough to keep her unconscious. She startled awake, uneasy, in the darkest hours, her senses wobbly. What had she heard? Was Will up? She slipped groggily out of bed, blinking to clear her vision as she crossed the gloomy hall to Will's room.

He'd been having such vivid dreams lately, almost nightmares they were. She hoped that wasn't the case tonight. Perhaps he'd just kicked off his blankets. Such a wild sleeper he could be. Maybe all this thrashing in the night, these frightening dreams, were because he was growing.

She bent over the bed in the darkness and reached out a searching hand. "Hush, my sweet boy. Mam's here." She touched the pillow and patted the blankets, feeling about the bed for him, expecting to find him curled near the foot as she so often did. "Will?" Her sleep-sodden brain surged awake. "*Will?*"

All the memories of the past few days burst forward with the speed and devastation of a gunshot. She braced both hands on the edge of the bed and drew a series of quick breaths. A low moan escaped her. Will was gone. She must have dreamt that he cried out for her.

Was it not enough that the loss of him plagued her daylight hours, but now her nights were haunted as well? Was this how it would be the rest of her life? She bowed her head and brought her hands together, but her soul was empty of petitions. The law had spoken. Her son was gone. And no amount of prayer would bring him back.

She slid beneath the quilt on the bed, wrapped her arms around her son's pillow and wept.

AILISH CLIMBED the stairs to the third floor, her legs so tired from standing all day it took effort to lift them step after step. Three days she'd had Liam, and her long work hours meant she'd barely seen him in all that time. She stopped outside the flat, leaned a shoulder against the wall and rubbed the back of her neck with both hands. Faith, but the smell in this hallway was surely bad enough to kill rodents. How had it come to be that after a lifetime in the fresh air and open hillsides of Ireland she was living like this?

She plastered a pleasant expression on her face to mask the fatigue of another twelve-hour workday, steeled her resolve not to crack beneath Will's unrelenting anger, and went inside. Meg's four children were chasing about the room, giggling and roughhousing, jostling Ailish as they tumbled over one another. Meg stepped in from the kitchen and wiped her hands on her apron.

"Enough with all the noise, now," she admonished. "Quiet down, all of you."

Ailish glanced around. "Where's Will-Liam?" She'd begun calling the boy by both names so he would get used to hearing Liam. Gradually, she planned to use Will less and less, hoping that if she didn't force the name overmuch, the transition to Liam would be easy.

"He's asleep," one of the children shouted.

"Aye, and that's why you should be keeping quiet," Meg said, irritation underlining her words. "Else you will all be going to bed right now."

"How was today?" Ailish asked hesitantly. "Did it go any better?"

"Let me ponder that a bit." Meg pulled two wooden chairs close together and dropped down onto one. "Ah yes, now I recall. He threw his dinner all around the room, screamed about wanting his Mam and Papa, and wouldn't stop hitting and pinching the others. So I put him in the corner and when that did naught, I put him in bed hoping it might calm him down. He cried himself to sleep."

"Another fit?" Ailish sank into the chair next to Meg. It must have been bad if he'd worn himself out.

"'Twas his third today, this last one worst of all. I know it was late and he was weary by then, but he's getting worse, Ailish."

"I think he's testing us," she answered, grasping for an explanation that didn't lay blame on her taking him from the Montgomerys. "I'm no stranger to him. We've had fun together this past month. Sooner or later he'll come to accept that he lives here now."

Meg scowled. "But he hardly knows me, Ailish, and I'm the one he spends his days with. I know you love the boy, but—"

"I promised my sister." Surely Meg could understand.

Though her husband saw little of his own children because of the long hours he worked, no one would ever expect he should give them up because of it. "I'm the only relation Liam has left. I owe it to him."

Meg pursed her lips. "You owe him something, that's true. But it would do you well to consider what exactly that is. He's having tantrums in the day, nightmares at night—"

Ailish waved a hand to cut her off. She had no energy to be entertaining Meg's doubts. No interest in them either for that matter. Though each day had become a battleground, she was confident Will would adjust in time. "He's mine now," she said. "I fought for him and won. My sister would be glad. Other children have lost their families, become orphans. In time, they come to accept the change in their lives. He will too."

KATHLEEN PASSED the open door to Will's room, then took a step back. Jack stood beside the bed, hands clasped around something, shoulders hunched with grief.

Her heart wrenched, and she stepped into the room and wrapped her arms around him from behind, leaned her head against his back and wished for an end to their torment.

Rain slashed against the window, and the spring wind rattled the pane as if to say the peace they sought would not be easily found. Jack turned and opened his hands to show her what he held; a blue-uniformed tin soldier lay on his palm, musket at the ready.

She touched the soldier with one finger as though it were something miraculous and fragile. "Where did you find it?"

"I didn't," he said in a rough voice, his face as bleak as the day outside. "I kept it. Slipped it into my pocket when we packed his toys in the satchel. I wanted to remember...to never forget..."

"The wars?" Her throat tightened.

The corners of his eyes crinkled. "All the battles he won with the General in charge."

A strangled sob slipped out of her. "Sometimes I thought if there was no war by the time he grew up, he might want to start one." She took the soldier reverently into her hands as though touching it might connect her with her son. "And then I'd remember him insisting we rescue the worms after the rain and bring them to the dirt, and I knew his heart would be too big to wage real war."

"I shouldn't have kept it," Jack said. "I've been thinking about him lining up his men and discovering one blue-coated soldier missing, all because I wanted—"

"He won't even notice," she insisted, though she knew he would.

"I just want him to be happy," Jack said so quietly she almost didn't hear him.

She nodded and brought the soldier to her chest above her heart. "One soldier won't be making a difference to him. I'm sure it won't. But to us...I'll thank you for keeping it. This wee link to him might make these next months a bit more bearable."

"There's something I want to talk to you about." His words were almost lost beneath the clatter of rain on the window.

She ran a finger over the toy soldier, memories flooding over her as heavily as the water was running down the pane. "Not some other bad news, is there?"

"No. I've been talking to Sean." His eyes met hers, then he glanced away. "My grandfather is gone. Will is gone. This room...his bed...there are so many memories. Too many, I've come to think."

"What are you saying?"

He took the soldier from her, turned it over in his hands as though carefully choosing his next words. "What this house meant to me, to us, is gone. There's nothing holding us here, Kathleen. Nothing that truly matters."

"Why would you say that?" She'd never heard him speak like this. "My family is here. Ma and Da—"

"A poor choice of words. It's not what I meant. Sean tells me your parents may be going with him to the Oregon Territory."

Her mind reeled. "I thought they'd put that idea aside. Da's not said a word of it since that first night. And Ma? What does she say?"

"She's leaving the decision to your da."

Afraid of where the conversation was headed, Kathleen dropped her head back to avoid Jack's eyes. A crack stretched across one corner of the ceiling forming a shape Will had once declared to be a duck's bill. The devil take her, even the cracks held memories. "When did you learn this?"

"Sean told me last night, after you retired. It seems he and your Da have been talking of it all along."

"And no one saw fit to tell us?" The air almost crackled with her anger.

"They thought we had enough to think about with Will and the hearing."

Kathleen huffed. "Because we'd be less upset learning it *after* losing Will? A week before Sean is to leave? A week before they're all leaving it seems?" She threw both hands in the air. "Were they planning to say anything at all or just disappear one day? My whole family, just gone?"

"Be fair, Kathleen. No one was trying to hide it. They were waiting until after the hearing. None expected the judge to award Will to Ailish." He set the soldier on the bureau, a lonely plaything in a room empty of joy, and rubbed his fingertips across the faint dust on the smooth surface.

"I've been giving a lot of thought to this past year," he said. "It's not been a good one for us—not yet anyway. My grandfather passed on. Our son will soon to be back in Ireland. The Know Nothing party is growing strong on a platform of hatred of immigrants, especially the Irish..."

It struck her then how much he was still the whaling captain he'd once been, a man who had rescued her from the ocean, his shoulders broad, his jaw strong, his countenance determined, his dark eyes filled with compassion. The sharp edges of her anger began to soften.

Jack lifted both hands palm up. "Kathleen, what's holding us here? Perhaps we should consider going as well."

She took a step back, and another, horrified. *What was holding them here?* He shouldn't even need to ask that. *Leave?* How could he be suggesting such a thing, let alone speak it aloud? Grief must be making him senseless.

"Start fresh somewhere far away," he was saying. "Raise the other children we'll have—for Kathleen, I'm sure we'll have them. Begin again someplace where we won't be reminded every minute of every day that we once had little boy named Will." His voice cracked, and her heart began to shatter anew.

She let his words reverberated around her as she groped for a response. "Leave Boston?" she finally asked.

"Yes. Either we spend our days thinking we see Will 'round every corner and in every crowd, or we start over somewhere else. Make fresh memories in a new place."

"We could never close this house up by next week," she protested. "And your business. What of your business?"

"I'll start over on the west coast."

How could he be thinking like this?

She went to the window and pressed her forehead to the pane, let her gaze linger on the street below, at the people going about their day, hurrying to get out of the rain, unaware that within this home lightning had struck and fractured their lives. So many memories were here, embedded in the walls and the floor and the air around them. People didn't just pack up and leave in the span of a few days. *Like they did in Ireland.*

Aye, she'd done that already, she didn't wish to be doing it again.

"Would you want to get land too?" she asked as though she were seriously considering the proposition. Which she wasn't.

"It only makes sense."

"And become a farmer?" she asked, incredulous.

"I'd have Sean farm it. And your da." He frowned and ran a hand over his jaw. "If they're giving away land in the Territory, we'd be foolish not to take it."

She lowered herself into the wooden rocking chair near the bed, ran her hands over its glossy armrests. "So many nights when Will was cutting teeth, I rocked him in this chair. And when he had nightmares..." Her eyes teared. "In this very spot, I soothed him back to sleep." She pushed off with her feet and slowly rocked back and forth, back and forth. "So many memories you're asking me to leave behind. I don't think I can do it. I'm sorry, Jack. Not yet. Not so soon."

AILISH WALKED through the cemetery in Cohasset, her eyes on Liam as he ran in and out between the gravestones and trees, slapping each one and calling out a number—any number, not in sequence—as if keeping some sort of count. Only God knew what an almost three-year-old kept count of in a cemetery. She didn't want to ask, lest she send him into one of his tantrums.

The tranquility of the place helped calm her mind. It had been a relief these past days to know the hearing was over and Liam was hers for good...but despite her elation over the outcome, it had been so very trying. Again and again he'd asked —demanded—to see his Mam and Papa, and she'd had to explain over and over that he lived with Ailish now and couldn't see them anymore. The exchange inevitably led to an outburst. He'd had so many this week, she'd lost count. And once his temper flared, not even his soldiers could mollify him.

All along she'd believed it best to make a clean break with the Montgomerys, especially since she intended to take Liam back to Ireland. But sometimes when the boy was in the midst of temper, a part of her wondered if perhaps it might help for him to visit with Jack and Kathleen a time or two.

And truth be told, she missed Sean. After a month of twice-weekly visitations, after the time they'd spent together in Concord, she was finding it hard to accept that she would never see him again, never laugh with him again, never—

She sucked in a breath, appalled at her own weakness. "How can you be missing him?" she chided herself. "So many fish in the ocean, how is it you'll be wanting the only one you can never have?"

For God's bright sake, if things had been going better with Liam, she wouldn't even be thinking of Sean. She knew what the problem was. The long hours she spent at the store meant Will spent most of each day with Meg and her children, people he never known before. Even the two half-days she got off each week left little time for her and Liam to get used to one another.

She stopped on the bank overlooking the shore. In front of her, the ocean sparkled sapphire and emerald, stretching all the way to the horizon beneath a clear blue sky. At her feet, a light surf unfurled to darken the sand of the beach, each gentle wave adorned with a cap of white like dabs of frosting on a cake.

She could hardly reconcile the serenity of this scene with the image she held of the day her sister died...the heavy gray cloud cover, the furious wind, the violent seas.

"If you haven't yet noticed, sister, we won. I've got Liam," she said into the breeze. "Your own son. Five days already I've been raising him." Her mind returned to the life they'd had in Ireland, when their family was together. "Don't you worry. I'll make sure he grows up knowing of you. And his brothers and his da and all of our—"

"Angels! Heaven!" Liam shouted, running toward her. "Found angels!"

She grinned at his excitement. "Angels? Show me, Will-Liam."

He pulled her across the cemetery to a large sandstone marker topped with a sculpted angel kneeling in prayer. It was the resting place of a child, a lass who passed on when she was nearly two years old.

She set a palm against the white stone. Why was it that no matter what the country, there were always children dying long before they should? She felt a flush of sympathy for the girl's parents, a wave of the pain they must have felt over losing her. *Like Jack and Kathleen Montgomery must be feeling now.*

She shoved away the thought and crouched down to draw Liam into her arms. He twisted away and pointed to another nearby marker, also adorned by a large angel. "Heaven. It heaven," he cried, dancing impatiently from foot to foot.

"Aye, she's in heaven."

He patted his chest. "I in heaven."

"Nay, not you." She stood and brushed a hand over the

headstone. "*She's* in heaven," she said about the dead child, realizing none of this would make sense to him. How was she to explain death to such a young child? How much could he possibly understand?

"Mam's baby died. Papa say...he went with angels." Will drew a long inhale as if sharing the information had been an effort.

Her breath hitched. Talking he was, of Kathleen's last miscarriage. She let her eyes roam over the angel standing guard on the child's grave. "That's right, he went to heaven."

"Couldn't see Mam or Papa."

"Aye," she said in a gentle voice. "But now he sees other children...in heaven. And the angels. He sees the angels."

"Granddad went to heaven."

"Grandparents do that sometimes." Though this wasn't what she would have chosen to talk with him about, she was relieved to be getting on with him so well.

"I want to see Granddad." Will stared up at her.

"I know, sweetheart. But Granddad is dead. You can't see him."

"He with angels."

"Aye." She nodded.

"I with angels. Want to see Granddad."

"Will-Liam, you're not in heaven."

His face reddened and he stomped a foot. "I am!" He pointed at the angel.

"Nay, you're not," She knelt and reached for him. "It's a statue. Stone—"

"Want to see Mam's baby," he cried, swinging his arms wildly. He smacked a hand against her head. "Want to see Granddad." He swung at her again and she caught his wrist before the blow landed.

"No hitting," she snapped. "This is a cemetery, not heaven."

Her gaze swept over the rows of gravestones, so many sleeping dead longing for life, while her nephew seemed suddenly to be obsessed with embracing death. She had a fleeting wish for the chance to ask Sean what to do, how to handle this moment. He had such a way with the boy, and she seemed to be failing at every turn.

Will's lower lip puffed out, quivering. "Mam's baby not see Mam or Papa." His words tumbled out of him. Tears streaked down his reddened cheeks.

"Because they're dead." Ailish glanced at the ocean. Perhaps distraction would work since he wasn't yet in a full outburst. "Shall we go down to the beach and take off our shoes?"

Liam's stance was wide in defiance, his eyes narrowed. "Granddad not see Mam or Papa. I not see Mam or Papa."

Her heart stilled. Nay, he couldn't be thinking...

He raised both arms up toward the angel kneeling on the gravestone. "I with angels. I dead too."

"It's not a real angel, Will-Liam," she said, her patience fraying. She stood and patted the angel's wing. "It's stone. You're not dead. You're not in heaven. Come to the beach now." She took hold of his arm and tried to pull him away, but he fought back, screeching, swatting at her with his free hand and kicking at her legs until she finally let go.

Granddad!" he wailed, running back and forth between the markers as the carved angels smiled beatifically down. "Granddad, where are you?"

Ailish put a hand to her mouth in horror. Had she done this? Had she made Liam think he was dead because he couldn't see his parents? He wasn't even three yet. Holy Mary in heaven, was she harming this child?

She banished the thought as soon as it came to her. He was her nephew; how could she possibly be hurting him? "Will-

Liam, you're not dead!" she said quickly as if to convince him before he could react. "You're not in heaven. Granddad's not here. The baby's not here. You're alive with me. And I love you." She tried to draw him close to reassure him—to reassure herself—but he wrenched out of her arms and threw himself to the ground.

"Want to see Granddad," he said though great gulping sobs. "My Granddad. Please Aish, please I see Granddad."

CHAPTER THIRTY-THREE

Five days. Will had been gone just five days and already it felt like a lifetime. Kathleen heard the door to the Irish Relief Society open, but she didn't look up from the clothes she was folding. Let someone else help this customer; she had nothing left to give.

Slow footsteps moved in her direction across the wooden planks of the sales floor, and though she wasn't in the mood to be helpful, she put a pleasant expression on her face and lifted her head.

Ma? "Ma, what are you doing here?" she asked.

"Och, Kathleen, sorry I am to be bothering you here of all places, but I've been working round the clock and I wanted to talk—"

"About you and Da going west with Sean?" she asked in a bland voice, though barely-contained fury roiled her stomach. She had finally gotten over Sean lying to her about going to Concord with Ailish. And now this.

"You know already? I wanted to tell you myself."

"I can't believe you're doing this, Ma." Kathleen crossed her arms. "Will has been gone but days. And already you're making plans to leave."

Ma's face fell. "I know it hurts. Feels like a betrayal, don't you think I know? I'm sorry it's happening so fast. Your da and I have talked it over and over. If we don't do this now, we'll likely never have the chance again. I wish it could be different, for us to have more time..."

But what about me? Kathleen wanted to cry as though she were young again and in need of consoling. *If you're gone, who will carry me?* She glanced around to make sure no one was near enough to overhear them. "This is not the place to be having such a discussion."

"Aye. But I've had no time off to visit you at home and I knew it could wait no longer."

Kathleen began to refold and straighten stacks of trousers on a nearby table. "Seems to me you're all being quite...impulsive," she said petulantly, unwilling to give her mother even an inch.

Ma helped her fold. "'Tis not impulse, but urgency that drives this. Whether we'd had months to decide or only days, we would have chosen the same. I know you're hurting, Kathleen. Losing a child is..." Her forehead creased and her eyes glistened. "None should ever have to go through it." She blinked several times. "We will carry Will in our hearts every day of our lives. Every day."

Despite her determination to hang onto her anger, Kathleen felt the pressure in her chest yield. Ma and Da's first child had not been Sean, but another wee boy who died in his sleep at only three months. They marked his birthday still.

Ma cleared her throat. "We could wait a year to go, but who's to say there'll be land left to get by then? *Ní fhanann trá le fear mall.* An ebb tide does not wait for a slow man." She folded a pair of boy's trousers, set them on the stack, and folded another.

"We've always had so little, Kathleen, despite how hard your da works. Knocked about by fate we've been, more often than others who have so much more. I'll not be complaining, just stating fact. Your da and I had but one day to decide whether to leave Ireland. Just as you did when Sean returned from Newfoundland and found Ireland in famine."

A woman came up holding a men's shirt. "Have you any larger shirts in this fabric?" she asked.

"Over here." As Kathleen led her to a nearby table, she motioned with one hand for Ma to go into the back room.

Everything was happening so fast. If they could only gain some time to pause, to consider, to reflect, to breathe. But nay, Sean's departure in a week made everything urgent. The wagon trains leaving in May made everything urgent. The snow in the mountains made everything urgent. She was sick to death of the word *urgent.*

She joined Ma in the back room, picking the conversation up without missing a beat. "Leaving Ireland was not the same as this. Then it was a choice of living or dying," she said.

Ma put a hand on Kathleen's arm and reached out with her other to draw Kathleen's head near hers. "One can live and still die, lass. Never will I forget saying goodbye to you that morning in Ireland, knowing I'd likely never see you again. Then next sending Sean across and thinking the same."

Kathleen's tears broke loose and she sank into her mother's arms.

"Your Da works fourteen hours every day in that factory. I'm working nearly the same as a domestic. Two children still at home we have...and never enough money. If we stay in Boston, our only future will be to fall ever further behind. Starting fresh somewhere else is a chance to reclaim hope."

Kathleen pulled away and swiped a frustrated hand across her eyes. "How many times have Jack and I offered to help? And yet you always refuse."

"Not being able to take care of your own, it's another kind of death. A slow one. Especially for your da. Grateful we've been that you were kind enough to offer, but don't be discounting pride, lass."

Kathleen felt her anger seep away, her arguments crushed by the truth in Ma's words. "Will you be leaving when Sean does?"

"Aye. We've both given notice on our jobs. Your Da told the landlord we'll be going." Ma's voice was so tranquil she might have been saying that she and Da were going to take a stroll because the weather was so lovely.

"And Tomás and Nora? They'll not be minding?" Kathleen couldn't help but remember how long it had taken her youngest siblings to adjust to city life in Boston.

"They're excited for a life better than what we've found here. A chance to leave the slums."

"And Rory? Does he know?" Kathleen asked, her desperation rising.

"I've posted a letter to him up in Lawrence. Old enough he is to get land of his own, so I'll not be surprised if he joins us. Especially with how dangerous his job is."

Kathleen pretended to study the floor. Aye, Rory would not miss the chance to own land and leave that godforsaken machine shop behind. He was twenty now, a man grown. As soon as he got Ma's letter, he'd be here. They were going, all of them.

"Jack wants to go, too." She wondered if there was something wrong with her because she had no desire to leave. "Wants to pick up and move as though the life we have here doesn't matter."

"It's not that, lass. I think he fears it would be impossible for the two of you to begin anew if you stay." A line appeared between Ma's brows. "I know how hard it is to face such a decision when your heart is raw. But sometimes the starting over is easier once you accept that the fight is done."

"Don't be preaching to me, Ma, trying to force me on this," Kathleen snapped. She felt as though the air was being squeezed from her lungs. "Not after the loss of me son. You're asking me to forget him—"

"Nay."

Kathleen waved her hands between them to stop Ma from saying more. "You're asking me to leave the very place where he came into our lives, where he grew from infant to child. Nearly kills me, it does, to think of another family living in our house—in Will's room—covering up our memories with their own."

Voice shaking, she strode out to the sales floor. "You can be telling the rest of them—Jack, too, if you want—I'll not be going. Shame on you all for trying to push such a thing on me."

SHOULDERS HUNCHED, hands jammed deep into his pockets, Sean headed home along the empty night street. Gas flames flickered above him in the street lamps, his path lit by their soft yellow glow. There was a time he would have thought the scene charming, romantic. But no longer.

He'd spent the evening with Ma and Da, going over the details and costs for the upcoming journey—first, from Boston to Missouri; and next, from Missouri to the Oregon Territory. They'd reviewed the list of the supplies they would need to purchase once they reached Independence—a covered wagon, oxen to pull it, provisions enough for the four-month journey, warm clothing. They'd hashed over the amount of money they had between them and discussed ways to make it stretch further.

But no matter how much he threw himself into the planning, he couldn't shake the guilt he felt over Ma and Da deciding to come along. It hung over him, heavy, this fear that leaving Kathleen and Jack behind with their memories and no family for support was straight-out abandonment.

He should have tried harder to convince Ailish to withdraw her petition for custody of Will. Should have pressured her more. "Instead, you played both sides of the coin," he muttered to himself in disgust, "pretending everything would somehow work out and no one would get hurt."

What had he thought would happen once he'd spent the night with Ailish?

He came to a sudden halt and dropped his head back as if an answer would be scrawled across the night sky. *What in the devil's name had he thought would happen? That she would suddenly decide she didn't want Will, and instead wanted...Sean*?

Nay, not that, he insisted to himself, but the truth hit like a blow to the chest.

Overhead, a half-moon dipped in and out from behind scattered, fast-moving clouds, and the stars twirled like dancers on a darkened stage taking one curtain call after another.

If new moons portended new beginnings, what was prophesied when the orb was half bright and half dark? Uncertain beginnings and harsh endings? He let out a bitter laugh.

He'd never expected the judge to remove Will from Kathleen and Jack's home. Never thought Ailish would actually take him if she won. Never considered she might go back to Ireland.

Never expected to fall in love.

Love? He wasn't in love, there wasn't even a chance he could fall in love. Not with the woman who'd torn apart his sister's family.

Nay, he'd never love her.

He clenched his jaw as if biting down on the thought to finish it off.

The moon disappeared behind another cloud and he waited for it to return. But the clouds, moving even faster now, piled up upon one another until not just the moon but all the stars had gone missing.

KATHLEEN SAT on the edge of the bed in her nightclothes and watched Jack, bent over the newspaper at the round table in their bedroom, reading to the light of an oil lamp, a tumbler of whiskey in hand. A question kept repeating itself in her mind: how could he think they could leave this place?

Intent on reading, he didn't notice her gaze, nor the frown that creased her forehead as she remembered the night he'd brought her to his home when she'd had nowhere else to go; the day, months later, when he'd asked her to become his wife; the moment, years later, when he'd taken Will into his arms and embraced the orphaned babe as his own.

In a shadowed corner, Will's small rocking chair sat abandoned.

For as long as she'd known Jack, he'd rarely made impulsive decisions. Even those that might seem so at first, were usually grounded in serious deliberation. So the fact that he now wanted to uproot their lives in the span of a week meant, perhaps, she owed him another hearing, a second discussion about leaving.

"These past days I've been thinking," she began, "about what you talked to me about."

He lifted his head and surprise flitted across his face. She swallowed hard. "It's not an easy proposition you've laid before me," she said. "Five years ago, I had to decide whether to cross the ocean, to leave behind my country, everything I knew, everyone I loved. Making that choice about tore my heart out."

She tightened the belt on her wrapper and slid into a chair beside him. "Now I find that my family is leaving *me* behind—and I am forced to make a choice again. Only this time, it seems my heart will be torn apart whether I go or stay."

"Kathleen..."

She held up a palm to stop him as she gathered her thoughts. The light in the oil lamp flickered, casting shadows across his face, and she was once again reminded of those days on the ocean, the dark stubble on his jaw, a lock of unruly hair falling onto his forehead. So many plans they'd made since then, so many paths they'd traveled together.

"I can hardly think of leaving this house and its memories," she said. "And yet, with Will gone, with all my family leaving..." *What was it she wanted? What did she want besides her son back?*

Blinking back tears, she crossed the room, more uncertain about her answer than she'd ever been. "How can we be leaving Will behind?" she whispered.

Jack was at her side in an instant, his body encircling her. She leaned into the safety of his nearness, the protection of his arms. He stroked her hair and kissed her head, and for a fleeting minute she let herself pretend that everything was as it had been before, that Ailish had never come into their lives, that Will was in his bedroom sleeping and at the first light of dawn would burst into their room screaming like a banshee—a happy one.

An ache was always with her now, jagged edges that pierced with agonizing swiftness if she let herself think too long about what had happened. "More than once now I've called his name aloud, pretending to myself he was just in the other room though I knew that he wasn't. I just wanted to...I miss him so much." The despair in her own voice frightened her.

She felt a shudder run through Jack, a rare expression of his grief. "Sometimes I forget he's gone," he admitted, his voice hoarse. "Yesterday, I saw a rabbit outside the window. Only after I turned to beckon Will, did I remember I no longer had a son."

His words landed like arrows in the place she kept locked tight, the dark hollow in her soul where her disappointment lay, her guilt over not being able to give her husband a child.

"We should have fought harder to keep him," she whispered, struggling to fend off the accusations of failure assailing her from every corner of her mind. "Should have run like your grandfather told us to do."

"You know we could never have done that."

An ember sparked inside her. *Truly?* Knowing what was to happen, would he not wish to go back and make different choices? The spark flared, and her thoughts came at her from every direction, like hungry crows swooping in to pick clean a cornfield.

She should have insisted they leave. Should have stood up for Will and their family.

"Don't be speaking for me." She hit him in the chest with both hands to push herself away, fury spreading through her like a flame licking along a branch. "Perhaps you couldn't have left with Will. But I could have."

Jack gave her a sympathetic smile, enraging her. She jammed

both hands against him again, harder this time, embracing the fierceness of her actions, the power of them. "I could have," she snarled. Her world felt out of control, tilting and wild.

"We should have taken him to California." Her hands were fisted, her blood burning, her breath rapid. "We'd be together...happy...but for you always having to do the right thing. 'Tis your fault. Yours. Your fault we have no child." She pounded her fists against his chest and he did nothing to stop her. "You did this to us. You did this, you did, you did, you did," she cried, welcoming the pain in her hands with each blow.

And then she broke along with her heart, uncontrollably sobbing, gulping for air, hanging on him as though her knees would fold without him there. God save her, what was she saying? Jack had given her a life filled with love, and she was blaming him without reason.

"I'm sorry," she murmured against his chest, her tears wetting the front of his robe. "I'm sorry, I'm sorry," she whispered, her apologies as much to the son she no longer had, as they were to her husband. "It isn't true what I said. I couldn't have stolen Will away from here any more than you. 'Tis not your fault we lost him. 'Tis not your fault I cannot bring a child to term."

"What? Hush, Kathleen," he murmured. "Do you think I blame you for the loss of our babes? Never. I never have. I never would. We know so little in this world. Who is to say what causes one child to be born perfect, another to be malformed, and another not to make it to birth at all?" He wiped her cheek with the sleeve of his robe, the fabric soft as the palm of child's hand. "Believe me on this, Kathleen, I've never blamed you. Do not blame yourself."

His heart beat steady and strong against her cheek, like that of a steadfast soldier in the face of adversity. "And what of us?" she asked in a strangled voice. "Will made us a family."

He bent his head to press his mouth to hers, to nuzzle his lips over her eyes and cheeks, along her throat. "Ah, Kathleen. We're a family, you and me. If the two of us are the only family God sees fit to bless us with, I will be grateful every day that he sent you to me." The catch in his voice drew a fresh round of tears to her eyes. "What we have, nothing can harm," he whispered. "I won't let it."

"But a child—"

"Not a child, not the lack of one, or the loss of one, will harm us. It's not your fault we don't have a child. I will love you until the day we leave this earth, children or not." His voice dropped low. "And I will love you all the days after that, though you and I will be part of them in spirit only."

Deep in that hollow where her dreams had gone to die and guilt stoked a bitter flame, she felt an easing of her pain, a surrendering...forgiveness. As though the scab that kept her failures and self-blame contained had finally healed enough that she could stretch the wound and not have it hurt.

Will was gone, all her babies were gone, she had done everything she could to keep them, and yet life, as it should, was demanding that she go on.

"I love you," Jack said.

"And I you," she whispered. "Always you." She undid the tie on his robe, slid her hands up the dark hair of his chest, felt his muscles tighten beneath her touch. Pushing up on her toes, she pressed her mouth to his, teased him with her lips and tongue, her kiss an apology, a declaration of hope, a demand for their future together.

He pulled her close, hands skimming down to cup her buttocks and mold her against the length of him. She felt his need, as urgent as her own. His tongue stroked a trail of heat over her throat as he tugged open her wrapper and shoved it off her shoulders.

A cool draft skimmed over her and was quickly replaced by the warmth of his fingers tracing the curves of her breasts, making circles, smaller and smaller, sending fire to her core. A whimper escaped her.

"I love you," he murmured against her breast as he skimmed the tip with his tongue, drew it into his mouth and lingered there until she was gasping. He blew gently upon the moistened skin, then kissed his way to her other breast, his rough jaw and gentle mouth rousing every nerve to a restless edge. His hand stroked softly along the inside of her thigh, his thumb brushing over her, teasing, circling, insistent, his touch searing, driving her higher, breathless, until she broke beneath waves of sensation, and the world and all its troubles burned away.

He lifted her into his arms and kissed her hard on the mouth as he lay her across the bed. "I love—"

"You," she finished and reached for him, their bodies melding in love and shared grief.

CHAPTER THIRTY-FOUR

THE ROOM WAS DARK SAVE FOR A SLIVER OF LIGHT FROM THE barely open door, just bright enough to illuminate Liam's soldiers scattered about the room, still lying where he'd flung them in a fit of temper. Ailish sat on the floor beside the straw mattress where the boy slept and wrapped her arms around her bent knees.

Such a sweet child when he wasn't angry. And once he got past his anger, all was forgiven. But his outbursts were getting longer and more frequent, and she didn't know what to do.

Yesterday he'd cried and raged at the cemetery in Cohasset until he almost made himself sick. Wept on the train ride home. Had been unmanageable once they got here. No matter how she tried to reason with him, he remained convinced that he was dead.

Because in his mind, only death would keep him from seeing his parents.

Too young he was to understand what death actually was, its

finality, its agonizing permanence. She ran a hand over his hair, still damp with sweat from the tantrum.

Surely, if she just held out long enough, eventually the two of them would turn a corner and things would get better. He would forget his other life.

But would he? *Had she forgotten the life she used to have*?

If she let herself look at life through his eyes, it wasn't hard to see why this felt like death to him. It was the end of everything he'd known before, the absence of everyone he loved.

Remorse chastened her. On hands and knees, she began to gather his toy soldiers and line them along the baseboard, one row of red and one row of blue, both generals on horseback at the front, prepared for action when Liam awoke.

He would adjust, she knew he would. He was young and children were so...adaptable. If she waited him out, in time he would forget all of this. He would forget Kathleen and Jack, just as he'd forgotten his real parents. Eventually, he would come to see Ailish as the only mother he'd ever had.

She just had to be patient for a few weeks, perhaps a month. Or two. No longer than a year, surely, though the child had a stubborn streak worse than his brothers.

She set up the final soldier and frowned. There was one less blue than red. Faith, but the boy would be beyond destitute once he discovered the loss. She searched the room without success, then took one of the red soldiers and hid it beneath the mattress so he wouldn't notice the discrepancy before she'd been able to find the missing man.

Better to hide the problem than experience another tantrum like he'd had today. Out of control he'd been, begging for his parents and grandfather. Though she'd tried to keep her feelings in check, his grief had devastated her. She knew what it was to long for the people she loved. Fate had foisted that agony upon her.

And now she had foisted it upon Liam.

The thought landed so hard, she lifted her head and whispered, "No." But conviction was lacking in her heart.

She had forced this pain upon Liam not because she wanted to save him—he'd needed no saving from the Montgomery home—but because she wanted to ease the grip of grief on her own life. She wanted a family again.

Her thoughts spooled back over the past years—so many heartbreaking events she thought she'd never be happy again. And then came the miracle of learning Liam was alive. For the longest time, she believed that finding him was a sign she was meant to have him. She'd imagined their lives together, pictured telling him of the family he had lost so he would grow to love them as much as she did.

She'd been so intent on what she wanted, she'd never let herself consider what it would be like for Liam to lose the life he knew, to start all over. She'd let herself believe that a month of visitations would make the transition easy.

Sure as the moon appeared each day, she'd been a fool.

Liam's chest rose and fell, soft and steady in the tranquil rhythm of slumber, all the troubles of daytime replaced by pleasant dreams. He seemed so peaceful, it was almost possible to convince herself he would awaken happy to be here with her, not a care for his previous life.

But she full well knew that what appeared to be placid slumber was merely rebellious exhaustion.

If she waited long enough, someday it might be different. Someday his sleep might be serene. Someday. *After she'd put him through hell on earth first.*

She brushed her hands over her face. A month now she'd

known him. Almost a week she'd had him. Six days. She loved him now as much as the day he was born, when she'd promised her sister she would always take care of him.

Yet she knew her sister would have been impressed by the Montgomery's lovely home. She would have been pleased that her son was growing up in such comfort and with opportunities for schooling and life only afforded to the upper classes. Aye, she would have noticed all that.

But what her sister would have seen first—and cared about most of all—was that her son was loved, that he had a mam and da who adored him.

For it was hard to miss; it was exactly what Ailish had seen from the very first day.

Her shoulders sagged with weariness. Who was she serving by taking Liam away from the Montgomerys? She tucked the blanket around him, brushed a soft hand over his hair. He sighed in his sleep.

"I tried to do right by you, I did," she murmured, tears closing her throat. "Only now I'll be thinking I might have been wrong all along."

She'd been running toward this child as if he was the balm that would heal her wounds. But she'd laid her own misery upon him—a child—and had devastated his life just so she could feel complete again.

How had she become so selfish...and cruel?

She thought of Sean, on his way to Missouri by now. He'd lost two children. His wife. Yet he was making a new life for himself.

She could do the same. Not in the Oregon Territory, surely, but here in this country she could start over.

But first she had to set right the things she had torn apart.

Which meant she had to talk to the lawyer. Nay, better the judge. Get this to the decision-maker as quickly as possible.

Liam rolled in his sleep, thrashing enough to kick loose his blanket. "Aish," he murmured. "Aish."

Her gut twisted. "I'm right here, Li-" She swallowed hard. "I'm right here, Will. Right here." She drew the blanket over him.

Someday when he was older, he would want to know about his early life, and as all children are wont to do at some point, he would ask, "*Tell me about the day I was born.*" She prayed he would be told about the mam who had birthed him, about the da who had kept him alive in a satchel. And if she were to ask God for one wee favor, 'twould be that Will would also learn of the aintín who loved him so much, she gave him up.

KATHLEEN LAY in Jack's arms, content. She sent her gaze across the ceiling and down the wall, to the hearth where a low fire burned, past the tall draped windows facing the street. This room was nicer than some, certainly not as nice as others. But at the end of the day, it was just a room. An unremarkable room made exceptional because of the presence of one thing—Jack.

She looked into his dark eyes and knew there was only one place in the world she wanted to be—wherever he was. "I've been thinking..." She faltered and began again. "Contemplating...that if ever we should conceive a child who finally joins us in this life—or if we adopt one who needs a family—it might be best if we were somewhere else, beginning fresh. Somewhere far from Boston, where every room in our home won't be reminding us of what we've lost, but instead be showing us what we have."

Jack pushed up on one elbow, grazed her earlobe with his

mouth and nuzzled her neck. She gave his shoulder a playful swat and felt him smile against her skin. "Be paying attention now, I've things to say," she said in a stern voice, though she couldn't keep the corners of her mouth from twitching upward, nor her hand from brushing over the dark hair curling across his chest and tapering down his belly.

Never would she tire of loving this man.

"Pay attention now," he warned, his eyes heavy-lidded. "Or I'll not be paying attention either."

She tangled her fingers in his hair and tugged his head down to kiss him. When finally they broke apart, breathless, she plumped the pillows behind her back and sat up. Jack opened his mouth and she pressed a hand to his lips to still his protest.

"What I'll be trying to say is this," she hurried to say. "After leaving Ireland in the hold of a timber ship and crossing the ocean aboard a whaling vessel, I'd thought I was done with adventures. But I've come to realize something." She gestured wide with both hands. "My home is not these walls, these floors, these rooms, this roof. My home is not in Boston or County Cork. Me Ma said to me before I left Ireland, *An áit a bhfuil do chroí is ann a thabharfas do chosa thú. Your feet will bring you to where your heart is.* They have brought me to my heart, Jack. Wherever you are, I am home. If you still want to be leaving next week with Sean, I'll be at your side."

"YOU WANT to give him back to Mr. and Mrs. Montgomery?" the judge asked in disbelief as he entered his office with Ailish on his heels.

She'd been waiting outside his door for half an hour, hoping to talk with him before she was due at work. Now she had less than twenty minutes to spare.

"You mean for a visit."

"Nay." Her answer came quickly, driven by both her resolute need to right this wrong and her lack of time. "I want them to raise him."

Eyeing her warily, the judge propped a hip on the corner of his expansive desk and waved a hand at the leather chairs facing it. "Please have a seat. To say I'm taken aback might be an understatement. A week ago, you were adamantly opposed to giving up your rights to the boy. What has changed in so short a time?"

She perched on the edge of the chair. "I don't believe I was thinking straight about what this meant for Will. This past week, I've come to realize the Montgomerys are his family now. It wasn't fair of me to pull him away from the only people he knows."

The judge watched her in a cool, unhurried way. "How are things going otherwise? How is his behavior? Are you two getting along?"

She had no time for long discussions. She couldn't be late to work, couldn't risk losing her job again. "We get along fine. He's a spirited lad, stubborn some might say, but I'd call it *determined*. I'd be lying to you if I said he was easy. He's not." She clasped her hands together in her lap to contain her nervous energy. "Has a fierce temper, he does. But I knew that before I got him, he showed it on many of our visitations. Please don't think that's why I want to give him back."

She thought of her grandmother. And her mother. And her sister. And Kathleen. "Much as I was wanting to become his mam, it's become clear to me that he's already got a fine mam.

And a da. He's got parents that he knows." Her voice cracked. "Parents that he loves."

"When did you come to this decision?"

"Last night. Quite late."

"And here you are, first thing the next day." The judge settled into his chair, frowning. "I'll admit to you, Miss Sullivan, your request leaves me troubled. Jack Montgomery is a respected man in our community. I would expect nothing irregular from him, and yet, I would be remiss if I didn't ask...have you been contacted by any of the Montgomerys or a representative of the family?"

She tensed. Not a word she'd had from Sean, not that she'd expected one or even deserved it. But the part of her that longed to believe in the messages of the moon and the mischief of the faeries had held to the faintest whisper of hope that she might hear from him again. "Nay," she said, shaking her head.

"No one offering money or something of value in exchange for the boy?"

It took a moment to realize he was asking whether she was selling Will to the Montgomerys. *Trading him for money.* Jesus, Mary, and Joseph, what kind of person did he think her to be? She squared her shoulders. "On my sister's grave, nay," she said, insulted. "How can you think such a thing of me? Or of them? Nay, none have contacted me."

The judge dipped his head in apology. "I don't mean to offend, but please understand, I have to ask. A child's welfare is at stake here."

"Since the start of this, all I've wanted is to do right by my sister's son. I thought that meant he should be with me. But I needed no visits from the Montgomerys, no money from them, to discover I was wrong. Last evening, I realized that what's best for Will is not a new mam, not a different house. It's the mam he had, the home he knows."

The judge opened a desk drawer and shuffled through the files inside, drawing one out and setting it on the desk. "Since you're voluntarily giving up your rights to the boy, I expect my ruling can be reversed with minor effort. But the law is new. I want to consult with a colleague to ensure my interpretation is correct." He frowned at her, his eyes appraising. "And while I do that, I want you to think carefully about—"

"But I have!" What more would it take to convince him her words were genuine, her motive pure?

He raised a hand. "Longer than one night. This cannot be an impulsive decision, Miss Sullivan. The new law is very clear...once you relinquish your rights, the adoption becomes permanent. If you go through with this, it will be final. You'll not be able to get the boy back later."

"I've thought of that already." She fought to hide her exasperation. Did he think she hadn't paid any attention this past month?

"You and the boy are getting along?"

"We are, but that isn't why—"

"Then I see no reason to rush this. I will not disrupt the boy's life again unless I'm confident this is not a momentary impulse on your part." He set his palm on the file. "I want you to take several days to thoroughly consider your decision."

Frustration spiked into her. She knew her mind today, knew what her answer would in a few days, knew what was right for Will. "I'll be needing no more time. My decision will be the same whether I give it today or in a week."

"Not a full week. Next Monday will be fine."

The blood rushed in her ears. "Could you...would you please...at least tell the Montgomerys of my change of heart?"

His brows snapped upward. "Out of the question. I will not give them false hope. Nor will you. The family must learn nothing of this until you've taken the necessary time to think it through." He set his mouth. "You may be convinced that you won't change your mind, but I am not. From my side of the desk, this has all the signs of an impetuous decision made because the boy is prone to fits of temper."

Ailish leaned forward, tears of frustration blurring her sight. "Nay. It's what I want for *him*."

"Then four more days will only make you more resolute. After all the boy has already endured, you owe him the certainty of a reasoned decision. One you'll not wish to overturn a day later." He sat back in his chair. "Come back Monday if you still wish to move forward. I promise the paperwork will be prepared and waiting."

CHAPTER THIRTY-FIVE

Awake with the sun, Sean muttered to himself, though it wasn't the sun that woke him this Monday morning. His sleep was severed by the noise of activity in the house—doors banging, voices and footsteps in the halls. It had been this way ever since Jack and Kathleen decided to join the family going west; with less than a week to prepare, the house had been frantic from dawn until well past dusk.

Emma arrived early each day to help sort through the family's belongings, dispose of most of them, and pack the things they wanted to take along. Today would be especially busy because their train departed Boston early tomorrow—and Kathleen and Jack still had much to put in order before then.

Sean dressed and went downstairs to find out what he could do to help.

"I have a list," Kathleen said. "But would you first check on Ma and Da? With both working today to make a last bit of money, I'm certain they'll be needing some help. Just make sure they're ready to go and will be meeting us at the station bright and early tomorrow."

"For being the last to join the adventure," Sean said, "you're as bossy as if the whole thing was your idea."

Kathleen laughed, and he was glad to hear the lightness in her tone. He hoped the trip would keep her from dwelling overmuch on Will, though he knew from experience that staying busy provided only a temporary reprieve from the pain of loss.

The stop at his parent's flat went quickly. Their belongings were few and already packed. Nora and Tómas each had a list of errands to run while Ma and Da put in their last day of work. And all four of them assured him they would be at the train station the next day with plenty of time to spare.

"Grand of you to be worried about us, but no need," Da said before he left for his job, his grin as broad as Sean had seen in years. "Nothing will keep us from being on that train tomorrow."

Sean walked with Ma toward the big house where she worked as a domestic. "Hard to believe this will be my last day here," she said. "That we'll soon be traveling as many miles from Boston to Oregon as we traveled from Ireland to Boston. We'll be twice as far from our country as we are now." Wistfulness wove through her words.

Sean looked ahead down the street, luminous and fresh beneath the early morning sun. Sometimes he wondered whether he should be going to the Territory alone, to make sure it was all that they'd heard it was before the whole family uprooted itself again. "I hope I'll not be dragging you across America only to have your dreams die in Oregon."

Ma put her arm around his waist. "Och Sean, don't even think it. Life feels to have purpose again. *Is fhearr fheuchainn na bhith san duil. It's better to try than to hope.* Your da and I are glad to be reaching for a new life instead of just dreaming of one."

His fingers brushed against something in his pocket, then closed around the small stone Ailish had handed him at Walden Pond. He rolled it in his palm, then brought it out into the sun. He'd barely taken notice that day, had thought it just a gray stone like so many others and forgotten all about it. But now, with the sun glinting off the black speckles, he saw that Ailish had been right; it looked like a sparrow's egg.

"What have ye there?" Ma asked as they neared her workplace.

"Nothing. Just a stone." He remembered Ailish reaching a hand back for him, beckoning as she stepped into the pond. How he suddenly hadn't wanted her to go without him. *Not then, not ever.*

He wondered if she was happy with her new beginning. How she and Will were getting along. Whether she'd already booked passage back to Ireland.

Ma took the stone and turned it over in her fingers. "Where did you get it?"

He considered lying, then decided there was no point. "Walden Pond, the day I went there."

"With Ailish."

"Kathleen told you?" He cursed under his breath. There was no reason for her to have told Ma. No reason for Ma and Da to know. Just gave them one more thing to worry over. "It didn't mean anything. Betrothed she is, and I was going anyway—"

"'Tis all right if it meant something," Ma said softly. "It couldn't have made things worse. And there was always a chance it might have made things better."

He shrugged and looked away, no longer caring what it could have meant or not.

Ma gave a sharp exhale. "May God and Mary save you, lad," she said, watching him. "You fell harder than I even guessed."

She set the stone in his palm and folded his fingers back over it. "I wish, och, I don't even know what I'll be wishing for."

They stopped outside the servants' entrance to the grand house where she worked. She took hold of Sean's arm. "Life can become so knotted...and hard it can be to find a path out of its tangles."

"It's not yours to worry about," he said. "I have a path out. The Oregon Territory. A three-thousand-mile journey across America."

"Did putting three-thousand miles between you and Ireland make ye forget Moira?" Ma shook her head. "Ah, Sean, the best journey brings ye home. And home...is wherever your heart is."

Sean dropped the stone into his pocket. "Three-thousand miles is the best I've got. I've no choice but to make it work."

AILISH WAITED at the judge's door, more determined than ever. She'd spent the last four days reconsidering her decision to give Will up. Had thought about it until she feared she might go crazy, talked to Meg until she couldn't bear to speak of it any longer. Yet despite all her mandatory second-guessing, she'd not wavered in her decision. Not once.

"I laid a wrong upon that family and my own nephew," she said the moment the judge opened the door. She kept her voice neutral, emotionless, not daring to show even a hint of regret or sadness. She couldn't risk the man thinking she had doubts. For she didn't—and she wouldn't.

"You're certain this is what you want?" he asked, leading her into the room.

"Aye. It's not about me. It's about Will. He should not twice have to lose his parents."

After a heavy silence, the judge gave a single approving nod. "As I promised, the paperwork is ready." He took a document off his desk and handed it to her. "This says that you relinquish your rights to young Will and agree to his adoption by Jack and Kathleen Montgomery. Please take a few minutes to read it. Make sure it's truly what you want to do."

She grasped the arm of a leather chair in front of the desk and lowered herself down. This was real. It was actually happening.

Aye, and that was good.

She bent over the document, managing to get through only the first few lines before tears blurred her sight. It made no difference. She probably wouldn't understand the words even if she could see them. She didn't need to read this paper to know she would sign it. Chin still down, she blinked her eyes clear, then raised her head and nodded at the judge. "I understand what it says and it's what I want to do."

Before several more minutes passed, the judge had brought in a colleague to serve as witness, and both he and Ailish had affixed their signatures to the document. When it was over, she sat back in her chair, all the tension of the last month gone, only exhaustion remaining. And the confidence that soon Will would be where he belonged.

The judge was watching her closely. "All that's needed to complete the adoption are signatures from Mr. and Mrs. Montgomery and, of course, a witness to their signing. I know this couldn't have been easy for you, Miss Sullivan. I commend you for your selflessness. May you find blessings in your life ahead."

His kindness gave her the courage to make a request, one she didn't actually expect him to grant. "I'm wondering if I might ask, sir, would it be possible for me to be the one who brings

Will to the family?" Heat rose up her cheeks. "I'll not cause any trouble, I promise you that. I've just been wishing to ask their forgiveness. And to thank them for taking Liam in and loving him."

The judge steepled his fingers and considered her request for so long she knew he was trying to figure out how to kindly refuse her. Instead he smiled and said, "I think there's a way we could do this that won't create turmoil in the process."

He dipped his pen in the inkwell and wrote several sentences on a clean sheet of paper. Then he rolled that page with the adoption documents, tied them with a length of string, and secured the knot with wax impressed with his seal.

"Give these papers to the Montgomerys when you take the boy there. They are your proof that you've legally given him up. I've included a note to Mr. and Mrs. Montgomery instructing them to sign the documents in front of a witness and return them to me or their attorney. Either of us can file the papers so the adoption becomes a legal record—and they become young Will's legal parents."

WILL'S LEGAL PARENTS. The phrase echoed through Ailish's head as she filled a satchel with Will's his clothes. She gently folded each garment as though her careful attendance to his things would weave her love, her family history, her remorse into the texture of the fabrics.

She'd left the judge's office and gone right to work at Chandler's, spent the whole of the next twelve hours standing, smiling, serving—all while suppressing any outward signs of joy and grief.

Not a doubt did she have that this was the right thing to do for Will, but now that it was to actually happen, she found herself longing for just a wee bit more time with him. She closed the top of the satchel and began to fill a second bag with the rest of his clothes and toys, saving the box of soldiers for last. After setting it on top and closing the bag, she sat back on her heels. All of his things were there, everything he'd brought from home.

Home.

Her throat constricted. Though he didn't yet know it, he was going home. The tears she'd fought all day finally broke loose, and she surrendered to them, dropping her head into her hands and weeping quietly as she finally accepted the death of her dream. There would be no family for her.

And yet, better her dreams to die than his, for he had an entire lifetime ahead of him. She wiped her eyes on her sleeve and went into the main room where Will was lying on his stomach looking at his book of fairytales, while the other children roughhoused nearby. Meg ceased her mending.

"Aish, read me?" Will asked, not a speck of his typical temper to be seen. "Bo-Peep? Three Bears?"

His good-natured demeanor was almost her undoing. "In a bit, lad." She went over to Meg. "It's the right thing to do, I know that," she said, her tone muted. "But would you mind telling me so once more?"

"Aye, as often as ye need to hear it. 'Tis the right thing to do." Meg pressed her lips together, subduing her emotions. She gestured at the stained walls of the shabby apartment, the cracked glass in one of the windows. "What sort of a place is this for children to grow up? What sort of a life is this, so many of us living in one flat, barely surviving week to week? It will be my sorrow forever to know that the hope that drove us from Ireland died on America's shore."

"But not for Will," Ailish said in a voice as tattered as the tenement she lived in.

"Aye, not for Will. Perhaps he'll do something great one day. For he'll will have opportunities you could never give him."

"And will he forgive me when he learns I gave him up, his own living relation?" she asked, already knowing the answer but wanting reassurance nonetheless.

"Aye. Ailish, he hardly knows you. How fair would it be to take any child from a loving home and give him to a stranger?" Meg echoed words they'd each spoken many times over the past few days. "All the love in the world you have for him, and still, you're no more than a stranger to the lad. Don't be doubting yourself. 'Tis a brave and compassionate thing you're doing." She put her arms around Ailish and pulled her close. "Will you be taking him now?"

Will rubbed his drooping eyelids; his mouth opened in a wide yawn. She'd intended to take him tonight but, faith, what was one more day? "So late already. And well past his time for bed." Her voice caught. "Tomorrow will be soon enough, once I've finished working. Everything is packed. Will you come along to help carry his things?"

"Aye. And to hold ye up once you leave him there."

CHAPTER THIRTY-SIX

KATHLEEN WATCHED FROM THE OPEN DOORWAY AS THE DRIVER loaded their bags and trunks onto the carriage. Two weeks ago, she and Jack had a son and a life in Boston. Today, they were childless and leaving on a journey to begin a new life on the opposite coast. Uncertainty pricked at her mind and she refused to grant it entrance.

The street was empty, so early they were. The sky overhead low with gray clouds. She'd expected the day to be alive with excitement, but instead it almost seemed forlorn.

Sean came up to her from behind and put an arm around her shoulders. "The ship's ready to set sail," he said in a jaunty voice. "All aboard for the American west."

American west. The words made her panic anew.

What was the matter with her? She was acting as though she'd only just learned they were leaving, when she'd known about it—and willingly agreed to the journey—a week ago.

"It'll be all right. A better future we'll have there," Sean said as if knowing her thoughts. He gave her shoulders a squeeze.

"You'd best not be wrong."

"I wasn't wrong about coming to America now, was I?"

She let out a snort. "I almost drowned on the voyage."

"But then ye met Jack. Admit it, Kathleen, I was right."

"Pah! Lucky is what you were."

Sean threw back his head and laughed, the sound of his joy so contagious she gave him a grin. "We're running late," he said. "Ma and Da are probably already at the station waiting on us."

As he ran down the steps to talk to the carriage driver, Kathleen contemplated the future...and the past. Though this house and city had been her home for just five years, she was finding it nearly as painful to leave behind as Ireland had been.

Jack came out the door with Emma and set two more satchels on the stoop. "That's the last of it," he said.

Kathleen's stomach leapt. A new life lay ahead. Everything unknown. What if it didn't work out?

"We've made the right choice, I'm sure of it," Jack said as if she'd spoken her fears aloud. He cupped her cheek with his hand. "Do you think we're doing the right thing?"

"Aye." She wanted to weep. "It's the best thing we could do."

Emma dabbed at her eyes with the corner of her apron. "I can't believe you're going. So quickly it's all come to pass." She clucked her tongue. "And so much left to do. But don't worry, I'll get the house emptied and everything settled before the new owners move in." She tried to smile, but her mouth twisted and suddenly she was crying, tears streaming down her creased cheeks as if a raincloud had opened above her alone. "All the years I worked for this family, all of it to be memories now."

Kathleen gave her a hug. "You can still come with us."

"Pah. I'm getting up in my years now. No time be moving away from my family."

"I don't know what we would have done without you,"

Kathleen said, her words snagging in her throat. "Thank you for being my friend from the very beginning."

"You'll let me know what you learn of Rory, won't you?" Emma asked. "So I can quit worrying over him."

Kathleen nodded. "We'll find out soon enough." The first leg of their journey was north to Lawrence where Rory was living and working. Though Ma had written him twice, she'd not received any reply. They'd spent the last couple of days assuring one another that he must not have received the letters because his address, *Shanty Town South*, was too vague.

But in truth, they were worried. The company where he worked was known for having little care for its workers. No matter which of the company's endeavors one looked at—textile mills or canals, construction or road building projects, and especially the machine shop—people got hurt, maimed, died. It was just a matter of course for the Essex Company.

The carriage driver came up to the stoop, lifted his cap and plopped it back on his head. "We need to be going if you're to catch the early train to Lawrence."

As Jack handed the man their last two satchels, Kathleen pushed the entrance door open with her shoulder. "Give me just a moment," she said, dashing inside and up the stairs.

She stopped in the doorway to Jack's grandfather's room. "Wish us well, Grandfather, and keep us safe," she said. "For as you well know, the best laid plans of mice and men often go awry."

She crossed the hall to Will's room and let her memories bathe the ache in her chest. "Forever I'll love you, my Will boy. May you be blessed with all that is good," she whispered, sending the message into the universe so on nights when Will's sleep was unsettled, her words might slip into his dreams and calm him.

Blinking hard, she went into the room she shared with Jack. Their life together, their love, had begun here. The children she'd conceived and miscarried. So many memories of Will. Yet though the furnishings were still in place, the room felt empty. As though the spirit of their life had somehow been packed into their traveling cases along with their belongings.

She lifted the front of her skirt and hurried downstairs to the kitchen, let her eyes run over every inch of the room, imprinting a picture on her memory. Then she did the same for the dining room and parlor. She hoped it would be enough to carry her through the homesick days she knew lay ahead.

"Kathleen." Jack waited in the foyer, the place where he'd first told her he loved her. He reached out a hand.

Suddenly she was eager to be gone.

"I'm ready," she said, twining her fingers with his for courage. Together, they stepped out the door, down the steps, and into the carriage with Sean.

THE TRIP to Lawrence took longer than Sean hoped it would, the train wheels clacking away the minutes as the sun climbed above the trees. Though the family's spirits were high, their conversation was limited. In part, because they'd been up since so early in the morn, but mostly because the nearer they got to Lawrence, the closer they got to finding out about Rory. Why hadn't he answered Ma's letters? Was he all right?

Sean let his head drop back, his worry over his younger brother crowding out all other thoughts. Rory had always been such a gentle soul. Had he been born in an earlier era, he might have become a bard. Instead, he was working long, backbreaking days in a machine shop for a company that worried not at all about the safety of its employees.

He pushed aside the thought and let the rhythm of the train and the steady clatter of the wheels on the rails lull him into a drowsy slumber. A sudden shriek of the whistle shattered his sleep and startled him awake. He swore under his breath as he scrubbed his hands over his face and cleared his throat. "Must have fallen asleep," he muttered to no one in particular.

"Aye, ye did," Nora said. "Snoring with your mouth hanging open."

"Nay, I wasn't—"

"Spittle running down one side of your chin," Tómas added.

"And a loud rumbling—"

"Have done with it now, you two." Da chuckled. "They're just playing with ye, Sean. Sleeping like a babe you were."

Sean shook a playful fist at his younger siblings. "Best you be watching your backs. For I'll be waiting to repay you."

As the train began to slow and the conductor came down the aisle bellowing, "Next stop, Lawrence," Nora leaned over Tómas to peer out the window. "I can hardly wait to see Rory's face when he discovers we've all come to get him."

"We can't all go to the shop." Worry etched a groove between Ma's brows. "Not all seven of us."

"Serve him right for not answering," Nora said with bravado, as if daring them to challenge her certainty that Rory was alive. She pursed her lips. "Fine. You and Da go. But tell him we all wanted to come and you wouldn't let us."

As the train came to a halt, Sean flung himself off the wooden bench. "Nay, I'll go. Alone." If there was bad news to be had, he didn't want his parents learning it from anyone but him. "Let's be hoping he's still working there."

"He'd have written if he moved on," Tómas offered.

Unless he'd been killed. Common it was for Irish laborers to die and be buried, their families never learning of their passing. A chill slithered down his spine as he exited the train.

He found the machine shop without any trouble and soon was standing stiffly in the shop office, hat in hands, heart in throat, asking the man behind the desk whether he might see Rory Deacey on an urgent matter. The sounds of metal grinding and sanding and milling echoed from deep within the building; the smell of heat and grease sifted through the air. He prayed that his brother was here so he could save him from this hellish life.

The man looked at him with an expression that was hard as the rock Sean had blasted in Virginia. Fear began to pound a beat in his ears. Rory couldn't be gone. He couldn't have died.

"What is the urgent matter?" the other drawled, standing. "I can't just call him off the floor."

"He's on the floor?" Joy spiked in Sean's chest and a smile cracked his face.

"Where else would he be?"

Sean sobered. "Our mother has taken ill," he said, adopting a grim tone. "I've come up from Boston to tell Rory. If you could spare him for a few minutes, it would be much appreciated."

The man didn't answer, just exited through a door at the back of the room. Minutes later, Rory charged through the same door, eyes dark with fear. "Sean? What are you doing here? What's happened?"

"Did ye get Ma's letters?" Sean pulled his brother outside.

"Not since March have I seen anything from Ma. Is she all right? What's wrong?"

"Nothing that knowing you're alive won't cure." Sean hit his brother in the shoulder. "Write home once in a while, will you? She's fine."

"What about the emergency?"

"There isn't one. Listen, Rory—"

"What about Da? And the others? Are they—?"

"Everyone's fine."

"Then why are ye dragging me off the floor?" Rory smacked Sean on the arm. "Jaysus, are you wanting to get me fired?"

"Be shutting your mouth Rory, and listen for thirty seconds," Sean said through gritted teeth. "Much has happened these past six weeks and you'll be knowing nothing of it. We've scant time, and I'll be needing an answer from you when I'm done."

Rory crossed his arms over his chest and stayed silent through Sean's entire retelling—until the moment he learned the entire family was waiting at the Lawrence depot. Then his jaw dropped and he let out a small laugh. "It wasn't enough adventure for this family to come across from Ireland, eh?"

"You won't be coming with us?"

"Are you daft? Of course I'll be coming with ye. I'll be finished at seven. 'Twill take but minutes to pack my bag." Rory started for the door.

Sean grabbed his arm. "Are you not understanding me, Rory? Everyone is here. We're ready to go now."

"I can't. If I walk out now, I leave my area short one man." He held Sean's gaze and bent forward as if to impart a secret. The sun illuminated his face, his eyes shone with the strength of the principles he'd upheld even when he was a wee thing. "They run lean here. My leaving in the middle of the shift puts other men at risk. If I tell them now that I'll be leaving at the end of the day, at least they'll have time to put someone in my place for tomorrow."

Sean dragged a frustrated hand over his hair. Everything Rory said was right. But if they waited for his workday to end, they'd have to be staying the night in Lawrence. "There's no train out that late. We'll lose this whole day."

"Then leave me behind if ye can't be waiting. I'll not leave my group short-handed," Rory said. "I'll follow you, find you in Independence. Ar scáth a chéile a mhaireann na daoine."

Under the shelter of each other, people survive. Ah, but Rory was their mother's son, through and through. Sean clapped his brother on the back. "Nay, we'll find an inn for the night. We'll not go on without you."

CHAPTER THIRTY-SEVEN

AILISH STARED AT THE BRASS KNOCKER ON THE DOOR OF THE Montgomery home, an eagle's head with a ring in its mouth polished to a glossy sheen. Though the air had grown cool as the sun dropped below the horizon, sweat prickled over her shoulders and under her arms. She clutched the rolled documents with both hands, unable to force herself to knock, to take the final step. She knew she was doing the right thing, so why, in Mary's name, had it suddenly become so difficult?

She glanced down the block in the direction of the small park where Meg and Will waited. It had been Meg's idea, and a good one it was, not to bring Will to the house until Ailish explained why she was there and delivered the adoption papers to prove her intent. "Besides," Meg had pointed out, "imagine what could happen if no one is home. Think of the fit he'll throw once he's at the front door and we have to take him away with us."

Ailish fixed her gaze on the eagle's curved beak and

tightened her grip on the documents. As long as she didn't knock, she could still change her mind.

Faith, but now she was being an idiot. She grasped the heavy brass ring and made three sharp bangs against the door as if to crush the temptation. Will belonged with these people. He had become their son as much as he'd once been her sister's son. She would keep them apart no longer.

After waiting for what felt like several minutes, she banged the knocker with vigor again. Suddenly the door swung open and a stout woman filled the doorway. "A little patience is of benefit to us all," she muttered as her eyes swept over Ailish, the corners of her mouth curving downward in disapproval. "It's a speck late for shopping," she said. "Are you here for the table and chairs?"

Ailish frowned back at her. "Nay."

"The settee, then?"

"I'm here to see Mr. and Mrs. Montgomery."

"About the house?" the woman's voice rose in disbelief.

Ailish squared her shoulders and raised her chin. "It's a private matter. I assure you, they'll want to be talking to me."

"All well and good, but they're gone."

Could nothing ever go smoothly? "Might I ask how soon they'll be returning?" She hoped they weren't attending a late gathering, for she didn't want to keep Will up until the wee hours. And she most certainly didn't want to return here in the morning before work. Jesus, Mary, and Joseph, now that she was standing at their open door, she just needed—wanted—the whole thing over with.

"But don't you know?" The woman tilted her head. "They've gone west. To the Oregon Territory."

Ailish felt her jaw drop. Her thoughts twisted into so many knots she couldn't force a response from her mouth for several long seconds. *Oregon?* "I thought—only Sean—was going west." Her words staggered out of her like an unseasoned sailor on the deck of a ship.

"You know the family?"

She hesitated. "Sean, mostly. He told me he was going to Oregon to get land. But I thought he was going alone."

"He was. Then suddenly they all decided to go." The woman stepped onto the porch as though eager to talk with someone who knew the family. "All of them," she said as though she still couldn't believe it. "Sean, the Montgomerys, Micheal and Anna, their other children..." She rubbed her fingers beneath her eyes. "I've been a cook for this family a long time, and if you ask me, it was too quick a decision."

As the woman spoke, Ailish watched the sky darken from deep violet to indigo, growing bleak and hostile like the ocean beneath a fast-moving front.

"I thought it just idle conversation. Them being supportive of Sean," the woman continued with a tsk. "And now they're gone."

"Ideas can be contagious." Ailish remembered how quickly she'd warmed to Sean's plan to find the spot where Thoreau had launched his boat on the river.

"They decided so quickly...and still I didn't believe it until the captain said he'd divested himself of his business interests." Her voice quavered. "Did you know of their son?"

Ailish's heart stilled. She gave a nod.

"A terrible thing. Worse than a death, I think it was for them... They didn't leave because they wanted to get land. They left to start over." She let out a long sigh. "Asked me to come along, but I'm too old for new beginnings."

New beginnings. This couldn't be what the new moon had promised that night on Walden Pond. Nay, not this.

She had caused this. *She* was the reason the family had left. She had driven them from their home, from Boston, from the life they'd built here. It was her fault Will would grow up without his parents. God be forgiving her for what she'd done to this family.

"When did they leave?" she asked, knowing the query to be futile. One day or ten, they were gone all the same.

"This morn. They were up with the sun."

"Today?" Ailish closed her eyes briefly as her thoughts tumbled. "What time was their train? Perhaps I can catch them."

The woman let out a laugh. "Catch them? It's nearly dark. The train left before nine this morning."

Ailish's heart sank. The sweat on her skin had grown cold in the chill air. A shiver rippled through her. She could have brought Will last night—had planned to—and selfishly decided against it. After already having him four extra days because the judge had insisted she give more thought to her decision, she'd chosen to keep him one last night. "You're sure?" she asked.

"As sure as I know this house is echoing in its emptiness."

The last of daylight was sifting into darkness above the rooftops, and Ailish wished futilely that it was this morning's dawn she was looking at, and she had arrived just as the family was leaving. "Will they be writing? To give ye a new address?"

"They said they would. But the trip will take four or five months, so I don't expect I'll hear from them for at least half a year."

A lamplighter lit the nearby street lamps with practiced efficiency, reached his long pole up into each lamp, the wick at the end igniting the gas. For as far down the street as Ailish could see, there were circles of light around each lamp and pockets of dark between them.

Light and dark. Good and bad. Joy and sadness. Up a while

and down a while. Life was more a challenge than ever she'd thought it would be, with heartrending decisions she'd never expected to have to make.

And once again, she had chosen wrong. One night and everything had changed. Will would never have his room again, never have this home, never have the people he loved most in the world. *Because of her.*

She'd won him—and he'd lost everything.

She pressed a hand to her throat to hold back the wail that wanted to escape.

"What of the matter you've come about?" the woman asked. "Is there something I can help you with?"

Ailish started down the steps. "Nay," she said. "'Tis no longer an issue I'm afraid."

THE TRAIN RATTLED along the rails that would eventually bring them to New York, the countryside rumbling past in shades of tan and brown and pale green. Though they'd departed Lawrence early when the day was still cool, the temperature inside the train had risen steady from the sun on the roof and the number of people inside. Now, even the breeze through the open windows wasn't enough to keep them comfortable.

Kathleen shifted on the seat and wondered whether she'd let herself be drawn too impulsively into this decision. The second day of their trip and already she was homesick.

Though she knew it wasn't home she was missing so much as Will.

"The conductor said we can get off at the next stop and walk around a little." Jack slid onto the bench next to her. "We're not far out."

She nodded. Anything to distract her from what they'd left behind. Hard it was to believe this was only the beginning. That before the journey was complete, they'd have traveled by train and stagecoach and steamer and wagon. "I know it's not wise for me to dwell on such things, but Will would love this a-venture."

"*A great a-venture* he would call it," Jack said. "Part of me hoped he never learned how to properly pronounce the word."

Kathleen could tell by the squint of his eyes that he was remembering previous a-ventures with Will, perhaps thinking ahead to all those that would never come to pass. Her vision blurred with unshed tears.

Jack bent his head close to hers. "We did everything we could," he murmured against her cheek as if trying to convince himself as much as her. "She's taking him to Ireland. And we're beginning anew in the west. We have to."

The train whistle shrieked, the conductor called out, "Hartford. Hartford, Connecticut," and the train slowed as it rolled past scattered buildings on the outskirts of town. The station platform came into view, a sparse crowd waiting, some with satchels at their feet and dressed for a journey, others empty-handed, eagerly searching the train windows for the faces of those they'd come to meet. The train screeched to a halt and steam sifted past the windows, blurring the view for several seconds before dissipating into the air.

"Hartford, Connecticut," the conductor called again. "Watch your step if you're getting off."

Kathleen stood and stretched her lower back, then followed Jack into the line of passengers already in the aisle preparing to exit the train. She exchanged a smile with Ma and motioned her to join them. The rest of the family was fast asleep, lying against one another like a collapsed row of dominoes—Da slumped against the window, Nora into him, Rory against her, and Tómas into him. It had been a long day of travel already; they'd started early and had changed trains twice along the route, moving all their baggage each time.

Outside, as Kathleen strolled with Jack and Ma along the edge of the platform, beneath a day glimmering with the promise of summer ahead—a summer they would spend crossing prairies and mountains—she tried to shut her ears to the heartfelt greetings and farewells circling around her.

But the emotion filling the air crept past her defenses like a faerie of evil intent, sneaking into her consciousness to show her the joy in the laughter, the despair in the weeping, the longing in the embraces, the affection in the gentle touches, the love in the hands clasped together as if wanting never to let go.

She felt it all.

And though she had vowed to put aside her thoughts of Will, in that instant she was back in Boston giving her son away. And then she was back on the quay in Country Cork, the day she'd left Ireland. And then she was at her home yesterday morning, running from room to room in a mournful, private farewell.

She stopped at the edge of the platform to compose herself and take in a view of the dusty town, its hard-packed dirt streets quiet and nearly empty. From somewhere behind her came the voices of families parting ways. "Don't forget to write." "Tell your grandparents hello." "If you find gold, send us some." "Don't be forgetting where home is." "Seems like just yesterday you were knee high, and now you're leaving on an adventure."

An image of Will as a young man stole into her mind. Will, stepping onto a train. Waving goodbye. Going on a-venture. A great adventure.

Grief mingled with regret, and she shifted her position so she could better see this family sending their son off on his own, so she could feel their pride and their worries and let herself pretend that she and Jack would be doing the same one day.

As the young man bent to pick up his suitcase, a view opened across the platform and Kathleen glimpsed a dark-haired boy bouncing from foot to foot, chin lifted high as he waved at the train and let out a screech of joy.

Her breath caught. "Will?" she whispered.

CHAPTER THIRTY-EIGHT

AILISH LIFTED THE FRONT OF HER SKIRT AND FLEW UP THE NARROW stairwell of the run-down building she called home.

She'd slept fitfully, spent the morning at work barely able to think, her thoughts bouncing between chastising herself for keeping Will and extra night and searching for a solution.

And then it had come to her. How to fix this. How to make sure Will wouldn't pay for her bad decisions the rest of his life.

Flying down the hallway, her spirit invigorated by her newfound solution, she threw her shoulder against the door to the flat and blew it open on the first try. Will and the other boys were playing with the soldiers, red versus blue, lined atop battlements of wooden blocks. "Want a war, Aish?" Will asked.

Her heart wrenched, missing him already. "Where's your mam?" she asked the oldest boy.

"Down at the water closet."

She let out an impatient huff and paced to the window overlooking the alley. When she heard the door open, she spun round, nearly bursting with excitement. "Meg!"

Meg stopped. Her eyes widened. "Ailish, what are you doing here?"

"They let me off early." She hadn't intended to lie, but suddenly her plan felt shaky at best. Her confidence wavered. "How has he been today?"

Meg's brow creased and she joined Ailish at the window. "Wept on and off all morning," she said, her words hushed. "Insisting he was, that I take him home."

"Fools we were for bringing those satchels with us last evening, even if he didn't know what was in them. The boy's no idiot. If only I'd taken him one day earlier..."

"Perhaps 'twas the Good People intervening, wanting Will to stay with you."

"For God's bright sake, Meg, and what if they do? You know the faeries have only their own interests in mind. They'll not be hoping to help young Will Montgomery unless there's something in it for them." She frowned. "Besides, all along you've been saying I should let him stay with the Montgomerys—and now you're saying the opposite?"

"Just trying to be helpful. What else can you do but keep him now?"

"What else?" Ailish went to kiss the top of her nephew's head. Now that fate had intervened, it would be so easy to justify keeping him.

Easy. But not right.

She tousled the boy's hair and went back to stand beside Meg. "I've been mulling this over all morning. And I've found an answer." She held back, nerves jittering, afraid that Meg might point out all the flaws in her plan. And today she had no patience for it. "More than once, Sean told me he would be joining the wagon train in Independence, Missouri."

"And how will this be helping you?"

"The family will be there a week, perhaps two. Buying supplies, getting what they need for the trip." She sifted through her memories of Sean describing the preparations. "Don't you see what this means? It gives Will and me time to get there, to find the family in Independence before the wagon train sets off."

"Have you gone mad?" Meg burst out. At the sound of her raised voice, the boys froze and locked concerned eyes on the two women. "No cause to worry, lads," she said, pretending to be busy in the kitchen. As soon as the boys returned to their game, she faced Ailish again. "You can't be racing across the country on a hope and a prayer," she said under her breath. "What if you can't find them? And think of the cost? How will you be paying for such a trip?"

"I've the money I saved to return to Ireland."

"But you'll be giving up everything. If ye spend all you've got —if you leave your job—"

"I've left it already. It's why I'm home early."

Meg gasped. "You've decided already? Ailish, this is too fast—"

"I haven't time to spend days pondering it." She raised her chin and crossed her arms over her chest as if to block Meg's words.

"Aye, but surely it deserves more than just one morning's scrutiny. Think, Ailish. Whether you find the family or not, you'll have to be coming back here in the end." Meg threw her hands wide. "You'll not have the means to return to Ireland. You'll have no work. *And if you still have the boy, you'll have spent everything for nothing.*"

Nay, it would not be for nothing. If she couldn't find the family at least she would know—could tell Will when he was old enough to understand—that she'd done everything she could, spent everything she had to try to return him to his family.

"You're saying nothing I haven't already thought myself," she said. "I've made my choice, already checked the train schedules. I've enough money to get the two of us to Independence." She was leaving a bit of detail out, but that was just as well. She didn't need Meg to point out more ways the idea was unsound.

Stunned silent, Meg searched Ailish's face. "But have you enough money to get home?"

Leave it to Meg to get to the truth. "Sure there are jobs to be had in Independence," she said with an impatient shrug, eager to end the discussion. "At least I'll have done right by Will. And I'll be thinking it's what my sister would want most. Indeed, if I were dead on the ocean and Will was my natural son, it's what I would want most."

"How soon?" Meg's face began to crumble. "What are your plans?"

"The train departs in less than three hours. We'll get into Providence in time to take the overnight steamer down Long Island Sound. In the morning we'll dock in New York, ready for the train to Philadelphia."

"I dare say but you've gone and truly lost your mind now, haven't ye?" Meg pulled Ailish into her arms, and the two clung to one another knowing it was likely they would never see each other again.

"Lost my mind?" So often these past few years she'd felt she was losing her mind with grief. "Nay, Meg, I think I've finally found it."

~

KATHLEEN PUSHED up on her toes, hoping to get another glimpse of the boy, but he was swallowed by the slow-moving crowd congesting near the tracks. Was she imagining what she longed to see or was Will really here?

She took a couple of steps to the side and, for a heartbeat, the boy came into her line of sight again. Recognition jolted her. *Will.* How could this be? If he was here, where was Ailish? She scanned the platform, her eyes meeting Jack's for an instant before certainty propelled her forward. She pressed through the crowd, bumping shoulders and elbows, leaving a trail of "*Pardon me*," in her wake. Nothing mattered except that Will was here. Whatever Ailish had done, whatever the reason Will was at this station without her, it could be fixed.

She spotted the boy in line to board the train and hurried forward to drop to her knees beside him. "Will!"

He pressed back into the woman behind him, took hold of her skirt in his fist.

"Will!" Kathleen repeated as she looked directly into the face that was...almost Will's. Her thoughts collapsed. She blinked, disoriented, and struggled to put her world back on its axis.

"Can I help you?" The woman placed a protective hand on the boy's shoulder.

Reality rammed into Kathleen's brain with agonizing force. She pushed herself to her feet, the shock of her mistake squeezing her throat to the point that she could hardly speak. "I am so sorry," she choked out. "I thought...he looks so much like...I thought he was someone else."

As she backed away, Jack's arm came around her waist, holding her steady as he steered her toward Ma. "I thought it was—"

"I know."

"Jack, what's happening to me? I wanted it to be him so

badly. Just wanted it to be him. I'm seeing Will in other children..."

"It's happened to me too."

Ma took hold of Kathleen's arm. "'Twill get better, lass, I promise. Time will bandage the wound."

"And what of Will?" she asked. Would time bandage the wound until he no longer remembered it at all? Would their son forget his life with them? Their home in Boston? How much they loved him? "Will he remember us, do you think, when he's been back in Ireland for years?"

"I'm sure he will."

"And if he crosses the ocean hoping to find us and we're no longer in Boston? What if twenty years have passed and no one remembers us or where we've gone? What if he searches and can't find us?" she asked, her voice ragged.

Ma drew Kathleen into her arms, cradled her head and smoothed her hair as if she were a child again. "You're tired, Kathleen. So much has happened so fast, and we've been traveling a long day, twelve hours already. You need to let go of these worries. If you keep thinking *what if?* you'll drive yourself mad." She brushed the back of her hand across Kathleen's cheek, wiping away tears Kathleen hadn't even known she was shedding.

"You did everything you could to keep him. Now let yourself cry," Ma murmured. "*An rud a ghoilleas ar an gcroí caithfidh an t-súil é a shileas. What pains the heart must be washed away with tears.*"

The train whistle blew sharp as a blade, slicing through Kathleen's thoughts as it announced its imminent departure. She stepped back from her mother and saw Jack watching her, the man to whom she had pledged her life, the man with whom she was starting over once again. She gave him a watery smile. "If we don't hurry, we'll be left behind."

He twined his fingers with hers, brought her hand up so he could kiss her knuckles, then pressed their clasped hands to his heart. "You'll be all right. We both will," he said as they headed for the open train door.

"Just don't be after forgetting," Ma said from behind them, "*Tiocfaidh an lá fós a mbeidh gnó ag an mbó dá heireaball.*"

"The day will yet come when the cow has use for her tail?" Kathleen asked. She threw a look at Jack. "Jesus, Mary, and Joseph, Ma. Now exactly what is that supposed to be meaning?"

"Just what it sounds like." Ma followed them onto the train. "There are better days ahead."

CHAPTER THIRTY-NINE

"Riding a boat," Will clapped his hands and bounced on his toes. "Big boat."

As the steamer's whistle blew a long, low-pitched sound and the ship slipped softly away from the Providence dock, Ailish lifted the boy into her arms. The setting sun misted the shore with a light so pale gold it glowed, almost otherworldly, as if magic had been sprinkled over the buildings, the road, the wagons and carriages and horses, even the American flag hanging still on a pole near the water's edge

"Goodbye, goodbye," Will shouted, waving at the people on the quay as if departing from dear friends, though he knew none of them. Nor did he know where he and Ailish were going, or why. She'd told him only that they were having an adventure—and he'd taken to the idea with unbridled enthusiasm.

She gave him an affectionate squeeze. For all the outbursts he'd had in the short time she'd known him, he'd behaved perfectly on the train ride from Boston to Providence. If the rest of the trip went half as well, she would consider herself lucky indeed.

Will's head swiveled back and forth as he checked out the passengers scattered across the deck—from those of average means who had paid for sleeping berths in the general quarters, to others so wealthy they would spend the night in private staterooms. "Having a-venture," he announced to an older woman beside them. The quality of her coat disclosed her membership in the moneyed class. He held up a tin soldier. "This my soldier."

Ailish touched her chin to the top of his head. "Will, don't be bothering—"

"And a fine soldier he is." The woman smiled. "Do you want to be a soldier someday?"

"Captain. My papa a captain."

"Is your papa in the army?" the woman asked.

His papa? Ailish thought of her sister's husband. And then of Jack Montgomery. Twice blessed this wee lad was. "Nay. On the ocean. His father is a ship's captain."

She stayed at the rail with Will as the crowd thinned and the night's darkness swallowed Providence away. Waited there until all that remained of the glowing shoreline was a row of shimmering gold spikes shooting into the sky like castle spires in a faerie kingdom.

A deep weariness settled over her. So many decisions in the past week, so many changes, and now a long trip with uncertainty as their final destination.

The moon rose, round and full, brightening the sky as the steamer cut a path through the water, its huge paddle wheels driving them forward into the unknown. Her grandmother would say the full moon was a time for gratitude. Faith, but what she wouldn't give to talk with her once more, to ask how

Ailish was to be grateful after all that she'd lost. Grateful for what?

Will wrapped himself around her and lay a sleepy head on her shoulder. As she pressed her lips to the top of his head, the answer came to her unbidden.

Grateful she was that Will had survived the shipwreck. That she'd been able to see him again. That he had been taken in by a fine family, a stable family, a family that loved him—and that he loved.

And Sean...grateful she was to have met him. To have had enough time to get to know him. To have learned about Mr. Thoreau and his way of seeing the world. A smile kissed her heart. To have that day at Walden Pond, and that night. The gods had gifted her something special in that time, something she'd not expected nor thought she even wanted—the knowledge that she could love again.

For indeed, there was no escaping the fact that she'd fallen in love with Sean. And she would hold that love, fresh and free it was, like a flower on the forest floor, for a very long time.

A whisper of a sigh slipped out of her. If they'd met in some other way at some other time, perhaps they might have found a way forward together. Ah, if only wishing made it so.

She turned away from the rail. "Are you ready for bed, lad?"

"Not tired," he mumbled and snuggled in closer.

She carried him below deck to the berth in the women's bunk room where their bags had been deposited, changed him into his nightclothes, and put him to bed. He fussed not at all, asked only once for his Papa, then drifted to sleep, one arm thrown up so sweetly over his head it made her heart hurt.

She stripped down to her shift, neatly folded her blouse and skirt and tucked them into her bag, then slid under the covers beside him. The ship rocked gently as it cut through the water of

Long Island Sound, the steam-powered paddlewheels tapping with each powerful turn.

Ailish's mind drifted, fatigued, as she vaguely heard the sounds of other women taking the berths around her, tucking their children into bed, whispering endearments and promises, their murmurings gradually filtering away as one after another fell silent with slumber.

A gift, a voice in her head whispered, *a gift it was to know that love still flourished despite the horror of the famine and England's neglect, despite America's prejudice.*

"Papa," Will breathed in his sleep. "Papa."

An ache squeezed her breastbone, and she was grateful once again—this time for the privacy of darkness and the innocent confirmation from Will's own lips that her decision to give him back was the right one. She closed her lids and drifted into a sound sleep for the first time in days.

"FOUR O'CLOCK IN THE MORNING," Jack said, as the family filed off the train into a damp New York night, steps leaden, shoulders drooping.

"Six hours late." Kathleen rubbed her eyes with a fisted hand. Why had she thought moving to the west coast would be simple? Or smart for that matter.

"They're building railroads so fast they're cutting corners," Sean said. "That's the problem."

"I'll not be thinking a cow on the tracks is the fault of the railroad," Kathleen muttered uncharitably.

"Nay, of course not. But the tracks should be able to hold up if the train runs into a cow. The rails shouldn't be breaking so easily."

A middle-of-the-night chill sent a shiver down Kathleen's spine. Only the second day and already things had gone wrong. They'd spent hours stuck in the countryside waiting for help to be summoned and the tracks to be repaired. Patience had been tested, tempers flared. Nora had wept over the cow's untimely death, and soon all the other children in the car had joined her. Their cacophony of wailing had been like an inharmonious funeral choir. For a cow.

Thankfully, Ma had put a quick end to it.

Once they'd gotten underway again, spirits had risen, only to plummet upon reaching New York. For now, it seemed their troubles were only continuing. The family was exhausted, hungry, disheveled—and the men were especially dirty because they'd gone out to help with the track repairs.

As they piled their trunks and bags together, her doubts grew. Perhaps she and Jack should have let Sean and the rest of her family go to Oregon first. And if it the land giveaway turned out to be all they expected, she and Jack could have followed in a year.

"Are we going to a boarding house now?" Nora asked.

Da patted her shoulder. "It makes little sense, it being so late," he said as Jack nodded agreement. "We'll be paying for the full night and getting but a couple of hours."

"Up all night we've been," Nora protested. "I couldn't even fall asleep once."

"Aye, ye did. Snoring you were with your mouth hanging open," Sean said, teasing her with the words she'd thrown at him the day before.

"Spittle running down your chin," Rory added, grinning.

She stuck out her tongue, then turned back to Da. "If we're not going to a boarding house, what are we to do then?"

"Follow me." He started toward the depot building, its

windows showing not a light inside. “There are benches in the waiting room—”

“Da!” Nora stared, her mouth open. “We’ve been rattling in a train car all day and night on a seat hard as all the stones littering Ireland and now ye say—”

Ma took hold of Nora’s arm. “Be still, lass. Your da is right. No reason to pay for beds when dawn is near upon us.”

Nora let out a whine. And though Kathleen kept her own mouth shut, she found herself feeling much the same, her fatigue breaking down the mental barriers she’d erected to protect herself against memories of Will and all that they’d left behind.

“Ye sound like a dying cat,” Tomás said.

“Be done with this, all of you,” Ma snapped, her own patience as frayed as the rest of theirs. “Into the depot with you. We’ve blankets in the trunk, enough for all of us so we won’t be cold. ’Twill be a blessing indeed if we’re all tired for the train ride tomorrow. Means we’ll sleep the whole thing away.”

CHAPTER FORTY

KATHLEEN WOKE, CHILLED AND STIFF AND HALF-SITTING, STILL IN the position in which she'd fallen asleep, one arm around Nora who was curled against her side. As she pulled the blanket higher over the two of them and tried to slide a numb arm from beneath her younger sister without waking her, she spotted Jack across the waiting room, staring out the window at the breaking dawn, hands clasped behind his back.

On this third day of their trip, was he wondering, like she, whether they'd made the right decision?

The rest of the family still slept, wrapped in blankets and sprawled across benches throughout the room, heads resting on makeshift pillows of folded clothing. Sean stirred, then sat up and rolled his shoulders. Spotting her awake, he quirked a brow. "Second thoughts?" he quietly teased, not realizing how close to the truth he was.

She chose not to answer. "Tell me again about our next train, for I think I've blocked it from my mind," she whispered. "Will we have to be walking to another station?"

"Aye." He gave an apologetic shrug.

"I've had enough of walking between stations," Nora croaked, her voice loud enough to cause the rest of the family to begin to rouse. She brushed her hands over her hair and face. "How hard can it be to figure out that one train should let off where the next begins? Not halfway across town."

"If you'd been listening yesterday, you would know why," Sean said. "Every railroad is owned by different investors. Rushing they are to stake claims to the routes and lay down the tracks."

"With not a care as to whether it works for passengers." Kathleen muttered as she folded her blanket and tossed it onto the bench. She knew Sean was watching her, but didn't look up.

"Imagine how bad it must be with cargo." Jack crossed the room to join in. "Goods have to be unloaded from one train and carted across town to be loaded onto another."

"If I were rich," Nora declared, "I'd buy up all the railroads and connect them. I'd make it easy for passengers to move from one car to the next. I'd have beds for long trips and a kitchen so everyone could order food. And I'd—"

"Mother of God, Nora, quit talking." Tomás pulled his cap down over his eyes.

Da let out a laugh. "Be glad we've not yet taken the stagecoach. They say the roads are so rutted that when it rains, passengers have to get out and carry their own bags. Sometimes they have to push the coaches free of the mud."

"Sounds perfect for you, Tomás," Nora sniped.

"We shouldn't be needing a stagecoach until Ohio and Indiana," Sean said.

Nora grinned. "Unless something goes wrong."

Kathleen folded another blanket and let her family banter, her mind wandering in the comfort of their camaraderie.

"How long to Philadelphia?" Rory asked.

"Barring any cows on the tracks," Sean answered, his eyes on Kathleen, "about six hours with stops."

"And then we turn west," Nora announced, as if she'd planned the trip herself.

"We're going west today." Tomás pulled his cap up and let out a smug snort. "Philadelphia is west of New York."

"Don't be stupid. You know what I meant."

As the two began to bicker, and Ma ordered everyone to pack away the blankets so they could go find a place to eat, and Da and Jack went to the ticket window that had just opened, and Kathleen spotted Sean watching her with concern, a wave of contentment washed over her.

Jesus, Mary, and Joseph, this family of hers. This husband. This life. This adventure. This future. She'd lost much with Will, had lost much with each miscarriage, was giving up much by going to Oregon. But Ma had been right as usual. Starting fresh was like reclaiming hope.

"Ye haven't answered me yet," Sean said in a muted voice. "Are you wishing you'd decided otherwise?"

She smiled as they followed the rest of the family out to the street. "For a while, I was," she admitted. "But not this morning. Today I know it was a good choice, the best choice...even if we're forced to be hauling our trunks from depot to depot, waiting in the middle of nowhere for tracks to be repaired, and pushing stagecoaches from the muck."

She looked ahead down the main street of a town through which she would likely never pass again. There would be many places like this on the journey. Her heart began to thrum a beat, excitement and anticipation and fear rolled into one, and she sent up a prayer that the Oregon Territory would be as happy a place for them as Boston once had been.

~

"SURE THERE'S a great many people wanting to take the train to Philadelphia," Ailish muttered. She adjusted the satchels over each of her shoulders, took hold of Will's hand and pulled him through the crowd, eager to get onto one of the passenger cars and claim a window seat.

The air was cool and fresh, yet sweat trickled down her back. Though she'd packed only a small bag for each of them, she'd not been able to carry both bags and Will too, so their walk from the steamer dock had been at a child's pace. And the bags had grown heavier with each step.

She ran her gaze along the Philadelphia-bound train—locomotive, baggage car, five passenger cars, and caboose—and wondered which offered the best hope for a window. If it was true that the end car was the least desirable because it bounced more than others, perhaps they'd have the best luck there. With so many people already boarding, she had only one chance to get it right. 'Twould be a fool's errand indeed to exit and try a different car when the train was filling up so fast.

Setting her sights on the last car before the caboose, she scooped Will into her arms and hurried across the platform, apologizing again and again as the bags on her shoulders bumped people in the crowd. At least they'd not need to deliver their satchels to the baggage car; she wanted Will's toys with them to keep him entertained.

Once inside the car, a quick scan down both sides of the aisle told her they were too late.

"My soul to the devil," she grumbled as she shoved their bags under a bench near the front. Hopefully Will would be so busy watching people on the train, he'd not even notice he couldn't see out the window.

She sank onto the upholstered seat, anticipating plush comfort, only to discover it was little more than crimson fabric over wood. Faith, but 'twould be a long, uncomfortable ride ahead. "Here's a lovely spot, Will," she chirped as she lifted him into her lap. "Just what I was hoping for."

Within minutes, the whistle sounded and she could hear the chuff-chuff-chuff of steam as the locomotive crept forward, the sound coming faster and faster as the train picked up speed. Silver gray smoke slipped past the window and disappeared, left behind like memories one choses to forget.

The train's conductor, lean and spry in his dark suit and cap, moved through the car checking tickets and collecting fares. "Good morning, young man," he said to Will. "Are you having fun on your trip?"

"Can't see." Will stuck out his bottom lip.

"Hush lad, there'll be more to see later," Ailish said. The conductor tipped his head at her sympathetically and went to the next row.

"Can't see," Will said more loudly and clambered off Ailish's lap to stand on the bench beside her, arms stretched out to either side along the back.

Before she even knew it was happening, he was sliding sideways, pressing his small body into the shoulder of the man nearest the window and leaning forward across his chest to watch the countryside pass by. Mortified, Ailish apologized and brought him firmly back to her lap. "We haven't got a window and ye can't just be climbing over people to get there," she scolded.

Minutes later, Will wriggled down to the floor. "Hot," he announced. He fanned his face with both hands, exaggerating the motion.

"Such a nice breeze through the windows," she said, though

she could feel only a hint of fresh air. She patted the bench. “Come up here by me and you can feel it.”

He ignored her. “Hot. Hot. Hot-hot-hot-hot-hot,” he sang out, marching in place to his made-up song. “Hot-hot-hot-hot.”

Ailish’s breath seeped out from between clenched teeth. Faith, but what had happened to the perfect child from yesterday? If this was to be his behavior, it would be a *very* long trip indeed.

Hours later, by the time the conductor came through the car announcing, “Next stop, Trenton,” she was nearly worn out. The man at their window had been nice enough to let Will sit on his lap and look outside every now and then. And Will had made friends with two older children and shared his soldiers until they’d lost interest. But most of the time, he’d simply jabbered and sang and talked to strangers about anything that came to mind. Mostly his soldiers. And his papa.

Always his papa. If she couldn’t find his family in Independence, she would never forgive herself.

The conductor stopped at the front of the car. “We’ll be refilling with water and taking on wood here. If you’d like to get off and stretch your legs, you’ll have about twenty minutes.”

Ailish closed her eyes in profound gratitude. Perhaps twenty minutes would tire Will out so he would nap on the next leg.

As soon as the train stopped, she had Will in her arms and was out the door, carrying him to a short row of steps leading from the platform to the street. Determined to wear him out, she led him down the steps and back up, down and up, down and up.

Will let out a belly laugh. “Jump now,” he demanded.

Ailish took his hand, lifted the front of her skirt, and bounced up the stairs beside him, both of them chanting, “Up, up, up," as they went. Spinning round at the top, they bounced all the way down and then back up again.

Stopping to catch her breath, Ailish put her hands on her waist and stretched her lower back, twisting left and then right. Will made a great show of copying her, then whirled suddenly and jumped down the steps alone.

"Just look at you," she said, affection kissing her heart. "Such a brave lad you're getting to be. What will I be doing without you someday?"

Her smile faded and guilt pricked at her. How had Jack and Kathleen been able to bear losing him?

CHAPTER FORTY-ONE

The moon. Sean could see the moon, just a sliver against the dark sky, the evening star shining bright off to one side. It was high in summer, leafy tree branches whispering on the breeze, the air laden with the scent of pine and wildflowers, crickets spinning a fiddler's tune.

He was with Ailish again, at Walden Pond. She wrapped her arms around him from behind and rested her head against his back. The heat of her swept through him, twined itself around his heart. And at that moment he wanted for nothing.

"'Tis again the new moon," he said, pointing upward. He brought her into his embrace, let his forehead come to rest against hers. "When first you told me it meant second chances, I wasn't sure I could believe you. Wearied I was of so much of this world. But now..." Hands on her arms, he gently pushed back, wanting to see her face.

She smiled at him. Her lips, her eyes, almost shimmered, her skin was oddly iridescent. Then a brittle sharpness came over her features, and her flesh darkened to the color of ash.

And as he brought a hand to her cheek, she crumbled into nothingness.

The forest stilled to total silence.

His breath caught. He spun from one side to the other, eyes darting over the beach, the black woods, the path around the lake, the pond. "Ailish," he called. "Ailish, where are you?"

Overhead, the stars gleamed, suddenly overly bright, like torches in the sky. And the moon that had been just a sliver, now glowed with so much light the pond shone like a snow-covered hill reflecting a full moon.

A sudden chill skittered through him. What was happening? "Ailish," he demanded. "Where are you?"

From the edge of the pond a white swan rose, powerful wings silently lifting it into the air up and over the trees until it was gone from sight.

And then the gleaming stars settled and the moon's glow quieted and the breeze began to rustle the leaves. And as Sean sank to his knees in the sand, the crickets began to mourn.

SEAN WRENCHED AWAKE, head bent against the train window, neck cramped. His shoulders were damp with sweat, his breath hitched with each inhale. He stared unseeing at the people coming and going on the platform, their chatter through the open window a gentle background murmur. *Like leaves whispering in trees.*

It hadn't been real. He'd been dreaming. Back at Walden Pond he'd been. With Ailish. He squeezed his eyes open and shut to clear his vision and waited for his heart to calm.

A sign on the depot wall told him they were in Trenton, New Jersey.

"Remember, I get the window next," Nora said close to his ear.

He dragged his mind back to reality.

"Seanie, we agreed. You need to move."

Burying the memory of his dream, he scrunched up his face at his sister. "We agreed you get the window on the next leg. But the next leg hasn't yet begun." He set his head against the glass as if there were much he still wanted to see outside.

At the far edge of the platform, a woman caught his eye, dark hair twisted into a knot at the nape of her neck. The crowd shifted and she disappeared from view, appeared again for a blink, then vanished once more behind a cluster of people. He pushed to the edge of his seat. Though her back was to the train, there was something familiar about her, the way she stood, the manner in which she moved her hands...

Ailish.

Cursing himself silently, he turned away. First he was dreaming of her. And now he was seeing her, like a ghost, just as Kathleen was seeing Will where he wasn't.

After what Ailish had done to his family, he should be despising her, not conjuring her up in his sleep—and now awake.

He'd tried to hate her, truly tried. Yet he'd not been able to, for he understood far too well her grief and desperation.

"Ma, Sean won't move." Nora slammed his shoulder with a flat hand.

"All right, all right, it's yours." He pushed himself off the bench and threw a glance at the rest of the family, most of them napping. "I'll be getting some air."

As he stepped down from the train, his eyes slanted of their own accord to the far corner of the platform. The woman was still there at the top of the stairs, speaking to someone at street level. Then she skipped down the steps and out of view.

He pursed his lips, relieved she was gone. God save him from wishful thinking and dreams of Ailish. From seeing her in places she could never be.

And God help his immortal soul. For what did it say about him that he still longed for the woman who had plunged his family into such pain?

He stomped on the thought and headed for the stairs.

What does it say about you? his mind asked when he reached the bottom step and looked in both directions down the street. *What does it say that you can't let her go, even three-hundred miles away from Boston?*

I just want to make sure it isn't Ailish, he silently protested, though he knew the real truth was, he wanted it to be her.

Spotting the woman striding away down the street, he took several quick steps after her, then stopped. Obviously she was on her way somewhere.

And he was an idiot.

He let his head fall back and absently noted a wisp of clouds sifting across the sky high above him. "She lives here," he muttered to himself. "This is her home."

A force barreled into the back of his knees almost knocking him to the ground. He staggered, cursing, and reached back to grab hold of a child's arm and drag him forward.

"Uncle Sean!" Will screeched.

The world ground to a halt. His thoughts scrambled. *Will?*

The woman spun and sprinted toward them, the front of her skirt grasped in one hand, dark hair tumbling down from its knot. Her gaze swept over him, landed on Will, then snapped upward again, as if she'd only then registered his presence. Her steps faltered; her mouth silently formed his name.

He swung Will into his arms and waited as she slowed to a walk. Waited until she reached him and lifted her eyes to his.

Ailish.

Jaysus, what a dream this was.

He had to be asleep, for how else could he be holding Will and looking at Ailish as though it was common as rain in Ireland to happen upon one another in a train station in New Jersey, three-hundred miles from Boston?

Ailish blinked several times as if he were an apparition, then shook an angry finger at Will. "How many times do I have to tell you? Don't be hiding like that. My heart almost—"

She broke off, touched a hand to the base of her neck. Her mouth moved but nothing came out until finally she said, "Sean? What are ye doing here?"

'Twas the best of dreams, it felt so real. Like it might truly be happening. He hoped he didn't wake for a while. "I might be asking the same of you."

Will bounced in his arms and waved an excited hand at the depot. "Riding a train! Big train."

"Ailish, how do you come to be here? In Trenton."

"I'm following you," she said softly.

That was when he knew for certain he was dreaming.

Surely God had conspired with the faeries to create this moment, for not once in all her planning had she ever thought they might catch Sean before he reached Independence. "Your family, are they with you?" she asked hopefully.

"Aye." Sean's brows pulled together. "But how would you be knowing to ask that?"

Her soul ached, not from grief, but from deep joy tinged with melancholy, like leaves when they are still green with life, their tips beginning to curl brown as summer gives way to a different beauty in autumn.

She had succeeded. Will would soon be back where he belonged. "The cook told me—"

"Emma?"

"I went to the house in Boston. I'd had time to think, you see, about what my sister might have chosen for Will if she could."

Will wrapped his arms around his uncle's neck as if trying to glue himself to the man. Regret returned, hard and ugly and unforgiving, over what she had done to this family.

"All along, what I wanted was to keep my promise to her...to make sure that her son was raised by his family." She roughly cleared her throat. "But I've come to realize—too slowly, I'll admit, and I'll be forever sorry because of it—my nephew was already being raised by his family, one that loves him as much as my own sister and her husband did."

She examined the dirt street, rubbed a toe in the dust. "I've come to see that it was not young Will who was in want of a family. 'Twas me."

"Ailish—"

She shook her head, needing to say her piece before she found herself unable to speak. "I thought the best place for him was with his own blood." Her mouth quivered and she blinked back tears. "But it came to me that Liam had no need of a new mam, for he already had one...and a da and an uncle and a whole family. There was a truth your sister spoke in court that first day, a truth I refused to accept for a long while. *It isn't blood that makes a family, but love.*"

"Ailish, what are you saying?"

"You ride the train?" Will asked. "Uncle Sean?"

"Aye lad, he'll be riding the train." Ailish smiled and patted the boy's arm. "Sean, I love him more than you can know, but I'll be thinking..." The words caught in her throat, wrapped in her pain and unshed tears. She started again. "I'll be thinking the best way to keep the promise I made my sister is to leave Will with the family he already has."

"You're giving him back?" Sean asked in a strangled voice.

"Aye. Tried to do it in Boston I did, but I was a day late. Then I remembered you said you'd be a week or two in Independence. And I had a wee bit of money saved to go back to Ireland, so Will and I, we set off on an adventure—"

"On a-venture," Will echoed. "A-venture, Uncle Sean." He clapped his hands.

"You're giving him back?" Sean repeated, as if he couldn't quite believe her.

"All aboard," the conductor shouted from the platform. "All aboard for Philadelphia."

She jerked her head up to look at the train and her stoic demeanor cracked. "His bag. Let me get it. I have adoption papers—"

She dashed up to the platform and onto the train, retrieving both Will's satchel and hers from under the seat. Now that she'd found the Montgomerys, there was no reason for her to continue on this journey. A pang of loneliness hit like hunger in her belly.

"The papers are right on top with a note from the judge," she said briskly as she handed Sean the bag. "I've put me own signature on them already, giving consent. They need only sign and it will be legal." *Finished. A circle complete.*

She dug a small package sheathed in brown paper from her own bag and tucked it inside Will's. "This is for Will. We lost one you see. Please be telling the family I'm sorry, it's not exactly the same—" She knew her words were making little sense, but there was no time for long explanations. Bending forward, she lay a hand on Will's back to feel the warmth of him one last time, then pressed a kiss to his cheek. "Goodbye Liam."

She picked up her satchel and took a step back, both hands tightly clutching the handle. "Go on with you now."

Sean didn't move. "Ailish, I don't...thank you—"

"Last call for Philadelphia," the conductor called.

She took another step back, wiped her hand across her damp cheeks. "They'll be closing the doors, Sean. Take him. Get on with ye." Her voice cracked and she fought to keep from breaking down. "Please."

He hesitated, then ran for the train with Will hanging over his shoulder waving and shouting, "Goodbye Aish, goodbye."

CHAPTER FORTY-TWO

ACROSS THE AISLE FROM HER THREE YOUNGER SIBLINGS, KATHLEEN folded her arms over her chest and anxiously tapped her foot. What had happened to Sean? The train was about to leave and he was nowhere to be seen. "Where did he say he was going?" she asked again.

"To get air," Nora replied as if having to answer the question a second time was an imposition of the worst magnitude. She turned her back on Kathleen and rested her forehead against the window. Without warning, she let out a shriek that startled everyone in the car.

"Nora!" Ma admonished.

Nora clambered over Tomás and Rory's legs, swatting away their complaints with her hands as she lurched into the aisle. "Kathleen! You'll never guess if I give you a hundred tries." She pointed to the front of the car just as Sean charged up the steps, a satchel dangling from one hand, a child clasped to his chest with the other.

Recognition struck instantly, and Kathleen gave a fierce start.

"Will," she breathed, her fingers tightening around Jack's arm. She shot to her feet and stumbled into the aisle, confusion and disbelief and questions tangling her thoughts. "Sean? What are you doing—"

"Mam, mam, mam!" Will cried, arms outstretched as he tried to launch himself out of Sean's arms.

She grabbed hold of him and gathered him close, curled her body around him as her eyes overflowed and her tears dropped onto his head like fat drops of dew. "Oh, my Will," she whispered. "I've missed you so." She didn't care how he came to be with them, didn't care if it was only for a minute or two. All that mattered was that he was here.

He stroked her face. "No cry, Mam. No cry." Spying Jack, he let out an earsplitting screech and threw himself toward his papa with such force he almost fell from Kathleen's grasp.

Jack scooped him up and pulled him into an embrace so tight Will shouted, "Squashing Papa, squashing!" and laughter exploded from the whole family, a burst of elation edged with agony. Will reached up with both hands to roundly pat his father's cheeks and touch his glistening eyes. "No cry Papa. No cry. Sean find me," he insisted.

"That makes twice he found you," Jack said in a ragged voice.

Da took hold of Sean's shoulder. "Is Ailish outside?"

Fear rumbled through Kathleen with the thunder of a passing train, a reminder that Will didn't belong to them anymore, that this was but a momentary reprieve. She reined in her joy, determined to protect herself from feeling too much. She couldn't let these few short minutes become a searing repeat of the day they'd been forced to give him up.

Ma took Will from Jack and snuggled him, kissed his neck and whispered silly things into his ear as he bent in half, giggling.

"Where is she, Sean?" Jack glanced at the door.

Sean shook his head. "She—"

"Seats please!" The conductor called from the back of the car. When no one moved, he started down the aisle toward them.

"Ailish is gone," Sean said quickly. "Will is yours now."

Through the open windows came the sound of steam hissing from the engine as the train prepared to depart. "What have you done?" Kathleen whispered.

"I've brought you a child. *Your child.*" Sean's mouth curved up in a roguish grin, an expression that had precipitated trouble since they were children. "Why do ye always think I'm up to something, Kathleen?"

"Because so often ye are," Da interjected.

"Seats please." The conductor herded them out of the aisle, waiting until all were seated before he moved on.

Kathleen leaned over Jack and jabbed a finger at her brother. "Be telling me now and be quick about it. What have you done? In Mary's name, Sean, what is going on?"

He held up both palms in surrender. "I saw Ailish—"

"Where?" Jack asked.

"Just outside. Said she was on her way to Independence. That she was trying to catch us to give Will back."

Give him back? Sean's next words were lost to her as she fought to make sense of what he'd just said. 'Twas not possible. Just a week ago, Ailish had told the judge. *He is my blood. He belongs with me—*

"...said she was sorry," Sean was saying. "Told me that you were right, Kathleen. That families are made not by blood, but by love."

She swayed as if Sean's words were a gust of wind that had blown in the door and struck her alone. "She said that?"

"Aye. Said she realized it wasn't Will who was in want of a family, but her."

Kathleen's guard began to crumble. In all of eternity, she would never have expected this. Ailish understood.

Sean opened Will's satchel and brought out a roll of documents, tied with a string and sealed with wax. He handed them to Jack. "She said these are adoption papers. That she signed them already."

Jack had them open in seconds. "It's true. She signed away her rights."

Kathleen sucked in a gasp.

The car jerked as the train began to crawl forward, its powerful engine exhaling like a great beast on the prowl. Two short blasts sounded on the whistle. Kathleen dropped her chin to her chest and let her long-held tension seep down her arms and out the tips of her fingers. "Do you mean to say, Sean, that he's ours? *Legally*?" She raised her head.

"As soon as you sign the papers. And file them."

She couldn't speak. No one could. Nora began to bawl into the silence, great choking sobs one after another until Tómas, blinking hard, roughly cleared his throat and snapped, "Have done with the dramatics, Nora."

"No sad," Will cried as he bounced on Da's lap. He poked a finger at each member of the family in turn. "No sad, no sad," he shouted.

"That's our boy," Jack said with a laugh. "He's home."

Kathleen reached across him to put a hand on Sean's arm. "I can't believe you did this—"

"Not me. It was Ailish's doing. And a bit of luck, I suppose. I just happened to see her..." He took a small package from the satchel. "She sent this for Will."

"A farewell gift?" Kathleen tore back the wrapping, then bit her lip at the sight of a blue uniformed tin solder, rifle at the ready. Nearly the same as Will's it was, not different enough for him to notice.

"She said they lost one," Sean explained. "That she was sorry it wasn't exactly the same."

Kathleen's stomach wrenched. These soldiers were costly, each one individually made and painted. How much had Ailish spent to replace a soldier she hadn't actually lost?

"She didn't lose one, Sean." Jack exhaled and shook his head, obviously as troubled as she was. "I kept one. Put it in my pocket the day he left, to remember him by."

The train jolted along the tracks, the wind whistled through the windows, and behind them, Will was jabbering something about angels to Nora. Ma leaned forward from the bench behind them, rested both hands on the back of their seat. "'Twas a selfless purchase Ailish made," she said over the noise. "As was the trip, itself. A fair amount of coin it would have taken her to bring the two of them all the way to Missouri."

Jack took the soldier from Kathleen and folded his hand around it. "I would venture," he finally said, "that she'll not be returning to Ireland anytime soon."

The conductor stopped to check their tickets, and in the moments that followed, Kathleen let her thoughts slip away from the conversation, let herself listen to the open windows rattling and the passengers around her talking and Da teasing Will...and Will giggling, his laugh a sound she'd never expected to hear again. She peeked over her shoulder at the two of them and smiled at their noisy joy.

And acknowledged all that Ailish had given up.

She'd sacrificed her own dreams for Kathleen's family. Likely spent all the money she'd saved in order to give up a child the court had ruled belonged to her...a child of her bloodline. *Her only living relation.*

She wondered, would she have been strong enough to do the same if their places were reversed? Pain cleaved her heart at the courage necessary to do such a thing.

She's not evil, she's alone, Sean had once said.

Kathleen leaned forward to peer toward the small window at the end of the row, a sliver of the countryside appearing and then gone, just a glimmer, like opportunities not grasped. The train wheels clattered a noisy beat beneath her thoughts: Ailish only wanted what they all wanted—a place to belong and people to love.

But was knowing that enough to forgive her?

"*Níor chuaigh fial riamh go hlfreann.*" Ma set a hand on Kathleen's shoulder from behind. "No generous person ever went to hell."

"Purgatory perhaps," Kathleen muttered. Ah well, she'd been praying for years that Sean would find love again. What right had she to complain about God's answer? She reached across Jack to punch her brother in the arm. "Will ye be knowing where Ailish is going now?"

He gave a detached shrug. "Back to Boston, I'd be guessing."

"And you're going on to the Oregon Territory?"

"Where else would I be going, Kathleen?"

"Don't play dumb with me, Seanie." Jesus, Mary, and Joseph, why were men ever so daft?

"Don't play clever with me, Kathleen. If you've something to say, be coming out with it."

She huffed and rolled her eyes. "Fine, I'll lay it out here. I know you've fallen for Ailish—"

"Kathleen, sometimes you need to stop telling yourself fairytales."

"It's all right, Sean," Ma said. "Kathleen told us—"

"Told you what?" He looked across the faces of his family. "That she's writing love stories in her head? Like Nora?"

"Mine are better," Nora said, offended.

Kathleen reached over the seat to take Will from Da. She brushed a hand over his fine hair and down his back. "It's a long time I've prayed for love to find you again, Seanie," she said. "And now ye have—"

"Are you forgetting? She's betrothed."

Kathleen bit back a laugh. "As was I. As was Jack. And not to each other, don't you remember? Yet you see how well that story ended."

"Trust me, Kathleen, she's not the answer to your prayers."

"Perhaps not exactly," she admitted. "But she's the perfect answer to yours. I was wrong that day when I asked you whose side you were on. I knew as I said it, there were no sides—only one wee lad who was blessed to be loved by so many."

Sean slouched into his seat, hands clasped in his lap, eyes locked on some spot on the floor. The windows clattered a rhythm as the train put Trenton behind them.

"You should bring her," Jack said. "At least ask." He handed the soldier to Will and the boy took it eagerly.

"He's talking of Oregon," Kathleen added, just to make sure Sean understood.

He narrowed his eyes. "Have you both gone daft? She tried to take your son. And now you want her with you every day?"

"We want her with *you* every day, Sean. For the rest of your life." Kathleen bounced Will on her lap as he waved the soldier in the air and barked out, "A-ttention men. 'Tention."

"Kathleen, look past this single moment when you've gotten Will back," Sean said. "Could you actually have her there? Knowing that she—"

"She's my son's only blood relative," she said fiercely, meaning every word. "'Twould be a blessing for Will I think, to grow up knowing her. To learn of his brothers...and his other grandparents...and his first ma and da—"

"Easy to say such words, but far harder to live. I suspect you would always—"

"Och, Sean," Ma said sharply. "*Ná bris do loirgín ar stól nach bhfuil i do shlí.* Don't be breaking your shin on a stool that's not in your way."

The train whistle sounded as they neared a crossing, splitting the air like a blade separating the future from the past. Sean looked to Kathleen, and she smiled and gave him nod of encouragement. His gaze shot to the exit door at the head of the car. Da was on his feet in an instant, clamping a hand on his son's shoulder.

"Be waiting for the next station now, lad," he growled as the train chuffed forward. "Better to present yourself to her alive another day, than in a casket this afternoon."

CHAPTER FORTY-THREE

Long after the train rumbled out of sight and the gray steam from its stack had dissipated, Ailish remained on the station platform looking down the empty tracks stretching to the horizon. Melancholy etched a scar into her soul.

She'd been so intent on achieving her goal, she'd not taken more than a minute to consider what it would feel like once she'd succeeded. Once Will was gone. *Once she was alone.*

A bit like death it was, like someone she dearly loved had passed on and she was in mourning. And yet not exactly that, for at the center of her grief there was happiness, a burst of contentment that Will was finally back where he belonged.

Where she belonged, though, was another question entirely.

She walked to the top of the stairs where she and Will had been playing less than an hour ago, went down to the street and retraced the path she had trod earlier. The town was busier now, more people moving about. She waited for a horse-drawn wagon to pass, then went out to the spot where she'd been when she heard Will screech.

Pivoting, she relived the moment she'd spotted Sean with Will, feeling again the thrill that had rushed through her at the sight of him, the relief that she'd found the family. *Found Sean.*

Her stomach clenched. *Found Sean and lost him.*

Nay, she'd not ever had him.

So what did she do now? The thought of going back to Ireland no longer held any appeal. If she was honest with herself, it had never been a good choice, she'd wanted it only because she was homesick and felt so alone. But Ireland would never be the same, not with all her family gone and the country devastated by years of famine.

She returned to the platform, set her satchel beside the wooden bench that ran the length of the depot and sank wearily down. High above her in the rafters, birds chirped a chorus, songs of warm days softened by the scent of lilacs. She tilted her head back to seek them out. Sparrows. Tens of them. *The little brown mice of the bird world* some called them.

But she knew better. Sparrows represented protection, for they lived in clusters to keep one another safe. And their cheerful spirit spoke to the joy of a simple life.

There were far worse tokens she could have come across as she pondered her future, as she mulled a return to Boston, a city where so many saw the Irish as nothing more than sparrows.

Perhaps she'd not go back. Rumor had it that New York was better. She had some money to begin anew since she and Will hadn't gone all the way to Missouri. And New York was but a train ride away along the rails she'd just traveled.

Anticipation sent a flutter of excitement through her stomach. *New York.* It even had the word *new* in its name. She'd have check the train timetable, get a ticket. But there was no rush. A minute or two would be soon enough. Or maybe a few after that. There was no reason to hurry for no one waited for her, none would wonder what had happened if she was late.

The thought tightened her throat and she pushed defiantly back against her self-pity. It was nothing unusual for her to be on her own. She'd been alone in Ireland. Came to Boston alone. New York could be no worse.

Hopefully.

She pushed herself off the bench, went into the depot and bought a ticket to New York on a train departing in less than three hours. Then, with time to spare, she took a leisurely stroll through Trenton, stopped at a small restaurant to get a bite to eat, and finally returned to the depot to wait.

Fatigued in both body and soul, she closed her eyes and let her thoughts drift with the symphony in the rafters, let herself remember the best of Will. And of her sister and her parents and her husband...and Sean.

"Excuse me madam, have you missed your train?"

"Oh, nay, I just—" She opened her eyes. Her stomach flopped at the sight of Sean standing not three feet away.

Everything faded away except him—his lean frame, his blue eyes, his mussed hair, the dirt on his cheek, the rip in his trousers over one knee. She rose slowly. "Did I not see you get on a train bound for Philadelphia?"

He brushed a hand over his dusty trouser legs and let out a sigh. "Aye, indeed you did. But what you didn't see was me jumping off it." He frowned. "Much further away from Trenton than I realized."

"Have you a wish to die?" she asked, taken aback.

"We weren't going so very fast at the time. There were cows on the tracks—"

"Sean! What could you be thinking? Did your family not try to stop you?"

He grinned. "They thought it a grand idea. Told me to do it."

"To leap off a train?"

His expression grew serious. "Nay. To come back for you."

The birds were singing so riotously, she could hardly hear him.

For her? Had something gone wrong? "Is Will all right? Is this about his clothes? I could only carry two satchels, so one had to be for my own things. His soldiers took up so much room, I had no choice but to leave some of his clothing behind."

"You think I would jump off a train over a child's clothes?"

"What then? Are they not happy to have him back?"

"Ailish! Yes, of course. They're overjoyed. But they were thinking..." He looked past her through the windows of the depot building. "All of us were thinking...I was..."

She waited, confused.

"What I'll be trying to say is...I'm wondering, are you still going to Ireland? To wed?"

She winced. Sure as the sun rose, she'd known that lie would jump out and trip her someday. She just hadn't expected it to happen at a railway station in New Jersey. "The dry goods stores won't hired unmarried women," she said, hoping he would surmise what she was leaving unspoken.

A minute ticked away.

"The thing of it is, Sean, never did I expect you to find out," she said with a huff. "But once you did, I couldn't risk you knowing the truth, lest you should tell—"

Confusion creased his brow. "Are you to wed or not?"

"Nay. 'Twas a falsehood...to get hired. I have no betrothed."

He ran a hand over his head as he considered her words, then let out a small laugh. "You lied about it?"

She nodded in defeat.

He straightened his shoulders as if throwing off a weight. "In that case, I've a second question for you. Would you like to come to the Oregon Territory?"

His words caught her by such surprise, she couldn't form a reply for several seconds. What exactly was he asking? "And...do what?" she replied, caution underlining her words.

"Have you forgotten? They're giving away land. Every man and woman who wants it can get a hundred sixty acres."

He'd come back about...land? She bit the inside of her lip, the pinch warning her not to be a fool. "Ahh. And are *you* forgetting, Sean, that women must be wed if they are to get any land at all?"

"I've not forgotten." He studied the wall of the depot as if planning to build one himself. "It brings me now to my next question." A smile unfurled across his face like a flag in a fresh breeze. "Would you come to Oregon and be my wife?"

She gaped at him. "So you can get an extra hundred and sixty acres?" she said, her tone soft but the edges sharp. She picked up her satchel. "Nay, I'll not be going to Oregon. If you'll excuse me now, I'll wait for my train inside."

"Ailish, wait," he said, grabbing her arm. "I'm saying it all wrong. When I saw you today standing in the street, and you told me you wanted Jack and Kathleen to have Will...I felt like we were back at Walden Pond, late that night when you told me of the new moon."

Her cheeks heated at the memory.

"You said it promised new beginnings." He took her satchel and set it on the ground. "But the truth of it is, Oregon won't be a new beginning for me unless you're part of it. I don't know what it was...the magic of the moon or the mischief of the Good People or just my own good luck...all I know is I've lost my heart when I was determined it would never happen again."

She let out the breath she hadn't known she was holding.

This was everything she'd hoped for, and yet, it wasn't just the two of them in this—and never would be. She regarded him in silence, refusing to let his words touch her. "And your family? What say they on this?"

"I told you, they sent me here."

"Well, maybe they had other reasons for telling you to jump off a moving train."

He barked out a laugh. "My own sister Kathleen said it would be a blessing for Will to grow up knowing his aunt and learning of his other family."

Her mind reeled. "I don't understand."

"I told them what you'd said, why you were giving Will back. Wasn't but a minute before the whole of them turned on me, asking to know why I'd left you behind."

She wanted to believe him. More than anything, she wanted his words to be true. "You're not a very good liar, Sean."

"Because I'm not lying. It's true. All of it."

"Are you saying they've forgiven me?"

"I swear it." He took hold of her hands and kissed each palm. "Ailish Sullivan, will you come with me to Oregon as my wife? Will you come with me to join my family? Not for the land. But for the love."

Love. Her heart lifted, her throat thickened. A husband. A family. A home. She'd never expected to have any of that again. But it was happening so quickly. Perhaps too quickly. "We hardly know one another," she said, finding her voice.

"But we're friends. It's a fine place to start."

Her eyes misted. "*My friend shall forever be my friend, and reflect a ray of God to me*," she murmured, quoting one of her favorite passages from the book Sean had lent her.

"Thoreau," he said, impressed, his smile wide. He squeezed

her hands. "I'll not be saying it will always be easy for us. But don't you know, a new moon rises again in just a few days—"

"Aye."

"You asked me that night on Walden Pond...*how often can a person be expected to start over?* I couldn't answer you then, not when I'd spent five years mourning Moira. But I can answer you now..." Silver flecks shimmered in his blue eyes. How had she never noticed the silver before?

"How often can a person be expected to start over?" he repeated. "As long as life gives you breath. It's a gift, it is, the chance to begin again...to plant seeds for the future, as your grandmother said." He took hold of her hands and touched his forehead to hers. "As I love nature," he murmured, "as I love singing birds, and flowing rivers, and morning, and evening, and summer, I love thee, my friend."

"Thoreau," she whispered. As he nodded, her tears overflowed. "Sean Deacey, I can think of no new beginning I would want more than this one with you." She reached up to pull his head down, to draw him close and press her mouth to his.

And in the background, the sparrows sang a chorus of joy.

If you enjoyed this book...

I would be forever grateful if you would post a review online.

AUTHOR'S NOTE

AUTHOR'S NOTE

Many of the historical events in this book are true, others are products of my imagination. Though I have done a tremendous amount of research to ensure historical accuracy, if there are any errors, they are surely my own.

In 1849, the Great Famine in Ireland was in its fourth year. On October 7th of that same year, the Brig St. John, carrying sixteen crewmembers and more than 100 refugees from the famine, was caught in a furious nor'easter and broke apart on Grampus Ledge, a rocky outcropping a mile off the coast of Cohasset, MA. As people along the shore struggled to retrieve bodies and goods from the mountainous waves, John Lothrop salvaged what he thought was a bundle of belongings (some said it was a rolled-up mattress) and discovered an infant inside. That story became the inspiration for *A Rush of White Wings*.

Only twenty people survived the wreck, eight of them crewmembers. Forty-six bodies were recovered and buried in an unmarked grave in Cohasset Central Cemetery, the rest were lost to the sea. In 1914, a 20-ft-tall Celtic Cross was erected in the cemetery as a memorial to the victims.

Adoption in that era was not a legal process; it involved simply bringing an orphaned child into one's home. Unfortunately, many children were "adopted" or "apprenticed" into families that were looking for free labor, and were often denied the rights of biological children, such as inheritance.

In 1851, Massachusetts became the first state to pass a law designed to protect the welfare of adopted children. By 1929, all states had enacted adoption laws and most put the welfare of the child at the forefront.

Concord, MA was indeed a hotbed of literary talent in the mid-1800s, with many famous, or soon-to-be-famous writers in residence, including Henry David Thoreau. Unable to find a publisher for his first book, *A Week on the Concord and Merrimack Rivers*, Thoreau published it himself. Not many copies were sold and he was left with hundreds of extras.

Thoreau gave several lectures in the spring of 1852, including one at Cochituate Hall in Boston titled, *Life in the Woods*. Due to a sudden snowstorm, few attended the lecture. Mr. Thoreau was introduced that night by his friend, Bronson Alcott, father of Louisa May Alcott, the woman who would eventually write the beloved classic, *Little Women*.

Thoreau was, at that time, in the middle of writing *Walden*, a book inspired by his two years (1845-47) living alone in a one-room cabin in the woods on Walden Pond. Though no transcript of his lecture at Cochituate Hall survives, I borrowed from the text of *Walden* to recreate what he might have said that night.

During this time period in New England, hatred for immigrants—especially Irish, Italian, and German—was growing. In the early 1850s, the secretive American Party rose to prominence on an anti-immigration, anti-foreigner, anti-Catholic platform. Members considered themselves to be "true Americans," defending the country against the rising influx of what they considered to be ignorant immigrants bringing crime and disease.

The party earned the nickname *Know-Nothings* because whenever members were asked what they stood for, they replied, "I know nothing." As their ideas spread, the Know-Nothing party elected more than 100 members to the US Congress; one even became Speaker of the House. They also elected eight governors; the mayors of Boston, Philadelphia, and Chicago; and thousands of local officials.

The group was particularly successful in Massachusetts. In the fall election of 1854, they took 99 percent of the state government, including the governorship.

The beginning of the end for the Know-Nothings came in 1856 when the party ran former president Millard Fillmore for president, and he placed a very distant third (he won only one state). As Americans grew disenchanted with the Know-Nothing platform, the group's members also split over beliefs about slavery. The Know-Nothing American Party dissolved in 1860, just before the Civil War began and Americans went to war against one another.

Congress passed the Donation Land Claim Act in 1850 to encourage settlers to locate in the Oregon Territory (which was made up of the current states of Washington, Oregon, Idaho and parts of Wyoming). The law, one of the first to allow married women to own land in their own name, was passed to benefit white people and half-breed Native Americans. African-Americans and Hawaiians were excluded from participating.

To meet Congressional requirements, Native American title to the land had to be removed before the land could be settled by others. So before passing the Land Donation Act, lawmakers first voted to negotiate treaties with Native American tribes in order to gain title for white people to the most desirable land.

Native Americans who resisted leaving their traditional hunting and gathering grounds were ruthlessly driven off by volunteer forces. By 1853, the U.S. Military got involved and forced the remaining Native Americans off their traditional lands and onto reservations.

There are a great many other smaller details in this book that are accurate to the time period including the unpredictable weather in the spring of 1852, the phases of the moon, every railroad branch having a different set of owners and few railway lines connecting to one another, and even the refusal by large stores to hire unmarried women because of the fear that they would be too much temptation to male customers.

It was a fascinating era, as I guess all are in their own way. Thank you for joining me on this journey!

ABOUT THE AUTHOR

Pamela Ford is the award-winning author of contemporary and historical romance. She grew up watching old movies, blissfully sighing over the romance; and reading sci-fi and adventure novels, vicariously living the action. The combination probably explains why the books she writes are romantic, happily-ever-afters with plenty of plot.

After graduating from college with a degree in Advertising, Pam spent many years as a copywriter and freelance writer before inserting a plot twist in her career path and writing her first book.

Pam has won numerous awards, including the Booksellers Best, the Laurel Wreath, and a gold medal IPPY in the Independent Publisher Book Awards. She is a National Readers' Choice Award finalist, a Maggie Awards finalist, a Kindle Book Awards finalist, and a two-time Golden Heart Finalist. More than a half million copies of her books have been sold worldwide.

Sign up for Pam's mailing list at: www.pamelaford.net
Contact: pamelafordbooks@gmail.com
Facebook.com/pamelafordbooks
Instagram.com/pamelafordbooks

Made in the USA
Monee, IL
19 May 2021